SCHOOL OF THE AGES

The Ghost in the Crystal

Matt Posner

Vitasta

Let Knowledge Spread

Published by
Renu Kaul Verma for
Vitasta Publishing Pvt. Ltd.
2/15, Ansari Road, Daryaganj,
New Delhi - 110 002
info@vitastapublishing.com

ISBN 978-93-80828-83-1

Reprint 2013

Layout and Cover Design by Vitasta Publishing Pvt. Ltd.
Character Design by Dipjyoti Lahkar
Printed by Vits Press, New Delhi

Contents

Preface

To young people reading this: magic is making things happen. You don't need wands or broomsticks or cauldrons. You need knowledge, will, focus, and courage. Sadness and loss are elements of life, but we are resilient, mighty beings, and we do endure, and we do triumph. The fact that this book is in your hands has proven that to me.

— Matt Posner

March 2012

December 2000: I Light a Candle

I was not a typical teenager, so if you expect that, you are going to wind up in a stranger place than you were imagining. Call me Simon, or even Simon Magus. That's my magician's name. You will learn my birth name soon, and more details about me. There is a lot, covering many years.

Yes, I said my magician's name. This is the story of when I was thirteen going on fourteen and I began attending a magic school in New York City. Not silly magic or playful magic that makes little kids smile. Real magic. Magic as it is. Magic as it has always been.

Simon Magus, the "real" one, if you want to put it that way, was in the Bible, in the New Testament book of the Acts of the Apostles. He fought with the disciples of Jesus and lost, and died. By the end of this book you will know why I say: although I did not die, I know how he felt. I should have been afraid when my battle came; I think he must have been afraid going into his. But if I tell you about my battle now, you will not be prepared. Let me tell you how it started.

I was a serious kid who kept to myself and never made very strong friendships in elementary or middle school. Both of those were public schools, in Bayside, Queens. I used to sit and think a lot. I liked my parents and was close to them, but spent a lot of time alone. There was always a kind of buzz in the air I felt, but being young, I thought everyone felt it, and didn't realize it was different for me. When I was a little kid, I read fairy tales about knights and dragons and wizards, like a lot of kids do – those who read – and I always liked the magicians. So when I turned twelve, I started reading about historical magicians, and how people who believed in magic did it. And I started trying that stuff, as best you can, when you're twelve. And I felt like it was working.

A year later, I was sitting on the upstairs porch of my room in my parents' house in Bayside, Queens, New York, drowsing in the winter afternoon's diminishing sunlight, poring over the latest copy of a new age magazine I had subscribed to for lack of much that was better. I had read all the articles at least twice and was down to the classified ads in the back, mainly because I was too lazy from the cold and inertia to get out of the chair and find something else to read. And there, amid the usual crystal-sellers and psychic readings by mail, I found an advertisement that somehow I had not noticed on my first review of the classifieds.

There was a small icon that looked like a castle, and beneath it the text read,

> If you can see this advertisement, you may have what it takes to be a student wizard at School of the Ages. School of the Ages is the oldest magic-based prep school in the U.S. Magic is about making the world the way you see it. Time travel our specialty. To contact our recruiters, burn an inscribed candle.

If you can see this advertisement, you may have what it takes to be a student wizard at School of the Ages. School of the Ages is the oldest magic-based prep school in the U.S. Magic is about making the world the way you see it. Time travel our specialty. To contact our recruiters, burn an inscribed candle.

I was thirteen going on fourteen. Like any teenager into magic, I had candles, incense, and other stuff in my room. My first thought was, inscribed candle? Inscribed how?

My second thought was obviously doubt. It must be a joke or a gimmick. I'm a savvy American teen. I can't fall for something so obvious.

My third thought was, why not? TV was boring. I had already read all my books a dozen times, it was too cold to go outside; my parents were both at work, the cats were all asleep in their hiding places and wanted to be alone. "I'll burn a candle," I said.

I went into my room, shut the balcony door, and switch on the heater. I got a candle from my top drawer and my folding knife from the top of my dresser, a novelty item from a Renaissance Fair. Laboriously, I carvezd "School of the Ages" and a couple of random Hebrew letters into the candle. By this time the heater was working. I put the lit candle in my brass dragon-headed candleholder, left it on the dresser top and lay down in bed to watch it burn. Soon I was asleep.

I awoke to the shock of the balcony door rattling violently. I propped myself on my elbows and stared at it as it banged back and forth within the frame as if forced by a violent gale. After several moments this stopped. I checked my candle; it was still burning; the sun was setting, making it about five in the afternoon. My parents would be home soon. I was groggy from the cold and sleeping, and decided to go down to the kitchen to make some tea.

It then occurred to me that it didn't make sense for me to be cold. I'd been sleeping just two yards from a blazing heater. I looked at it. It was off. I got up and checked the switch. It was turned on.

After some fumbling, I found that it was unplugged. But even so, there should have been some heat left over; after all, I'd only slept about thirty minutes.

Rubbing my eyes, I went down the narrow staircase to the ground floor. Whichever cat ran away when I approached was probably the cat that had knocked the plug out of the socket. All the cats seemed asleep. They would rise from their deep slumber in quest of food at precisely the moment my mother got off the bus down the block.

A few minutes later, with the tea in hand, I went back up to my room to look at the heater again. An arctic blast from the balcony drew my eyes in that direction, and I noticed that the balcony door was open a crack. That couldn't be. I had shut it and locked it. I set my mug on my dresser next to the candle and went to shut the door.

On the floor just by the narrow opening was a business card. Someone had dropped it there when he entered the house.

I was surprised. I ran down the stairs, bumping into the walls, left and right. At the bottom was Cheetah, our tabby kitten, who scrambled out of my path with just seconds to spare.

I considered running out of the front door just in my sweatshirt, jeans, and socks. There was someone in the house. But first I would wait a while, listening for the sounds of the intruder.

There were no sounds except the traffic outside, the clocks ticking, and Cheetah in the kitchen litter box.

It wasn't the first time something spooky had happened to me, but I didn't like it. I decided to go back up, get my tea, and blow out the candle and then watch TV downstairs.

No one jumped out at me when I re-entered my room. I went to my dresser to blow out the candle.

The business card was leaning against the candle.

I was sure I hadn't seen it before. I had started running the moment I saw it on the floor. There was no way I'd put the business card on the dresser.

So for the first time, in the candlelight, I read the card.

Mr. N.Otis	Northeast Regional Recruiter
Mr. South Wind, Esq.	Fallen Power Lines a Specialty

There was a small icon on the card that showed a man's face with full cheeks, violently blowing out air.

"Recruiter," I said aloud. Then it hit me. "Recruiter for School of the Ages?"

A violent winter wind blew up outside. The doorbell rang.

I went down stairs to answer the door.

The Recruiter

Through the peephole I saw a short man with a big nose and red cheeks, dark-haired but with a lined, weather-beaten face, wearing a black overcoat and a black fedora hat that shadowed his eyes. He was holding a leather case in one hand and using the other to prop himself up against the outer door. He appeared to be out of breath.

I looked at the face on the card. The same man.

"All my life I've wanted to see some real magic," I said to myself. "I never thought it would be like this. But I want to know it, whatever it is."

I opened the door.

"Hello, hello," he said. His voice was deep, but with a high, shrill note in it. "Mr. N.Otis, South Wind Esquire, Northeast Regional Recruiter, School of the Ages. Thanks for calling. Mind if I come in?"

I thought back to what I had read about dealing with magical beings. "I think I should draw a pentagram or something," I said.

"No no!" said N.Otis. "Waste of time, waste of time. A pentagram contain the South Wind? Nonsense. Anyway, you called me. Not a bad job, but not the best of candles, judging by the smell of it. Lucky I was already in the area, bringing you a storm tonight. Let me in, won't you?"

Cougar, a gray tabby, sauntered into the foyer, rubbed his chin on my leg, and went down the hall. I had always heard that cats and dogs were sensitive to supernatural beings, but Cougar didn't even acknowledge that Mr. N.Otis was there.

I had a strong feeling N.Otis wasn't planning to be dangerous, so I stepped back and waved him in.

"Thank you, thank you," he said, and whisked past me into the living room. I followed and found him already seated with his briefcase open. He looked up at me and said, "Take a seat, take a seat. Let's begin. I have a few questions to start with."

He crossed his legs, setting a pad on his knee, holding a quill pen. The ink jar was on the coffee table in front of him. I couldn't help checking to see if he had split any ink, but he hadn't. I sat on the couch, leaning forward. "Do you want some tea or something?" I asked.

"Later, later," he said. "To business first. As to your aptitude, how did you come by it?"

"I read about magic a lot. I just find it interesting. But I thought the ad was a joke."

"My lad," said N.Otis, "it's in the best interest of magicians to appear to be a joke, at least these days. If anyone knew what they were really capable of, how dangerously and subtly they can change the world when they really work at it, why, they'd be exterminated, trust me. But in reality, magic is no joke." He looked down at his pad and began to fire off questions. "So, your parents are magicians?"

"No."

"Grandparents or other relatives?"

"I don't think so."

"Were you born on a solstice or an equinox?"

"October 31, 1987."

He did some counting on his fingers. "All Hallows' Eve. Close to the autumnal equinox. A favorable conjunction of planets, no doubt, whether you're aware of it or not. History of family curses?"

"Of course not!"

"Lived in a haunted property in your youth?"

"When I was a little kid out on Long Island, our neighbors had a ghost."

He cocked his head at me. "Not Amityville, I hope."

"No, Hicksville."

"Good, good. What sort of ghost?"

"The fiancé of a Civil War soldier who never came home. She locked herself in a room and cried herself to death. They find puddles of tears on the floor, and the curtains keep opening as if she's trying to look up the road for him to appear."

"You saw the ghost?" asked N.Otis.

"No, but I saw the curtains move sometimes when I was playing outside."

"Good, good." He scratched some notes. "Back to my list now. Lived near an intersection of ley lines?"

"How would I know?" I asked.

"Lots of tornadoes in the area? Local people have high instance of insanity?"

"I live in New York. The whole city is insane."

"But not too many tornadoes," said N.Otis. "I should know that myself without asking."

"You're really the South Wind?" I asked him.

"Well, I have George MacDonald at back of me, and my brother Boris is a colder individual than I. But he's usually surprised to see me in this neck of the woods."

"Boris is the North Wind?"

"Enough, enough. Back to the interview, if you please, boy. Not much so far to qualify you. Say, you aren't the seventh son of a seventh son, are you?"

"I'm an only child," I said. I thought a minute. "My father has five older brothers."

"When we allow for children from previous alliances, byblows if you will, back in your family history, then it might be possible. I had a feeling, looking at you. Seventh sons of seventh sons are usually loners. We'll ask your father about it."

I panicked at that point. This was odd enough as it was, with just him and me, but my parents would be home soon, and they wouldn't be particularly happy to find the South Wind in the house.

"Maybe you should go," I said. "Maybe we should forget about this."

"Scared of your parents, huh?" said N.Otis. "Tough break, kid. Let's keep going."

Leo, the largest of the five cats, trotted in from the dining room, jumped up on the couch next to me, and stared darkly at my guest. At least that told me I wasn't hallucinating this recruiter. Some cats will look at things that aren't there, but Leo wasn't the nervous type.

"All right, all right. I'll fill in no for the rest of these birth and residence questions. Past experiences. Attended any other magic schools? Obviously no. Taught by family members? No. Taught by school friends?"

"No," I said. "Just skip to 'self-taught.'"

"Approximate number of spells cast, and their results?"

"Nothing serious. Just messing around. I don't think I ever did anything really."

Mr. N.Otis puckered his cheeks and then let out a long, frustrated breath. Across the room, a lamp rattled on its table, and the curtains momentarily flattened against the windowpanes.

"Simon, child, I'm not the one to tell you, but listen; you can do magic without spells, too. Just having a certain kind of attitude can be magic. Unskilled magic, I grant you, but magic all the same. So if you were just messing around with some spells, but you're the right kind of candidate for a magic school, something must have happened, whether you knew it or not. Okay?"

"Okay," I said.

"So I'll put you down for 'modest success rate' and 'native talent,' all right?"

"Sure."

"Good." He flipped over the page on his pad. "Special connections with animals. Cats, obviously. Any other kinds of animals that especially like you? Or especially don't?"

"When I meet stray dogs or cats, they always like me. I used to have gerbils and guinea pigs. The parrot at the pet store always makes a lot of noise when I go in to buy the cat food. Maybe I'm not good with birds."

"Not good with birds. No problem. It's a rare student who's good with every kind of animal. Moving right along. Precognitive dreams?"

"Sorry?"

"Dream about something and it happens?"

"That happens to my mother a lot."

"Good enough. Read tarot?"

"No."

"Tea leaves? Crystal balls? Palms?"

"No to all three."

"There's a long list here. Let's see, entrails, flight of birds, probably not. Those are Greek, only Hugh ever got any of those."

"Excuse me. Hugh?"

"Hugh Russ. My brother the East Wind. He used to recruit in the Mediterranean for Citadel D'If, back when he was willing to do much of anything. No to those for you. Look, I don't need to run through the list. Do you do any divination?"

"No."

"Do you dowse?"

"I never tried."

The key turned in the front door lock. One of my parents was home. My stomach hurt.

N.Otis Talks Up a Storm

I heard my mother come in. The high heels clicking and the rattling shopping bag were the giveaways.

I called, "We have company."

She went around the stairs to the kitchen and put the bag down, then came into the living room.

My mother was a tall woman with blond hair, light blue eyes, and the pale, chiselled features of a Roman statue. Except for the same small nose, I didn't look like her.

"This is Mr Otis," I said. "He's a recruiter."

"Mr N.Otis," he said, rising to offer a handshake. "South Wind, Esquire. Representing School of the Ages, America's oldest boarding school for promising magicians."

My mother wasn't quite ready to shake his hand yet. She gave me a foul look. "You and I will discuss this later." Then she turned to him. "My son should not have let you into the house. I think you should go."

"Before I go," said N.Otis, "maybe I should tell you both a little more about School of the Ages."

"No thank you," said my mother.

"School of the Ages was founded in New York City in 1858 by the wealthy industrialist, Elihu Danvers," he said. It sounded like a memorized speech. "He had made his money in railroading and was a member of the Fraternal Order of Masons. A highly moral man, Danvers was a capable citizen: his resources and reputation for fair dealing with people of all ranks enabled him to mingle with workers and presidents alike."

"Get out."

"His wealth and his connections in Europe and the Middle East enabled him to establish along with the school, one of the most formidable collections of magical artifacts and spirits ever possessed by an institution of higher magical learning."

My mother paused. Even if she found it to be nonsense, it was interesting nonsense.

"Danvers himself, though a magician of small powers, was the school's first Dean. Upon his death in 1919 at the age of one hundred twenty-one, the school admitted its first female students and hired its first female instructors under the leadership of Dean Aloysius Roosevelt. At this time its formal connection with the Masonic Order was also dissolved. In 1960, at the retirement of Dean Roosevelt, we admitted our first coloued students. In 1978, we formed a strategic exchange partnership with AAC in Brooklyn, leading to a merger of the two institutions."

"What's AAC?" my mother asked.

"American Academy of Cabala," said N.Otis.

"So the school is right here in New York," I said.

"At the moment it is," said N.Otis. "And most of the time it is. But that question brings me to the most exciting aspect of School of the Ages. We do occasionally shift in time and space for a while."

My mother must have been holding her breath, because at this point she sighed so loudly they could probably hear her next door.

"That's enough," she said. "It's time for you to leave."

"Last year's seniors took a field trip to the Lincoln-Douglas debates," said N.Otis. "The year before that, they watched St. Patrick driving the snakes out of Ireland."

"Go," she said.

"Watched Gabriel blow his horn at Jericho?" said N.Otis. "Acquired a bottled djinni from King Suleyman? Helped to raise a Neanderthal child?"

"Out," said my mother.

The front door slammed. My father was home. Everyone who wasn't already standing up stood up. Cheetah came barrelling into the living room, tail swishing. My father came directly to the living room. A short, dark-haired man, he was trim and handsome. In a moment he looked from my mother, who was quite annoyed, to me, with my forehead furrowed with worry, to N.Otis.

"Well, well," he said, and smiled. "Did we win the sweepstakes? Or maybe you're with the police."

"He says he's a recruiter with a magic school," my mother said.

Mr N.Otis introduced himself.

"Oh, that school," my father said. Born in India, he spoke with a mixture of British and Indian pronunciation. "Yes, I used to see the advertisements in my science-fiction magazines while growing up. I thought it was a mail-order witchcraft course or something."

"We're no correspondence course," said Mr N.Otis. "School of the Ages is the premier magical boarding school in the United States, in the grand tradition of the European academies such as..."

"You teach stage magic, right? Penn and Teller, David Copperfield?"

"Prestidigitation? Not at all. At School of the Ages, we teach a combination of European, South Asian, and Cabalistic tradition. Meditation, divination, sorcery, construction, conjuration. Acts of magic that can and regularly do change the world. And of course, in partnership with Manhattan's elite Smoot Preparatory, we provide a high school diploma widely respected in the non-magical world."

My father had a devilish look in his eye. He had seen that my mother was annoyed, and he was indulging N. Otis in order to play with her. I would still be punished once N.Otis had gone.

"And exactly what is the tuition at this fine school of yours?" he asked.

"Our endowment," said N.Otis, "means that we are tuition-free. Just give your son pocket expenses. Everything else is provided."

I had no idea what an endowment was, but "tuition-free" would have been good news if my father were serious. He was grinning.

"How about some tea?" he asked my mother.

She gave him a meaningful look as she went to the kitchen. The meaning was, "I'll get you for this later."

My father sat on the couch, gesturing for me to join him. I did, and he put his arm around me. Not a good sign. N.Otis also sat.

"If you did indeed see our advertisements," said the recruiter, "then you yourself missed an opportunity to receive training at School of the Ages. Only those with significant potential are able to see our advertisements. They are an admission test of sorts in and of themselves."

"Really." My father caught my eyes, then rolled his own. "Then you are saying, Mr Otis, that I could have engaged in divination and sorcery and construction and conjuration."

"If motivated, certainly."

" Can you prove this to me?"

"Perhaps," said N.Otis. He put both his hands behind his back. "How many fingers am I extending?" he asked.

My father closed his eyes and put one hand on his forehead, as if concentrating deeply. "Left and right index finger only," he said when he had opened his eyes.

"Exactly right," said N.Otis. He brought his hands back out, and it was so.

"No," I said. "That doesn't prove anything. You could have changed the fingers before you showed us your hands."

"I see," he said. "All right, young man, then how many fingers did I really have extended before?"

I thought about this for a moment. "None," I said. "You were waiting with your fists closed for him to guess."

He took this opportunity to smile, although the smile didn't seem sincere to me. "You see," he said. "The boy has talent."

My mother came back in, still standing. "That still doesn't prove anything," she said. "You could still be lying, just playing along and agreeing with whatever we say."

"I could," he admitted. "Well, then, my dear, how many fingers do you think I was extending?"

"Just the index and middle on the right hand," she said. "and the thumb. Because that's the most comfortable position. Look, you're doing it like that even now, unconsciously. Unless you're doing that on purpose to mislead me."

"Right again," said N. Otis. "Truly, this is a magical family."

"They can't all be true," I said.

"In a way they can," said the recruiter, "because magic is a matter of creating reality to accommodate your perception. Whatever each of you believed became true, especially considering that I don't really have fingers. I am the South Wind, after all."

My mother glared at my father. "This is all your fault," she said. "This stuff comes from your side of the family."

My father shrugged.

"So tell me," said N. Otis. "Is Simon here the seventh son of a seventh son? Looking at you, sir, I think perhaps you are one of six boys, but your mother lost a child when he was very young. Yes, there's something in your eyes. A brother died before you were born. He had a different father also."

My father lunged out of his seat. "How did you know that?" he cried.

"I'm calling the police," my mother said. The cordless handset was in her hand.

"Don't bother," said N. Otis. "The line is dead. The wind has just blown a heavy branch into a nearby telephone wire and thoroughly disrupted this service area."

My mother was clicking the cordless handset on and off. "No dial tone," she said.

"And no cellular signal either," he said. "We winds can cut those off without even thinking about it. But how did Simon here get six brothers, I wonder? What has his father been up to?"

"That's enough," my mother said. "Seriously, it's time for you to go."

Mr N.Otis opened his coat pocket and took out a card. He scribbled a few words on it and handed it to my father. "Here is the date and time for Simon's second interview," he said. "You are both welcome to come with him and see the school for yourself. You won't regret it. School of the Ages changes lives for the better – or the worse. One way or the other, if you don't come, you will be curious and regretful forever."

In a few strides the recruiter was into the hall and out through the front door. I went to the window. There was no sign of him outside. The windowpanes rattled.

"You are grounded," said my father, raising one eyebrow, "until you are twenty."

....

A Family Discussion

We talked as a family about what had happened and had to agree that we wouldn't soon forget it. My apologies for causing such a disturbance through idle play were eventually accepted.

"I was stupid," I said. "It says in all the best books that if you don't take magic seriously, it can cause terrible problems. I guess I never really believed that until now."

"Well look," my father said. "Enough strange things happened to all of us and we can't just pretend they didn't and forget. Anyway, we have the business cards, and Mr. Otis did know things he shouldn't have known."

"Such as what you were up to before we met," my mother told him.

"The Village in the mid-70's," my father said. "Come on, you know how it was."

"Not in front of our child," she said.

"But I meant, he knew that I had an older brother from my mother's first marriage," my father said. "And not even you knew that."

We decided to try one further experiment. I got my copy of Enchantment, where the school advertisement was, and we all looked at it. We could see the ad, so we went next door to see Mr. and

Mrs. Verne, a nice old retired couple, to ask what they saw printed there. They saw an advertisement for imported Greek olives. We kept trying. Ron Cheng, the postman, saw scented candles. The supermarket checkout woman, Reetu, saw a travel agency website. The clerk at the New Age Bookstore where I bought the magazine saw a subscription offer.

"So it's real," my father said when we sat down again to discuss it, "and all three of us have the potential to be real magicians, which is why we can see it. It's true, my side of the family have always been a little odd. But not yours, Magdalene."

"Honest hard-working salt-of-the-earth types," my mother said. "Except my aunt Silvana, who was always saying she saw the Black Dog of San Gimignano walking around in Astoria. But she was ninety years old by then, so we didn't take her seriously."

"All the same, there you go," said my father. "Aunt Silvana's pioneering spirit is with you still, Magdalene."

"But the question is," I said, "am I going to the second interview or not?"

"Do you want to?" my mother asked.

"Well," I said, "I was thinking about it. You're always telling me about how teenagers rebel by doing things their parents wouldn't approve of, and you're always saying that my magic study is just an example of that. But what if it isn't? I mean, what if it's what I'm supposed to do?"

"We can't know that," my mother said.

"We can't know that it isn't either," my father said. "And there's no point in trying to discourage him now. We weren't trying too hard when we bought him the magazines and the candles."

"You bought him those ?" my mother asked.

"And the subscription to the New Age Book Club," he added.

"Well, I wanted to encourage him to read more."

"I hate TV," I offered. "I mean, except for *Charmed*."

After raising and lowering his eyebrows a few times, my father took his wallet from his back pocket and carefully slid out the appointment card and passed it to my mother. "Looks like a safe enough place and time," he said.

"Midnight of Christmas Eve in the parking lot outside Irish Pete's Smokes on Avenue J?" she read. "Give me a break, Martin."

He shrugged. "Well, I think it's up to our son, Magdalene. What's it going to be?"

There is a peculiar thing about being a teenager: sometimes you want things so much that you think you will die without them. But then at other times, you don't really know what you want, and when you keep asking yourself, do I want this or not, no one answers. And the only thing that you know is that you want to find out if you want it. But parents don't understand that kind of thing. You have to know how to talk to parents.

"I'd like to go and see what happens," I said. "I mean, I like magic, and it's free tuition for a prep school degree. Smoot's a good school, right?"

"That's good enough for me," my father said. "I'm all for going."

"But you don't know what you're getting into," my mother pointed out. "And you don't know why they want you."

"I have to go there to find out what I'm getting into, right?" I said.

"It could be dangerous," she said. "In fact, I'm sure it is. Look what happened right here in this house."

"Your father was in the Navy," I said. "That was dangerous. But everyone was proud of him, right? And if these people wanted to hurt us, couldn't they do it any time they wanted?"

"All right," she said. "I see your point. We can go and see what happens."

The Parking Lot and the Ride to School

At 11 PM on Christmas Eve, 2000, we piled into my father's ten-year-old Cadillac. All three of us were wearing business suits. Mine was a blue pinstripe. My father's was gray, double-breasted, with a red tie. My mother wore a black pantsuit.

We figured there would be real magicians there, who were too strong for any kind of magical protection I could copy out of a New Age magazine. All the same, just for comfort, we wore pendants with our star signs on them. I had burned some incense over them and just sort of said they were there to keep us safe from hostile magic. My parents sat with me while I did it. That was weird, having them take the magic seriously when they used to treat it like just a passing phase. The ritual with the pendants was more to keep us from getting too nervous while we were waiting. During the couple of hours before it was time to leave, my father kept cleaning his glasses, my mother redid her make-up twice and her hairstyle three times.

I found it a little scary that as we were going out of the door, all the cats came and sat together on the stairs and watched us silently. I guess they thought so much activity at that time of night was unusual for us. If so, they were right.

It was a long way to drive, but since it was Christmas Eve, the streets were empty, except for NYPD and the very rare bus.

When we pulled into the parking lot, we were surprised to see that we were not alone. There was a large limousine pulled up there, crossing several spaces, and in front of it stood a group of men in dark suits and white shirts, with wide-brimmed hats. One was a short man with a huge white beard. There was a taller, heavier man around my father's age with a big black beard. The third person was actually a boy my age, much taller than me, with black eyes and furrowed eyebrows, bent slightly as if his head and shoulders were too heavy to hold up straight. He looked directly at our car with a mixture of suspicion and scorn.

We sat in the car, the lights off, and studied them. Even I knew what these three were: Chasidic Jews, probably from Flatbush or Borough Park, members of a deeply religious and private branch of the Jewish faith, generally distant and unfriendly to people with different beliefs.

My father said, "Do you think they're here for a second interview, too?"

"I can't imagine why on earth they would be here otherwise," my mother said. "Didn't that recruiter say something about that?"

"He said School of the Ages had merged with some kind of Cabala school," I said. "Maybe that's what they're here for."

We each thought about it quietly for a while. Finally I realized, and my father realized at about the same time, that if there was any hope of them being friendly, we would need to stop just sitting in the car and staring at them.

"I think we should get out of the car," I said, and my father said "Yes" so quickly I hardly had time to finish my sentence.

"You stay, Magdalene," he told my mother. "They don't like women in pants."

....

"Give me a break," my mother said.

My father and I eased our car doors open, got out, and waved hello.

The old man nodded and looked away, but the younger man smiled slightly and waved back. The boy my age gave me such a mean look that I thought I saw shadows coming out of his eyes.

"You first, or me?" my father asked.

"I'll do it," I said. With him following, I walked toward the limousine. When I was a few yards away, I looked at the three faces to see whose eyes I could catch, and found the younger man the best choice.

"I'm Simon," I said, "and this is my father, Martin. I think we're all here for the same thing." I offered a handshake.

"I'm Rav Aharon Mermelstein," said the man, taking my hand. He had a soft, cold grip. "My father is Rav Yehudah Mermelstein of Yeshiva HaTorah. This is my son, Yakov."

Closer to Yakov Mermelstein, I found him even more dark and menacing. There was a certain savagery to his expression that frightened me. All the same, I offered him a handshake. But he stared at my extended hand like it was a rotten fish, then turned away.

"Yakov," said Rav Aharon. I guessed 'Rav' was short for 'Rabbi.' "That's not right."

The boy addressed his father in a language I could not understand. I didn't think it was Hebrew, so I guessed it was Yiddish. The father replied in the same language, in a reproving tone. After a brief exchange, Yakov Mermelstein took my hand, squeezed it violently for a moment, then let go and looked away. Meanwhile, my father shook hands with Rav Aharon. The older man, Rav Yehudah, looked off down the street.

I felt like massaging my hand from the ferocity of Yakov Mermelstein's grip, but I decided to keep my cool and observe him.

"Did you meet this Otis fellow?" my father asked Rav Aharon.

"No," he said. "We have… certain contacts in the school. Alumni in the family."

"Then you've seen the school before?" my father asked. "Did you go there?"

"No," he said, a little stiffly, "Actually, I had my schooling directly from my father. But I don't think that's right for Yakov, although he doesn't seem to agree with me."

This bothered the boy, who complained in Yiddish to his father once again. His voice was hoarse and reedy, as if it was halfway to its adult deepness.

"This is our first experience with a magic school," my father said. "Do you have any idea what we can expect?"

"This school has a good reputation," said Rav Aharon. This comment didn't seem very useful to me, so I turned to his son.

"Big night for us, huh?" I said. "I'm not even tired."

"You don't know what you're talking about," was his answer.

"No offence," I said.

He gave me a dirty look and turned away. He was looking in one direction and I noticed the old grandfather looking the same way, so I watched also. A pair of blue krypton bulb headlights appeared in the otherwise deserted street, came toward us and pulled into the parking lot.

It was a large, dark green school bus with "Smoot Preparatory" painted in white letters on the sides. The driver flipped the lights off and opened the folding door. Seeing that something was happening, my mother climbed out of the car and came to join us, taking my hand and my father's in each of hers. Along with the Mermelsteins, we watched as the driver climbed down.

He was a man in his seventies, with grayish hair and deeply tanned skin. He was wearing a dark suit and an old-fashioned chauffeur's cap. His front teeth were white and prominent.

"My name's Mr. Saluto," he said. "Come aboard, and I will drive you to the School of the Ages."

"Our driver will watch your car," Rav Aharon said to my father. I noticed he and his father did not look at my mother, but Yakov Mermelstein did, again with dark disdain.

One by one we climbed onto the bus. Mr. Saluto offered my mother a hand up, but she said "thank you" and climbed on her own.

Once we were all settled, with my family on the right side and the Mermelsteins on the left, Mr. Saluto returned to his seat and flipped the headlights on again. Then he turned back to look at us. "We will drive into the Battery Tunnel," he said. "But we won't come out on the other side as you've seen it before. There is a side tunnel you can take if you know where to look, that comes out by the school when the stars are right."

We drove for some time, the dim streetlights reflecting from the dribs and drabs of snow that remained from the previous week. My parents were watching out if the window as if they expected something strange to happen any minute. The Mermelsteins seemed to be looking at nothing.

When I saw the green signs marking the entrance to the Battery Tunnel, and then the row of toll booths, I got a rumbling feeling in my stomach. I thought it was nerves and looked at Yakov Mermelstein to see if I could read the same in him. It was hard to tell, on the dark bus, but my guess was that if he was nervous, he showed it by getting even more cold and stiff.

Just after we entered the tunnel, it became pitch dark. The usual tunnel lights were gone; there was nothing except the faint bus headlights.

"Not long now," said Mr. Saluto. "Wait for it." And as he said that, I could feel the pain in my stomach growing, as if I could tell what was coming, and then abruptly it eased as he turned the wheel sharply to the left. He seemed to go over a series of bumps, and then there was the rattle of stones underneath and the rustle of grass and we were no longer on a road at all, but going through trees, and then across a starlit field. Ahead of us loomed a large stone building that stretched beyond the scope of my vision through the window, and in front of it stood a small group of people in what looked like monks' outfits.

Mr. Saluto gave the bus horn a weak toot, swung the bus sharply to the left again, and parked it. "Here we are!" he cried, and opened the door.

"My God," my mother said, looking out of the bus windows across from us at the building. "Is that Romanesque Revival?"

I was going to make for the bus door, but the Mermelsteins, moving more rapidly than I expected, were already in the aisle. After them went my mother, my father and I followed.

"Thank you," I said to the driver. My voice was weak; I could hardly breathe.

"Not a problem," he answered. "See you for the ride back."

As I took my first step off the bus onto the grass, I half expected an electric shock from the ground. But there wasn't one. Instead, in just a moment, two prospective students and four parents were standing stiffly, awaiting the approach of a group of five hooded figures.

One of these, slightly shorter than the others, stepped in front and put down his hood. He was a middle-aged man with a goatee, his mostly bald head reflecting the moonlight, with dark glowering eyes and wire-rimmed glasses.

"Welcome to School of the Ages," he said. "I'm the Dean."

The Visit

The Dean and the other robed people led us through double doors to a large domed entrance hall where we walked over a tiled floor with an inscribed wheel with seven spokes.

"Each spoke of the wheel has a name and a meaning," said the Dean, naming them in clockwise order from the closest to the door. "Balance. Faith. Perception. Wisdom. Receptiveness. Judgment. Discipline. You will learn to rely on these principles as you walk through this space each day."

The domed room was lit by a gigantic chandelier overhead stocked with dozens of tall candles. Descending from the center of the chandelier by another chain was a large metal fixture which contained a large quartz crystal.

"A most prized and honorable Memory," said the Dean, gesturing. The way he said 'memory,' I knew it was the name of something special.

The Dean led us to a small metal door somewhere going along the wall, produced a large key, and soundlessly opened it. Beyond we saw a staircase up, narrow and dimly lit. "The conference room," he said. "We'll stop off there to explain a few principles."

We climbed the stairs, which creaked, and came into a squarish room with a large oak table and several matching chairs. The Dean took one at the head of the table, and his companions sat beside him on either side. We two families took the opposite sides of the table.

"Dr. Archer," said the Dean.

One of the robed people put down his hood to reveal a gray-haired man in his fifties with serious light-blue eyes and a square jaw. He wore severe looking glasses with dark rims. When he spoke, his voice was sharp, practiced and even.

"If you speak to non-magical people about what you've experienced tonight," he said calmly, "you will face what we call the Cassandra Curse. Does anyone understand what I mean?"

After a moment's silence, my mother spoke up. "Cassandra was the Trojan prophet that no one would listen to," she said. "Is that the one you mean?"

"Exactly," said Dr. Archer. "Cassandra was a prophet who always told the truth, but she was cursed so that no matter how true were her words, no one would hear or heed them. Perhaps this drove her mad. But as you all should know, this is the fate of anyone who talks about what the average person has been taught not to believe. I'll give you an example. There are thousands of people who say they have been abducted by UFOs. Thousands. But unless you are one of those people, you are almost guaranteed to think that they are foolish, mistaken, or mentally ill, or that they are deceivers. And that is exactly what you will be up against if you try to reveal School of the Ages to the world. It has been tried before; however, the fact that still no one in the world at large knows about us, should demonstrate to you what came of those efforts."

"Are you saying the school has a curse to protect it?" I asked.

"No, I am not," answered Dr. Archer. "It is the society you live in that will curse you. The will of people not to believe what does not suit them, is as powerful as their will to believe what they wish for. You are under no form of compulsion or threat from School of the Ages. Quite simply, we do not require any, because the world at large does not want to know about us."

"But there are a lot of people who have said they were magicians," I interrupted. "Were they really?"

Dr. Archer looked at me as if my question made no sense. "Specifically whom?" he said. "We have to deal in actualities here."

"Allow me Dr. Archer," said the Dean. "Simon is asking how the curse of Cassandra applies to historical magicians. The answer is that they are transformed into myths, and their lives are publicly rewritten. John Dee saw angels reflected in crystal, and through them knew the future, but he has been recorded in history merely as a trickster and an adulterer who hoodwinked Elizabeth the First, and came to a sticky end. Books still propound his angelology in every large bookseller in the West, but they are dismissed out of hand as mere commercialized lies. In time, John Dee will become, like Merlin, someone whose very life is held to be a matter of folklore. But I should not begin this sort of lecture today. I asked Dr. Archer to explain why it is advisable for you to maintain secrecy."

"We had a girl a few years back," said Dr. Archer, pursing his lips for a moment, "who insisted upon telling all her cousins about her studies here. The cousins told the aunts, and the aunts told the doctors, and within a few months she found herself within a health care facility, receiving Thorazine."

The Dean looked at me. "This warning is mainly for you, Simon, and your family," he said. "Now, I would like you all to meet Rabbi David Shulman."

Another of the robed people lowered his hood, revealing a man about Dr. Archer's age, plump, with a round, well-combed beard. He was wearing a plain black velvet skullcap. I realized then that the Mermelsteins had taken off their larger hats, revealing the same type of skullcap beneath. Later I understood that this small round skullcap is called a yarmulka, pronounced 'yah-mik-uh,' or a kipa.

"Rabbi Shulman is the Assistant Master of Cabala," said the Dean.

At this the oldest of the three Mermelsteins, Rav Yehudah, spoke sharply in Yiddish to his son.

"He is saying," said Rav Aharon, "he would like to meet with the Rambal this evening."

Judging from Rav Yehudah's tone, and his face, I felt sure that he was saying something more strongly worded than that. While Rabbi Shulman replied, somewhat more patiently, I looked at the other faces I could see and chose Dr. Archer as my best bet.

"Who is the Rambal?" I asked.

"He is our most distinguished instructor," Dr. Archer said carefully. He chewed his lip for a moment, then added, "Perhaps you might ask me other questions on this topic at a more opportune time."

I nodded, trying to make sense of the odd name on my own. A glance at Yakov was met with an unfriendly and spiteful glare. After a little more of what sounded to me like bickering, the Dean spoke commandingly: "I should like to introduce you all to our instructor in meditation and music, Maestro Morgan."

Another of the hooded people put back his hood, revealing a shock of white hair and large, rheumy eyes. When he spoke, even though he looked worn and shaky, Maestro Morgan's voice had the balance and pitch of song.

"I will supervise your daily morning meditation," he said. "This meditation is mandatory before breakfast for all students. No student at School of the Ages sees the sun before he has seen my face. These daily meditations will transform you from sporadic and sentimental beings into creatures of deep focus and awareness. The music of the mind is music of true feeling."

"We have morning prayers of our own," said Yakov Mermelstein. "What about tefillah?"

"Tefillah is completed before meditation," said Rabbi Shulman. "We rise earlier than the other students."

"Pardon me," my mother said, "but what exactly is the purpose of the meditation?"

"It strengthens and harmonizes the mind," said Maestro Morgan.

"The evening is wearing on," said the Dean suddenly, "and we still have a great deal to discuss. We turn to the question of our course offerings. Here is our Registrar, Ms. Roosevelt-Wilson."

The smallest of the hooded people put down her hood, revealing a dark-haired woman in her forties with gray eyes and a smile that seemed to be covering some feelings of annoyance.

"All of our first-year students carry a minimum of two history courses, mathematics, and a science," she said. "Your other required course is theory of magic. You then select, in consultation with your advisor, four electives in the magical arts. For you, Yakov, one of these electives is non-magical Talmudic studies, one is first-year Cabala, and the other two you are free to choose. For you, Simon, your electives include divination, astrology, numerology, construction, elementary summoning, introduction to Hebrew, and this year's special offering, workshop in Memento Analysis. You may discuss the specifics of your selections with your advisor."

"Can I study Cabala?" I asked.

"Actually," said the Registrar, "that is an unusual request from a student with a non-Jewish background. The Dean will..."

"I'll explain it to Simon," Dr. Archer said. He gave me a look that I took for a warning to shut up.

"If you don't mind," my mother said, "I have a few questions. First, School of the Ages isn't an all-boys' school, is it?"

"No," said the Registrar. "We became co-educational in 1951."

"But you must understand," said Rabbi Shulman, "the girls, they are not admitted to Judaic studies. This is a matter of very firm religious conviction."

"All right," my mother said, "and the other question is, is this school all study, or are there sports and clubs and field trips?"

"Yes, although we have a small student body, we offer a range of extracurricular activities," said the Dean. "Allow me to introduce our activities director, Mr. Bannerjee."

The last hooded person revealed his face: he was an Asian Indian man, slight, thin, and unsmiling. He wore gold-rimmed spectacles, and his lips still quivered slightly whenever he was not speaking.

"We have several sports and many clubs," he said. There was a very slight accent, as of someone who had been speaking English as a second language for many years. "Our selection of seasonal sports include indoor hockey and basketball. These are most popular with students. All sports with magic are allowed of course. Also, depending on the amount of interest from students, variable from year to year, there are clubs for many branches of magic including astrology and construction. In previous years, boys and girls performed in band and concert chorus, but these have been discontinued recently participants being very few."

"What about housing?" my father asked. "School of the Ages is a boarding school, correct? But how often will we see our son once he's enrolled?"

"During holiday weeks," said Mr. Bannerjee, "Your son will visit you in your home. Summer is school, months off are November and December. Housing is in the main building, electricity and hot water not being available. Each student is housed with one roommate of the same sex, except for graduating seniors who receive individual rooms if requested. Our Cabala students maintain individual dining facilities due to religious conviction. The dormitory rooms are furnished. They are clean but not very large, I am afraid."

"We have a kosher kitchen and dining hall," said Rabbi Shulman. "The non-kosher facilities are closeby, as the students are permitted to meet and study together during meals."

There was a pause. Rabbi Aharon asked Rabbi Shulman something in Yiddish and received a reply in which I heard again the name "Rambal." Finally the Dean rose and said, "With your permission, we'll move on to individual interviews for our young students. Simon, if you will go with Dr. Archer. Yakov, you will go with Rabbi Shulman. The rest of us will remain to answer additional questions."

Dr. Archer rose and gestured toward the door. "Shall we?" he said to me.

The Personal Interview

Several stairs and cold gray corridors lay between the meeting room and Dr. Archer's office. The varnished oak door to his office had a triple lock, and he mumbled some words over each of his keys before turning it.

A blast of warm, dry air crossed my face as the door came silently open. The office was all stone, high-ceilinged, with roaring flames in a fireplace at the far end of the room. Dr. Archer had an oak desk, two identical oak chairs, an oak bookshelf containing a small, neat collection of books, and a large oak armoire which was shut and which I felt sure was locked. The walls were bare except for a small tapestry near the curtained window. Only a pile of papers on the desk demonstrated that the office was used for work.

Dr. Archer took the chair closer to his desk. When I didn't sit, he gestured to the other chair.

"I was expecting to meet with you, about a month ago," he said. "I usually know who my students are going to be."

"You can predict the future?" I asked.

"Not with absolute certainty," he said. "I am not a visionary. But you will learn that a high sorcerer is attuned to celestial rhythms. I am conscious of what is about to transpire because I am aware of how the energies in the universe are at play." He gave me such a piercing stare that I forgot the heat of the fire and felt like I'd been thrown into ice-cold water.

"You are going to enroll," he said. "I anticipate little opposition from your parents. When you enroll, I will be your advisor."

He said this, not with a tone of command, but with calm understanding.

"What do you teach?" I asked.

"I am a high sorcerer," said Dr. Archer. "My responsibility, in addition to instruction, is protection of the school. I am Principal Defender, as it is said here. I will see about enrolling you in my course in Memento Analysis. Although there will be significant demand, I should be able to prevail upon the Registrar. Now, I am certain you have some questions for me."

"Who is the Rambal?" I asked. "Is he very powerful?"

"Very well, I will explain that," said Dr. Archer. "The Rambal is Rabbi Moshe ben Lichtman. He is one of the most respected Cabalists of this past century and one of the major sources of the school's current reputation."

"Why is he called Rambal?"

Dr Archer pursed his lips and shook his head. "You need to be more perceptive," he said. "His initials are R-M-B-L. Simply add A. It's a principle in Hebrew naming. Similarly, the great Jewish philosopher Moses Maimonides was Rabbi Moshe ben Maimon, or Rambam."

"Can I study with him?" I asked.

"Your request poses numerous difficulties," said Dr. Archer. "They are both problems for the school and problems for you individually. While School of the Ages creates a measure of social interaction between its student Cabalists and its other pupils, there are certain types of interaction which are discouraged. A certain religious single-mindedness is necessary for that type of study. For the non-Cabalist arm of the school to thrust someone like you into the mix would be politically messy."

"You lost me," I said.

"It doesn't matter," said Dr. Archer, "as no doubt you do not have the Hebrew skills yet. Don't let it worry you. We have plenty of other things to keep you busy."

"Do you know why Yakov Mermelstein is so unfriendly to me?" I asked.

"I doubt that he has ever met a non-Chasidic boy before. It will change. I've a feeling his father wishes him to overcome that particular prejudice.

"But now I have some other things to explain to you," he said. "You should understand that your life at School of the Ages will have few of the sorts of distractions you are currently used to. There is no television, no radio, no newspapers. Selections of food are very few. The dress code at the school allows for the flamboyant, but this does not apply to you because I require that all my students dress simply."

"That's not a problem for me," I said.

"I know," he replied. "Now, you will have a roommate and an assigned study partner who shares most of your classes. It is rare that this is the same person. We are careful at School of the Ages to make certain that no one becomes isolated when studying, since a harmful frame of mind can result from an immature person practicing magic alone. You are to work together with your assigned partner, regardless of whether you believe yourselves to be compatible. Your ultimate compatibility and ability to aid each other will have been determined by use of divination."

"Who does the divination?"

"I do, or the Dean, or Dr. Chatterjee," said Dr. Archer. "But you don't need to trouble yourself with that right now. In fact, while I am confident of your future enrollment, do not question the appropriateness of your admission, I have some questions for you. How you answer them will help me to form an opinion of your character."

I wasn't accustomed to having my character judged. Ordinarily I would have objected. But this wasn't an ordinary situation. This man had identified himself as a high sorcerer whose job was to defend the school from magical attacks. His eyes on me were like cold blades.

"What are your goals as a magician?" he began. "In other words, what do you wish to accomplish, in your adult life, using your magical abilities?"

I took a while to think about this question. I realized, as he watched me closely, that I hadn't really thought about it before.

"I guess so far I just was curious about what I could do with magic," I said. "I never thought I wanted to do that much with it. Maybe use it to get rid of my problems, like find things I've lost, or get over being sick, or get money in an emergency, or make annoying people leave me alone."

"You don't crave power?" asked Dr. Archer. "Or wealth?"

"Well, whenever I've read about magicians who tried to get these things, it never seemed to work out for them. They always wound up in prison, or were executed. So I figured I would just use magic in a quiet way to make life easier."

"So you believe that magicians can't be truly powerful in the world?" Dr. Archer asked. His tone was so flat that I couldn't tell whether he approved of this opinion.

"Well, you would know better than me," I said. "But it seems like the strong guys, at least most of them came to a sticky end."

Dr. Archer tilted his head slightly, looking away for a moment as he thought. Then he turned back to me again. "Here is the truth of the matter," he said. "The truly powerful magician can achieve success in the world most effectively, when he is not known to be a magician. The founder of School of the Ages, Elihu Danvers, was a man of this type. He attained great worldly wealth and power, but was virtually unknown outside the social circles in which he moved. Upon his death, he was immediately forgotten in the non-magical world. You will not find his name in a history book, nor will you find it on the wall of a museum or art gallery or wing of a university. That he achieved all that he did, without being known as a magician, is actually testament to his power. But it seems that it is not your goal to be powerful."

"Should it be?" I asked.

"It is presumed that you possess a certain potential," said Dr. Archer. "As you realize more of it, many options will occur to you. To be powerful is among them, but it is not the only option. Still, I notice that you are attempting to answer my questions with questions. You do not wish to reveal yourself to me. Why is that?"

I decided after a moment to answer this honestly. "I don't know what there is to reveal," I said. "I really don't know the answers to your questions. I just never thought about these things much. I guess I thought magic was real, but not as real as it actually is. So if there's this much to it, then I need to do a lot more thinking."

"Magic is power of the will," said Dr. Archer. "If you do not know deeply what you want.... I mean, have a deep knowledge of that thing you want...then you cannot will it. We must teach you how truly to know things. Very well. That will do at present." He started to rise.

"What sort of things can you do?" I asked. "I mean, how powerful are you?"

Dr. Archer looked at me coldly. "When next you sleep, you will have a dream. The contents are recorded on a slip of paper in an envelope under your pillow. Do not open the envelope until you have awakened. If you do, the demonstration will be of no use to you."

Admission

We got home at dawn, dead tired, slept a few hours, then got up and sat for hours like zombies on the couch, watching Macy's Christmas parade on TV. No one said much, other than "Who wants tea?" or "Who wants toast?" or "Did anyone feed the cats?"

After the parade was over and we were finished dozing through *Miracle on 34th Street*, I decided to start the conversation we all knew was coming.

"I have to go to STA," I said.

"Why?" asked my mother. She tried to smile, but was too tired.

"Well, Dr. Archer said he knew I was going to," I said. "But that's not the real reason. How can you know a place like that exists and not find out more about it?"

"If I hadn't seen it and met the people, I wouldn't believe it," my father said. "Everyone there seemed sincere enough, but the whole idea of a magic school seems crazy to me."

"Me too," my mother said. "I wonder if it was a hallucination. You know, if we were hypnotized or something, and were just sitting on the bus the whole time."

I thought about this for a while. I was very tired, so it hurt to think. "We can't call the school," I said. "You know what, though? Let's call the Mermelsteins."

My mother groaned. “Good luck.”

But my father was excited by this idea. He went into the kitchen. Our phone books were in a cabinet above the refrigerator. He came back with the Brooklyn white pages. There were a lot of Mermelstein families in that phone book. We found two Aharon Mermelsteins. One was in Flatbush, the other in Far Rockaway. We dialled the number in Flatbush.

It rang many times. I was going to hang up when someone answered.

“Yes?” I thought the voice was that of Yakov’s father.

“Hello. Rabbi Mermelstein?”

“Who’s calling?”

“This is Simon. Do you remember, from last night?”

This was the moment of truth. If he remembered, maybe it was real.

“We don’t speak of these things over the phone,” he said. “Why are you calling?”

I didn’t want to tell him we were calling to find out if School of the Ages was real, so I bluffed. “I want to ask your son Yakov something.”

“God willing, he will answer,” said the rabbi. He called out in Yiddish, and from the sounds, he had put the receiver down. There was more arguing in Yiddish. Finally the receiver was lifted again.

“What do you want?” snarled Yakov Mermelstein.

“Just to ask how it went last night,” I said. “How did you like Rabbi Shulman? Did you meet the Rambal?”

“My father told you,” he grated, “that we don’t speak of these things on the phone. I have nothing to say to you anyway. Goodbye.” He slammed down the receiver, probably on a table. I heard more

Yiddish. Then Rabbi Aharon picked up again.

"Let me speak to you and your father together please," he said.

My father went and picked up the kitchen phone and said hello.

"I will say this to you both together," said Rabbi Aharon. "Please understand, I don't wish to be unfriendly. But this call you are making, this is not the way in our family. Simon, you and Yakov will see each other at school soon. Perhaps he will talk to you, perhaps not for a while. I cannot control that. But even if he does, it will not be talking the way you know it. Please Mr. Moore, we do not want more of these calls."

My father and I both said okay. Then Rabbi Aharon hung up.

That night I had a dream.

I was standing outside Bayside High, where fencing surrounded the basketball courts. In my hand was a cellular phone. I knew it was a memory phone and I should enter a date. I typed in numbers for date and time. I couldn't see them but generally felt what they should be. At that moment I found myself walking into the Bayside Mall theatre with its big peach coloured walls. My ticket for *Jurassic Park* was in my hand. I was going to see it once again. Some other kids were supposed to be with me and I looked around for them. The ceiling seemed lower than usual, and it was hard to turn my head I walked past the ageing arcade games, Tekken 2 and Ms. Pac-Man, past the giant cardboard poster of the vine-covered log gate of *Jurassic Park*, looking left and right, my feet getting heavier as I moved. I was trying to find the entrance to the theatre where the movie was, or to find the other kids. None of the doors were right; all the brightly-coloured posters seemed to stare at me. I was lost, and again found myself entering numbers on the phone.

My father had me by the hand and we were in Manhattan. The

buildings rose through a layer of dark clouds. My head spun, but I could feel my father's sweaty hand as he led me through creaking glass doors into a huge room full of confetti and balloons and the blare of "Happy Days are Here Again" from trumpets and trombones. A crowd of people all waving wine glasses and paper horns. It was election day and we were in the winner's New York headquarters. My mother was there, but we had to find her. So we moved through the crowds of men in suits and women in dark skirts and silk blouses, till I felt myself almost drifting, drawn on only by my father's hand. I let go, took the phone and dialled again.

Now I was where I was when I was eleven. This terminal at JFK airport was like a big barn, where I waited with both my parents, behind a metal railing, watching a doorway. Around us were Indians, women in saris and men in shirt sleeves and dark trousers, some turbaned, a few boys and girls my age some younger, chasing each other through the crowd. "When you see your grandmother Devi," my father said, "remember, fold your hands and say Namaste." I said, "But you told me she speaks English." "She'll like that all the same," he said. People were coming out of the doorway – old men first and a girl in a wheelchair, then more white-haired people, a few businessmen, and then grandmother Devi hovering above everyone with her mouth hanging open, her eyes bulging, her gray hair floating around her head, her hands extended like claws. She was shrieking in anger and pain, but no one seemed to see her hanging there overhead her eyes saw me and she turned to face me and pointed with a claw and I dialled

I was in my bed, with dawn breaking. It was 2000 again. I was thirteen going on fourteen and awake, chilled to my bones.

A dream full of plain memories had become a nightmare at the end. I had to think hard to convince myself that my grandmother Devi was not a flying rakshasi, but merely an old and tired woman who wore sombre colours, smiled often, and had a lot of opinions.

I lay there shivering for a while, gathering my wits. It was a while before I remembered that Dr. Archer had told me to look under my pillow. I did, and found an envelope, sealed with a wax stamp with the School of the Ages logo. I got up and broke the seal. Inside was a brief typed note.

You will dream about a device that lets you revisit your past, but the dream will end badly.

My heater was off; probably my father had come in and turned it off to avoid the risk of fire. I switched it on, then lay down in bed and pulled the covers up to my shoulders. I lay thinking for a long time.

Goldberry

The letter came in the mail with the logo of the School of the Ages. I tore open the letter. The school logo was again at the top. The letter read:

We are pleased to accept your request for admission to School of the Ages. Your advisor is Dr. Archer. He has selected the program below for your first year. Your study partner is Goldberry Tinker. Your roommate is Robert Ravitz. The bus will arrive at your house on Jan 1 at 6 AM. You may bring one small valise of personal effects.

The Dean

I hope you don't mind me not giving their full addresses and phone numbers here. I wouldn't want you to bother them at home.

I was not surprised that Dr. Archer had chosen my courses. He seemed to feel that his skill in sorcery showed him what was best.

I knew the name Goldberry, of course: it was from *Lord of the Rings*, the name of a beautiful female nature spirit. So my study partner was a girl. This was the last thing I had expected. What sort of girl had a name like Goldberry? The parents had read the books and liked the name. Would she be as gentle and sweet as her namesake? Would I fall in love with her? Maybe the Dean was matching us together so we would become lifelong…

This thought was spoilt by the ringing of the phone. My mother, who was off from work, picked it up downstairs. She came and called up to me, "It's for you. Someone asking for Simon."

I picked up the phone. "What's up, dude?" said a boy's loud voice at the other end. "This is your roomie, Robbie Ravitz!"

"Oh hey!" I said. So you got the letter today?"

"Just got it," he said.

"Me too," I said. "Funny how that worked out."

"It's magic," he said. "You big on the old hocus-pocus?"

He didn't seem too serious. He was the first person I'd met who was into magic but sounded relaxed about it. I wondered if I should trust him.

"I just do a little," I said. It was true, but I hoped he'd think I was being modest.

"Me too," he said. "I've been trying to summon stronger elemental spirits, but I just keep getting their servants. Kind of like calling the boss and not getting past the secretary."

If he was summoning elementals – beings made of fire, water, earth, and air – He was beyond what I'd ever tried. Of course, it was possible he was lying or exaggerating to impress me.

"No, I never did that," I said.

"It's cool, man. We should team up and try to get one of these guys."

"Where do you do this?"

"Oh my dad gives me lots of allowance, so I save it up and get a hotel room in Chinatown. No one bugs you there. You clocking any ducats?"

"What?"

"Money, man? You have any? Let's do it tonight. I want to get Lazar-el, the Duke of Water. He knows where there's sunken treasure."

If he was bluffing, I didn't want to call his bluff. If he wasn't, he was doing something that sounded too dangerous for a beginner. Since he said he hadn't been successful, I figured he was mostly talk.

"Let's wait till school starts," I said. "Who's your advisor?"

"Maestro Morgan," he said. "Creepy old dude. Looks kind of like Christopher Walken."

"So what are you taking?"

"Let's see. Magic Theory, bio, European History, Asian History, Astrology, Intermediate Hebrew, Construction, Elementary Summoning. What about you?"

I read off my schedule to him. "We might have a few classes together, but you're ahead of me in Hebrew."

"Yeah well, I had a bar mitzvah. You scored a first-term seminar. How come?"

"It's my advisor's course. Dr. Archer."

"Whoa. You got that guy, huh? I don't envy you. He's stiff."

I felt a little annoyed hearing him openly criticize my advisor, so I changed the subject. "Tell me, Robbie, how did you find out about School of the Ages?"

"I was trying to summon a spirit of elemental air," he said. "Nicholotus the Sky-Dancer, who's supposed to teach you how to fly. Instead, if you believe it, I got his dad, the South Wind."

"Mr. N.Otis?" I said.

"Yeah. You know him?"

"Sure. He recruited me."

"He's cool," Robbie said. "He knocked out our electricity, but my dad still wanted to take him out to dinner and stuff. But he wouldn't go."

"So do your parents like you doing magic?"

"Yeah, they're all, follow your own heart, chacun á son goût and stuff. I'm not so good at regular school. It's boring. So they figure if this gets me all jazzed up, why not? How 'bout your folks?"

"I think it makes them nervous," I admitted. "Like they keep expecting to find out it isn't real."

"Real? Man, I could tell you some stories. Listen, we just have a couple of days before school starts. You want to get together?"

We made plans to see *Crouching Tiger, Hidden Dragon* at Union Square the next evening, then hung up. I felt that he knew things about magic that I didn't, and he was a good-hearted guy, but also a little bit of a show-off . All the same, they'd made him my roommate for a reason, so I'd better get used to him and make the best of it.

I went down to tell my mother who he was and what we were doing. She thought a minute and then decided to accompany me on the subway and hang around in the area, shopping, until the movie was over.

"I wish you wouldn't," I said.

"Well," she said, "you may be grown up for a thirteen-year-old, but you're still thirteen, and so is this boy you're meeting, right?"

I didn't win the argument. A little annoyed, I went upstairs and picked up the phone. I was going to call Robbie to cancel, but then I changed my mind and dialled the other number.

The phone was answered by a man who sounded well educated and British. I asked for Goldberry.

"Who's calling?"

"This is Simon. I'm her study partner at School of the Ages."

He made a slight coughing noise and put me on hold. I waited a long time.

The voice that responded was British and female and did not sound thirteen. "This is Goldberry. I've just gotten my letter today. I can't say my father is all that pleased that you're a boy. We rather thought it was Simone."

"Sorry to disappoint you," I said.

"Me? No, you haven't disappointed me. I don't know what his problem might be."

The father, in the background, offered a quick retort I could not make out.

"Oh please! What do you think I am, really?"

The father commented again.

"Is this a bad time?" I asked.

"Oh, what isn't?" said Goldberry. "Honestly! Are you at home today, Simon?"

"So far," I said.

"All right, stay. I'll be along in a while." She hung up.

While still annoyed with my mother, I knew I had to tell her company was coming.

Goldberry had not been what I expected; She was not shy and gentle but seemed outgoing and smart. She had our address from the admission letter, but how she would get to us I had no idea.

I waited an hour. She didn't show up. I thought of calling, but that had gotten her in enough trouble the first time. I thought about calling Robbie, who seemed better now that I wasn't talking to him. I thought about calling some people from my public school to tell them I wasn't coming back in the spring. But I was nervous to say anything because of the Cassandra Curse that Dr. Archer had talked about. So I sat rereading my letter. I knew that numerology was the study of how numbers are magical. But what was construction? And what was memento analysis? I wished there was a way to contact Dr. Archer and ask him. But there was no phone number, and I couldn't get there on my own.

It took me a while, thinking, before it occurred to me to make contact with magic. I didn't know if it would work, but what was the point of being a magic student and not trying? So I got out another candle and my special iron knife and carved "Dr. Archer" into it and lit it. While I was watching the candle burn, the doorbell rang. As I was running down the stairs, I half expected it to be Dr. Archer himself.

But on the other side of the door was a tall, pale girl with delicate features and shoulder-length light-brown hair. She was well dressed in dark slacks, white blouse, and dark jacket, with a fur-trimmed parka and elegant leather boots. Her eyes were hazel, greenish gold, and they were quite simply the most striking eyes I had ever seen. Their brightness and their intensity made me feel as if I had never seen such beautiful eyes before.

"Simon," she said, and offered a handshake. "I'm Goldberry. Let me in. It's bloody cold."

I stepped aside and gestured for her to enter. There's an issue about etiquette and power with magicians and thresholds, so an invitation is necessary, and I was glad to give her one. The reward was that she gave me her coat to hang in the hall closet.

"How'd you get here?"

"I took a cab. It took only an hour to drop me."

"A cab from Manhattan? Isn't that a little expensive?"

"My father doesn't need his money all that badly," she said.

I showed her to the living room, where my mother set down her magazine and rose.

After introductions and handshakes, my mother said she would serve some tea and went to the kitchen. Goldberry opened her small knapsack and took out her letter. "Let's see yours, then," she said.

I went upstairs and got my letter, and we traded. Except for names and addresses – her roommate was a girl, Leah Ritz, from Park Slope – they were identical.

"That Archer is quite a wit, I must say," she commented. "We make an odd pair, and not a hint of it at the interview. How much magic do you know?"

"Mostly history," I admitted. "I've only done very simple experiments besides that. What about you?"

"I used to read palms and tea leaves for money," she said. "And I healed my gran's rheumatism. But my father was clear when I was growing up that a magician's life was not for me. Too dangerous and too full of horrible people, he said. He has all sorts of magician friends I have never met, members of other alumni families. He was infuriated when I applied to School of the Ages behind his back, he being the head of the Alumni Board."

Goldberry said, "He was angry enough that I got in, then twice as angry I got a boy for a study partner. Wait till he learns you're a novice."

This stung. "Well, I do know something," I said. My mother brought in a tray with tea and Oreos. Goldberry eyed the Oreos with disdain, but took tea with milk and no sugar.

"Oh, don't get cross with me," Goldberry said as my mother withdrew to the kitchen to continue eavesdropping. "I don't mind you at all. But my father is a different matter."

I imagined having a full-fledged adult magician as my enemy. "Should we change partners, then?"

She sipped her tea and looked at me puzzled. "You can't, you know," she said. "They're ever so stubborn about it at school. So you're scared of my father, are you?"

"No, I'm not scared. Are you saying I should be?"

"He grumbles a lot," said Goldberry, "but my mother won't let him do anything."

"Then both your parents are magicians?"

"After a fashion," she said. "Mother was a fortune-teller, till my father made her respectable. But it's all rather different in Britain. Honestly, I get enough of this talk at home. What about you?"

"We can all see the ad," I said, "so we all have talent. But my parents don't know very much about magic. They just have a lot of odd relatives."

"Well, my father says Dr. Archer only takes students with promise. So you can't be a total waste."

That reminded me of something. "I need to run upstairs for a moment," I said, and did. Jag, the kitten, ran upstairs after me and jumped on my bed as I came into the room.

As I came into my room, the candle sputtered and smoked. As I looked at the smoke, I felt dizzy – I got a sense of Dr. Archer's presence in the room: a flash of memory, of his serious gaze, and a feeling that he wanted me to be patient. I sat down on the bed to shake off the dizziness. Cheetah rubbed against me and purred.

A moment later Goldberry came in, carrying the tea tray with the cups, but no Oreos.

"What are you up to?" she said. "What's all this smoke?"

"From my candle."

"Smoke like this from a candle? Not likely."

"Maybe I did something stupid," I said. "I was trying to call Dr. Archer. I wanted to ask about my schedule. So he made the candle smoke to send me a message to wait."

"You burned a candle and he answered you with smoke. Not bad. Hold on a tick." She took a buzzing pager out of her knapsack, looked at the number, then gestured at the telephone in my room.

"Go ahead," I said.

She dialled, and when someone picked up, had a conversation in excellent French. "That was Cook," she explained after hanging up. "She was calling to ask what I'll have this evening. I told her I'll eat here. You don't mind, do you?"

"I'll see what we're having."

It turned out to be curry chicken. Anticipating that Goldberry would stay, and eager to make something good on one of her rare days off from work, my mother was making one of her best meals.

My father was home about an hour later. He raised his eyebrows when he met Goldberry, who was taller than me. "You're my son's new friend?" he said. "Well, I expect you'll keep him in line."

He went to freshen up. When he came down, we sat at the table for a meal of chicken curry, jasmine rice with peas, chopped cucumber and onion salad, flatbread, and plain yogurt. Goldberry ate sparingly and politely praised the food.

"It's like my mother used to make," my father said.

"Your mother was Indian?" Goldberry asked.

"She still is. And my late father was English," he explained. "I'll tell you our family history, since my son is so secretive about it. My father, Stringfellow Moore, was an importer from Leicestershire, thus my son's real name, Leicester. L-e-s-t-e-r for Americans. My father ran an office in Bombay, where one of his secretaries fixed him up with her niece, who became my mother. Mother had cut her hair and was wearing pants, which in the 40's was pretty scandalous in Bombay, so it was hard to find her an Indian husband, and a British one, while less desirable, at least got her out of the house. Things worked out nicely between the two young people. They had many children of whom I am the youngest, and in the 1970's, I left India on my own to settle here in New York.

"My wife, on the other hand, has New York in her bloodstream. How I got her out of Manhattan is anyone's guess. She sings 'Give My Regards to Broadway' in her sleep."

"Not quite," my mother said. "I grew up in Soho, and my parents were actors. That's about it."

"Oh, not really,' Goldberry said. "There must be more to tell."

"Shall I tell you why my son is called Simon?" she asked.

"No," I said.

"You tell her, then."

"After Simon Magus," I said.

"No, I mean why do you hate your real name," my mother scolded.

"I don't," I said. "But it is a deliberate joke, after all. Leicester S. Moore. Les S. Moore. Less is more."

My father said. "But we were thinking of the Golden Mean. Everything should be done in moderation. Not too much work, not too much play. Not too much food and drink, but don't starve yourself either. Rich is bad, poor is bad. Stay in the middle."

"I quite agree," Goldberry said. She turned to me. "What does the S stand for?"

"All my grandfathers have S names," I said. "Stringfellow and my great-grandfather Sriram on my father's side, Saul and my great-grandfather Salvatore on my mother's side."

"This is a real melting-pot family," my mother added.

The doorbell rang.

"Never rains, but it pours," my father said, and went to answer it.

A booming voice could be heard once the door was opened. "I'm looking for my daughter."

"Oh bother!" said Goldberry.

The Bargain

Mr. Tinker was very tall, six-two at least, and had neatly groomed dark brown hair. He wore a dark suit, alligator shoes and a long black overcoat.

"Join us," my father said, offering a handshake. "I'm Martin Moore, and this is my wife Magdalene and my son… er, Simon."

"My daughter is here without my permission," said Mr. Tinker. He remained standing outside and did not accept the offered handshake. Cold air was making its way into the warm dining room.

"I didn't know," my father said. "But she's safe, as you can see, and you and she are welcome here any time."

"Will you have some dinner?" my mother said, gesturing to the table. But he gave her a cold, dismissive look.

Goldberry was quieter than I expected during all this talk.

"Already eaten," Mr. Tinker said. He looked at his daughter. "If you're quite done," he said.

"At least stay for tea," my mother offered. Mr. Tinker still had not crossed the threshold.

"Let's go, Goldberry," he said.

"Honestly," she said in a low voice. "They're quite nice, you know."

He gave her a stern look. "Get your coat."

I decided it was time for me to do something. By refusing the invitation to enter, Mr. Tinker was giving a magician's signal either that he was our enemy or thought we were his. Both were unacceptable. As the only magician in the house, only I could respond to his signals. Also, as Goldberry's partner and host, I owed her whatever protection I could give against her angry father. I decided to take a risk.

I stood up. "Stay for tea," I commanded.

Anywhere but at home, I would have no chance to command a magician with this power. But within my own home, I would be stronger than anywhere else.

Mr. Tinker and I stared at each other eye to eye. I felt a wave of cold energy wash over me, the concentrated power of his will. If he had wanted to, maybe he could have sucked my life out, or bounced me from wall to wall like a handball. That didn't matter. I was doing what I had to do. In my own home, I should win. Feeling his power, I tried to send some of my own back at him, although I had no idea if I was really doing it.

At last Mr. Tinker blinked, turned his head aside to end the conflict, and finally stepped over the threshold.

"Not bad, Moore," he said to my father. "Your son has potential." He offered his hand this time. "Clive Tinker."

I stole a glance at Goldberry, but so many emotions were flickering over her face that I didn't know what to think. I looked at my mother, who mouthed, "What happened?" I mouthed back, "Later." She said out loud, "I'll put the kettle on."

While my father was hanging Mr. Tinker's coat, he came and crushed my hand in his powerful grip. "You have courage," he said. "You'll need it to take care of my daughter. She's impulsive."

"I think she can take care of herself as well as anyone," I said.

"She is your daughter after all, Mr. Tinker."

He gave me a long look, then chuckled and sat at the table at what would be my father's right hand. "After Goldberry left, I had it out with Archer," he said. "He told me you'd some spine, but I had to see for myself."

I wasn't ready to trust Clive Tinker yet, so I didn't tell him that I was surprised by what Dr. Archer had said. I'd had no idea I could do what I had tried to do, or that I was courageous enough.

"You didn't have to be rude," Goldberry said in a low voice.

"I'll deal with you later," was his reply.

This seemed like normal father-daughter talk, so I let it go and focused on my father, now coming to the table. Did he have any idea what was going on?

"Mr. Tinker," he said, "I hope you don't mind me saying that School of the Ages was a big surprise to all of us in this house. So I have to be curious about how you felt when you first heard about it."

"Well, I was expecting to go to Cambridge Philosophical Prep," said Mr. Tinker. "Just as well I didn't; it closed down a few years later. Citadel D'If was possible, but I don't care for Parisians, and the headmaster, Godinot, was a wanker. Then my father met Dr. Cornelius Archer at a conference in Brussels."

"The same Dr. Archer?" I asked. "Our advisor?"

"No, his father," said Mr. Tinker. "Your advisor is Solomon Archer."

"So you always knew you were going to attend a magic school?" my father said. "You see, we only found out they existed a few days ago. Are we the only new kids on the block?"

"I'm sure Simon can tell you that most magic is learnt by

apprenticeship," said Mr. Tinker. "So it tends to pass from individual to individual, at least at first. Most students with potential don't develop it from books or instinct, as perhaps Simon has. It follows that most magicians know the territory early on."

"Then he's at a disadvantage right now?" my father asked.

"What he can do is limited by what he knows he can do, and by what he dares to do. As an example, when I was on the threshold of your house, he dared to order me to enter. He knew he could try that because he is stronger in his own territory than he would be outside."

My mother gave me a startled look, but my father played it cool.

"Mr. Tinker," I said, "perhaps you could tell me what Memento Analysis is?"

"Perhaps I could," he answered. "But such knowledge is not lightly given. I am not your teacher, and so there must be a bargain."

"Please don't," Goldberry pleaded.

"I'm sorry," I said, "but what are you asking me?"

"If I give you the knowledge," said Mr. Tinker, "you must give me something in return. What do you offer? What we agree to exchange is the bargain."

"Does it have to be something magical?"

"Not in general terms, no," he said. "But in this case, that is what I will require."

I looked at Goldberry, trying to ask with my eyes whether I should make this bargain. I was going to learn the answer to my question from Dr. Archer in a few days anyway, but then, having dealings with a full magician might be good experience. Goldberry seemed to understand my question, but she was embarrassed and lowered her eyes. I had to decide alone.

"Name your price," I said darkly, trying to meet his gaze.

"Then I propose a greater bargain," he replied. The whole room was still. "A service bargain. I will aid you three times. The first time is to answer this question. The other times are as yet unknown. And in turn, you will pledge to give your life three times to my daughter."

I wasn't sure what that meant, but it sounded important, and it meant a lot to me that he would ask me to take such responsibility. To agree and to bargain with him on these terms would make me a man.

"Agreed," I said.

"Oh, crikey," Goldberry whispered.

Mr. Tinker reached inside his suit jacket and took out a gold pocket watch. It was small enough to fit in his palm. The back of the watch was engraved with a lion and a dragon, each leaning on opposite sides of a plain shield. He extended his palm. "Here is the thing that binds," he said. "Touch it and pledge."

I put my hand on the watch. I felt very still and cold. "I pledge to give my life three times to Goldberry."

"And I pledge to aid you three times according to your need and my skill. The covenant between us ends only upon its completion, to extend if necessary beyond death."

"Agreed."

Goldberry hung her head.

"Come with me, then," Mr. Tinker said as he put the watch away. "We will go apart, and I will explain."

We went upstairs to my balcony. Since there was only one chair, I left it for him and got a folding chair from the hall closet for myself. The night was chilly, but I was already feeling so cold that being in the open air didn't seem much different. Mr. Tinker didn't seem to notice the cold either. His full attention was on choosing his words.

"When a person dies," he said, "the spirit leaves the body and enters the spirit world. But the bonds of that spirit to the world that we know are not wholly broken. It is possible still to make contact with some spirits and to communicate with them to gain knowledge and power. Many spirits do at last travel so far from our world that we can no longer know them. In order to prevent this, magicians create mementos. The name is short for the Latin memento mori, memory of the dead. A memento is an object that enables a magician to make direct contact with a dead person."

"Is that difficult?"

"To make slight contact is not difficult," he said. "To make a fulfilling contact, or a complex one, requires more skill. To compel a spirit bound by a memento to perform some action it does not desire, or to betray what it holds secret, is far more difficult."

"And dangerous?"

"Of course. It may even come to pass that you are instead commanded by the spirit."

I had heard of such things before, only not in the context of mementos. "What is memento analysis?" I asked.

"This is a complex question," said Mr. Tinker. "Some years, School of the Ages temporarily exchanges a portion of its memento collection for a selection from another stronghold, library, or magic school. Most of the mementos arrive unlabelled and generally unknown. The first task in memento analysis is to find out which spirits are bound to the objects. Next to be determined is, whether the spirits are too malignant to be controlled. If they are not, then it is determined how the spirits may be employed to advantage, generally by giving information."

"What happens to the bad ones?"

"Different institutions have different policies on that matter.

To release a spirit from its momentary binding may enable it to be used to cause greater harm elsewhere. For this reason, at School of the Ages we do not destroy mementos."

"So if I understand correctly," I said, "the memento analysis course is about making a catalogue of who's inside a bunch of random objects."

"Don't bloody oversimplify like that," said Mr. Tinker.

"Well, what does a memento look like?"

"It is generally metal, stone, or crystal," he said, "and is rarely too large to lift. Some are crafted objects, some in shapes created by weather or geology. The longer an object has held its shape, the better memento it makes. A memento is not instantly recognizable by sight. Touch is more reliable, if you are a person with ability."

"What does it feel like to touch a memento?"

"That is for you to determine."

"Well.... It sounds like mementos can be easily hidden."

"They can," he said, "and they can endure for centuries."

I paused to think. There were more questions to ask, dozens, but my mind was racing too fast for me to focus. I decided to finish up. "Just one more question," I said. "How are mementos made?"

"It would be unwise for me to tell that to a thirteen-year-old," said Mr. Tinker. "A badly crafted memento can be a harmful thing. Now if you're quite done, it's late and I should like to go home."

"How?" I asked. "How do I give my life for Goldberry three times?"

"Give your life to her," he corrected. "That was the pledge. I don't know that either. But when the time comes, I expect we will know." He took out and opened the pocket watch. "And now my daughter and I must go. Good-night."

Robbie

In the morning the ringing of the telephone woke me up. I was thinking of Goldberry, who had been whisked away by her father before I could say good-night. I wanted but feared to see those eyes again. In case it was her, I grabbed the receiver.

"I am very troubled by what you did last night," said Dr. Archer. "Your impatience disappoints me. Of course you were bound to come to grips with Clive Tinker eventually, but why would you bind yourself to him inside your own home?"

"I guess I just thought it would be helpful, or something."

"You thought it would make you feel like a grown-up, I expect," said Dr. Archer disapprovingly. "You know, it was not easy to select a study partner for Goldberry Tinker. Much thought went into the decision to assign you. You must be more careful in the future. I will see you on the first. Good-bye."

He hung up. I did star-69. The number it gave for the last incoming call was my own home phone. So much for that idea.

I spent the morning going through my belongings to decide what I would pack. One small bag would not hold much. My mother came in and pressed me about underwear and socks. My father came up before leaving for work and gave me his new overcoat, which was too long for me, but had large pockets I could stuff with extra clothes. In the end, the only things besides clothes I decided to take, were a few items of magic paraphernalia, none of which I wound up ever using again.

When I was done packing, I called a few people from Bayside High and told them I was going away to a boarding school in Vermont and they should write to me care of my parents. One or two guys said they would write I found out that one girl liked me, but overall there was not much of a reaction.

By then it was time for my mother and me to catch the bus to the subway to Union Square. She fussed over me with advice most of the way. Here is a summary of it. Don't get into trouble. Don't fight with anyone. Don't try too hard to impress your teachers. Just be yourself. Be nice to that girl Goldberry, but try to avoid her father. Change your sheets often and make your bed every morning. Don't eat too much, drink alcohol, or smoke anything. Don't smoke anything, Leicester; I don't trust some of these magic types. You let us know if you're in trouble. We'll get there somehow. Be sure you get enough sleep. Dress warmly all winter.

Partly to cut off some of this, I asked her what she thought of Goldberry. I had barely talked to my partner and was interested in seeing her again. It wasn't falling in love, as I had imagined it. In a way, I felt too serious for that. Falling in love is worth it, but Goldberry was too interesting to fall in love with. She was smarter than anyone my age I'd met before, and very different. Putting her on the potential girlfriend list wouldn't be doing her justice. The partnership would be more rewarding.

It's not that Goldberry wasn't cute; she definitely was, although she was taller than me. She seemed so interesting that cute didn't matter.

Anyway, I asked my mother her opinion and she said, "Well, she's a very nice girl. You know, she was so outspoken until her father came. She seemed so afraid of him."

"Anyone would be," I said. "He's a strong magician."

"I can't pretend to understand that," my mother said. "But sometime, I'm going to tell you some stories."

We rode for about twenty minutes more without speaking. Then the subway stopped at 14th Street, and we made our final arrangements about meeting later and went in separate directions.

Union Square is four large streets, one of them Broadway, forming a box around Union Square Park. The park is always busy with people taking breaks from work to eat and smoke. There are fewer people in the winter, of course, but it wasn't too windy when we got off the subway at the southeast corner. I had about two blocks to walk, around that corner and down a side street to the theater. Robbie had told me he would be outside the theater wearing a gray overcoat and a gray felt hat. I got to the theater, went in and bought my ticket, and returned outside to wait. When it was close to the movie time, I went back in and bought his ticket so we could go right in when he showed up.

It was five minutes past the start time when I saw the gray hat and coat jogging up the street toward me. They enclosed a tall and very chubby boy with dark brown hair and red cheeks. I stepped forward to meet him and extended my hand. "Robbie," I said. "I'm Simon. I have our tickets. Let's go get seats."

Robbie walked inside with me with lots of smiles and "Good to see you"s and "Oh, man, I never figured it was such a long walk from the Village." Then he said, "Grab us two in the back and the popcorn and sodas are on me. You like Junior Mints?"

The movie was several minutes underway when he showed up with two sodas in his hands and an enormous tub of popcorn cradled against his chest. He handed me a box of Junior Mints from his pocket.

I am a moderate eater. By the time the movie was over, all the popcorn was gone, as well as his own box of candy.

"You were hungry," I said as we got outside.

"Nah," he said. "I'm just a pig for popcorn is all. Want to head over to the park for a while?"

I agreed to go.

"Man, I can't wait to go to school," Robbie said as we walked toward the square.

"Me too."

"Hey, who's your study partner?"

I told him a little bit about Goldberry, and then, about our encounter with the Mermelsteins.

"I don't know much about Cabala," he admitted. "But it's supposed to be strong magic. This Mermelstein kid might be someone you don't want to cross."

I didn't feel like continuing with that, so I asked, "Who's your study partner?"

"Balaram Dass," he said. "Indian dude from Yonkers. I haven't met to him yet. They said he's coming back from Bombay tonight."

I explained to Robbie that I was one-quarter Indian by way of my father's mother and had relatives in Bombay also. His reply was his usual "That's cool." Then he asked me again if I wanted to go with him to summon an elemental spirit.

"I think I'll wait till they teach us about it," I said.

"Sometimes the summoning doesn't work out," he said, "but sometimes they give you cool powers and stuff; I mean, if you ask them nicely. Hey, watch this. See that patch of snow there, by the fire hydrant?"

I looked at the nearest dirty-green hydrant. There was a small patch of snow there. "Okay."

Robbie said some nonsense words and gestured at it. As we watched, a trickle of water emerged from the bottom and flowed over the curb edge into the street. The trickle continued until the whole patch of snow loosened and flowed into the street.

"It's not much," Robbie said. "I mean, it only works on little pieces of ice and stuff. But it's nice to know you can do that kind of thing. I like to do it when I'm bored and looking out of the window, like in school."

I had gotten used to thinking Robbie was all talk, so his display surprised me. Whether he'd really melted the snow, or just predicted what was going to melt on its own, it was impressive.

"The spirits won't usually give you any powers that people would really notice you using," Robbie explained. "Not the spirits I can get, anyway. Maybe the big ones could. But the spirit that gave me that, Nilofer the Lily, said what she was really doing was awakening something in me that was always there. You should summon her some time. I mean, she kind of makes fun of you, but she explains things too."

"What do these spirits look like?"

"Nilofer kind of looks like a female David Bowie, with the spikey hair and the different coloured eyes. Elemental spirits usually look just like people," he said. "You could pass them in the street and not realize it. You know, like Mr. N.Otis. Any time you run into some stranger who helps you out, it could be a spirit. And strangers who mess with you could be some spirit in a bad mood or who doesn't like your face."

"Does that happen to you a lot?" I asked.

"Who knows?" he said. "I hope so. I like things to be interesting."

New Faces

I was up at 4 am on the first. I lay in bed a while imagining the faces of the people I would see again that day. The stern Dr. Archer, the wry Goldberry, the jovial Robbie, the brooding Mermelstein all passed before my eyes like phantoms.

Finally I got up and went downstairs to the kitchen to feed the cats. Leo, Cheetah, and Cougar were all awake and eating already. I went into the dining room to discover my father sitting at the table in his usual chair. In the soft illumination of the night light in the kitchen, I saw him very still and thoughtful in his pajamas and bathrobe.

"You should get some more sleep," he said. "Big day today."

"That's why I can't sleep."

"Don't blame you. Big change to make at a few days' notice." He asked me if I had called any classmates from Bayside. Then he said, "I know you're not going to be far away, but it still feels like that. Can I tell you a story?"

I sat down in the chair next to him.

"Your grandmother," he said, "was married before she met my father. He was a bank manager or something, a very important man in the town he was from. But in Bombay he was a nobody. He'd transferred there and then arranged to be married. They were married three months, but they were both unhappy. He felt uncomfortable in the big city, and he began to mistreat her. She got her two brothers to help and they moved him out of their apartment and out of Bombay altogether and told him not to come back. It was after that, that she found out she was pregnant. It was a big problem, you know, to have a baby without a father. So they got a divorce and got her married to Stringfellow Moore, my father, as soon as they could. The real reason she married an Englishman, besides liking him of course, is that no respectable Indian man would marry a divorced woman with a child on the way.

"Somehow, I don't know how, the father found out about the child, a son named Rajiv, and he came back to Bombay a year later, to demand the boy be given to him. There was a lot of trouble I won't go into, and he was refused. My two uncles thrashed him and left him at the train station.

"The next night my mother woke up in a cold sweat, feeling something was wrong. Rajiv was in a crib at the foot of the bed. She saw a dark shadow standing over it. She shook my father, but he didn't wake up. Her eyes adjusted to the dark, and there was the baby's father, with a cold, faraway look in his eyes. He reached down into the crib and picked up Rajiv. She couldn't move, but she screamed and he vanished.

"Finally she could move again. She went to the crib and found Rajiv there, only he didn't feel right in her arms. He didn't seem to know her, and he never made a sound again, and a week later, he died.

"Of course, long before this, my father rang the police. This is where it becomes troublesome, son. It was confirmed beyond a doubt that Rajiv's father was in jail that night, for disorderly conduct, at the exact time my mother saw him in her bedroom.

"My grandmother, who was a clever woman in her own way, said that what my mother Devi saw was an evil spirit that could take any physical shape. These spirits were always given to kidnapping mothers and children in the old legends. My grandmother also said that the real Rajiv was gone, and that the dead infant was a changeling. In this case, that meant an evil spirit that was exchanged for my real elder brother.

"My father was very angry at what my grandmother did next: she sent some servants to the father's village to see if he had Rajiv with him. They came back and said that he did, that they had seen the infant with their own eyes.

"So my grandmother went to the village herself with the police and went to his house, but they found that he had moved away, and he was never heard from again. They said he had become a Muslim and was living in Karachi, a city that is now part of Pakistan."

He paused, considering his words. Then: "So what do you think of that story, Leicester?"

"Well," I said, "There are lots of stories like that, if you know where to look for them. It's hard to know which ones are true, if you didn't live through them yourself. But what do you think?"

"When I was a boy, I believed it, because my mother told me," he said. "Then when I grew up, I decided it was a story they'd made up to cover something else, such as giving Rajiv to his father because my father didn't want him, or putting Rajiv up for adoption. But now…" He seemed to be waiting for me to speak.

"But now," I guessed, "you're starting to wonder if it was true after all."

"Exactly. There are a lot of strange stories about my family,

Leicester. But it's only after this last week that I've started to think seriously about them. If you're going to get into this kind of business, you should know." He got up, and went into the kitchen, and began to fill the kettle. It felt like he wasn't done.

"Tell me more," I said. "There's something else on your mind."

"Nothing specific," he said slowly. "Just be careful. The weird stuff is closer to home than maybe you realize. Your mother..." Again he struggled for words.

"Does she know all this?"

"Of course. She... Well, every mother wants her son to have an easy time in life. And what you're doing...is not going to be easy I think. You're going far off the beaten path." He put teabags in two mugs. Leo was crunching dry food on the countertop nearby.

"She doesn't like it."

"You're being brave," he said, "and she likes that. The rest, she'll get used to."

After a moment, the kettle whistled, and he poured the water and spooned the honey.

"Are you okay with it?" I asked my father.

He thought a while as he stirred my teacup. "The thing is," he said, "I wasn't really surprised."

*

About an hour later, I went out on the porch to wait for the bus. We had a short, steep front lawn cut by some crooked slate steps. I shut the door behind me and carried my bag down to the curb.

In a moment the bus came chugging out of the street two blocks down and rambled up the block. It stopped with the door just beside the base of the yard steps. The door creaked open Mr. Saluto stepped down in his driving cap, took my bag, and shook my hand. "All aboard," he said with a grin and a wink.

It was dim inside the bus. I peered at the shadowy figures in the nearest seats and they peered back at me. There was a solemn-looking Orthodox Jewish boy with a woven wool skullcap who gave me a nervous nod and then returned to his leather-bound prayer book. In the next seat sat, a short boy with dark curly hair and a warm smile. Behind him, another Orthodox boy, a big redhead, fast asleep. Across from him, a short, thin Asian Indian fellow in faded jeans and a white shirt. And behind him…

"Coo-ee," someone. I recognized Goldberry's voice and went to sit by her.

"You didn't half notice me, you prat," she said as I got settled. "Too early for you, is it?"

"No, I've been up for hours," I said. "Listen, I would have called, but…"

"It's all right," she said. "We were both chatting up our roomies. That one there is yours, right?"

She gestured a few seats back, where I saw Robbie dozing with his face against the window.

"How'd you know?" I asked.

"He introduced himself, just before he began snoring," she said. "I thought he fancied me, till I saw he fancied himself quite a bit. My roommate's called Leah. She's very shy. We'll pick her up on the way. She's a Park Slope girl."

The bus rumbled and rattled and started to move. I realized I didn't have my bag and got up, but then found it on the rack above my seat, next to a leather valise that had to be Goldberry's.

"Next stop Brooklyn," Mr. Saluto called.

"Anyway, you're a prize fool," Goldberry said. "Taking on my father, like that." She smiled.

"You think I surprised him?"

"You might have done," she said. "But he's dead clever, you know. I wouldn't go thinking you got the better of him."

"I didn't," I said. "Dr. Archer called me yesterday and let me have it for taking that oath with him."

"Yes, why did you do it?"

I had been thinking about that, and now that I was with her, I realized the answer. "I think whatever I promised to do, I would have done anyway," I said. "I think you're going to be a great partner, and I won't regret it, whatever it is."

This answer surprised Goldberry, and she looked away, out of the window at the dim street.

"What's the matter?" I asked.

"Nothing," she said. "Except I feel bad. I had my doubts about you when I met you. I thought you were nice enough, but that was about it. But you didn't half surprise me there. And I'm a fortune-teller at that."

I saw she still wasn't looking at me.

"I'm sorry if I said something wrong."

"Wrong?" she answered. "Oh, it was perfect. That's the problem, you see." She was still looking out the window, so I did as well.

We got onto the Grand Central Parkway, and after a few miles got on the Jackie Robinson towards Brooklyn. A lot of this highway was narrow and wooded, so I stared at the bare trees and patches of snow. Whenever I glanced back at Goldberry, she had her eyes closed.

"I'm going to talk to Robbie," I told her. She didn't respond, so I just got up and went back to where Robbie was sleeping. I sat next to him and nudged him. After a moment he blinked, looked at me, and grinned.

"Hey, man," he said. "Great, you made it. Where are we?"

Outside the window I saw brown buildings and cracked streets. "Somewhere in Brooklyn," was all I could say.

"Well, I met a couple of guys when they were getting on," he said sleepily. "The Indian dude up front is my study partner, Balaram. The other guy with the black curly hair is Rocco. The Jewish guys are Max and Daniel. Rocco's from my neighborhood, and the other guys are from Flushing. That guy in the back, with the Renaissance Fair cloak over his head, no one knows who he is."

I looked to the very back of the bus. Someone had a velvet cape covering his head. I couldn't make out anything.

"And I met your partner," Robbie continued. "You talk to any of those guys?"

"Not yet," I admitted.

He closed his eyes. "I'm going back to sleep," he said. "Wake me up when we get there."

He went to sleep, and after a few minutes I closed my eyes too. I didn't sleep, but I rested until the bus rocked to a halt. The door opened, and three Chasidic boys got on in a group and made their way to the back. One was Mermelstein, but he went by so fast that I couldn't catch his eye. There would be plenty of time for that anyway. I closed my eyes again, and this time dozed.

When I woke up, the bus was stopping again. The door opened, and a small girl with long, tied-back black hair climbed on. She was petite and pale and had eyes as dark as the night sky. She was wearing a long black dress and a wool coat. I realized this was Goldberry's roommate, Leah. As she walked down the aisle, I saw the curly-haired boy, Rocco, offer to help with her bag. She turned him down and looked away. I had been thinking of making the same offer, but now decided not to. Instead, I went to Goldberry's seat, saw she was asleep, and gently tapped her on the shoulder to wake her. "I think this is your roommate," I whispered.

"Yes, I think so," she said. She stood and gestured, and the girl came toward us. I realized I was in the way and got out of the seat, standing in the aisle.

After they said 'Hello', Goldberry introduced me. "This is my partner, Simon. Simon, this is Leah."

"Good to meet you." I offered my hand, but she didn't accept it.

"Good to meet you," she answered in a painful whisper.

"I'll let you guys talk," I said, "but tell me if I can help out."

She said thank you and sat, looking away from me. That was happening a lot this morning. The bus clanked away from the curb, and I looked up front and saw Rocco looking around the edge of his seat at Leah. I shrugged at him, and he smiled and shrugged back. Then I went and sat by my sleeping roommate. In about twenty minutes, we entered the Battery Tunnel.

Just as during the first visit, I felt a rumble in my stomach, an uneasy feeling that we weren't moving forward anymore. It was like we were going sideways at the same time.

The bus came out of the tunnel and bumped across the grass. The bumping disturbed Robbie, who lifted his head sleepily. "We're here," he said. "Way cool."

The sun was starting to rise behind the clouds, turning the sky dry and white. The bus pulled up in front of the building, precisely where it had on our last visit. The other students began to stir, gathering up their bags and books and moving into the aisle. I collected my bag, stood and smoothed out my coat. It was warmer here than it had been riding through Brooklyn.

As I stepped into the aisle, someone thrust past me suddenly and violently, throwing me back into Robbie, who was still not alert.

"Ouch!" he shouted. "Look out, dude!"

I dropped my bag and got up. I rushed into the aisle to confront the boy who had knocked me over. I recognized him even from behind.

"Mermelstein!" I called to him. "Wait a minute."

He stopped, turned only halfway, looked over his shoulder at me with narrowed eyes, and said nothing.

"You knocked me down, Mermelstein," I said. "You need to take it easy."

He turned a little further and raised one hand with the index finger extended. "You are no one to talk to me," he said in a low voice. "No one." Then he turned again, and went up the aisle toward the bus door.

"What a grouch," Robbie said. "You know that guy?"

"Yakov Mermelstein, from Flatbush," I said. "He's got something against me, but I don't have a clue what it is."

I entered the aisle, followed by Robbie. As we passed the seat where Goldberry and Leah had been, I saw them still sitting there and stopped, gesturing to them to go.

Goldberry looked at her roommate, then said, "Go on. We'll be along in a bit."

Leah looked at us for a second, then lowered her eyes. Robbie caught this and bent over, trying to look at her face and catch her attention.

"How's it going?" he asked. "We haven't met. I'm Robbie Ravitz." He offered her a handshake, but she didn't take his hand, although she looked at him and gave a weak smile.

"It's OK," Robbie said. "I don't bite."

"I know," she said very quietly. "Just excuse me for now."

He shrugged. "Just tell me your name and we'll save the rest for later."

"My name is Leah. Please excuse me."

"Yeah, shove off," Goldberry said harshly. "Simon, get him out of here, would you?"

I took Robbie by the elbow and guided him toward the bus door.

"What the heck?" he said to me.

"She's really shy," I said. "She wouldn't talk to me much either."

"I have got to get to know her," he said. "Your partner's cute, but that Leah has got to be the prettiest girl I ever met."

I had a feeling that Robbie, big, round and brash as he was, was going to get nowhere with Goldberry's shy and diminutive roommate, but I decided not to say this to him. We climbed down from the bus into the chill air.

The other students were standing around in small groups, clustered around stacks of bags on the grass. The one with the cape was now revealed as a tall boy with a colorless face, uncombed hair, and a sharp nose. He was standing near Rocco but not looking at him. Aside from Mr. Saluto, who had taken off his shoe and was shaking some pebbles out of it, there were no adults visible yet. I looked at the broad entrance doors and the mostly shuttered windows of the sprawling building in front of us. This was my new home.

"OK, now they're coming," Robbie said. I thought he meant some teachers had arrived, and looked around to see where they were coming from. But I realized that he meant Goldberry and Leah were finally getting down from the bus. "I'm going to go talk to her again," he added.

"I'd give it a break if I were you," I said. I looked him in the eye and shook my head. The weight of my gaze seemed to get him to think things over, as I had intended.

"OK, OK," he said at last. "I'm just nervous, man. Got to do something. Hey, where's that Mermelstein guy? I'm going to set him straight."

Mermelstein was several yards away, talking to two other Chasidic boys. Not waiting to discuss it with me, Robbie strode quickly in his direction.

Mermelstein caught the motion immediately, turned, and raised that index finger again. He said something under his breath that I couldn't understand. Whatever he said was effective, though. Robbie stopped in his tracks, then took a step back breathing heavily and retreated to my side.

"What happened?" I asked him.

"It was like an electric shock or something, all through my legs," he said. "I just couldn't take another step. Wow, that guy knows what he's doing! But I know a few tricks, too." He shook himself, looking like a big wet dog in his ragged gray coat. He was going to have another go at Mermelstein.

"Robbie," I said. I caught hold of his shoulder. "Robbie! You really need to chill out. Let me deal with him."

"Okay, Okay," he said.

I wasn't sure what I was going to do, but I wasn't about to let Mermelstein bully anyone, no matter how much Cabala he knew already. I stepped in front of Robbie, and then slowly walked toward Mermelstein and his comrades.

The other two Chasidic boys saw me coming and rolled their

eyes. But Mermelstein turned sharply again, raising his hand once more.

"I'm not attacking you, Mermelstein," I said. "I'm not looking for a fight, so your trick won't work on me, will it?"

I had no way of knowing that, but somehow I did. Maybe I wasn't powerful, but my instincts were good. He lowered his hand, but squared his shoulders and loomed over me as I came closer. His hard eyes, his shaggy hair, and white skin against the black suit, all made him menacing, but I was sure he wasn't going to hurt me just then.

"I have nothing to do with you, *apikoros*," he said, using a word I didn't know. "I told you that, and my father told your *goyish* father the same thing. Stay out of my way or you'll regret it."

"Why don't you try being polite?" I said calmly. "Just because you don't like me doesn't mean you have the right to knock me down. And you had no business using a spell on my friend either. You can have whatever friends you want, but I don't see why you'd make enemies."

"Because," he answered, "it's bad enough already to have to go to school with your kind. I don't have to talk to you."

"My kind?" I looked at the other Chasidic boys, but they were expressionless, staying out of the argument. "I don't have a kind, Mermelstein. And I think anyone who does is limiting himself too much."

"Break it up, guys," one of the other students called to us. "Here come the teachers."

The main doors had opened, and a group of six hooded figures was coming toward us. The bus engine roared, and the bus pulled away. I watched it disappear around a clump of trees. Then I turned back to the teachers again.

At the front of the group of teachers, the Dean lowered his hood and told us, "Each group of partners will have a brief meeting with its advisor. Then we will go to the Great Hall for meditation, and then breakfast."

The other five teachers lowered their hoods: I quickly found Dr. Archer, then recognized Rabbi Shulman, Maestro Morgan, and Mr. Bannerjee. The last was a younger man who also had the same beard, skullcap, and long black coat that distinguished Rabbi Shulman.

Goldberry and I went with Dr. Archer. Robbie and Balaram went with Maestro Morgan. Mr. Bannerjee took Rocco and the kid with the cape. The young rabbi took the redhead, Max, and the other Orthodox guy, Daniel. Mermelstein and the two other Chasidic boys went with Rabbi Shulman. I didn't see where Leah went.

Orientation

Dr. Archer had a fire burning in his office. We took off our coats. "I know you have gotten acquainted, as have your families," he said. "This year will be challenging for both of you. You will have noticed from your schedule that mathematics has been omitted in favor of numerology. This seemed prudent because our first-year mathematics course would not be challenging for Simon. As to each of you individually, with whom shall I start?"

I waited for Goldberry to speak, but when she didn't, I said, "You can start with me."

Dr. Archer narrowed his eyes for a moment, peering at me as if he could see through me. "You have changed a great deal in a short time," he concluded. "Your knowledge of School of the Ages has awakened your courage and your ambitions. These traits will certainly be useful, but you must moderate and balance them. Because you did not do so, you have become overly entangled with Clive Tinker, a powerful magician whose motivations you do not know. Your enmity with Yakov Mermelstein is more understandable. Dr. Chatterjee predicted it when charting the future of this fresher class."

He paused, so I took the chance to speak. "He's obnoxious," I said.

"Perhaps so," said Dr. Archer, "but I submit that you are the greater cause of the conflict."

I was not expecting this. It cut off the complaints about Mermelstein that I was planning to voice. Instead, I said, "I don't understand."

"Then you must learn," he said. "The morning meditations will assist you in gathering your scattered perceptions. Now, what questions have you regarding your subjects of study?"

I did have one. "What is Construction?"

"It is the preparation of objects for use in magic. You might charge them with a particular energy in order to assist in a ritual, or you might impart to them permanent magical properties. I believe you have done this before?"

I remembered the small protective pendants I had made for my parents and me before visiting School of the Ages for the first time. "I don't think I did it so well, though."

"Rabbi Horn will enable you to perform construction more effectively," Dr. Archer concluded.

"How do we know where to go and when?"

"You will get a printed schedule after breakfast." He turned his gaze on Goldberry. "You may be concerned," he told her, "that you will be expected to achieve a certain level of success because of family connections. I do not speak of myself when I say this, for my expectations of you are based upon my investigations of your own character. On the other hand, I do not think it wise to intervene. You must yourself find a solution to the expectations placed upon you by others. I must also commend to you the care of Leah Ritz during her first year at STA. The reasons for this will become clear to you in time. Now, what questions have you?"

"I have one," she said. "Why am I not enrolled in Divination class?"

"Unfortunately," said Dr. Archer, "Simon currently lacks potential in that area, and the schedules of study partners must be identical in the first year. You may enlist in the Divination Club in order to develop further in Divination this year."

"I don't mind taking Divination, even if I fail it," I said. "You can take us out of Numerology."

"Your opinion is noted," said Dr. Archer.

I asked him a few more questions. The boy with the cape was called Corby Crow. He was supposed to be Rocco's study partner, but he was a loner. The young rabbi was named Rabbi Zylberberg.

When all questions were answered, Dr. Archer said, "Now, let us go to the Meditation Hall."

He led us down a set of wide stairs I hadn't seen before. In a large gray room, many robed and hooded faculty members stood outside a pair of broad wooden doors. Dr. Archer departed, and after a quick look at each other, we headed for the doors.

The Meditation Hall had a high ceiling and was supplied with pews like a church. There was a platform at the far end of the room. The only light came from many dozens of taper candles arranged carefully on the pews and the platform, and from battery-powered lanterns that some of the older students had brought. Among the pews nearby, at least fifty students were gathered. I found that I didn't feel like talking. No one else was talking, and the only sound was some shuffling and some pages turning. Goldberry and I joined the group and stood waiting.

The other students were a mixed group. Besides the ones I knew, there were more Chasidic and Orthodox boys, two or three Indians, the others white, some formally dressed, others in what looked like specialized wizard garb like robes and pointed hats. They looked odd to me in my plain buttoned shirt and dark slacks, next to Goldberry in her blue skirt and red cashmere turtleneck and elegant leather boots.

However, it was hard to concentrate on these thoughts for long. The room was hot and stuffy, and I found myself light-headed and sleepy. I made my way to a pew, losing Goldberry who was headed towards her roommate Leah. The latter was already seated at the end of a different pew, far from the others, although not unnoticed, as some of the boys in the room were turned slightly in her direction.

I sat, swiftly locating everyone else in the room that I recognized: Robbie with his partner Balaram; Mermelstein and his cohorts, now holding what looked like small embroidered pillows in zipped plastic holders; Rocco, Max, Daniel.

"Be seated."

The voice was from the platform. Maestro Morgan was now standing there, though I had not seen him arrive. The students moved to the nearest pews, the older ones smoothly, the newer ones with some bumping and confusion.

"An equilateral triangle without colour," Maestro Morgan said. "The perimeter three colourless lines, void within the perimeter. Visualize."

Equilateral triangle: three sides all the same length. It would be easier to visualize that if I shut my eyes, I thought, so I did. It was still very difficult to imagine something without color, and I felt color drifting into it, green, pastel-blue.

"Without color," Maestro Morgan repeated. "Hold the image. Second-years, rotate the triangle round a bisecting line to form a cone. Third years, double the triangle and rotate opposite directions.

Seniors, flatten the cones dorsally. First-years, retain the triangle."

He said nothing else for a long time. I struggled to keep the triangle in mind while my thoughts drifted. How long till I would see my parents again? Would Mermelstein fight me? Would I be able to learn Hebrew? Why was Leah so shy? What would studying with Goldberry be like? With each of these thoughts, faces and possible future events drove the shape of the triangle out of my mind, and I had to struggle to recapture it. I would call the image back into my mind, but always with black lines, like in my maths textbook. "Get rid of the color," I told myself. I tried to imagine the color draining away, as if the bottom of the triangle were leaking.

"Dorsally, Cohen," scolded Maestro Morgan. "Dispose of that clown face, Dempsey! The triangle, first-years! The triangle!" With these last five words, it was as if he was singing. The sound of his voice as he cried out "The triangle!" drove away my fog of useless thoughts, and for a flash of a moment, I saw the triangle in my mind, so sharply it might have been a memory.

"Can't visualize void," Corby Crow whispered to himself. "Idiot, what is he saying?"

"First-years," said Maestro Morgan, "the triangle is the first stage of disciplining and ordering your mind. We will continue the triangle daily until you master it. In any quiet moment, perhaps before you sleep, remember the triangle. Older students are dismissed. First-years remain."

I kept my eyes closed, trying to hold onto the triangle despite the rustle of the older kids leaving the hall, its doors creaking open and slamming shut. Maestro Morgan had shown it to me, but without his help it was slipping away.

"First-years," he said, "it is common for students of your age to neglect your meditation, as it is both painful and frustrating before you become used to it. I must urge you instead to give extra attention to this work. Should your skills at meditation lag, you will find that your overall growth as magicians will suffer as well. At present, meditate upon the triangle as often as possible. And this advice as well: meditation is not a matter of fierce concentration. It is instead a matter of inner peace. Dismissed."

Outside, we found the activities director Mr. Bannerjee, and the registrar, Ms. Roosevelt-Wilson, waiting to guide us to the breakfast room. As we walked, Robbie and Balaram came over to me. I shook Balaram's hand, and we said hello. There was little talk; most of the first-years were overwhelmed by the newness.

As we passed through the stone corridors, I tried to learn my way. It was hard to tell the halls apart. But soon the smell of food told us we were getting closer. Finally we came into a small foyer where we were met by the young Rabbi Zylberberg we had seen earlier, who led about a third of the group toward the kosher dining room. The rest of us went with our current guides, and in a moment arrived at a long high-ceilinged dining room with many large, round wooden tables.

A selection of breakfast food was on each table: tea, coffee, juice, pancakes, French toast, scrambled eggs. The older students were already busy with forks and spoons; the rest of us dug in.

"Man, that meditation was freaky," Robbie said. "But I liked it. Seeing the triangle just floating there."

The curly-haired boy named Rocco introduced himself. His real name was Scott Vitello, he said. "This is crazy stuff, all this," he added. "My dad's a fireman, and my mom stays home. I never saw this kind of thing before."

"Me too," I admitted.

After that we were all busy eating, especially Robbie, who took three times what I did. As I was starting to feel full, I sat back in my chair and then spotted one of the older students coming to our table. He had handsome but stern features and serious eyes. "How are you doing?" he said. "I'm looking for Simon."

"I'm Simon."

"I'm Donovan Archer. My dad's your advisor. I thought I'd just say hello and let you know I'm around if you need any help." We shook hands. "Same for the rest of you guys. By the way, if you like kosher food better, it's just down the hall."

He shook everyone's hand, then went back to his own table. Now that I was finished with breakfast, my mind turned to Goldberry. I hadn't seen her since meditation. I got up and walked around the dining room. Some of the older students said hello, but most ignored me.

Finally I found Goldberry and Leah sitting at a table with two older girls who were ignoring them. I sat by them. Leah looked down and away.

"So how did you guys like meditation?" I asked.

"Quite relaxing, really," Goldberry said, twiddling her empty teacup. I took the hint and passed her the teapot.

"What did you think, Leah?"

"It was good," she said faintly, still not wanting to look at me. "I used to do it with Appa when I was little."

"Oh, did you learn a lot of magic from your father?"

"I don't know," she said. "I don't know what would be a lot. He used to teach me." Her voice trailed off, and she looked at her plate. I didn't think I had ever met anyone so shy in my life. My parents had taught me to be bold when meeting new people, but with Leah

I felt shy too. She was so pretty that it was hard not to stare at her. It was also hard to know she didn't feel good with me around. I decided to let it go.

"If we can't stay together," I told Goldberry, "maybe we could meet to talk after dinner?"

"Can do," she said. "Want to copy my notes, do you?"

"More like to compare notes."

"Right."

A little while later, Ms. Roosevelt-Wilson came in to hand out schedules and maps of the school building. While we were peering at the maps, which had large areas grayed out as "off-limits for first-years," she explained that there were no bells and that we would have to keep track of time with our own wristwatches. Mr. Bannerjee would show the new students to the dormitory area, where we could get settled in our rooms, nap a little, and then assemble in Amsterdam Auditorium for a one-time special Theory of Magic lecture by the Dean.

Mr. Bannerjee warned us that our rooms did not have windows, and we would have to rely on candles and lanterns till we got the windowed dorms in our fourth year. Then he walked us to the dormitories, in a more sunny upstairs part of the building, where gray winter light shone through large windows. The corridors were decorated with posters advertising club and team meetings. Many older students were already in their rooms, and I heard Beethoven's Fifth Symphony coming from one open doorway, and "Stairway to Heaven" trickling out of another. Since there was no electricity, they had to be using battery power.

Robbie and I found our bags and coats already in our rooms. We had very little to unpack. I laid my books and my few magic paraphernalia on the small wooden desk, put my clothes in the pull-out drawer built into the bed frame, and lay down on the bed. Robbie dumped his bag onto his desk, then lay down on his bed and was comatose in minutes. I felt myself drifting off.

I ASK FORGIVENESS said a voice directly next to my ear.

....

I jumped up and looked around, but there was no one else in the room other than me and my snoring roommate. The voice had been hollow, as if I was hearing it come from the bottom of a well. I was sure it was no dream. Dreams grow vague with time, but this voice didn't fade from my memory. I got up and shook Robbie awake.

"What? What?" he said impatiently. "Oh, come on, man. Let me sleep."

I described the voice to him: a young man, a tenor, with a harsh undercurrent.

"Spirit," he said.

"What kind?"

"Spirit of a dead person."

"You're kidding."

"Look, Simon. There's got to be all sorts of spirits hanging around a place like this. I wouldn't let it worry you."

"Forgiveness for what?"

"Probably nothing to do with us, but all about what he did when he was alive. Look, I told you, man. There are spirits around us all the time that we don't recognize. Don't forget that we were both recruited by an elemental spirit."

*

About an hour later, Robbie and I followed some older students to Amsterdam Auditorium, a large high-ceilinged room with a dais at one end. There were about a hundred folding chairs. A podium stood on the dais. The room was heated by firepits in the floor, burning a relatively smokeless fuel. What smoke there was rose to large ventilation shafts in the ceiling. As we came in, we took legal pads and pens.

Many students and faculty members I didn't recognize were already assembled. I saw Goldberry alone and went to sit next to her and told her about the spirit voice. To my great relief, she took it more seriously than Robbie had.

"I can't belief ghosts just go randomly whispering in people's ears. Right, let me see your palm, then." She took my hand in both of hers and held it steady. "Well, then. Very long life line, I see. Runs in the family?"

"I have a grandmother who's eighty-seven."

"Right. Lots of breaks in the love line. A lot of friendships, but a lot of loss. Moderate in wealth and business, very large family. Adventurous life. I think what I see here is that an awful lot will happen to you from now on. You don't seem an adventurer to look at, but looks can be deceptive. So odds are Mr. I-Ask-Forgiveness is up to something."

She let go my hand. "You're good at that," I told her.

"Good enough to make some money out of it," she said. "But not good enough yet to do anything really useful. Palmistry's not much for solving immediate problems."

"So do you think I should talk to a teacher?"

"Could do," she said.

I was starting to look around for Dr. Archer, but then I changed my mind. "Forget it. I'll try to deal with it myself."

"Fair enough."

A tall, light-haired boy was now approaching us. He came to Goldberry first and said, "Hello. I'm William Goodenough, from the second year."

"I'm Goldberry Tinker. I think my father knows yours. This is my partner, Simon."

I shook hands with him, but he scarcely looked at me.

"Take a walk later on?" he asked her.

"Business or pleasure?"

"I'll show you around the school."

"Show us both and you're on."

"All right." It wasn't what he'd had in mind, but he kept his cool, shook hands with her, gave a wide smile, and went to sit somewhere else.

It was strange to have someone basically ask my partner out right in front of me. I guess my feelings showed on my face.

"What's the matter?" Goldberry asked.

"He doesn't waste any time, does he?"

Goldberry rolled her eyes. "My father probably arranged it."

"What if he didn't?"

"Well, I've nothing to be afraid of all the same."

The noise in the room rose, followed by a noticeable hush. I looked to the front and saw that the Dean was now standing on the dais at the podium. All the students and teachers began finding seats. I got my pad and pen ready. Gradually the room fell silent, and the Dean began to speak.

"As I have said before, in fact as I say every year, it is important that School of the Ages be a place ruled by respect. You will respect your instructors for a number of reasons. An important reason is their greater experience and ability. Another is that to do otherwise will harm the life of the school, and this will not be tolerated. The principal reason, however, is the character of your instructors. Armed with the knowledge one comes here to gain, an individual can choose to garner great wealth or worldly power. Your teachers have chosen instead to dedicate themselves to sharing their knowledge. In effect, they have decided that to assist in your growth and spur your success is more worthwhile than to secure their own. This is an act of nobility and courage to which you must aspire, and not one which you dare to scorn. You may dispute with your instructors; you may contend with them when your cause is just; but you must always respect them.

"The same is true in your relations with one another. Whatever your differences, you share two common bonds. One is that you are alike in your choice to center your life upon the philosophy that we call magic. The other is that you are alike in your choice of School of the Ages, as a place to develop your potential. Because of these two bonds, you must always hold one another in high esteem. It is not expected that you will always like one another. You will often find yourselves in conflict. This is permitted within certain boundaries. These are: cause no lasting harm to body, mind, or spirit; and do not further attack a defeated foe. Should you find yourself in a conflict you cannot manage, you may end that conflict by admitting defeat to your opponent.

"School of the Ages is not subject to any law but its own. No authority exists beyond what we ourselves impose. There are no police; there is no government. Those forces cannot find us here. Your safety is dependent upon our law. Fortunately, we are not tyrants, and your safety from outside forces is virtually assured within these walls.

"Now, on another topic, many of our older students have come to me pleading to be told of our annual school trip. I have heard many excellent suggestions. Bear in mind as always that certain locations and events do repel our means of travel. Thus we cannot venture to Bethlehem in the year zero B.C.E. to test the veracity of a certain birth. Nor can we hear the teachings of Gautam Buddh, nor follow Mohammed on the Hijra from Mecca to Medina. An amusing suggestion, Mr. Lambert, to pose as Bedouins and give the Prophet wrong directions, but I believe we all know better.

"Our School of the Ages trips avoid battles for reasons of student safety. Thus the Norman Conquest in 1066, Napoleon's defeat at Waterloo, and the evacuation at Dunkirk have all been excluded.

"My apologies to Miss Dunham, but as the wedding of Prince Charles and Lady Diana is within living memory, we cannot approve it. And I thank Chatterjee Minor for his well-researched suggestion, but we will not go hunting for a gorgosaurus this year."

Several of the older students laughed.

"We will, however, consider several suggestions from Renaissance Europe, including the court of King Louis XIV and Versailles, the painting of the Sistine Chapel, and the first performance of A Midsummer Night's Dream. The construction of the Great Wall of China was of sufficient duration for a suitable moment to be found. The trial of Socrates is also an option. More suggestions remain on my desk awaiting review. I shall examine celestial influences to assist with the selection."

I couldn't believe what I was hearing. Was the Dean really talking about visiting such great moments from the past? I wondered where I would choose to go.

....

"Yes, Rocco?" said the Dean.

"Sir," said Rocco, "I mean, I know I'm out of order and all, but why don't we go into the future?"

"We are continuously doing so, young man," said the Dean. "It is only that we are not skipping over anything."

The older students laughed again. Perhaps they'd heard that question and answer before.

I was lost in thought and hadn't noticed Goldberry standing up beside me.

"Yes, Miss Tinker?"

"If I may, sir. I know it's possible to get glimpses of the future, but they never last long. So I think maybe if we went forward, we'd just get thrown back again, so quickly it wouldn't be worth the trying."

"A fine speculation, Miss Tinker. Perhaps I may explain it by the example of the man who claims he can run around the world in less than a second. He then makes a small motion, thus." The Dean twitched slightly. "He then announces that he has returned."

"That's stupid," Yakov Mermelstein shouted. "Of course he didn't run around the world."

"Logic dictates that he did not," said the Dean. "It is easier to believe that all he did was twitch his head in an effort to deceive you. This is what time travel to the future is like. You enact the mechanisms of transport, you feel as if perhaps you have moved, but you find yourself exactly in the place and time where you began."

"Then I'm right," Goldberry said. "You just get snapped back again."

"Perhaps," said the Dean. "Or perhaps you simply cannot remember your journey. Now, if our first-years can withhold their questions on the most challenging of topics, I may speak of the most basic. All of you, upon your first visit to School of the Ages, became aware of the seven values represented in the floor tiles of our entranceway. We call them the seven pillars: faith, perception, balance, wisdom, receptiveness, judgment, and discipline. As with the branches on the *Sefiroth*, so will you often contemplate our seven pillars. First-years, be certain to visit the entrance hall, and to spend some time familiarizing yourself with the relationships among these pillars. Students of Cabala, you will find that the *Sefiroth* is also represented there, as Rabbi Shulman has doubtless informed you. I turn everyone's attention now to the four fundamental principles required of a magician trained at School Of The Ages. They are meditation, concealment, universal language, and continuous defense. The combination of these four is on its own quite useful, and will give you significant advantages in daily life.

"Meditation is, of course, part of your daily routine, and you should practice it as often as you can, not only in the morning. To master the skills we teach here requires great mental and emotional stability. It also requires advanced powers of visualization. Our program of meditation is designed to create both. I stress this for our new students, who may fall into the fallacious belief that results are more important than means."

"Say it again in English," called an older student. He was medium height, had a reddish, friendly face, and wore jeans with brightly colored suspenders, giving him a jaunty look.

"Manners, Dempsey. What I meant to say is that if you only care about reaching your goal, and you don't pay attention to perfecting the technique that will get you to your goal, you will get an unsatisfactory result."

"Like what?" called the same student.

"See me after the assembly, Dempsey."

Dempsey, stood up and raised his hand. "What would the unsatisfactory results be, sir?"

"Most commonly, the result would be failure," said the Dean. "On some occasions, the result will be corrupted, a distorted version of what was intended. The analogy is to a skater. She may attempt a triple axel, but if her technique is not perfect, then either she will fall, or her performance will appear clumsy."

I thought I understood what he was saying, but decided to be sure and raised my hand.

"Yes, Simon?"

"Sir, do you mean that powerful magicians concentrate better than other people?"

"I would say, rather, that they are more concentrated. You do not succeed by clenching your will, as you might clench your fist. Rather, you succeed by remaining stable and emptying your mind of competing thoughts."

This I didn't quite understand, but I sat down.

The Dean looked from one side of the assembly to the other, then continued. "The second principle is concealment. It holds that you take action without attracting notice. Here is the reason for that. The more noise you make about your intentions, the more competing interests may interfere. As an example, suppose your goal is to make it rain in your immediate area. If you attempt this privately, the primary obstacle is your own ability to complete the work. If you predict on the television news that you are going to create rain, and you set up a circus tent and shoot off fireworks as part of your method, then you attract opposition. Anyone who does not believe in magic is, in effect, willing you to fail. Anyone who dislikes you wills you to fail.

Anyone who does not want rain is also opposing you. If they are not magicians, these people may individually not contribute greatly to your difficulty, but taken all together, they may well hold off the rain.

"Today's third principle is the principle of universal language," the Dean said. "This principle is specially taught at School of the Ages. It is the belief that communication between people can supersede the individual tongues with which they are familiar."

"We're all familiar with just our own languages," said Dempsey. "Except the French, of course."

"Excused, Dempsey," said the Dean. Dempsey left, dragging his feet and smiling at his friends. "We each speak different tongues-different languages-but these are merely overlaid upon a mental pattern of communication that can be understood directly and which does not truly require words. It is not mind-reading. You understand only as well as during an ordinary conversation. Universal language is no protection against lies or poor communication. However, using this principle, you may talk with anyone in any time, the same way you would converse with anyone you presently know. Universal language is an ability possessed by all spirits; therefore you will learn to access this ability by using your own spirit.

"Our final principle is defense. Briefly, it means that you will always maintain some degree of protection against surprise attack. It is both a slowing of time-perception at the moment of attack, for purposes of general threats, and also an actual shield against purely magical assaults. About this you will learn more later on. All of these principles will be emphasized repeatedly in your classes. Mastery of them is what distinguishes a School of the Ages graduate.

"This concludes my remarks for today. My office door is generally open, but remember that most matters about which you may ask me are better brought first to your advisor. Dinner will be served in approximately one hour; you are free to move about the building till then."

The Dean stepped down from the podium. I tried to watch where he went after that, but I was distracted by some noisy conversation nearby, and while I was distracted, the Dean apparently left the room. Some of the other teachers remained to chat, however, and the older students mostly scattered. My head was whirling from all the information I had just received. I had copied it down as best I could, I went over my notes to fill in whatever else I could remember. When I was done, I nudged Goldberry, who was also looking at her notes thoughtfully, and said, "I wonder who all these teachers are. Do you think the Rambal was at the lecture?"

"Who? Oh, I doubt it. I hear he's not usually seen outside of class. Why are you so curious?"

"I don't know. Maybe it's just strange to feel that half the school is totally secret. I wonder if anyone here has met him." I looked around for someone to ask and spotted Donovan Archer and waved to him.

"How are you doing?" he asked when he'd joined us.

"It's a lot to take in," I said, "but I like it so far. I wanted to ask you about the Rambal. Have you ever met him? What's he like?"

"I've met him," Donovan said. "I first met him when I was a boy. He doesn't talk very much. Usually his assistants do the talking, or else you can just tell from his eyes what he thinks."

"Then he's not friendly?"

"Words like that don't really apply to the Rambal. He's not mean or unfriendly. It's just that he doesn't pay attention to things that aren't his concern. He sees a lot of things we never see and thinks about things we can't even guess at."

"So if I want to meet him, I need a really good reason."

"They won't let you near him without a good reason," said Donovan. "Do you have one?"

"No, not at the moment. But it's good to know about him."

"If you have a problem you can't handle, you can ask my father," Donovan said. "At least that's what I do."

It was a tight schedule. On Tuesday, Wednesday, and Thursday there was scarcely time to breathe. Friday was a short day, apart from a basic Hebrew course Saturday was clear, probably to accommodate Cabala students. Class on Sunday was a new idea for me.

"We've a long weekend," said Goldberry.

"Are all these teachers magicians?" I wondered.

"If they weren't," Goldberry said, "they wouldn't be able to get here at all."

Dinner was good – chicken, salmon, and Caesar salad, rice pilaf, cider and coffee. Although there were school workers, adults, bringing the food from the kitchen, it was difficult to look at them or notice them; probably that was intentional. I sat with Goldberry, Robbie, Balaram, and Rocco. While Robbie explained his experiences with spirits, I sat trying to absorb everything I had experienced that day. Balaram described his activities as a sculptor of clay figures of Hindu gods. He would try to improve them by calling upon spirits of the earth. So he was a lot like Robbie.

"Do you think most study partners have a lot of things in common?" I asked Goldberry.

"Not always," she said. "Sometimes they do."

"Do we?"

She took a while to think about that. "I think we do," she said at last. "But I don't know what just yet."

....

We were interrupted by the arrival of second-year William Goodenough. Ignoring me, he greeted Goldberry and said, "Shall we?"

I considered whether it was worth the trouble to note his rudeness to me and decided it was not. I nodded to Goldberry, and we went with him.

Goodenough's tour of the building was comprehensive and useful. We saw every area students frequented and were told what places to avoid. We saw most of the teachers' offices, except for the American Academy of Cabala entrance, which was shut. Goodenough couldn't take us into certain areas which he said were off-limits to students below a certain age.

"What happens if we go there anyway?" Goldberry asked.

"You'll be very uncomfortable," he said, "and you'll run away."

Throughout the tour, Goodenough disregarded me. If I spoke to him, he gave the shortest and least informative answer that was polite. I was very annoyed by this, but I decided it wasn't good to do anything about it until I knew what he was up to.

We finished up the tour by the dining hall, said good-night, and went our separate ways. I fell asleep as soon as I got in bed.

....

The First Week of Classes

I should explain first how different life was in the School of the Ages building than life at home. No electricity makes an enormous difference. We were well-supplied with candles, battery-powered lanterns, and flashlights. The halls were lit with censers on tripods, the bowls full of burning smokeless coals. Our rooms were both dark and cold. Supposedly a large coal furnace supplied hot water and heated the classrooms, but there never was any hot water, and the classrooms were always freezing. The large central spaces, such as the dining rooms, had enough light that we could all see each other and study. Each dining room had both a firepit and a large fireplace, with utensils, that we could use for our own cooking, although plenty of food came out of the kitchens, and it was generally hot at the beginning of the scheduled mealtime.

Showers and bathrooms were communal, like in a gym – you had individual stalls which supplied some privacy, but could expect to see other kids of your own gender coming and going in bathrobes, towelling themselves off, and so on. The girls were the big winners in the bathroom department. Their bathrooms had windows that shone directly on mirrors since there were fewer girls than boys in the school, so the odds were better that they could get privacy.

Our first year dormitory rooms, which we had to stay in, for three years, were on the ground floor, close to all the gathering places, furthest from the classrooms. In the fourth year, we would move to second-floor rooms with windows and have more light. The rooms were supplied with the barest minimum of wooden furniture, but they were fairly large. There was space enough for half-a-dozen people to hang out in one room if they were willing to crowd onto the bed or sit on the floor. We had little brooms to sweep our floors, but Robbie and I and most of the first-year boys were lazy about it.

We had no phones, no computers, no TV, no Internet – only battery operated radios and games.

No one really minded. Magic was much more interesting to all of us than TV, and once you got into a routine, you weren't even bothered by the low light. Even cold showers can become appealing, once you manage to put out of your mind what hot ones feel like.

Let me tell you about the classes.

Construction I with Rabbi Horn was not what I expected. Rabbi Horn was a man in his late forties who wore a polo shirt, slacks, and tennis shoes instead of the dark suit, typical of the Cabala school rabbis. He smiled and sat in one place, droning on for a large part of the class meeting. The lecture was about "accumulating influences." He said magical objects were more effective if made under specific conditions favourable to you, the object, or the spell itself. He then gave a long and turgid list of correspondences, including astrological signs, seasons, equinoxes and solstices, compass directions, times of day, prevailing winds, birthdays, nearness to ley line intersections, if in Britain, and more. We were to begin memorizing these a few at a time, in preparation for various quizzes. I copied it all down, though I yawned a lot. One of our semester tasks would be to make a large "correspondences poster" which neatly arranged the information.

Asian History was supposed to be with someone named "Dr. Chatterjee," so I was surprised to see Mr. Bannerjee, the activities director, come in and begin the class. He was dressed very differently in a gray suit, and had his glasses at the tip of his nose. He started with a geographical overview of the areas that would be covered, and then went from one region to another telling stories about events in those places. There was also a very large and dry textbook which would be used for tests, but he was not going to teach the book because, he said, history is about how people lived in a time and how that time felt and what it meant to the future – no book could capture this feeling, and the feeling is what was really needed, the flow, to connect magic and history. He spoke more clearly, and with excellent English, but I was too busy taking notes to wonder about it until class was over. After class I went to his desk and asked, "How come you're teaching this class today?"

"I am assigned to teach this class this year," he said.

"But our schedule says that Dr. Chatterjee is teaching it."

"I am Dr. Naresh Chatterjee. I don't understand your question."

It was so strange that I just mumbled "Sorry" and left the classroom.

Biology class was focused on identifying categories of living things and knowing their properties and proper environments. Chemistry was about different substances and how they interact. Both courses, taught by Dr. Lehman, were stripped down to what most directly applied to the study of magic. This made them tolerable for me, although Goldberry hated both.

I thought Numerology was going to be a lot of maths, but I was wrong. It was more like a philosophy class. Professor Bright was a small, white-haired man with a twinkle in his eye. Each number has its own special properties, he told us. These are seen as diminished because the numbers are used for everyday purposes. But the fact is that magical numbers are not just numerals, like on a cash register, but they are different ways of understanding and naming God. Since real names have power, the real name of a numbered aspect of God lets you connect with the power locked into that aspect. Through practice, he continued, some versions of the name have become more charged with meaning than others. To take advantage of that, Prof. Bright constantly used the Hebrew words for the numbers to encourage us to respect them. But he said that that was just a way of reminding us to view the numbers in a sacred way. Once you can think "three" or "seven" and feel it in terms of power, he said, then any way of naming would work.This was hard and complicated.

Magic theory was a lecture course given by different teachers on different days. The idea was first to learn the standard ideas that magicians use to plan their spells, and then to examine a lot of special cases to see how the rules worked together. In some cases where something didn't seem to make sense but still worked, you would just say, "If it works, it works, whether it makes sense or not." This, our first lecture, was given to us by a man who looked like Dr. Chatterjee and talked in the less clear English of Mr. Bannerjee. I was very confused, but didn't know whom to ask. Asking the teacher hadn't worked during Asian History, so I wasn't about to try it this time.

It was definitely a new experience for me to attend a class at eight in the evening. This made me especially nervous about Memento Analysis. I already wanted to do well, first because I was a novice in an advanced class, and especially because it was taught by my advisor. It had been a very long day, but I found I was very alert as I made my way down to the basement.

The assigned room, which took some finding even with my map, was just a small parlour, with a padlocked wooden inner door across the room from the entrance. The parlour was lit by a single candle. The room was very chilly: I could see my breaths, the way you do on a frosty winter day.

Seated in one of the few wooden chairs was Yakov Mermelstein. He was reading a leather-bound Hebrew book and did not look up.

"What are you reading?" I asked, sitting down.

He looked up and glared at me. "This is not for you."

"I didn't say it was. It still won't hurt you to tell me."

"Why?"

"Because it's polite. Or because being friendly is better than making enemies."

"Enemies?" He laid the book on his lap and gave me the full weight of his stare. His eyes were so dark and cold, they seemed to suck out of me what little body heat I still had. "You don't frighten me," he said after a moment, and looked back at his book.

He hadn't frightened me either, but he had impressed me. "I'm not trying to frighten you. But let me make a suggestion. There must be a reason why your Cabala school merged with School of the Ages. There must be a reason why so many classes have students from each. I'm curious. Aren't you?"

"No," he answered, lowering his book momentarily. "I know what I came here to learn. Not like you, *apikoros*. You have no idea."

I decided I was getting tired of his nickname for me. "Why do you call me that? What does it mean?"

He snorted. "Go and find out. I'm not your teacher."

"I will find out," I said. "And maybe I'll find something to call you, too. Now please, if you want me to shut up, tell me first what you're reading."

Again he turned his dark, cold gaze on me, and again I felt my strength slipping away. There had to be some way to resist it, but I couldn't think of a way. I looked away. From the corner of my eye I saw him smile, then return to his book. I was not going to let him beat me.

"What is that book?" I tried again.

He looked at me again, angrily, but this time without the cold stare that had weakened me before. "This is Rashi," he said. "It is a commentary on Talmud. Talmud is a book of legal decisions made by rabbis of centuries ago. Rashi is among the most important authors of such commentary. That is the answer to your question, and it is all I have to say to you, so now, shut up!"

I was happy to shut up. Indeed, it was hard to talk. I opened my book bag, got out a notebook, and began to review some of its contents. My eyes wouldn't focus, so I closed them. It had been a long day, and I was tired, but I hadn't forgotten what Maestro Morgan said almost every morning: visualize the triangle. See the triangle, and you draw your energies toward its perfection. I did this, and I felt some of my strength returning. But I couldn't hold onto the image for long. After a moment I heard voices in the hall, and more students arrived. Most were older. Goldberry and Leah came last. All the chairs were full, so I gave up mine.

"Stretching your legs, are you?" Goldberry said. "Good enough." She took the seat, smiling wryly.

"Yes?" said an older student. I recognized William Goodenough. Not him again, I thought. I hadn't noticed him coming in before.

"Have you ever handled a memento before?" he asked Goldberry.

"I have. I took the 'Mystic Tour of North England' in '97. They have the memento of Edward Kelly in Lancashire."

"Edward Kelly," I said. "John Dee's young assistant."

Goodenough had been waiting for Goldberry to ask who Kelly was. It was my pleasure to disappoint him. He turned on me.

"Have you ever handled a memento?" he asked in a challenging tone.

I was about to admit that I had not, but then I realized something, or thought I did. "Goldberry," I said. "Your father's pocket-watch. Is it?"

Her eyes widened. "Don't know. Could be. He never lets people touch it, usually. Certainly I never have."

If the watch was a memento, and Clive Tinker had had me swear on it without telling me, then something bothered me about that.

At this point the hallway door opened, and Dr. Archer came in with his son Donovan. He looked around, counting us. "Good, good," he said. "Let's go to the sacristy." From his pocket he produced a large iron key, which he applied to the padlock on the inside door. The door opened silently, releasing a gust of cold air. "For future reference," he said, "warm clothing is recommended. Mind your hat, Miss Dunham," he added to a girl with a tall cone hat, who was about to knock it off stepping through the door. "With all respect to Mickey Mouse, that sort of garment will not really be helpful."

Some people chuckled. I was surprised to hear Dr. Archer joke.

Inside were a number of high tables. On each sat a small wooden box. There were also a desk and a chalkboard. The room was totally frigid, far colder than anywhere I had ever been before.

"Two to a table, please," said Dr. Archer.

I went with Goldberry and found Leah also standing at the table.

This was irritating, as I wanted to work with my own partner, but Goldberry had been told by Dr. Archer to help Leah, and he was in the room with us watching me, so I decided not to fuss about it. By the time I had thought this out, the only table with only one person was occupied by Yakov Mermelstein. He gave me a scornful look as I set down my notebook across from him.

"Just for tonight, okay?" I said.

He sneered, looking from me to Goodenough and then back at me. "Not wise to make enemies, huh?" he said very quietly. "You make me laugh, *apikoros*."

"Good," Dr. Archer said to the class, thankfully interrupting Mermelstein's nettling. "Open your notebooks and make good use of them. Does anyone here require an explanation of what a memento is?"

No one volunteered, so I raised my hand, and Dr. Archer raised his eyebrow. He knew very well that I knew what a memento was and what it had cost me to find out.

"Yes, Simon?"

"Are we going to learn to make new mementos?"

Dr. Archer shook his head. "That is a matter of advanced study, to be offered on a tutorial basis. Even in Europe, it is not part of the regular course. Any other questions?"

"What are we going to do with the bad ones?" asked Miss Dunham.

"At School of the Ages we do not destroy mementos, so we will label them for what they are and return them to HUN."

"These are from Eretz Yisroel?" asked Mermelstein.

"Our main course of study will be artifacts from Hermetic University of the Negev," said Dr. Archer. "Not the ones before you tonight, of course, which are School of the Ages' practice pieces. The mementos which are our primary study were retrieved by HUN staff as part of a cache near Bethlehem."

There was silence as this sank in throughout the chilly classroom. Bethlehem, Negev – I struggled to recall past geography lessons that might have told me where these places were. "Eretz Yisroel" and "Holy Land" sounded like Israel. If so, some of the mementos we were going to study might be remarkably old.

"Each of the boxes in front of you contains two mementos," said Dr. Archer. "The spirits bound to them are known to be agreeable, and are accustomed to interacting with students. Each of you is to try your luck this evening with at least one of the mementos in the box. Don't open the box yet, Mr. Goodenough. If, when you open the box, one memento seems to call to you more than another, trust your instinct in the matter and select it, if you can.

"Now, when you are holding your memento, feel free to examine it by sight and touch. Then you must still your mind. Use whatever meditation Maestro Morgan has set for you. But you must rid yourself of thoughts that are off-task. Feel open to new experiences.

"When you have achieved that state of mind, then redirect your attention to the memento, and say hello. You need not say it aloud. A greeting in your thoughts is sufficient. If you do not get a response at once, relax further and try additional greetings. These spirits are friendly and do not require much coaxing. Once they are aware of you, they will speak to you. They speak in your thoughts only, for they are not strong enough to do more. Are there any questions?"

"We haven't mastered universal language yet," reminded Goldberry.

"All spirits have that ability. The principle of universal language is for speaking to living people."

....

"What should we talk about, then?" asked Miss Dunham, the girl with the witch hat.

"Ask them to talk about themselves. Say little about yourself other than that you are a student at School of the Ages. Friendly they may be, but all spirits trade in information, and what seems to be of small consequence now may harm you in the future."

There were no more questions. Looking around, I saw that the class was perhaps evenly divided between the nervous and the eager. The eager ones were already fiddling with the box lids. The nervous ones seemed to be frowning and panting and whispering to their table-mates.

As for me, I tried to keep in mind what I'd heard in magic theory earlier in the week. Your ability to do something is partly determined by whether you believe you can do it. If you know you can do something, then you do it. If you doubt, you probably fail. So I said to myself, "You're here because you can do this. Don't wonder; just get started."

I reached for the box lid, but Mermelstein's hand was there first. He threw the lid back, started to reach for one of the objects inside, then paused.

Trying to figure out which one is kosher, I thought to myself.

He slammed the box lid shut. "Say it again, *apikoros*," he snapped at me.

"Say what? I didn't say anything." I was sure I hadn't spoken that comment aloud.

With a loud snort, Mermelstein threw open the box lid again and took out what looked like a jagged chunk of brick. I took the other object, a gold wedding band.

It was difficult to clear my mind with Mermelstein's harshness so close by. He was breathing heavily and shifting from foot to foot. Finally I took the ring and went to another table.

I studied the ring. There were no decorations or markings other than a few scratches from wear. It was cold and felt smooth. I could find no marks on the inside either. It was small, probably a woman's. I started rubbing it, like rubbing Aladdin's lamp. "Hello," I thought.

"Hello, young man," said an elderly woman's voice. "What's your name?" She didn't speak aloud: her voice was in my head, but it wasn't a thought. It was as clear and as individual as a person speaking.

"I'm a student at School of the Ages," I answered. It wasn't difficult to separate my private thoughts from the thoughts I wanted her to hear, but I could feel a light pressure for me to share those thoughts with her as well. "What's your name?" I asked. "Tell me about yourself."

"My name is Chastity Gray," answered the old woman's voice. "I'm from Philadelphia."

"Oh. Did you know Benjamin Franklin?" I joked.

"Well, bless my soul," she said. "Yes I did, just a little. The poor man, losing his son that way."

As the conversation continued, I was less and less able to see and hear what was going on around me. I felt my hands on the cold gold ring, I heard her voice and mine, and I couldn't sense anything else. "How did he lose his son?"

"Well, young William was the governor of Pennsylvania, so when the revolution came, he took up with the Tories. They never spoke again, so I heard. Mr. Franklin could not have been the same afterwards, I expect."

"I didn't know about that."

"Oh, I used to see Mr. Franklin in the street now and again, and I always did read *Poor Richard's Almanack*. But young man, it's a shame. My old eyes aren't good any longer. I really can't see around that school of yours. Do you suppose I could borrow your eyes for a while? Just to have a peek, of course."

This request startled me so much that I almost slipped out of the conversation. "Uh, no, Miss, uh, Mrs. Gray, I don't think we should do that."

"Well, all right, young man. You know best, I expect, although I would think you would show more respect for an old lady like myself. I do feel so alone sometimes, and I can just tell from us talking that it would be easy. Why don't we? Mr. William Cowper did write that variety is the spice of life!"

The pressure from her was increasing, and I wanted to end the conversation. But how could I? Dr. Archer hadn't told us that part. Not to panic, no… If you believe you can do it, you can. How would I end a normal conversation? Like hanging up a phone, maybe?

"Goodbye," I said, and imagined myself setting down a phone receiver and hearing it click.

The cold air came rushing over my skin, and I was back again. I let the wedding ring – that I now knew was Chastity Gray's wedding band, slip from my hand to the table and slumped forward.

Back at my original table, Mermelstein had put down the brick but was standing with a mixture of pride and slight dizziness. Elsewhere, I saw Goodenough and Leah holding their mementos, looking at nothing. Goldberry was also done: her memento, a silver dollar, sat on the table in front of her. She looked shaken. I went over to her, and we spoke in low voices.

"Are you okay?"

"Yes, I suppose," she said. "Such a sad man. I couldn't bear to talk to him. He died so young, fighting in the American Civil War. He asked me to care for his children. I hadn't the heart to say they are also long dead."

I picked up the silver dollar, looking for a date. The coin was worn, and the images on it difficult to read. There was a woman seated in a long gown, and the year on the coin was 1863. I put the coin back in the box.

Goldberry shook her head as if getting rid of cobwebs. "What happened to you?"

I told her about it.

"She asked to take control of your eyes?" Goldberry asked, surprised. "Did you know you were a medium?"

A medium is a person who can let the spirits of dead people speak through her or his mouth. Historically, most of them are considered phonies, but as I had just spoken to a spirit, I knew that some of them surely were not.

"I doubt I am," I said. "Mediums are almost always women." I looked at Leah, next to me, who was still involved with her memento, probably unaware of us.

"I doubt that, too," said Goldberry. "But she seems to be extraordinarily talented."

I remembered something else to ask Goldberry about. "Just before we started, did I say anything to Mermelstein?"

She pursed her lips. "I don't think so," she said, "but he certainly said something to you. I was wondering what that was about, really."

"Because, you know, I was thinking something nasty, but I didn't mean to say it out loud."

Around us, more people were finishing with their mementos. Leah was the last to do so. She set it down, and gave a sigh, and closed her eyes.

"I am pleased that everyone here was able to make contact with the bound spirit," said Dr. Archer. "Tell me what you observed. William?"

Goodenough said, "My spirit said he was lonely because the memento kept him from playing with other children. I don't understand that."

"Nor do I," said Dr. Archer. "But it is not necessary to understand. Miss Dunham, you have taken four prior years of summoning. Assuming your hat has not cut off blood flow to your brain, you will be able to tell us why that is so."

"Because you can't trust a spirit unless you bind it," said Miss Dunham tensely.

"It is not in the nature of spirits to be truthful," Dr. Archer confirmed. "A spirit will always use information to its own advantage."

I raised my hand.

"Yes, Simon?"

"Does that mean Chastity didn't really know Ben Franklin? She just said she did because I asked her if she did?"

"It is possible for a spirit to play-act in that way, yes," said Dr. Archer. "When we continue with more difficult mementos, remember that our only goal is to identify their residents, not to extract information or to seek favours."

He gave us instructions for several strategies to defend against unfriendly occupants in the mementos, then ended class early.

I walked out with Goldberry and Leah. "How did it go?" I asked Leah. "Who was in your memento? You were talking for a long time."

"I asked him to introduce me to some other spirits," she said quietly. "I was trying to reach someone… but it doesn't matter."

"Trying to reach who?"

"It doesn't matter," she said again, and quickened her pace.

"Who?" I asked Goldberry.

"So now you're an owl."

"No, I mean, who was she trying to reach?"

"I've no idea. But if you keep asking her, I expect she will tell you."

"Why?" I asked.

"Isn't it obvious?" Goldberry rolled her eyes. "She likes you."

Before the Field Trip

It means a lot more to say someone likes you if you're thirteen going on fourteen. I wanted to ask Goldberry "Likes me how? How do you know?" but I thought it would be embarrassing. If she liked me as in "trusted me," then I'd just be her friend, which I definitely wanted to be anyway. If she liked me more than that, it would be much harder. Leah was a girl that every boy looked at, not just because she was the prettiest girl in the school but because she was politely mysterious. The more she pushed people away, the more curious they got. I couldn't not like her back. But then, my roommate Robbie liked Leah, and I didn't want not to be friends with him. And Goldberry was only my partner, but still I felt being interested in Leah was like cheating on her. I disliked Goodenough always hanging around Goldberry. So how could I be close to Leah and make Robbie jealous and still be jealous of Goodenough at the same time?

The complications made my head spin. Lying in bed that night, I felt like throwing up. I kept going over in my mind every conversation I'd ever had with any of them until I finally drifted off.

YOU MUST GIVE ME FORGIVENESS, said the voice.

I snapped awake. Robbie was still snoring on the other side of the room.

I couldn't move or speak aloud, but I tried to think of my conversation I had with the spirit in the memento.

"Who are you?" I thought.

YOU WILL LEARN OF ME. THEN YOU WILL GO TO RAV YEHOSHUA AND HE WILL FORGIVE ME.

"Who is that?"

YOU MUST FIND A WAY.

It was if something in my head was wiped away. I knew the spirit was gone, and I could move again. This time I wouldn't wake Robbie. I would figure it out myself.

I got up and went down the candlelit stone corridor to the bathroom. I could see my breaths in the icy air. As I returned to the room, I decided I would keep practicing with the mementos, get better, and then figure out how to deal with this ghost. It still took me a long time to get to sleep.

I woke up in the morning thinking I would talk to Leah at breakfast. When I got to the dining hall after meditation, she was there, eating alone at a table, but I couldn't go over to her when so many people were watching. I sat with Rocco instead. He told me a funny story about Dempsey, the senior who had given the Dean a hard time at the assembly the first day of school. I hardly heard him. I'd failed at meditation, hadn't seen the triangle; I was being haunted by a nameless spirit; and all of a sudden I couldn't talk to a girl I'd been talking to without trouble for most of the week before. That was enough problems for one morning, but unfortunately another arrived: William Goodenough, along with King, a classmate I'd seen him with in the halls. He sat next to me, ignoring Rocco's cheerful greeting.

"I just wanted to talk to you," said Goodenough mildly. "We've gotten off on the wrong foot, you and I. I'm not sure why. Perhaps we can talk it out."

I looked at him, then at King, who was expressionless, and then at him again.

"That's not why you're here," I said. "I think you know what the problem is as well as I do."

"Well, I've learned, from my father as well as my teachers, never to underestimate a magician, even a novice. I just want to say that if I should not underestimate a novice, neither should that novice underestimate me."

"Whoa," said Rocco.

"This has nothing to do with magic," I said.

"Everything has to do with magic," Goodenough said. "Crowley defined magic as making the world change in accordance with your will. If you pick up that water glass and drink, it's magic. And if you advise someone to change his attitude, and he does, that's magic too." He stood up, winked, and went off with his friend.

"What a jerk," said Rocco. "What's that all about?"

"Never mind."

"Okay, but say the word, I got your back."

"Thanks. Same here."

I kept eating, but the food seemed dry and tasteless to me. When I finally set down my fork on a plate where plenty of food remained, and started on my now cold cup of tea, Robbie and Balaram came over to the table from where they had been eating elsewhere.

"Great news, guys," Robbie said. "We're going on a field trip!"

"On the first week of school?" Rocco said. "Whoa."

"We're going this Sunday," Robbie said. "All the kids taking summoning."

"Where to?"

"Canada! We're going to see *Ogopogo*."

It sounded like a Native American village. I had never heard of it, but I still got an idea. I needed to clear my head, and a field trip might help. "I want to go," I told them. "Who's the teacher? I'm going to go ask him."

"Mr. Phillips, the school's Master Conjurer. I'll walk you to his office."

We left Rocco and Balaram to chat and went up to the hall where many faculty offices were. I saw that Dr. Archer's office door was slightly ajar and wondered if I should ask him first. But no, why bother him with something I didn't even yet know to be possible? So I kept following Robbie to another door. He knocked, and the door popped open at once. A yipping sound drew my eyes down to a white toy poodle, standing in the doorway. It ignored Robbie and sniffed my leg. I knelt and offered my hand, which the poodle licked. I had never met a dog of any size that didn't like me.

"Come in," said a deep voice from within the office.

Robbie pushed the office door open. The inside was pleasantly warm but smoky. Having been invited, we crossed the threshold, stepping over the poodle. The smoke was from a large pipe in the mouth of Mr. Phillips, a very tall, broad-shouldered black man with a professional air about him. He was gray-haired and middle-aged, but his eyes were youthful and friendly.

"Murgatroyd likes you, young man," he said to me. He gestured at a chair with his pipe. "And Murgatroyd is a good judge. So you have my ear."

"This is Simon," Robbie said. "He..."

"Now, now, not so hasty, Mr. Radish. Let him speak for himself."

"I'm Simon." I offered him a handshake and was accepted. He was very strong. "I'm Robbie's roommate. He told me about the field trip, and I'd like to come along."

Mr. Phillips puffed on his pipe and then said, "You'll need your advisor's permission first. And before you rush off to ask him, is there anyone else I should be expecting to knock on my door?"

I hadn't thought about that. "I guess I should ask my study partner if she wants to go."

"And she is…?"

"Goldberry Tinker."

He tapped his pipe gently, thinking. "Then Miss Tinker is welcome under the same conditions. Let's not add further to the list, however, boys. A lot of students are stir-crazy at the end of the first week. Hm?"

"Yes, sir."

Murgatroyd was hovering by my ankle. I bent and scratched him behind the ears, realizing that I missed Cougar, Cheetah, Leo, and the other family cats.

"Mr. Radish, if you will remain a moment."

I took this as instructions to go. The door shut behind me. When I turned, I saw Dr. Archer waiting for me in the hall by his office.

"Very precipitous," he said. "You wish to go on a trip you know nothing about. May I ask why?" His hard gaze seemed to burrow into me.

"Well… This week has been hard. I just want to get away for a while."

"So long as learning is not your motive," he said coldly. "Permission granted. But not for your partner."

I was going to ask why not, but the look in his eyes told me he was in no mood to be challenged.

"Is there anything bothering you that I ought to be aware of?" he asked.

It would be stupid for me to lie to Dr. Archer. I knew he had ways of knowing what I was doing.

"I'm sure you're already aware of whatever it is," I said. "I'm going to try to handle everything on my own."

He frowned and stepped back toward his office, then turned halfway to look me in the eye. "When you require assistance with any troubles, you should come first to me before any approaching other teacher. Troubles, I mean, other than requiring assistance with the course work. Tradition dictates that your advisor be your first resort. It is also my preference." A moment later, he was behind his door, which was firmly shut.

As I went to my room to get my books for the day's classes, I went over my problems again to see if there were any I should go to Dr. Archer with. There was only one, the spirit that Goldberry called "Mr. I-Ask-Forgiveness." I would be smart to tell Dr. Archer about it. But I had decided to handle it myself. Rule one: if you can believe you can do it, you can do it. The memento class would teach me how to deal with the spirits of the dead, and then I would get rid of this one on my own. I hadn't even told Goldberry or Robbie that it spoke to me again.

When I saw my partner in class, I tried my best to pretend the previous night never happened. I didn't tell her about Goodenough's threat either, but I did tell her about the field trip and that Dr. Archer had refused her permission to go.

"Keeping my nose to the grindstone, I expect," she said. "He knows I'm behind on my Asian History essay. He always knows these things. It's annoying."

That night we worked together on chemistry problems and on drawing up a dietary influence chart for Construction. Did you know you shouldn't eat red meat before doing a major spell, because it takes so long to digest that it depletes your energy? And that you should also avoid beans and broccoli if you tend to … well, never mind that.

Goldberry was a little crabby, just enough to put a sarcastic edge on everything she said.

"Do you wish you could go on the trip?" I asked her as we added parsley to the list of useful herbs. "I can help you finish your essay."

"No," she said. "Wouldn't help. I'm behind on other subjects, too."

"We'll do some extra work tomorrow night."

"No. Leave it be, can't you?"

I couldn't figure out what was bothering her, and it was the wrong time to ask. Instead I went back to the homework. Goldberry was normal after that talk, but I still felt bad about going without her. On Saturday night, as we reviewed my Asian History notes, I said, "Listen, maybe I shouldn't go tomorrow."

"No, go on," she said. "I think I can muddle through well enough for twenty-four hours."

"It's not like that much is going to happen on the trip," I said. "Forget it. I'm being stupid, running away just because of some worries. That's why we're supposed to meditate, right?"

Goldberry gave me a very annoyed look. "If you've something worthwhile to say, say it. If not, then I've studying to do."

There was a lot more to say, but I decided to drop it. No so much could happen in one day, just from going to one Native American village.

Ogopogo

Sunday morning: Robbie's battery-powered alarm went off at 5 AM. He ignored it, but I got up and went to wash my face. When I got back to the room, he was still out cold, so I got dressed and then shook him awake. "Meditation at 6 today," I reminded him.

We made it to the Meditation Hall on time, along with the other people going on the trip. Maestro Morgan was not there; we were on our own. I struggled with the colourless triangle as usual, until I lost it entirely when I saw that Leah was in the room. Sitting alone in her pew, her head bowed in prayer, she made me feel strangely calm, as if no one was in the room but the two of us, cloaked in shadows by the candlelight.

Leah wasn't in Robbie's class, so what was she doing there?

Breakfast was toast and coffee. It was too early for the kitchen staff, so Dempsey, the senior, went back to the kosher kitchen and made the food himself. Sitting at breakfast with the dozing Robbie and his owlish partner, Balaram, I was struck by how alone Leah really was, not looking at anyone as she ate, intent on a small prayer book.

Seeing her with a book, I realized I hadn't brought anything to do on the bus, so I excused myself and went back to my room. I put a few schoolbooks and a pad into my new School of the Ages knapsack and returned to breakfast.

....

Mr. Phillips was there now, along with his pipe and his poodle Murgatroyd. Once he was sure we were all present, he led us outside, about thirty kids total, to where the green Smoot Preparatory bus and Mr. Saluto were waiting.

Robbie crashed into a seat and went to sleep, so I sat with Balaram. Mr. Phillips came on board last. Murgatroyd ran up and down the aisle, rubbing legs and licking hands.

"We have a long trip ahead of us," Mr. Phillips shouted. His booming voice filled the bus. "It's about eight hours to British Columbia. We will stop in Vancouver for a very late lunch. There are some drinks and snacks in the overhead racks, if you need them. Once everyone is a little more awake, I'll talk to you again about what we'll be doing when we arrive." He sat, and a cloud of smoke arose from his pipe.

Murgatroyd was now rubbing against my leg. I scratched his head. He went to Balaram. I watched Balaram pat him on the back.

Then I realized what I'd just heard. Eight hours to British Columbia.... Eight hours to the other side of the North American continent. How? It took that much time, or more, to fly that distance. We were going to British Columbia? I had thought we'd just go upstate to the Canadian border and this Ogopogo place would be just on the other side.

"Balaram," I said.

"Yes." He was very alert as Murgatroyd moved on down the aisle.

"Where is Ogopogo?"

"Lake Okanagan," he said. "North of Vancouver somewhere. I've even been there before, but most people think Ogopogo isn't real, so they don't see her much."

"Ogopogo is a she?"

Balaram took a moment to study me to see if I was teasing him. "You really don't know what this trip is about?"

"Not at all. I just wanted to get away for a while. I thought we were going to a Native American village." I realized as I said this how preoccupied I'd been, and what a stupid error I had made by assuming something without verifying it. Preparation is important. You can't prepare if you don't know what you're doing in the first place.

"Well, you're in for a treat," Balaram said. "Ogopogo is the legendary lake monster who lives in Lake Okanagan. Kind of like the Loch Ness Monster, only in Canada."

"We're going to see a monster?"

"Mr. Phillips says Ogopogo is really a water spirit. She only gets seen if she wants to he seen or if there are people around with the potential to be magicians."

I looked out of the window. There were woods on either side. I thought maybe it was the Jackie Robinson, but when a sign appeared, it showed we were on I-80, westbound, passing Hopatcong, New Jersey.

"How did we get here so fast?" I wondered aloud. "How can this old bus get us there in eight hours?"

"Not a clue," Balaram said.

I thought about where we were going. It made sense. A field trip for a summoning class should be about summoning something. I had been really clumsy about the whole thing, with no idea what I was getting into. No wonder Dr. Archer was so upset with me.

"Say, Balaram," I said. "Is Leah Ritz in your class? Robbie didn't tell me that."

"Lucky for him, no," said Balaram. "He'd never be able to

concentrate. I think she's in the with the second-year kids."

"Then she must be really good for her age."

"I guess." Balaram took out Theory of Correspondences, the construction textbook, from his bag and began studying. He didn't want to talk anymore. I could see why. I was bothering him with question after question. This is harmful to anyone's concentration, and you need concentration for magic to work well.

It was time for me to make some decisions. I could study, I could sleep, I could look out of the window and try to figure out how fast we were going, I could wake Robbie up, or… I could go and talk to Leah. The very thought of that made me dizzy and soured my stomach. But the only way I could stop feeling like that would be to find out more and then decide what to do. I'd already messed up with this trip, going to a major spirit summoning, completely unprepared. Why do that with a classmate? I had never been nervous talking to a girl before – or even talking to Leah before. But Goldberry had said she liked me, but I didn't know how much she liked me. If I guessed wrong, I could really embarrass myself, and as small as School of the Ages was, everyone would know. Robbie would know, and he'd be angry because he was crazy about her himself. And my enemies, Mermelstein, Goodenough, would find out and would mock me. And Goldberry wouldn't respect me anymore. A lot was riding on such a simple thing as a conversation. The whole point of this trip for me was supposed to be to get a chance to think it through. Now I was on the spot. If I did nothing on this, the perfect chance to speak to her, I would look like a fool. Or was that what Goldberry wanted anyway? Maybe she was angry with me for something that I didn't know about, so she had set me up to get embarrassed. But Goldberry was my partner. She couldn't do that!

....

I tried to tear myself away from all these tangled, stupid thoughts. The important question wasn't what anyone else wanted. It was only what I wanted. If you want to make something happen, you believe you can do it and you act. You compensate for obstacles and opposing influences if you can, and you accept that there may be good reasons if it doesn't happen, but the bottom line is you act. That's magic. I, Simon the magician, Simon Magus, would act. I wanted to get to know Leah better, so I would act.

I tried to see the triangle. The shape came and went, flickered in my mind's eye for a while. Then Leah's face replaced it, clean and lovely as shining crystal. For a moment, holding her image there, I felt connected to her, as if by invisible bonds.

That was it. I was going. I got up and scanned the bus for her. She was a few seats behind me on the other side, holding her prayer book. As I stepped into the aisle, holding the seat backs for balance, she looked up and met my eyes. I took this as a good sign and went to sit by her. She made room for me. I saw in her face that she had been expecting it.

"You knew I was coming?" I asked.

"Goldberry told me you were coming," she said. "I had a strong feeling you were on the trip because you wanted to talk to me." She said this so quietly that I couldn't tell how she felt about it.

"Maybe," I said. "But I didn't know that was the reason. I was just planning to think things through. A lot of things. One of them was talking to you."

"Oh? Then what were the others?"

"There are some people I'm having trouble with."

"Yes, I know."

"Goldberry told you?"

"I can see for myself. Some people think you're crazy to have such strong enemies."

"Really? How strong are they?"

"Both very strong. Yakov Mermelstein is from a family of cabalists. It's in his blood. And William Goodenough is descended from the founder, Elihu Danvers."

"So I'm in big trouble?"

"No," she said. "I don't think so. If you were, your advisor would tell you. Anyway, my father always taught me that even failure isn't a waste because you learn from it."

"So I'm going to lose if I fight them?"

"I don't know," Leah said. "I don't think it matters. The Dean told us that they expect us to fight. If you're in trouble, you just surrender, and whoever you're fighting has to leave you alone."

I had forgotten about that, and I was happy Leah reminded me. But I also knew I didn't want to surrender to anyone, unless I was wrong.

"Where are you from?" Leah asked.

"Bayside," I said. "Hicksville."

"And you were always a magician?"

"Not really. I always liked magic and stuff like that, but I never knew a place like School of the Ages existed."

We were sitting quiet for a while, not sure what to talk about next, when I noticed that Robbie was awake and coming toward us. I was not looking forward to that, but I smiled and said hello.

He offered me his hand, but his handshake was not as warm as usual. Then he sat in the seat in front of us, leaning over the back. "How are you doing?" he asked Leah.

"I'm all right, thanks." I noticed how she stiffened when he looked at her. I still wasn't sure why.

"So, Simon told me a lot about your memento class. How did you like it?"

"I don't know," she said. "It's hard to know after just one class."

"Do you like Dr. Archer?"

"Well, he seems very knowledgeable."

Robbie paused, struggling for something to say. Leah wasn't making it easy, and I didn't know how to help him, either.

"So have you done a lot of summoning?" he tried. "I've been trying to summon elemental beings at about the second rank. Azarrina, and Enkur, Nicholotus, Lazar-El, you know."

"I see."

"Since I was ten, I started reading the books on it."

Leah fidgeted, then opened her prayer book. I saw a beat of sweat run down Robbie's cheek.

"In the famous words of Foghorn Leghorn, I'm pitching them, but you're not catching them. What's up?"

She looked at him, and then me, with mild curiosity. "Who's Foghorn Leghorn?"

"He's a chicken," Robbie said. "A big chicken from the South, who always adds 'I say' in his sentences."

A blank look from Leah.

"In Warner Brothers cartoons...?"

"I've never watched TV," she said.

Robbie looked directly at me. "Simon, help me out of here."

"Can you do the Foghorn Leghorn voice?" I asked him.

He was quiet a moment, thinking about it. "I can do Kermit the Frog," he concluded.

Leah was immersed in her prayer book.

....

"Come talk to me, roomie," he said.

I said excuse me to Leah and then followed Robbie to a seat at the back of the bus, behind a pair of sleeping Chasidic boys.

"What are you doing, man?" he hissed at me. "You know I like this girl. Why are you moving in on her?"

I thought it was a fair question, and I didn't have a good answer. I stalled. "I was just talking to her."

"So? What did you find out? Did you guys talk about me at all? Did you put in a good word for me?"

"No, we didn't talk about you."

"So what were you talking about?"

"Nothing. Nothing, really."

"Bull," he said. "That's bull, man." His face reddened. "There's a lot more boys than girls in our year, and you're trying to keep the two best-looking girls all to yourself. What are you doing, man?"

"No," I said. "No. That's not right. I don't own anyone."

"Then what are you doing?"

"Look, Robbie, I don't design my life based on what you think or what you want. I'm just doing what comes to me. If I can help you out, fine, and I hope you feel the same way, but that's it."

He shook his head. "You're messing me up, roomie," he said. "I must admit that I am very disappointed. I wish I had never told you about this trip." He got up, still shaking his head, and walked away, back to where Balaram was, still dozing around the middle of the bus.

I didn't know what to say, or to think, so I just sat there for a while. I tried studying, but found it going slowly. Really I knew nothing about summoning or Ogopogo. My roommate was mad at me. I had abandoned my partner. My advisor thought less of me for going on this trip. I had taken a risk to talk to Leah, and it had paid off, but to go back now would just be too confusing. Leah wasn't someone to get mixed up with lightly, and Goldberry needed me. And I owed her father a debt. And Mermelstein, and Goodenough, and the mystery of Dr. Chatterjee and Mr. Bannerjee, and… I was going crazy with it all.

A teacher, Mr. Phillips, was on the bus with me. But Dr. Archer had said I should go to him first with problems. But I needed to talk to someone. Who could I talk to?

Finally I realized, and I went up to the front of the bus. "Mr. Phillips," I said, "do you have a cell phone I can use?"

I went to the cramped, shaky bathroom in the back of the bus to get some privacy for my call. My mother answered. I said hello. "Thank God," she said. "We thought we'd never hear from you. Where are you?"

"I don't know exactly. I'm on the bus." I explained what I was doing. She asked a lot of worried questions, which I answered as quickly as I could. Then she put my father on.

I wanted to tell the whole story, but parts of it – the ghost haunting me, how I was torn between Goldberry and Leah – I just couldn't say out loud. So I told him about Mermelstein. He was startled by the things I'd told him Mermelstein could do – create an invisible barrier with a gesture, drain my energy by looking at me, possibly even hear thoughts.

"I'd tell you just to steer clear of him," my father said, "but I guess that wouldn't help. You can't do any of these things, right? Or anything like that?"

"No, not so far. Not soon, either. Someone who knows Cabala really has an edge."

"Then I guess you're doing the best you can do. Just don't give in. He has to have a weakness, though."

"Sure, he does. He's...he's narrow-minded. He doesn't understand outsiders."

"Then that's your weapon, I guess. Use that. Listen, how's Goldberry?"

"About the same, I guess."

"You meet anyone else interesting?"

I thought about this a while. "No... not really."

"Now, Leicester. I know that tone of voice. Whom did you meet?"

"Look," I said. "I should go. It was great talking to you guys."

He sounded as if he was trying to hide sadness. "Keep in touch."

I put down the phone, left the bathroom, and wobbled back to the front to return the phone to Mr. Phillips. "Thank you."

He nodded, wiggling his pipe in his mouth. "I'll send you a bill," he joked. Then he added, "Something else I can help with?"

"No, not really. Except did you realize I didn't know what Ogopogo was? I mean, I really got into a mess coming along without knowing what the trip is about."

"True enough. But even if you aren't a summoner yourself, you have the right feel to you. That's what Murgatroyd told me. Ogopogo won't mind you being there. Just follow along with what we're doing."

"Okay."

By afternoon it was snowing and bitterly cold on the road. We stopped in Vancouver for a late lunch. Mr. Saluto found a kosher Chinese restaurant. We sat in small groups at several tables. I sat with Robbie and Balaram, but didn't talk or listen. Leah sat alone. Then it was back on the bus, about an hour more of travelling, and the bus stopped.

We were in a parking lot. The sky was azure, with no clouds. Frost crunched under our feet as we walked across the asphalt and onto the damp grass to a dock. The blue lake reached out to the horizon in two directions, more long than narrow. In the distance across the lake, we could see a line of blue mountains, and, built into the downward slope of the foothills, a small community of white buildings. Closer to us, but out of swimming range, was an island consisting of two brown earthen mounds, one larger than the other, both bare except for a few jutting evergreen trees.

"That's Rattlesnake Island," Mr. Phillips told us. "Peachland is on the other side of the water. We're not far from Kelowna."

"How come there's no one around?" Robbie asked. "Shouldn't there be, like, beaucoup tourists around here?"

He was right. The parking lot was empty except for our bus. There were no boats out on any part of the lake that we could see.

"Perhaps there's a wine festival," Mr. Phillips said. He winked at us.

He, Dempsey, and Robbie were carrying what looked like heavy trunks. That made sense: summoning sometimes required a lot of tools. I stood back and watched. Mr. Phillips had reviewed the procedure during the ride, but I had not understood it. Opening the three trunks, they took out and spread a large white tarpaulin on the dock and secured the ends with heavy quartz geodes. There was a sound like a hum or a chant, I wasn't sure. I was afraid to join in, not really afraid, but convinced it was the wrong thing to do.

Mr. Phillips made symbols on the tarpaulin with a stick of black charcoal. Then he removed jars of colored sand from a trunk and began to trace the symbols by slowly pouring sand along his outlines. If there had been any wind, this might not have worked, but the air was cool and still.

On a Sunday afternoon, there ought to have been some people around the resort, even in January. But there was no one. Still my fellow students were humming and chanting, and there was no other sound. I looked all around, at the parking lot, the trees, the sky, the lake. Other than us, no living thing was visible anywhere.

Pouring the coloured sand took a long time. Some of the students' voices wavered, but in time I felt I was hearing only one real voice, as if my classmates had summoned a sound that could exist without them. Soon I could hear nothing else, and I began then to watch the lake. At first I saw nothing in the blue waters. Then, in the far distance, a shadow broke the surface and quickly sank below again.

"She is near," cried Mr. Phillips. "Stay calm. Ogopogo has never harmed anyone during a lawful summoning. Now…quiet!"

The hum died down at once.

"Stay calm. We have issued the call. She is a thing of water and moves sinuously. Stay calm and keep her form in your minds."

I watched the water, aware I was doing nothing to help. Then, quickly, I looked at Leah, her head bent in prayer, and then at Robbie, his eyes closed, his lips parted, looking half asleep. Mr. Phillips was standing at the edge of the dock with Murgatroyd cradled against his body with one hand.

I looked back at the water. There were two dark shapes now, two shadowy, shiny bumps, flowing in and out of the water like a snake slithering over low rocks. I couldn't see any head. If there was one, it was submerged. The shapes came towards us at a strange diagonal, as if they meant to pass near us but not come all the way. Then, when they were near, abruptly they rose higher as the creature dived deeper into the water, raising a broad, flat tail like a whale's.

"It's gone," I said quietly.

"Not yet," said Mr. Phillips, though he should have been too far away to hear me. And just then, Murgatroyd yapped and jumped from his grasp onto the dock and from the water rose the most frightening head I had ever seen. It had a jaw like a horse and a mane made of reeds and bulrushes, the small sharp teeth that a jackal has, and its eyes were completely white and reflective, like the eyes of a cat in headlights.

Some of my fellow students uttered gasping sounds or single words of surprise. Only Mr. Phillips was not shaken. Robbie's mouth was open, Leah was grinning and laughing, Dempsey hooked his thumbs in his suspenders and his eyes twinkled. Me, I fell over backwards.

Ogopogo, with a head the size of a truck engine, snorted, spraying all of us with cold mist. She rose till her head was way above us, looking left to right and right to left with her shining eyes.

"My God," Dempsey said, as if only just realizing what he was looking at.

I got up, not sure what to do. Not every computer-animated monster in every movie ever made can prepare you for seeing a real one. It was like stepping off a bridge and falling uncontrollably down into an icy chasm and crashing onto the jagged stones of a totally new world. I didn't know what to do, and then I did. I got up and staggered over to Leah and put my arm around her shoulders.

"Now I know," I whispered to her. "Now I really know."

"I've always known," she whispered back. "But it's more beautiful than I ever imagined."

Ogopogo snorted again. Mist engulfed the dock. The cold sky turned gray. Then I heard the voice. It was high and thin, and it came, not from the monster, but from beside my ear, yet with a hollow sound, as if it was merely an echo of a voice from a distant planet.

(Why was I called? My occupations are far away.)

"You were called to demonstrate what is known," said Mr. Phillips. "That your magnificence be fully known, you must answer our questions as truthfully as you can."

(This is not without cost, conjuror.)

"The cost was paid, years ago, in anticipation of moments such as this: release from the ancient binding within this place, save when lawfully called."

(To lengthen chains does not remove them. Promise freedom, conjuror.)

"Not today, spirit."

(Very well, but I shall not forget.)

I could see little through the mist, but I realized, slowly, as if half asleep, that Mr. Phillips was advising us.

"Speak the spirit's name, and then ask your question," he called. "No one will hear if you first speak its name."

I heard whispering in all directions, but I could see no one through the fog except Leah beside me. She was whispering. For a moment, as she looked into the mist towards where the monster's head might be, her eyes were bright with hope; then they fell. I put my arm around her, and then removed it. She didn't seem to notice.

(You are full of questions, student.)

"Yes, I am," I whispered.

(Ask me not of love, for you are a child and cannot comprehend it.)

"What should I ask you about?"

(The future. Ways and means. The waters are an endless and

endlessly changing path, as is the time ahead.)

"Will I be in danger soon?"

(Your mortal kind is always in danger of death.)

I'd left something out. "Ogopogo, will I be in danger soon?"

(Before year's end.)

"Ogopogo, how will I defeat my enemies?"

(What enemies?)

"Ogopogo, how will I defeat my greatest enemy?"

(You will find Yehoshua ben Perachyah.)

The direct answer startled me; just like that. The voice was not near me. The whispering around me died down, and the mist began to clear. I realized I should have asked about my bargain with Clive Tinker. Still, somehow I had had little choice about what I said. Ogopogo had guided me to the question she wished to answer.

I sat down on the wet grass. Of course it was a strong spirit, stronger by far than me, and I had come unprepared to confront it and wasted my chance to learn something useful. I looked around. All my fellow-students, even the seniors like Dempsey, seemed similarly befuddled. Dizzy and not wanting to stand, I went on hands and knees to where Robbie was lying on his back in the grass.

He tilted his head to see who it was. "Oh, hey, roomie," he said.

Magic Ball

We got in around midnight. Robbie and I had slept several hours of the return trip, but he crashed out again as soon as he saw his bed. I was tired, but I went down the hall and around the corner. It wasn't Leah I wanted to see. Actually I'd avoided her on the return trip, wondering how the strangeness of that moment had let me put my arm around her. I wanted to see Goldberry if she was up. The light was on inside, so I tapped on the door with one knuckle.

Goldberry opened it. She was in her pajamas and robe. Her face was red, her amazing eyes wet from crying.

"What happened?" I asked.

"My father paid me a visit," she said. "Good you weren't here, or you'd have promised him a kidney."

"Let's get a snack," I suggested.

We went to the dining hall, where a late-night snack of cheese, crackers, and fresh fruit was set on the sideboard. A few other kids from the trip were there, and two or three huddled shapes of kids who had fallen asleep studying. Goldberry and I took some food and went to a table in the corner.

"What did he say?"

"Mother's been sick as usual. No, not as usual. Worse. And this is the time when she needs me helping her, not wasting my time here at School of the Ages." She spat a grape seed onto her plate – a sign of great anger, given her usual excellent table manners. "He had me packed and bound for the door, all my books left behind. 'Enough of this self-indulgence of yours,' he said. And then… And then…." She stopped and sipped her juice. "We were nearly to the door when we saw someone in the way, in one of those hooded robes. I think my father knew who it was before he put his hood down."

"Who?"

"Dr. Archer. I mean, who would expect him to be here on the weekend? And he said, like he knew everything, 'You know she can't leave, Clive.' And my father said, 'I'm on the Board. I'll arrange it.' Then Dr. Archer said, 'Do so, and I will give my resignation at once. I am pledged to the defense of students within the School of the Ages grounds. To withdraw a student against her will is within my mandate to prevent.'

"'She's my daughter,' my father said. 'No one may be compelled to leave our grounds without the consent of the Dean,' said Dr. Archer. 'The same protection was afforded us in our own time here. Violate it now, even once, and you will cause irreparable harm to our defenses.'

"My father was as angry as I've ever seen. I got the feeling this was not the first time they had it out. So I came back to my room, and he went out of the door with smoke coming from his ears." She paused and bit into a peach.

I was tired, but I still got an idea. "He knew it was going to happen."

"Who? My father?"

"No. Dr. Archer knew. That's why he wouldn't let you go on the trip with me. He must have known your father was coming. No, wait, not exactly. What did he tell me? He doesn't predict the future, but he knows in general what sort of things are going to happen. So he knew you needed to be here. And he knew I shouldn't be here, or I would have interfered. And your father and I owe each other, and that would have been a mess."

"And he wanted to handle it himself," Goldberry said. "They've bad blood between them, they must." She shook her head, then smiled, if weakly. "Enough of this, then. How was your trip?"

I had thought, during the trip back, about what to tell her. I told her about calling my parents, and about the ceremony, and about Ogopogo. And then, although it was hard, I told her about the time I'd spent with Leah.

"Seems like you made a decent job of it," she said. "I'd not go fast, though."

"I don't even know what I want," I admitted. "I guess I just want to find out what I want. Speaking of that, what about Goodenough?"

"Oh, him. He came by to help me study, since my partner abandoned me."

"And then what?"

"Not much, really."

"I did abandon you," I said. "I deserve whatever he said. But I don't trust him, Goldberry."

"Nor I," she said. "But he has a pretty face, and he's useful. Also, it's generally better to keep an eye on a spy so you know what he's going to report."

"Spying? You think so? For whom?"

"For my father, of course. But don't worry. Spy or not, I know what to do with a boy like him."

*

The next week of classes went by fairly easily. Robbie forgave me, and I spent most of my free time in my room or studying with Goldberry. I was nervous about Memento Analysis, but even that class went smoothly. It was mostly lecture, and the practice memento I got contained the spirit of a small boy who just asked me for toys. Leah and I said hello, but nothing else. Even my enemies were too busy with their work to hassle me.

Friday morning at breakfast, Dempsey, Lambert, Miss Dunham, and some kids whose names I didn't know put up large posters in the dining room over the sideboard. "Winter club sign-up," they called out casually. I went with Rocco to look at the posters. Most of the older students were ahead of us, writing their names. I had been seeing signs for the clubs for the past two weeks, but I wasn't sure what to sign up for. "What do you think?" I asked Rocco.

"Definitely intramurals," he said. "I'm getting crazy without exercise."

"I don't like sports much," I said, "but exercise isn't a bad idea."

"Plus you can use magic," Rocco reminded me.

That sounded interesting enough, so when we got up to the posters, I wrote my name down for intramurals, next to Rocco's. Then I put Goldberry's name on for the divination club, and added mine also.

The first club meeting for intramurals was Saturday night, after sundown so that the Cabala school boys could attend. It was held in the gym, a high-ceilinged, echoing room at the back of the building on the ground floor. The gym was supplied with high, narrow windows – clerestory windows, they're called – that would let in plenty of sunlight during the daytime. Since it was a night meeting, many lanterns were arranged around the room. Playing in that light would be like playing night ball under a bright moon. There were about thirty students there, all boys. The Chasidic boys had taken off their coats and were in shirt sleeves with their prayer shawls tucked into their black pants. The rest of us were wearing jeans and sweatshirts.

"Four teams," said Mr. Bannerjee, the activities director, who was there with a clipboard. "Captains please. Dempsey, Finkel, Solomon, Rocco. Choose your teammates and report to me in five minutes."

Team selection didn't take long. The older non-Jewish students were on Dempsey's team. Finkel, a big boy with a red beard, took all the Chasidic boys. Solomon took all the orthodox boys. Rocco got me and the other freshmen. The two extra kids were on our team. Mr. Bannerjee wrote our names down. "Basketballs," he said. "In the storeroom. Please to play half-court. Practice only. Dempsey against Finkel, Solomon against Rocco. Every player gets at least two minutes playing time. Basic hexes only today. That includes you, Mr. Rosenberg."

"Who, me?" called Rosenberg, a short, bullet-headed orthodox boy with a gold-embroidered skullcap.

We went to team meetings. "What's a basic hex?" was the question for most of our team.

"I think it means making the ball miss the hoop, or getting someone to drop it," Rocco said. "Anyone know how to do that stuff? 'Cause I bet Solomon knows."

"I could try," King said. He was a second-year; I had no classes with him and didn't know him, but he had been with Goodenough when Goodenough was trying to bully me, so I was surprised he was friendly now.

"Teach me," I said.

"OK," Rocco said, "You two guys sit out a couple of points and see what you can do."

I went off to the side with King.

"My dad told me a little about this," King told me. "You visualize the ball inside your head, and just kind of hold that picture there. Then watch the game, and when you want to do something, say a magic word and imagine the ball moving the way you want it to."

"What's your magic word?"

King blinked at me, surprised. "You don't know any?"

"Not really." Behind him, I saw the two teams move into action.

"Dad said everyone should have some word or name that sounds magical," he said. "I use my girlfriend's name, Eun Hee. That sounds like magic to me."

"Eun Hee? Where's she from?"

"She lives in Korea. I miss her all the time. Okay, let me try to hex these guys." He turned away, watching the game.

I also watched the action. Rocco was fast and energetic, but Solomon was good, too, and taller. I needed my own magic word. The ones I knew, like "Abracadabra," or "Ablanathanalba," were kind of overexposed in the kind of books you can buy in stores, so they seemed too phony to me. I ran through a few Hebrew words in my mind, but I knew so little Hebrew that I couldn't think of any words that sounded right. What to use?

USE MY NAME, said the voice. I hadn't heard it in a long time. The voice spoke into my thoughts, like a spirit bound to a memento.

Get out of my head, I thought back.

USE MY NAME, said the ghost. I AM YEISHU BEN PANDEIRA.

Just like that, the spirit was gone. I felt blood rushing to my head. I turned to watch the game, Rosenberg passing around Rocco to Solomon, and I tried to focus on the ball, to capture it in my mind. Cries of "Here, here," and harsh words echoed throughout the gym. Rocco covered Solomon; Solomon dribbled, passed back to Rosenberg, who dribbled around another of my teammates. "Don't see the faces," I said to myself. "Just see the ball. The ball is connected to me." The orange globe bounced and darted hand to hand. It wasn't an object separate from me – no, it was a shape resting within my mind. If I could only unite the two in my thoughts, what then?

Rosenberg went for two. The ball hit the rim and then rolled back off again. Max jumped for it, lost control and fell, rubbing his hand. "Hey, basic hexes!" he shouted. "That hurt!"

"You're out of shape," Solomon shouted, grinning.

I saw that grin, and something connected for me, and YEISHU BEN PANDEIRA flashed in my mind, and as if he had been shot, Solomon went flying backwards, landed on his behind, and slid across the court.

"Foul!" he shouted, rubbing his back. "Hey, who did that?" He looked at me and King, shaking his head.

Mr. Bannerjee blew his whistle. "Captains," he called. I stood there dizzy, wondering what I had just done, and how. I could hear Rocco denying he had anyone on his team who could do a hex like that. Eventually, Solomon got two free throws, and that was it. When Rocco put me in, I just covered my zone and barely touched the ball. When he took me out, I went and sat in the bleachers. There was no way I could do magic like that – no way. I could barely even see the triangle during meditation. Had that ghost helped me? But no, it was gone. Could just its name be so powerful?

Rabbi Mendy had taught us that different Hebrew names for

Hashem, or God, corresponded to different acts of magic. Dr. Archer had told us that the true name of a spirit gave you power over it. Had this ghost given me a powerful name? If so, why? What would happen if I used it again?

A part of me knew I should go to Dr. Archer for help. Yet I had told him I would handle my problems myself as long as I could. What would he think of me if I came begging for help just a week later?

After the practice, I was confused but not dizzy. On the way out I called to Solomon and went over to him.

"What was that hex?" I asked. "Any idea who did it?"

"Maybe one of the older guys," he said. "Rocco said no one on his team could do it. You guys are all pretty green, right?"

"I guess," I said. "Listen, tell me something else. What's an *apikoros*?"

"Someone who turned away from the right way of Jewish living," he said. "Who doesn't show proper respect for halacha, which is the way Hashem wants Jews to live and worship. Like your roommate, Radish, or that spooky Ritz girl."

"What's wrong with them?"

"Radish is reform, so he's hardly a Jew at all. And Ritz, she reads Talmud like a Yeshiva boy. Talmud is only for men. Must be from a whole family of *apikorsim*."

He smiled and walked off. I found myself hoping it was me who knocked him over. The apikoros label still didn't make sense. I had a Jewish grandfather, but had never been raised Jewish. Why would Mermelstein call me apikoros? Somehow, I would have to find that out, too.

Divination Club

Somehow the trip to Lake Okanagan really had cleared my head. I still had all the problems I had had before, but it was easier to forget about them. There were so many classes for so much of the day, and there were so many assignments from them, that the days blended together, and most of the time when I looked at people I just wondered if they knew the answer to whatever homework I was working on.

Sometimes Goldberry and I studied alone, sometimes together, sometimes with Leah or Robbie and Balaram in the room. No one's feelings changed, but we were all too busy studying and practicing.

I missed my parents a lot. I thought I wasn't being careful enough without my mother's traditional warnings. I missed hearing her heels clicking on the tiles by the front door. I missed her curry chicken and baked ziti. I missed my father's grin and his sarcastic moods.

My old school hadn't been too tough. There were kids I needed to stay away from, but I didn't have personal enemies there, people who knew me and thought about me and thought I was in their way. And there were kids there I liked, but not kids so important that I felt my whole life was about them. It's nice to be important enough that everyone cares what you do, but the pressure can be hard to handle. Overall, the real strangeness and suddenness of what I was doing really kept me feeling off-balance. In the world, as most people know it, if you say you're talking to ghosts, they get a doctor and lock you up. In the School of the Ages world, there are people for whom nothing could be more normal.

It was the day after the second divination club meeting that it happened. I was in meditation, and I finally saw the triangle and held onto it. But about the club…

Divination club was mostly girls. The student who did the most talking was the senior, Miss Dunham. She knew me from class but ignored me. There was Carol, a very tall, thin black girl who wore long, flowing dresses; and Mina, who named herself for and looked like the bride of Dracula, with lots of black and white clothing and lipstick; and Lakshmi, a short, plump Indian girl who wore shalwars and did astrology; and Irene, who had dark hair and wore jeans and Gypsy scarves; and Dwight, a skinny senior with blond hair, froglike eyes, and a stupid-looking half-grown beard; and Goldberry; and me. We were the youngest and the only new members. We weren't asked for our input.

"It was decided last year to begin this year with tasseography," said Miss Dunham. "We must each acquire a supply of cut plain black or green tea leaves. No added flavors or colors, if you please. Loose, not in bags."

"Is decaf okay?" I asked Goldberry too loudly.

"There must be an echo," Dwight said to Irene. "It sounds just like a rude child."

Yes, you do, I thought, but I kept quiet. I already had enough adversaries.

"Everyone needs a white or pastel-colored coffee mug," Miss Dunham continued, and then went on to give the details of a short ritual to prepare the mug. I made a note to ask Rabbi Horn to go over it in next the construction class.

"To remain a member in good standing, you must perform a daily divination," said Miss Dunham. "Until you are practiced with tea leaves, a tarot reading or I Ching sticks or casting runes will suffice. At each meeting, you will present a log and report as to accuracy and technique."

"When did this rule begin?" asked Carol. "I know I wasn't consulted."

"It's an attempt to prevent certain problems we are expecting," Miss Dunham said, and she looked directly at me.

"What?" I said. "What did I do? Isn't there anyone in the whole school who can stand to have me around?"

"You are without ability at divination," Miss Dunham said.

"I know that. I just joined to be with my partner. What's the problem?"

"I can't be exact," said Miss Dunham. "There shouldn't be any problem with what you're doing, but the forecast is bad."

"Well, if he goes, so do I," Goldberry said suddenly. "And you don't want that. I've read plenty of teacups in my time, more than some of you have, I expect."

"Give me the date, time, and place of your birth," Lakshmi said to me.

"You first," I shot back.

"Let's settle it with cards," said Miss Dunham. "Who will read?"

"I will," said Mina in a dreamy voice. "Come here, child."

"Child?" I said. "What are you, fourteen?"

"Child of God," she said in a more normal voice, rolling her eyes. "The spirits instruct you to come sit by me."

I decided to go along with that. Lakshmi traded seats with me.

"Shuffle and turn up a card," Mina told me, handing me a pack of brown-backed tarot cards. I did. The result was a young man with a stick across his back.

"This card is you, the Fool," Mina said. "You set out upon a journey of discovery knowing that you know nothing."

"Sure," I said.

"Turn another card. It is your past."

My next card showed a woman pouring water.

"Temperance," said Mina. "You were a well-balanced individual. Turn a card for your present problem."

The next card was a skeleton holding a scythe.

"Death," she said. "My favorite. Your old life is lost, and you face great change."

"Or someone will die," said Irene.

"You always think someone is going to die," said Carol.

"Turn a last card for the outcome," said Mina.

I did. I saw a robed man on a throne.

"The High Priest," said Mina. "A man wise in the ways of magic. You may become this, or you may meet such a person."

"So I'll see the Dean, or Dr. Archer. So what?"

"Throw another card on top of that," said Goldberry.

I followed her instructions. It was a man hanging upside-down by one foot.

"That's not the Dean or Dr. Archer," said Goldberry.

"A rabbi maybe?" Irene said.

"A very great rabbi," said Miss Dunham.

"The Rambal," I suggested.

*

That evening, as Goldberry and I were in my room studying for a magic theory test on the chapter about "applications of the law of contagion," I asked her, "Should we go try to see him?"

"Wouldn't mind," she said. "But I'll never get in. They don't like girls at American Academy of Cabala."

"Go see who?" Robbie asked. He was across the room at his desk, writing a composition about summoning circles.

"The Rambal," I said, and explained.

"Cool," he said. "I'll go with you."

"What reason will you give?" Goldberry asked. A tarot reading said you were supposed to meet a great man. Cheerio, Rabbi Lichtman, you seem to fill the bill."

"Why not?" I said. "I'm not going to make up a reason. He'd just see through that, anyway."

The next day at lunch, the three of us took the cold stone spiral staircase to the third floor where American Academy of Cabala was headquartered. The entrance, a wooden double-door, was at the end of a long hallway with few decorations other than some Hebrew posters. I couldn't read them, but they looked like announcements of events.

The hall was totally silent. Even our footsteps grew quiet. No one was there but us. The closer we got to the door, the worse an idea it seemed to be there at all.

A few yards from the door, we all stopped. I found that I was breathing heavily. Goldberry smoothed her skirt front and crinkled her eyes at me. Robbie was touching the air with his right palm, as if he had encountered a wall. He had to be joking. There was nothing there to touch. The wall was made out of doubt.

"Let's go," I said. It came out a whisper.

"Go on, then," Goldberry said.

I took a step. Bad idea, I thought. But I was a step closer. I took Goldberry's hand and tugged. She took a step also, but whispered, "I feel sick. William did tell us this place was protected."

"This is intense," Robbie blurted. I'd never heard him so quiet; he even breathed louder when he was asleep.

Ahead of us, the double doors opened and a tall, broad-shouldered figure came out, shutting them behind him.

Yakov Mermelstein.

"Get out of here, *apikoros*," he commanded me. His voice wasn't soft.

"Get out yourself," I said, able to speak better. "We're not breaking any school rules."

"You don't belong here."

"That's your opinion."

Mermelstein took a step forward. "Don't test me, *apikoros*. I'll make you regret it."

"He's not alone," Robbie said.

"He might as well be," answered Mermelstein.

Goldberry shook her head. "This is stupid. He can't stand here forever. Let's go and come back later."

"He's asking for it," Robbie said. "Come on, Simon. He can't handle all three of us, even on his own turf."

"No, I have a better idea," I said. "Who sent you, Mermelstein? Did someone send you to keep us away? Or did you send yourself?"

"I know you don't belong here. You need to go, *apikoros*."

"No one sent him," I said. "So why is he here? There's already magic in this hallway to drive us away."

"So who needs him?" Goldberry said. She snapped her fingers.

"Oh, wait. I see now."

"He's part of the spell," I said.

Mermelstein took a few steps toward me, then stopped, tilted his head, thinking it out. Finally he faced us again and came forward with rage in his eyes.

"Why doesn't the spell pick the strongest guy, like an older student?" I asked.

"Or the Rambal himself," Robbie said.

"Why Mermelstein? Is he that important?" I asked. "I think you're here for the opposite reason. You're expendable, Mermelstein."

A moment later, there was a blinding flash in my eye. I felt my back striking stone.

"You don't talk to me that way, you filthy boy," Mermelstein's voice said from somewhere far off. I was blind for the moment, not sure where my hands and feet were either. Then I heard grunting and shoes scraping across stone, and someone thumping into a wall.

"Will you hit me as well, then?" Goldberry shouted, distant as an echo. "Stupid boy!"

Then the door must have slammed open. A high, strong man's voice filled the hall. "Tchk! Yakov! Why do you profane yourself with this fighting?"

"Rebbe," he answered. "These goyim don't belong here."

"And we go freely to their places, so where is it written they can't knock on our door?"

"You can't let them, rebbe. This *apikoros*, he…"

The rabbi's voice grew sharper. "*Chutzpinyah*! Wait for me in my office."

"It's not fair, rebbe! You can't!"

The rabbi said a few words in Hebrew. I heard *Adonai*, which is a word for God used only in prayer. A moment later, I felt my vision and the feeling in my limbs both returning. A firm, cool hand took mine and helped me up. Soon I could make out the face of Rabbi Shulman, the Rambal's deputy.

"I'm sorry this happened," he said. "I'll speak to him. Is there some way I can help you?"

"We'd like to meet the Rambal," I said shakily.

Rabbi Shulman grinned. "Sometimes I have trouble seeing him myself. I can tell Rabbi Lichtman you asked to see him. Then he will call you on his own if he wishes. Is there a reason you are asking for a meeting?"

Goldberry and I explained the divination club. Robbie, who was slumped against the wall rubbing his head, gradually came to his feet.

"Cards and tea leaves are not our way," Rabbi Shulman said. "To know the future, we pray to Hashem to show us what he wills. You don't always find out what you want, but, nu, if Hashem tells you, you don't waste time wondering if you got it right." He smiled and gestured back toward the stairs going down.

Dr. Archer Investigates

The news that Mermelstein had punched me got around the school quickly. My black eye didn't help. Goodenough passed by our lunch table and gave me a wry smile. I avoided giving Rocco the details.

When I opened a book to study that night, I found a sealed envelope. Inside was a card in neat handwriting: "See me."

If he had meant the morning, he'd have said as much, so although it was late, I went to Dr. Archer's office. The fire was roaring. He was wearing dark slacks and a blue turtleneck. His eyes pierced me like spears. He did not gesture for me to sit.

"In case of difficulty, Simon," he said, "you are to come to me first. I am your advisor because I am best suited to help you, not Mr. Phillips, and certainly not the Rambal. I accepted responsibility for your education when I recommended your admission to the Dean. It perplexes me that you have so consistently avoided using me as an advisor. What explanation can you offer for your lamentable error in this regard?"

I couldn't look at him. "I suppose it's because you're busy," I lied.

"I am not as busy as I ought to be, given your recalcitrance," he snapped. "I have never refused you a meeting. In fact I have never excused myself from assisting any pupil of mine at any time on the grounds of being busy. I will not tolerate your obfuscation. An honest and direct answer is required at once."

"Why? You probably know everything anyway. Why make me say it?" I felt myself choking. I was about to cry and didn't know why. I didn't want to look like a fool in front of him, and that was just what was happening.

"I most assuredly do not possess intimate knowledge of the workings of your mind, nor am I so without competing worries that I may devote my entire day to monitoring the foibles of one thirteen-year-old."

"Well," I said, "some of us thirteen-year-olds have foibles, okay? We're not all perfect like you."

"I expect no perfection of you, nor of any student, not even Donovan. What I expect is that you will bring your troubles to me before any other teacher. In my day we had a credo at this school, under the acronym FPTA: 'first partner, then advisor.' I will ask again: why do you so consistently eschew use of me in the role of advisor?"

I was crying now. Dr. Archer finally gestured me into a seat.

"You're too good," I sobbed.

"Good? Define your terms. I have no use for such vagaries."

"You're too tough. You're always right. I'm always wrong around you. Okay?"

"Indeed," he said. "This last is true, but it is so because of late you have only come before me when you are wrong. Have you mastered the triangle?"

"Yes. Yes, but I mean, not right now. Yes, I can do it."

"Why not come to inform me?"

"Do you care." I knew I wasn't making sense, but I couldn't stop.

"Why do you suppose that I do not care? I did not take on your education in order to belittle you. Year after year I have endured such foolishness from adolescents. I can only hope you, unlike others, will be done with it by year's end. No sooner, given what you face."

"What I face? What do I face?" I coughed. "What are you talking about?"

"Within two years, we shall…" He stopped, gathering in his ferocity. "I don't know precisely," he said. "I know only that you will continue, as you have, to take on challenges greater than you are prepared for, and not all will end in triumph."

"You mean, like Mermelstein beating me so easily?"

"Beating you? Did you yield to him? I was unaware of your surrender."

"I didn't surrender." I wiped my eyes on my sweatshirt.

"Do you mean to?" He leaned forward, watching as if genuinely wondering.

"No, but he knocked me out."

"Why?"

"Because I wouldn't do what he said."

"And why else?"

"Did you talk to him about it?"

"No, Simon. Why else did he strike you?"

"I guess because I was saying he was being used by the spell."

"Spell? What spell?"

"The spell that guards the entrance to American Academy of Cabala."

"Nonsense. There is no spell there. Again, why did he strike you?"

"I guess I was making him feel stupid."

"And is that what you were trying to do?"

"I guess. I thought I could beat him that way."

"If so, then who was the winner of the battle?"

"He was. He knocked me and Robbie out."

"What was his goal?"

"To get rid of us, I guess."

"And what was yours?"

"To get past him and ask for the Rambal."

Dr. Archer nodded. "Whose goal was achieved? Yours, or his?"

I suddenly realized I was done crying. "I guess mine was."

"Then he struck you," said Dr. Archer, sitting straight again, "not to defeat you, but out of vengefulness that you were defeating him. I assure you, Yakov Mermelstein was sorely rebuked by Rabbi Shulman, both for his loss and for his pique."

"You mean Rabbi Shulman wanted him to win? But he took our side when he showed up."

Dr. Archer shook his head. "So it appeared. Rabbi Shulman is a good man. However, he is charged with maintaining the privacy of that place. It was his intent that you faced then, not the shreds of some antique spell of guardianship."

"You mean he was on the other side of the door trying to make us leave?"

"No need for that. A part of his mind, apart from his conscious thought, is constantly devoted to the task of discouraging uninvited visitors."

"Then his spells never wear off?"

"It has nothing to do with spells, or with time. A part of his spirit resonates with the overarching intent of the universe. Thus he is always present, just as God is always present, and always really means nothing at all."

It was the most incomprehensible thing I had ever heard. Looking at me, Dr. Archer realized I was lost.

"This knowledge is not yet for you," he said. "To answer more simply, when you were heading toward the entrance, Rabbi Shulman knew, and he sent Yakov Mermelstein to intercept you."

"What does he have against us?"

"Nothing personally," said Dr. Archer. "But American Academy of Cabala is an enclave. It is a community with set rules, and if you are there, you must comply. But then, it is the study of a lifetime to comply. One may think well of a person, and yet know that person cannot do what is required."

"Does that mean that Mermelstein and I will always fight? Or that I'll never meet the Rambal?"

"It means neither. What other questions have you?"

There were many questions in my mind, but still something stopped me from asking the hardest ones, the ones about the ghost named Yeishu ben Pandeira.

"Why does Mermelstein call me *apikoros*? It doesn't make sense, because I'm not Jewish, except my mother's father was."

Dr. Archer pursed his lips. "I don't know," he concluded. "At this time, only he can say."

"Then can you tell me more about Leah?"

"Perhaps. But would you have me tell others all that I know of you?"

"No."

I waited a moment to gather my thoughts. "Last question, I guess. How can I learn how to fight? With magic, I mean. Does anyone teach that?"

Dr. Archer thought a while before answering. “You are currently learning it, are you not?”

“I know, but that’s just by trial and error. Everyone else knows more about it than me.”

“If so,” he said, rising, “then as well you ask everyone else.” The door opened, on its own, I thought. Goldberry was waiting outside, holding an envelope like the one that had summoned me.

“Good day, Simon,” my advisor said.

Vasant Panchami

After her meeting, I saw Goldberry at dinner, and she looked as shaken up as I was. As we ate our lamb stew, I asked her how the meeting went.

"He's mad at me for not studying harder. I told him I can't help it, you know. My mother is sick. And he won't help with her bloody healing, and he forbade me to ask anyone else again."

"Like who? Did you ask someone?"

"I was going to ask the Rambal. That's what I went along for, you know. Dr. Archer says that 'the matter will be resolved by the end of summer,' but he won't say how or how it's going to come out. I'd try to heal her myself, if I thought it would do any good. But whenever I try, I just see my father's face in the way."

"Maybe if we try together."

"We could do," she said, "but I expect my father is too strong while he keeps her at home."

"Then," I suggested, "we could get Robbie to summon a spirit to teach us about healing."

"Robbie? All I've ever seen him summon is an appetite."

I thought this was a little mean, but I let it go. "What about Balaram then?"

Goldberry considered this. "Yeah, all right."

* * *

We found Balaram, Robbie's study partner, in his room. His roommate Max had just left for *maariv*, the evening prayer.

"You can keep something private, right?" I asked.

"Sure." Balaram smiled faintly, showing he had no idea why we were there.

"You'll strike a magician's bargain?" I asked. "Service for service?"

"What exactly is it you want?" he said slowly.

"We want you to summon a spirit to do something for me," Goldberry said.

"And keep it a secret," I added. "We'll tell you the rest after the bargain is agreed on."

"And what if I don't want to do it once I find out what it is?"

After some negotiating, we agreed to pledge him two services each, one for silence about the project, one for the summoning itself.

"My mother's sick," Goldberry explained. "My father won't tell me a bloody thing about it, and he has wards all around her. We need a spirit to heal her."

"How strong is your father?" Balaram asked mildly.

"He's not one to trifle with," Goldberry said. "He was Dr. Archer's schoolfellow."

Balaram picked up a summoning textbook from his desk and flipped through it. "I don't know if anyone in here can do what you want, but I can ask."

"Have you summoned any of those spirits before?" I asked.

"Yes, but I didn't bind them, so I couldn't command them, only talk. But these are pretty friendly spirits. Mr. Phillips said we don't do dangerous ones till third year."

After flipping through the pages a while, he said, "I need to work on this, as well as pick an auspicious time. Why don't you guys clear your schedule for…" He looked at a desk calendar. "Sixth February. That's Vasant Panchami. You can come to the *puja* at my parents' house, and we'll do it there afterwards."

"How do we get out of school?" I asked. A *puja* was a Hindu prayer ceremony, and in a family home would probably be followed by a party.

"My parents will pick us up. Get some yellow clothes, guys."

"And what about your partner?" Goldberry asked.

"He'll come along to the *puja*, but then we'll ditch him."

*

We had no trouble getting permission to miss class, so Goldberry and I found ourselves waiting outside the school, early morning of Sixth February. The air was losing some of its chill, and I found my overcoat a little warm.

Scrounging among the female students, Goldberry had secured three yellow scarves for herself, Robbie, and me. Balaram was wearing casual clothes but said he would change at home. "This holiday is about learning and knowledge," he said. "We pray to *Saraswati*."

"Who's he?" Robbie asked.

"*Saraswati* is a goddess," Balaram said. "She is the wife of Lord *Brahma*, part of the Tridevi, an aspect of the divine mother."

"So you really believe in lots of gods and goddesses?"

"For me, they stand for different things in the world. All the stories about them give us ways to understand life. It doesn't matter if you believe *Saraswati* is a goddess or if you just believe in what she stands for. The benefit to your life is the same." "Wait a minute," I said. "My grandmother, my father's mother I mean, always says the gods are real."

"Many Hindus would agree with her. I don't really disagree; I'm just kind of flexible is all."

I heard a rumbling sound and turned to look at the trees surrounding the building. As I watched, a blue minivan appeared amid the trees, as if coming around a corner I couldn't see. It broke through the trees and plunged across the grass.

The inside of the van was decorated with garlands of marigolds. The driver, a dark-skinned Indian man with a close-shaven head, braked, then jumped out. He nodded to us, then folded his hands in the traditional *'Namaste'* greeting used by Hindus. "Let's go," he said, opening the sliding side door of the van.

"This is my father," Balaram said.

"Hello, Mr. Dass," Robbie said. "We talked on the phone. I'm Robbie."

Mr. Dass shook hands. "Let's go," he said to his son.

We climbed in. The minivan was commodious, but cluttered with toys and the mess left by small children, as well as petals from the garlands. Balaram rode in front, conversing with him in Hindi, only a little of which I could follow. Soon we were merging into the Battery Tunnel. We came out by FDR drive and went uptown to the Triboro Bridge.

"How far do you live?" I asked Balaram.

"Yonkers."

Traffic was light. In about an hour we pulled up in the driveway of a red-brick duplex house. The lawn was immaculate except for a few children's toys. A yellow garland hung on the door.

As we entered, a young boy chased another boy up a staircase on our right. At the left was a tastefully decorated living room. Ahead of us were the kitchen and a sliding-glass door that showed a slightly snowy backyard with a shed by a wooden fence. Two women, an older one in a yellow sari and a very young one in a yellow shalwar kameez, emerged from the kitchen carrying trays with various types of rice pudding. "We're in the basement, said the older woman, obviously Mrs. Dass. She smiled and went down some stairs opposite the kitchen.

As we came to those stairs, we smelt the pleasant, heady odour of burning incense. Downstairs there was another living room with a large, tiled floor. The two women set the trays on a small table. In the center of the room, a table with burning incense, a basin of water, a box of Indian sweets, some fruit on a silver dish, and a silver cup of milk.

With the food set down, the two ladies were free to meet us. They were Mrs. Dass and Balaram's elder sister, Mrs. Chaturvedi. Soon we were joined by Mr. Chaturvedi, a round-faced young man with glasses, and the two boys, Vijay, ten, and Ajay, six, Balaram's younger brothers.

From a large cabinet in the corner of the room, Mr. Dass retrieved two statues. One was made of silver, and the other of glazed, fired clay. Both depicted the same being, the Goddess *Saraswati*, holding a *veena*. The silver one was obviously store-bought, but the other, I realized, was homemade.

"You made that?" Robbie asked before I could.

"My father helped," Balaram said. "It was difficult. He does a little magic, but not at the level of our teachers. Small pieces like the arms and the *veena* kept cracking in the kiln. We prayed a lot."

"Well done indeed," Goldberry said. She was right. The features weren't as fine and detailed as in the smaller silver statue, but they were remarkable for a figure made of clay.

Mrs. Chaturvedi decorated the two statues with small yellow flowers. We took off our coats but kept our scarves. Balaram went upstairs, changed into a yellow kurta pyjama, and came down with two wrapped packages. One he set down on a chair. The other, the larger one, he gave to me. "It's not from us," he said.

"It was delivered yesterday by a messenger," said Mr. Dass.

I looked at Goldberry.

"Go on," she said.

The package was lightweight. As I opened the brown paper, I realized I was holding a fur coat. I let the paper fall. It was an ankle-length coat of mostly dark-brown fur with white and auburn patches.

"Crikey," Goldberry said. "My grandfather's. I'd no idea Mum kept it. It's made from Canadian beaver pelts."

"Your mom must be cool," Robbie said.

"I wonder why she picked this to send," Goldberry said, tapping her chin in thought. "Or why the gift just now."

"Try it on," Robbie said.

"Can I use your phone?" Goldberry asked Mr. Dass. He walked her upstairs.

I pulled on the coat. It was a little too big for me, but amazingly warm and soft. The Dass' basement had been a little chilly, but now I couldn't feel that cold at all. I pulled up the hood. It covered my head completely and drooped onto my forehead.

With the hood up, I thought the room seemed quieter, more calm. I could still see and hear everything, but nothing really bothered me. I was at peace.

I put the hood down again. This wasn't the place to tell anyone the coat was magical. "Wow, it's really warm," I told Robbie, hoping he wouldn't ask to try it on. Then I took the coat off and folded it as best I could, set it on a chair out of the way of the family, and sat down.

Mr. Dass and Goldberry came back down the stairs. She rolled her eyes at me, because of her phone call, I think. I waved her over as Balaram deftly got Robbie involved in the preparations for the *puja*.

"My mother said," Goldberry whispered, "that the cards told her to get rid of an old possession and give it to a young man. My father hated this old coat anyway."

Before she could continue, the *puja* began. While Mr. Dass read aloud in Sanskrit, Mrs. Dass and Mrs. Chaturvedi washed the two images of *Saraswati* and hung garlands on them. Although I was a quarter Indian, it was the first *puja* I had attended in many years. I enjoyed the songs and sharing of food. The married women served rice puddings with raisins, cashews, and almonds. Balaram had brought down another wrapped package along with the coat; he gave this package as a gift to his elder sister. It contained an embroidered shalwar and two DVDs of Shah Rukh Khan movies.

After the *puja*, we all went upstairs for lunch. I had never eaten most of the vegetarian dishes they served, and found them too spicy. Robbie had no trouble with even the spiciest ones. We finished with tea. As most of the table talk was in Hindi, and I rarely practiced that language despite hearing my father use it on the phone all the time, I found my mind wandering back to the coat. Why had she sent it? And how would I use it?

I had wondered how Balaram would get Robbie out of the way. He used his brother-in-law, Mr. Chaturvedi, who asked Robbie to go with him to buy some groceries. Balaram then led Goldberry and me upstairs. He pulled a cord hanging from the ceiling, and an attic door opened, lowering a folded-up ladder.

The attic at my parents' house was similar, so I had no trouble climbing up. This space was low, narrow, and dark. Balaram lit candles, then incense. In the dim light, I saw that more of his clay images were arranged on shelves and the floor. He unrolled straw mats for Goldberry and me to sit on, then another for himself.

"I know you guys don't cast summoning spells," he said, "so just think about a door opening, and try to meditate on that. I'll do the rest."

In the flickering candlelight, my breath constricted by the heavy smoke, it was easier to meditate, as if the world and my memories drifted with the smoke, broke up, and faded away. Balaram was doing a ritual of some kind, but I didn't pay attention to it. The entire world was just the space inside that dark, cramped attic, and that attic had a door.

The door opened, in the wall on my right, and something came in. I could not call that something a girl, or a woman. It looked like a woman, but the way the smoke curled around it and clung to it, and the way it glowed – no, not a woman, not really. The loveliness and the wisdom of that someone were almost more than I could bear.

It looked like the sculptures of *Saraswati* down in the basement.

Balaram said, "Thank you for coming. But your shape is too magnificent for our eyes."

I stared at the thing that resembled *Saraswati* until its features flowed like water, and it became an ordinary Indian woman in a yellow shalwar.

"Thank you," said Balaram. "I will speak quickly of why I have called you. This girl beside me – her mother is sick. She wishes for a cure, but strong magic repels her. Perhaps you know what is happening."

The apparition tilted its head toward Goldberry, staring at her with childlike curiosity.

"*Deviji* says that your mother has seen something in the future that has frightened her," Balaram said. "The shock of that vision has caused her a wound of the spirit. To cure her, you must go to the place and time that she saw. *Deviji* has promised to return when that time comes. She will tell us where we must go, and when."

I had not heard the spirit speak, nor seen its mouth move. It was still staring at Goldberry. Then, slowly, it turned to look at me.

GET AWAY! cried the voice of Yeishu ben Pandeira.

At once the spirit that was a plain Indian woman frowned at me, leapt up and ran back through the door, and it shut with a snap.

"*Deviji*?" said Balaram. "*Deviji*?"

The smoke cleared. I looked at the wall where the spirit had entered and left. Of course, there was no door; the only door to this room was underneath the straw mats where we sat. I began to feel like part of the world again.

"I wonder why the spirit left so quickly," Balaram said.

I didn't say anything.

"So that's it, then," Goldberry said. "Just wait around for instructions, and then go see in person whatever horrid thing was in my mother's vision. Not what I was expecting."

"That spirit may refuse to answer," said Balaram, "but it never lies."

"But could it be wrong?" Goldberry asked.

"I doubt it. I'll ask Mr. Phillips. But I think if it came in looking like *Saraswati*, it must have wisdom, just like *Saraswati* does. Our summoning book says a spirit's first shape tells you what it's capable of."

Far down below, a door slammed.

"They're back," I said. "We'd better go down."

"By the way," Balaram added. "You guys owe me another service. I think you should entertain the little kids, right?"

With Leah

Goldberry tried to put her worries about her mother out of her mind and concentrate on our classes, but it was hard for her. Sometimes she'd look at a wall for a while, almost without blinking, and I knew what she was thinking about. Even so, every day she did a little to help me learn tasseography, the reading of tea leaves. I could understand the principle, that you find shapes in the tea leaves, and the shapes have meanings that you kind of have to memorize. For example, if you see a flower, you know that means someone or something new will come into your life. Understanding the principle was good, but when I looked in the teacup, all I saw was a bunch of soggy muck.

We were in her room practicing one nigh. Leah was out, as she usually was, when there was a sharp rap at the door.

"Yes?" Goldberry called.

In came William Goodenough, wearing a polo sweater and matching scarf. "Enjoying our tea, are we?"

"We're practicing tasseography," my partner explained.

Goodenough pulled over her desk chair, turned it around, and sat resting his arms over the back. "Do you see good news for me, Goldberry?"

"This cup is for me. You'll have to drink one of your own if you want me to read it."

He turned to me and smirked. "What does your cup say, Simon? I hope it says you were just leaving."

I looked in my cup. "Actually, it says someone really obnoxious is going to interrupt my study session."

He smiled. "Probably your roommate is on his way, then." Turning to Goldberry again, he added, "If you'd like to go to the dining room for two fresh cups, I'd be happy to have you read for me. And I have some news that might interest you."

"Maybe at breakfast," Goldberry said. "We've chemistry to do next."

"Well then, I can bring us two cups."

"Thanks," I said. "We could use a refill."

Goldberry set down her cup on the floor. "Oh, all right, let's go then. But no more reading the leaves for me tonight, William. Just tell me the news, and then I've chemistry. Back in a bit, Simon."

She left with him. I remained behind, still sitting on the bed, holding a teacup full of mush. I opened the chemistry book to a random page but didn't study. When the door opened again, I looked up, and saw it wasn't Goldberry but Leah, carrying her small prayer book in her hand and a woven bag of school books over her shoulder.

I saw Leah every day, of course, but I'd never been alone in the room with her. She nodded to me and set her bag by her desk.

"Goldberry went to the dining hall with Goodenough," I said. "To get tea."

She sat down at her desk and took out a book.

"I can go, if you want."

"No, that's all right," she said. "This is just Maths." She looked down at her book again, picked up a pen and opened a notebook.

"I feel funny," I said. "Maybe I'll go get some tea, too."

Leah didn't respond.

"Do you want to go with me?"

She set down her pen firmly. "Just for a few minutes."

Going somewhere with her, just her and me, was different. It was the kind of thing people talked about.

"We'll see the real mementos from Palestine this week," she reminded me as we walked.

"That makes me a little nervous," I admitted. "Spirits make me nervous."

"They should," Leah said. "They don't talk and think like people. You have to always be careful."

"Dr. Archer said that," I remembered. "But I think I knew it before, from everything I read. Or not just that. Sometimes I know what to do without thinking it through. Then it works, and I don't know how, or why."

"There are parts of us that don't think," Leah said, "because they already know. My father taught me that."

We were coming into the dining room. "I'd like to meet your father," I said.

"I wish you could but he died last year."

I made us tea and looked for a place to sit.

"Tell me about your parents," Leah said. "Are they magicians?"

"No. I'm the first in the family. But there's a lot of weird stuff on my father's side. I don't think he's told me too much about it."

We sipped our tea.

"Tell me why the orthodox boys don't like you," I asked.

"They don't believe girls should study Talmud. It says that in

Jewish law. Since I do it, that makes me an outcast in their eyes."

"Then why come to school here?"

"It's close to home," she said. "And if I went abroad, my mother says, it would be more dangerous."

That surprised me. "You're not in danger here, are you? I mean, everyone leaves you alone, right?"

"No, they attack me sometimes. Not so anyone can see."

"I'll help you fight them," I said. "Goldberry will too, and Robbie."

"No, they won't hurt me."

"Why not?"

She sipped again. "I know how to protect myself. My father taught me when I was little."

"But some of these guys know a lot of Cabala."

Her voice fell to a whisper. "So do I."

"You mean you're stronger than any of them?"

"Not stronger. Cabala isn't about being strong. It's about being stable. You just know where you are, and when people try to move you, you stay in the same place."

"Like meditating."

"Yes."

"I think I know what you mean," I said, and I told her about the beaver coat and how it helped me block out distractions.

"Yes, that makes sense, in a way," Leah said.

"I'll bring it by, so you can look at it."

"Oh, no!" she said. "Things like that lose their usefulness if you show them off a lot."

I felt that I'd tried to go too fast. "I guess I should go back to studying," I said. I drained my teacup and didn't look at the leaves at the bottom.

"Thank you for the tea, Simon." She was about to say something else, but then changed her mind and began to say the *bracha*, the Orthodox prayer after eating or drinking. I sat for a moment awkwardly, then went to put my cup with the other dirty dishes.

Goldberry and Goodenough were also rising from a nearby table.

"What's the news?" I asked her, trying to forget about Leah.

"I'll tell you privately," she replied.

"Excuse us," I said to Goodenough.

He caught me by the shoulder. Goldberry didn't notice and kept walking.

"Hands off, Goodenough."

"Oh, it has a temper," he said. "No, listen, good advice this time. I mean it in a friendly way. Goldberry won't listen, but the word around the school is that the orphan girl isn't safe to know."

"The orphan girl?"

His eyes went to Leah. She wasn't an orphan, of course; it was a nasty nickname.

"Says who?" I wrenched my shoulder away.

"Not me," he answered. "I don't care one way or the other. It's just what they're saying."

"You'd better leave her alone," I said.

"It was just a friendly warning."

"I don't need your warnings."

"Oh yes," he said, "you do."

Attacked

In the end, it was Robbie who told me the secret news, announcing "Guess what?" as soon as I walked into our room.

"We're doing a big school trip a few weeks after the break. They have picked the time and the place."

"Where?"

"Ancient Egypt, man. Some kind of famous lighthouse in the Mediterranean."

Ancient Egypt! Then this wasn't just a trip: it was a trip back in time.

The official announcement came a few days later, after meditation. I looked up from rotating the triangle and saw the Dean standing at the podium.

"For the next two months, your magic theory classes will be emphasizing the principles of concealment and universal language. As many of you are aware, we have scheduled a visit to Alexandria, Egypt, to observe the Pharos – the Lighthouse of Alexandria. Second-years and above will tour the city with their advisors. First-years must remain inside the school, but may observe from the roof and windows."

There were boos from several of my classmates.

"This policy is unalterable," said the Dean. "Younger students have not yet mastered the required skills."

He went on to explain more about the place and time. Alexandria was near the Mediterranean coast of Egypt. It was ruled by descendants of a general who had served the conqueror, Alexander the Great. It was a great trading city that attracted merchants and travellers from all over the Mediterranean and the east. Alexander the Great himself was interred there, in a glass casket in a gigantic monument of a tomb. All the literature, history and science that had been written down up to that time, in that part of the world was gathered in a gigantic library. The city also contained Africa's first museum. And then, of course, there was the Pharos, the famous Lighthouse, named after the island on which it sat. It was the tallest stone building in the ancient world, some 400 feet high, shedding a beam of light into the warm Mediterranean night that could be seen more than 30 miles away.

"What a waste," Robbie whispered to me. "Stuck inside the school. We probably won't even see any people."

"We can't do concealment or universal language yet," I reminded him. "By the way, where are you with the triangle?"

"Rotating it, red on one side and yellow on the other."

"You're a little ahead of me," I admitted.

*

That was the night we were scheduled to see, for the first time the mementos from the Holy Land. I was very nervous about that. Unlike the school training collection, these were complete unknowns, even to Dr. Archer.

I walked down to the classroom with Goldberry and Goodenough, who was speculating that there were mementos hidden in famous statues in Rome. When Dr. Archer opened the door to the sacristy, we were hit with a bone-numbing chill. Inside, our usual tables had been removed in favour of traditional classroom desks. On a very long table against the far wall were three large objects covered by brightly coloured rugs.

"I have sorted the mementos by difficulty and potential danger," Dr. Archer told us. "The principle of the traffic light applies. Those beneath the green rug you are permitted to attempt. Those beneath the yellow rug must be approached with caution, so do not use them this evening. The red rug denotes those artifacts which I consider too dangerous for students. It is from them especially that this terrible cold originates. There is power and malice in that pile. I display them to you so that you may see what there is to fear."

"Will you identify them?" asked Miss Dunham, patting her conical witch hat.

"That is not your concern," he replied. "Now, prepare yourselves for the task you are about to undertake. I advise meditation. Donovan."

Donovan Archer stepped to the table and removed the green rug. Beneath it were about twenty objects: bricks, stones, bits of jewellry, a pair of clay pots, a leather cap. Gradually, each student walked to the table and took an object. I took a dried clay brick and looked around for a good place to sit. Finally I went to one corner and sat on the floor. Dr. Archer spotted me and raised an eyebrow.

I closed my eyes and held the brick, clearing my head as best I could. Then, quietly, I said hello. There was no answer. I relaxed a little more, then tried again, and then a third time. Nothing happened. Frustrated, I started to get up, then changed my mind and sat again. Despite my efforts to relax, I was tense, and my mind was clenched tight like a fist. There in the room were almost all the people in the school most important to me: my partner, my advisor, my two worst enemies, and a girl I really liked. I had to get them all out of my mind. Maestro Morgan's morning lectures before meditation talked about visualization – creating a picture of something in your mind, and using it as a symbol for what you wanted. I imagined a door in a dark wall. It opened, and one by one I made them leave – Goodenough, Mermelstein, Dr. Archer, Leah. I made her smile and wink at me as she left – and then Goldberry, who gave me one of her sarcastic looks.

I'm alone now, I told myself. No one stands between me and the one I wish to speak to. And again I held the brick gently and said hello.

"What year is it?" asked the spirit. "Who are the consuls?"

"I don't understand," I answered.

"What month, at least?"

"March."

"That is no month," said the spirit. "Who are you? Yours is the first voice I have heard in many years."

"I am a student," I answered. "I want to know only what you wish to be called, and something of who you are."

"First give me news," said the spirit.

"First you will give me a name for you," I replied.

"I am Quinctus Varus Agrippa," came the answer. "I am of the equestrian rank, a Roman citizen, and a soldier of renown, a veteran of the Parthian War. Now, news for me, student. Who is emperor?"

I realized that the spirit knew nothing of how the world had changed in perhaps two thousand years. But I didn't know the names of any Roman emperors. Better to avoid the question.

"We'll speak of that later," I answered. "Where were you when you died?"

"I am dead?" said the spirit. "Then that is why I have so long lain in darkness. At times a voice calls to me from the blackness, as does yours. I had thought myself blind, but not dead."

"Where did you die?" I repeated.

"I recall a feast," said Quinctus Varus Agrippa. "Perhaps I was poisoned. The centurion, a lowly Osrhoennian, would have my daughter for his wife, but I would not allow it. He warned me that misfortune would repay my refusal."

"Who was the emperor then?" I asked. "And for how long?"

"Mad Commodus ruled, those ten years, since the death of August Marcus. And who is the emperor now?"

"America," I answered. "Americus."

"A strange name. But time changes many things. And what is yours?"

"If you want my name," I answered, "you must perform a service first, spirit."

"What service?" asked Quinctus Varus Agrippa. There was a strange and cunning note in his voice that I had not heard before.

"There is another spirit that haunts me," I said. "You must drive it away."

"That is a lot to ask in trade for a name."

The spirit's voice trailed off as I heard a human voice nearby me.

"Enough," Dr. Archer said sharply. I lost contact with the Roman and dropped the brick on the floor. "No long conversations," the teacher said coldly. "You're not ready for that."

I was dizzy. Dr. Archer was right, though. This was a spirit about which I knew nothing, and I shouldn't have tried to bargain with it. I closed my eyes, trying to clear away the cobwebs.

UNWISE, the voice of Yeishu ben Pandeira roared in my head. UNGRATEFUL YOU ARE, SINCE I HAVE GIVEN YOU POWER.

Go away, I answered.

I AM NOT SO EASILY DRIVEN AWAY. YOU MUST HELP ME TO WIN FORGIVENESS OF RAV YEHOSHUA, WHO CAST ME OUT WITH A WAVE OF HIS TWO HANDS!

Why me? I argued.

BECAUSE YOU ARE SIMON MAGUS.

No, I'm not, I answered. I just took his name.

YOU ARE SIMON MAGUS. YOU MUST TAKE FROM THIS ROOM THE STONE TO WHICH I AM BOUND. GUARD IT WELL. MY DISCIPLES TOO ARE HERE. THEY SHALL AID YOU ALSO.

No. Go away.

YOU MAY NOT SPEAK OF THIS. IF YOU ARE ASKED, SAY I HAVE GONE AWAY.

The voice faded. I was shaken.

A lot of what the spirit said still made no sense to me, but it was strong, dangerous, possibly evil. I needed help, but… I couldn't ask. Just the thought of talking to someone about it made my head pound. I was just sitting in the corner – I couldn't move. I didn't even know what was going on around me.

A very cold hand lifted my face and gently raised my eyelids. Slowly, the voice became clear. "I need two boys to take him to his room. Donovan. William Goodenough. Carry him, please. Miss Tinker, you ought to go as well."

After the Attack

Two pairs of hands lifted me by the armpits. They put my arms over their shoulders and hauled me out of the icy chill of the room. My vision was still blurry, and I wasn't sure how long it took me to get upstairs. Robbie was in our room, surprised and concerned.

"What happened?" Robbie yelled. "It was Mermelstein, wasn't it?"

"I don't think so," Donovan Archer said. "Something bad happened in class."

"He fainted," said Goodenough. "How sad."

"Goodenough," I said. Nearly a whisper. "Please don't make jokes all over school."

"I don't joke about this sort of thing," he replied. "But do me a favor in return, will you?"

"Too weak…now."

He whispered in my ear. "Just stay out of my way for once. I'm not going to hurt her. I'm trying to look out for her."

"My job," I said. "I'll do that."

"Just take a walk next time. One time, and if I don't torture her, let it go from there."

"Okay," I said.

Goodenough looked at Robbie. "You see?" he said. "Magic's

easy when you pick your moment."

When Goodenough was gone, Robbie pulled his chair up next to my bed. "What happened, man?"

"Not used to mementos yet."

"Oh, come on. It's got to be something more than that. *Was it Mermelstein?*"

"No."

"It was, wasn't it? You're not admitting it because you don't want me to go after him. That's okay, man. I'll be smarter this time."

"It wasn't Yakov Mermelstein," said Donovan. I had forgotten he was there. He seemed to have vanished, until, when he spoke, he drifted into view like a mist across a quiet lake. But then, I was pretty out of it, so maybe I had imagined that. "Yakov was still doing his own assignment," Donovan said. "It was something to do with the memento he was using, I think."

"Okay," Robbie conceded. "Thanks, man."

Donovan left, and a few minutes later, Goldberry came in with a cup of tea. I started to feel better as she gave me small sips. When the tea was gone, she took the mug back and balanced it on her knee.

"I don't like this at all," she said as she peered into the cup. "It's kind of like a skull shape, you see?"

"Are there crossbones?" Robbie asked.

"What?"

"You know. Skull and crossbones. The pirate sign."

Goldberry gave him a dirty look. "Have you a point? Or do you enjoy wasting my time?"

"No, I just thought, if you had both, it would mean something."

"Do me a favour," Goldberry said. "Change your sheets. They smell, and I'll be sleeping in that bed tonight."

....

"Um." He started. "Not that I mind, but…"

"Not with you in it. You can go sleep in Balaram's room. I'm going to stay here for the night, in case Simon has another problem." She set down the cup on my desk and went to the door. "I'm going to wash up. Change your sheets, please."

She left, and Robbie started changing the sheets. "It was Mermelstein," he said again.

"It wasn't," I repeated. "I'm absolutely certain. It was the spirit…" I couldn't say what I wanted to, what had happened – I got a feeling like claws at my throat. "Uh, the spirit in the memento tried to take over my body."

"Okay," Robbie said. "You don't want to tell me, fine, just fine. Don't let me help you."

"I'm sorry, I… Well, I can't talk about it yet. Tell me something else instead. When we were at Lake Okanagan, what did you ask Ogopogo?"

Robbie was struggling to even out the top sheet. "What makes you ask that all of a sudden?"

"I don't know," I said. "You don't have to tell me if you don't want to."

"No, that's Okay." He lowered his eyes. "I asked for some help with how to summon Lazar-El, the Duke of Water."

Just as he knew I was covering something, I knew he was covering something too. "Did you ask anything else?"

"Nothing good," he said. He fluffed the pillow. "You know, your partner is a real peach. I wish I had such a great partner."

"I like Balaram," I said.

"I like him too, but he hides stuff from me. He's done some

summonings and stuff without me. He doesn't say anything, but I see what books he's looking at, and I can tell."

Of course, I had been at one of those secret summonings, but I didn't reveal that.

"You'd tell me," Robbie said, "if you knew about that stuff? Wouldn't you? I mean, if you heard anything?"

"I'd… Well, I'd tell you anything I could tell you."

Robbie stooped and looked me in the eye. He knew I was holding back. "Forget it. You're tired. Get some sleep. I'm going to give my partner the good news."

Goldberry came in right after he left, wearing her robe over her pajamas, carrying her nightly cup of unsweetened chamomile.

"Now he's gone," she said, "you have to tell me what happened."

"A spirit attacked me," I said. "That's all I can tell you. I want to say more, but I can't."

"You really should share, you know." Goldberry sipped her tea.

I closed my eyes, pretending to sleep. The last thing I saw was my partner's eyes flashing over the rim of my teacup, and then I fell asleep for real.

Music of the Spheres

I woke up early. Goldberry was still sleeping. Her forehead was lined, and her lips were twitching. Perhaps a bad dream.

I was still in last night's clothes, but there was a blanket over me. I got out of bed, a little wobbly, and left the room as quietly as I could. Wandering toward the dining room, I suddenly found myself going down a different hallway, the one that led to the meditation hall. One of the double doors was open. The candlelight within cast lurid flickering patterns out into the hall. I went in.

Someone was sitting in the front pew. I went a little closer and saw that it was Maestro Morgan. "Good morning, Simon Magus," he said without turning.

"Good morning," I said. I sat in the next pew over, on his left.

"Consider the music of the spheres," he said. "Johannes Kepler wrote on the subject. The volume is not generally known, but I read it while studying in Vienna. Music as we generally think of it is the harmony of sounds. But there is a music in the ways of the cosmos. Every planet, moon, star is fitted within a celestial pattern. Do you understand, Simon?"

"Not really," I admitted.

"In science, in the outside world, they now talk about chaos. They say that some actions occur at random, but they will still try to tease out the causes for things."

"Like in *Jurassic Park*," I said. That was familiar.

"I have never been to that place," he said.

"It's a movie, Maestro."

"Ah! Well, what I am trying to say is this: there is no disorder. Nothing occurs that does not have its counterpart in another event. All is in harmony. It is only that man cannot see some forms of order. But the movement of celestial bodies reveals the design."

"You mean like astrology."

"True astrology," he said. "Not the tripe in the newspapers. True astrology is a pattern of infinite complexity. Do you know anything about atomic theory?"

"I'm just thirteen, Maestro."

"This is no time to be thirteen," he said. "I wish you were older. But there is a harmony, also, in atomic theory. All matter – all physical objects – can be broken down into smaller and smaller parts. As science adds skill, smaller parts are found. Molecules; atoms; protons, neutrons, and electrons; gluons, quarks. Always they will find smaller parts, but they can never find the smallest."

"Why not?"

"Because there is no smallest. Imagine the largest star that ever existed. Could you see it?"

"If I was far away I could see it. If I was close, it would blind me."

"Quite so. Now, multiply its size by a hundred. Now can you see it?"

"I'd have to go even further away."

"Will a time come when the star grows so large that it cannot be seen? When you cannot go far enough away to view it in safety?"

"If… um. It would have to fill up the whole universe, right?"

"Yes," said the Maestro. "And yet it is believed that the universe is without limit. It is infinite. It must be, for, think: if you reached the end of the universe, like a wall, then what would be on the other side?"

"There is nothing except the universe," I guessed.

"So you cannot imagine a limit to how large a star can be, because there is no limit to the universe. Thus there is no limit to how large any object can be. Do you not then see that nothing can be so small that it cannot be seen?"

I thought about this. It was very hard to understand, but the peaceful room made thinking easier. "No, I don't get it."

"There is no limit on hugeness," said Maestro Morgan, "so there is no limit on smallness either."

"I don't understand."

"Yet it is so. The very large and the very small are in harmony. Each balances and enhances the other. An atom is the shape of a solar system. Why? Because the great and the small are governed by the same forces. In the stars, you see these forces at work. But astrology can always become more precise. More influences can be found. Mastery is impossible. Discover a principle, and it leads to a dozen more. The Cabalists also know this, and it is part of the Talmud as well: always more to learn. Furthermore, some matters can never be understood; but then, some are so frighteningly right that they cannot possibly be accepted. In the life of a magician, these frightening harmonies are ever more common. And harmony in the universe is not constrained by time."

"Which means what?"

"It means that events can be bound to each other despite their separation in time. There is no rule to say that an event today cannot cause an event in the past."

He had more to say, but I couldn't handle any more. "Thank you, Maestro, but why are you telling me this?"

"You are deeply shaken," he said. "But you will tell no one the reason. We cannot help to confront what troubles you. Still, we can help you to become able to face it. They say time is like a river, always flowing forward, ever changing. Not true. Time is a wind. It goes in all directions, this way and that, moves many things, leaves others in place. A wind may carry you forth and back again." He tilted his head slightly. "But I hear that another guest is coming. You must excuse me."

I left the great hall. There was no one there when I came out, but after I turned the corner, I heard footsteps from where I had just been. Soon Maestro Morgan would start again with another student. I went back to my room to wake my partner for breakfast.

*

Magic theory class that day was given by Dr. Chatterjee. He talked about the electrical and psychic connections between people and the Asian concepts of *Kundalini* and *Chi*. I didn't grasp most of it. Rocco asked if it was true that you could steal Chi, or life-force, from other people. Dr. Chatterjee said you could, and showed us a simple technique for doing it. It was basically taking some energy from one person and adding it to yourself, very temporarily.

"This is only a basic energy-stealing method," said Dr. Chatterjee. "It was developed only as a practice exercise. More advanced ones are used, generally only for self-defense, or by wicked-minded people."

I didn't understand how to do it, but Goldberry understood it.

A Fight

Dr. Archer had left for Vienna shortly after his last class, so Goldberry and I weren't able to see him the next day. I was feeling better, so we went to class as usual.

Rabbi Mendy, a middle-aged orthodox rabbi with a round red beard, gave magic theory class that week for the entire first-year class, concentrating on the principle of concealment. It began with visualization exercises. We imagined heavy cloaks, and in our mind's eye we examined every fold. Then, still in our imaginations, we pulled the cloaks on and wrapped ourselves tightly in them.

"Did it work?" asked Daniel. "I can still see everyone."

"This exercise won't make you invisible," said Rabbi Mendy. "It makes you unobtrusive. People who do not know you will not notice you. But someone who is seeking you will not be misled."

"So we use this on our time travel trips?" Rocco asked.

"The principle is useful whenever you go among strangers," said Rabbi Mendy. "A magician often has cause to go unnoticed."

"Can you use it to steal things, or sneak up on people?" Robbie asked.

"Only if no one is opposing your will," said the rabbi. "An alert guard will see you, though not a lazy one. Also, anyone who is worried or nervous, and anyone who knows you, will notice you. So also will a person with magic talent who is in a calm and open mood, though not one who is weakened or distracted."

"Then how do we know if it works?" I asked.

"You must practice it in the outside world. Your spring intersession is approaching. Go into public places and practice. Now, let us try again. Visualize the cloak."

Dr. Archer came back on Monday. Goldberry and I went to see him. He asked if we were well and if we were learning the principle of concealment. Goldberry asked him about my fainting spell.

"Choose one of the practice pieces," he suggested, "and work with that for the next few days."

The three of us walked down to the sacristy. It was bitterly cold, as usual. The mementos from Israel were still arranged as they had been, under green, yellow, and red rugs. Dr. Archer opened a cabinet in the back of the room and took out the boxes of school practice pieces.

"Select one," Dr. Archer said. "I shall be in the refectory."

The refectory, the faculty dining hall, was two doors down. He was trusting us. I found myself wishing he wouldn't, because I had a feeling something awful was going to happen in this icy chill room.

Goldberry and I began opening the boxes and looking through them for mementos we'd practiced with. Eventually she found a small silver moon shaped pendant on a thin chain. "Leah used this one for a long time," she said. "I'm curious, I must admit. Do you mind?"

"Go ahead."

She began the work to contact the spirit connected to the moon pendant. Meanwhile, I kept looking through the boxes, remembering the spirits I had spoken to.

THIS IS YOUR TIME, said the voice of my enemy. YOU

MUST FIND THE CRYSTAL WHICH HAS ENSNARED ME.

No, I answered.

YOU KNOW WELL WHERE THE CRYSTAL LIES. TAKE IT. HIDE IT. WITH THE CRYSTAL IN YOUR HAND, I WILL BE ABLE TO TEACH YOU MORE.

Forget it, I responded. I was trying to be strong, but the spirit's commands were hard to resist.

FORGET? IT IS THIS MOMENT THAT I LONG HAVE PLANNED FOR. TAKE THE CRYSTAL. I WILL MAKE YOU STRONG, AND THEN YOU WILL WIN ME FORGIVENESS.

No. I don't trust you.

YOU MUST HELP ME, said Yeishu ben Pandeira. I WAS TO BE THE ANOINTED ONE, BUT I WAS UNFAIRLY CAST OUT. RAV YEHOSHUA MUST FORGIVE ME.

Where is he? When did this happen?

IN EGYPT, TWO THOUSAND YEARS AGO, MY DISCIPLES AND I WERE CAST OUT. RAV YEHOSHUA REPULSED ME WITH HIS TWO HANDS. OH, ACCURSED DEED! I WAS TO BE ANOINTED WITH OIL. THE GLORY AND THE POWER WERE NEAR.

I don't understand.

I YEISHU BEN PANDEIRA WAS TO LEAD THE CHOSEN PEOPLE TO THEIR TRUE INHERITANCE.

"The chosen people?" I asked aloud. "Do you mean…?"

Suddenly I snapped out of it. Goldberry was watching me closely. "What was that you said?" she asked. "You didn't have to interrupt me in mid-conversation."

"Nothing," I said. I was dizzy again. I sat down.

…………………………………………………………………………

"No, you said, 'the chosen people,' wasn't it?"

"I think I fell asleep," I lied. "I must have been talking in my sleep."

She didn't believe me, and I didn't blame her. I would have to make the lie more complicated. But how? The chosen people – Egypt – of course.

"It must be all these ancient artifacts," I said. "I was dreaming about the Hebrews enslaved in Egypt, building a pyramid."

"You fell asleep standing up? Please, Simon."

I wanted to tell her, but I couldn't force the words out. Claws at my throat squeezed as long as I tried to say the words, "I'm being haunted."

"Well, come on," Goldberry snapped. "Pick one, and let's get to class. You can go to sleep early tonight, lazybones."

I sighed with relief that she was going to let it go. I grabbed a memento, Chastity Gray's wedding ring, and put it in my pocket while Goldberry went to get Dr. Archer. While she was gone, I realized where Yeishu ben Pandeira's memento had to be: under the red cloth, among the forbidden, most dangerous of the objects from the Holy Land. And while I didn't want to take it, I began to think about how I could.

*

Later, in my room, I asked Robbie how to say "anointed one" in Hebrew.

"You don't know that?" He seemed surprised.

"Why? Is it important?"

"Absolutely. The anointed one is the Moshiach." He pronounced it muh-SHOCK. "He's supposed to be the one sent by God to save the Jews and lead them to a kingdom in Israel."

"You mean, it didn't happen?"

"Well, most Jews don't think so, except those Lubavitch guys, you know, with the trucks? But the most famous person who said he was the Moshiach was Jesus. And a lot of people believe in him now, obviously."

"Then what's Hebrew for Jesus?"

"I don't know," Robbie said. "My rabbi in the Village always used to quote Jesus, but he always called him Jesus. In Reform they think Jesus was a great teacher, just not the Moshiach."

I stopped talking, pretending to look at my schoolbooks, while I was thinking it through. Yeishu ben Pandeira was saying he was supposed to be the Moshiach – a leader sent by God to save the Jews.

After a minute I got up and went down the hall and knocked on Balaram's door. His roommate, Max, was Orthodox and knew a lot of Hebrew. Max was there. He'd just come back from *Maariv*, his evening prayers, and was hanging up his coat.

"Max," I said, "what's Hebrew for Jesus?"

He scratched his head for a second. "It's that word they use to mean a heretic. I can't remember it."

"A heretic. You mean somebody who tries to change the religion in a bad way?"

"Sure," he said. "No offense."

"No, that's okay. I asked you."

"What brought this up? It's in your homework somewhere?"

"Uh, yeah. Yeah it is."

I left after chatting for a while. I needed to know if the name was what I thought it was. With the evening prayer over, some of the Orthodox and Chasidic guys would still be by the shul. I knew where it was. Maybe someone there could tell me.

I went to the *shul.* It was empty except for some older students still praying, so I went to the kosher dining room. There was a strong, rich smell of chicken and oil, so I got a plate and got in line. I didn't know most of the boys here. Some nodded to me or said hello quietly, but no one seemed to want to talk. I sat down alone at a table and started to eat.

I was only a few bites into my meal when I heard footfalls behind me. I knew before looking up that it was Mermelstein. I turned. Meir Kupferberg, his roommate and friend, a short, thin Chasidic boy, was behind him.

"Why are you here, *apikoros*?" Mermelstein demanded.

"I'm eating. I wanted some chicken."

"Since when do you eat with us?"

"If I can find someone friendly, I need some help with Hebrew."

"Sure," Meir said. "What do you need?"

"How do you say…" I began.

"No," Mermelstein said. "You have a Hebrew teacher for that. Go and ask him. This is our place."

"Yakov, forget it," Meir said. "They have the right to eat here."

"I say he doesn't," Mermelstein growled. "He's bad enough himself, but he goes around with that whore, Leah Ritz."

I stood up. "Take that back, Mermelstein." My breaths were coming harder and faster now.

"He can't stand the truth," Mermelstein said.

"Take it back," I said, "or you'll regret it." For a moment I saw Leah's kind and gentle face, her long brown hair neatly tied back, her tiny prayer books, her lips parting slightly as she prayed, and I imagined Mermelstein, this great ugly thunderstorm of a boy, standing over her, threatening her, calling her whore. The image made me so angry, I almost forgot where I was. "Take it back," was all I could say.

"This is our place," he barked. "Here, I say what I want."

"Come on, take it back," Meir said. "You insulted his friend. Who can blame him for getting angry?"

I stepped up to Mermelstein. "Take it back," I repeated.

"Take your whore back to *Gomorrah* where she belongs," he answered, grinning, showing me his yellow teeth.

USE MY NAME, the ghost shouted in my thoughts.

No, I answered.

USE IT.

"Yeishu ben Pandeira," I mumbled, almost without realizing I had done it, and imagined punching in those rotten yellow teeth.

Mermelstein staggered back, holding his mouth. Blood ran through his fingers, down his chin. "You're a dead man, *apikoros*," he snarled, his words garbled by his injury. He made a gesture with his hand. A split second later, it was as if a huge pair of jaws had closed around my neck. I felt rows of pointed teeth digging into my flesh. My body went limp. Those invisible teeth were suspending me in the air.

"You dare to come to my school bearing the name of a false prophet," Mermelstein roared. "You stink of falsehood, you rotten mutt! You run shameless with a girl who steals *sefarim* like a rat steals breadcrumbs." He spat out blood. "And you come into our place, and you think I will do nothing. You dare to knock at the Rambal's door, smiling like a *ben torah* with defilement in your heart, and you think I will do nothing? And you attack me, in our place, and you think I will do nothing?"

"Yakov, stop," Meir said. I was so desperate for air that my eyes were full of tears, but I saw Meir try to grab his arm and get pushed away. I realized there was nothing I could do. I didn't know any magic that could stop him from killing me. Vaguely I sensed that, all around us, boys were shouting, hooting, cheering. I was bleeding now, from those invisible jaws, and I couldn't even draw a breath as drops of blood ran down my neck.

USE MY NAME, said Yeishu ben Pandeira. I WILL SAVE YOUR LIFE, AND YOU WILL WIN ME FORGIVENESS.

You got me into this, I thought, and you'll only make it worse.

Suddenly the jaws let go. Wobbling, I backed up into the wall.

"Enough," Finkel, an older boy, was saying. "Do you want to start a war with them because of your personal problem? Chamor! We're not here to fight to the death."

"Give up!" Mermelstein shouted at me.

I couldn't talk. I tried to shake my head, swallowed as hard as I could.

"Give up!"

"Take it back," I whispered.

"Give up!"

"Take it back," I said, gaining strength, "or I'll eat every meal here, until you take it back, or you kill me."

"I'll kill you," he said.

"No, you won't," said Finkel.

"Take it back," I whispered again.

He spat blood again. I saw now, as my vision cleared, that it was still pouring into his mouth. Then I saw that two of his lower front teeth had been smashed out of his face.

"All right, all right," Mermelstein said. "She is not a whore." He turned away.

....

Finkel and Meir helped me out of the kosher dining room and down the hall to the regular dining room. There were a lot of kids there eating. When they saw me, staggering and bloody-necked, a lot of kids jumped up and crowded around me. The boys handed me off to Rocco, who carried me to a chair. Finkel left.

"What happened?" he asked.

"I fought Mermelstein," I said.

"Did you give up? Who won?"

"I did," I said.

"Whoa," Rocco said. He turned away suddenly, nodding to Meir.

"I'm sorry about that," Meir said to me. "But you know you shouldn't let him get to you."

"Maybe not," I said.

"What was it you wanted to ask? About Hebrew?"

"What's Hebrew for Jesus?"

"Hmm. Well, most gentiles translate it Yehoshua, or Joshua. But in the Gemara the name they use for him is Yeishu. That means heretic. That's why Christians don't translate it that way."

That was what I'd been afraid to hear. I wanted to ask more, but I wasn't strong enough.

"Look," Meir said. "What your friend is doing is wrong. If she really understood Jewish law, she wouldn't do it, because she would know that it's against the wishes of Hashem. But Yakov was also wrong to do what he did. You're not one of us, so it's not your fight. I can even understand why you like her. But listen, some good advice. Don't get in the middle if you can help it."

"I stand up for my friends," I said, weakly though.

"Yeah, we all will," Rocco added.

"OK," Meir said. "Just a word to the wise. If you need any

Hebrew help, feel free to ask me, whenever Yakov's not around." He smiled.

I shook his hand. "Shalom," I said.

"Shalom."

The Concealment Test

Goldberry and I spent the weekend doing homework and practicing with our mementos. I told her about my fight with Mermelstein, but made her promise not to tell Leah.

"So you say," she replied. "The two of you, you and Mermelstein, are both so predictable. Can't even see each other across the room without starting something."

I got to know Chastity Gray much better, and Yeishu ben Pandeira left me alone. I even started thinking about ways to get him to leave me alone forever. But the translation of his name haunted me. What kind of power would it take to fight off an ancient ghost that wanted to be Jesus? And how could it be that this false Moshiach had singled me out the same day I arrived at school? He said I was Simon Magus. How could he think that? I reviewed what I knew about that famous magician.

Simon Magus, according to some stories, was a Samaritan – from Samaria, where the "good Samaritan" of Jesus' parable came from. He was worshipped as a god in Samaria and had a statue in Rome made by Emperor Claudius, for whom he performed magic tricks, the most interesting of which was flying. He had a female companion named Helen, who was supposed to be a reborn version of Helen of Troy, or of some kind of fallen angel. He was the founder of a religious group that died out a while after his death. In the Bible it said that he tried to buy from Jesus' disciples, Peter and Paul, the powers they got from God in the form of the Holy Spirit. They rejected his offer, of course, saying that God's power cannot be bought. One story said he died when he was flying, and Saint Peter prayed for him to lose the power, which caused him to fall to his death. Another story said he claimed he could rise from the grave like Jesus, but when he was buried, he never dug himself out.

Although I had chosen to name myself after him, none of it sounded much like me; to tell the truth, I had like the "Magus" part of the name better in the beginning. I had not the slightest idea how to do any of the magical feats he was said to have performed. Perhaps my slightly dark skin tone matched that of a Samaritan of his time, but I couldn't imagine any other similarities.

*

One day close to vacation, I came back to my room to find a large manila envelope on my desk. It wasn't sealed; I opened it and took out the contents, a stack of mail for me at my parents' address. There were some magazines, some junk mail, and a note from my parents. I read that first.

Dear Leicester,

We're very excited that you'll be coming back to stay with us for a week. It will be spring, and nice weather outside, so Dad and I will take a few days off and we can do things together. We booked a lunch cruise around Manhattan Island and sent an invitation to Mr. and Mrs. Tinker and Goldberry, and to Mr. and Mrs. Ravitz and Robbie. Is there anyone else we should invite? Drop us a line if you can.

Love you,

Your mother, your father, Leo, Cougar, Cheetah, Jag, and Pink Panther.

It would be great to spend some time with my parents. When I got home, I might be able to relax for a while. I only had to decide what I could tell them, and what I'd have to keep secret. My parents weren't magicians. What would happen to them if I made them enemies who were?

I wrote a note to my parents to invite the Dass and Vitello families. Then I showed the letter to Goldberry. "Should I invite Dr. Archer and Donovan?" I asked her.

"Not if you want my father there," she said.

"What about…" I wasn't sure if I could say it. "Leah?"

"You could do," Goldberry said. "With Robbie Radish there, though, could be tricky. I'll check with her, if you like."

"OK."

Later that night, I was alone studying when Leah tapped at the door. I knew it was her because no one else would rap so gently. I got up, ran my hand through my hair, opened the door.

"Thank you for the invitation," she said. "I won't be able to come, but I wanted to give you this to use during the vacation." She smiled, handed me a small package, and slipped off down the hall.

I opened the package. Inside was a small leather-bound book, only about twenty pages long, with Hebrew lettering on the back cover. It looked like her prayer book, but it was smaller. Inside, like a bookmark, was a folded paper. I unfolded it. It was a phone number.

*

The last magic theory class before vacation was a field trip with Rabbi Mendy and Mr. Bannerjee. They took the whole first-year class on the green Smoot Preparatory bus. Our destination was Green Acres Mall in Valley Stream, Long Island. The teachers had stacks of paper money for us, $100 each, but before you were given your allowance, you had to demonstrate use of the principle of concealment. The test was simple: just walk behind the counter of a retail store, stand near the clerk, and not be noticed. If anyone in the store saw you, except people from School Of The Ages, your allowance went down $10 and you had to try again. If anyone confronted you, you lost $20. If you ran out of money while still trying, you got an F for the class session.

"It's not really fair for everyone," Robbie said on the bus. "Like, the Chasidic guys stand out too much in the black coats and hats. And everyone will see the pretty girls like Leah and Goldberry."

In his long gray overcoat, with his big red face, Robbie would be hard to miss, too. "We'll see," I said. When we got to the mall, the teachers took us to the food court, where we stood by Arthur's Treacher's as they picked small groups of students to go with them for the first test. I wound up with Rocco and Meir. Rabbi Mendy led us to Macy's and then to the women's sportswear department.

It was busy. A long queue of women was waiting to make purchases at a checkout kiosk staffed by an elderly woman with gold-framed glasses and a dark-skinned girl in a turtleneck. They were working back to back, so we couldn't sneak in behind either one, and the many people in line were mostly looking at the kiosk to see how long till their turn came up.

"Oy vey," Meir said. "Come on, rebbe, this isn't fair. You're going to make me lose money!"

"What?" said Rabbi Mendy. "Diamonds you were going to buy today? Get moving."

Meir stood a minute to compose himself. I knew him, so he didn't seem different to me as he started walking.

"Don't watch him," Rabbi Mendy said. "You're not concealed. Someone might wonder what you're looking at."

Rocco and I looked away, browsing through some green sweat pants on a nearby rack. A few minutes later we heard Meir's voice. "Well."

"Nu, not bad," said Rabbi Mendy. He peeled ten $10 bills from his money clip. "Meet us at the food court in ninety minutes." Then he turned to me. "Well, Simon?"

It felt very different, here in a crowded shopping mall, surrounded by people for whom magic was not real. In a way it was easier to do magic with only magicians around. There was no one to doubt, and no one to remind you that you'd spent your whole life thinking it was silly and impossible. How do you fool people who don't believe?

They're busy, I told myself. The old woman, the dark girl, they have no reason to care. They'll keep looking at their customers and their registers.

I tried to imagine a cloak that covered me. In my mind's eye, I tried to pull invisibility all around myself. But I couldn't stop seeing myself there, seeing them stare at me and call security.

But Meir, in his black suit and black hat and white shirt, had gotten his money. He had gone unnoticed!

I couldn't imagine myself being impossible to see. What would that cloak have to be, the one I was imagining? Not invisibility! Then what? How could I pass in front of their eyes and not be seen? What makes a person look right at something and not see it?

Then I realized how I would do it. Instead of become invisible, I would become familiar. I would make myself seem like something they saw so often they never looked at it anymore. I would hide myself in a cloak made of being boring and usual.

So I began to form this cloak in my mind. I was the old woman's worn-out sofa, I was the girl's unopened junk mail. I was everything they ever got tired of looking at. It wasn't a cloak I could imagine seeing with my eyes, but a cloak made out of attitude, that I imagined pulling around myself. I told myself that all around me, winds were howling, and inside my cloak of boringness I was warm, safe, and nameless.

Then I started walking. I stopped, browsed through some clothes. No one was looking at me. I took down a blue blouse on a plastic hanger from a nearby rack. Ordinary, ordinary, I said to myself. I put it back and went to the counter, made a half-circle around it, to the gap between the two clerks' counters. Still no one noticed. I took a step inside, right behind the dark girl. She turned, and looked ... at the older woman, and said, "Marjorie, can you scan this?"

"You can reset your scanner, Najeeba. Point it at..."

And I kept walking, past both of them, and came out on the other side, and got clear of them, and went to Rabbi Mendy.

"Your first time," he said. "Not so bad. What were you thinking when you did it?"

I told him.

"You were specifically hiding from the two clerks," he said. "But no one in line saw you either. This is the law of part and whole. Affect a part successfully, and the whole will be affected. Why?"

I was waiting for him to give me the money, to prove he was satisfied, and I couldn't think.

"Forget the money," he said, perhaps noticing that I was looking at his money clip. "Answer first. If you affect a part, it affects the whole. Why?"

"I don't know."

"Rocco?" Rabbi Mendy asked.

"I never heard of the law of part and whole," Rocco said. "Is there one?"

"No," said Rabbi Mendy. "Why isn't there, Simon?"

"You don't need one," I guessed. "Uh… the law of… the law of, 'if it works, it's true'?"

"The law of pragmatism," said the rabbi. "Good guess, but you can use that law to explain anything. Once more: why is there no law of part and whole?"

It was starting to become clearer. "Maestro Morgan told me you can never find the smallest piece of anything. Particle physics, right?"

"Why not?"

"Uh…"

"Rocco?"

"Who needs parts anyway?" Rocco asked.

"Exactly," said Rabbi Mendy. "There are no parts, only wholes. And since many wholes side by side would only be parts, what do you conclude?"

"That there's only one whole." I guessed.

"Exactly. And that whole is called…?"

"God," Rocco said.

"That's right. And if Hashem is a whole, why do we talk about parts?"

This was a tough question.

Rocco looked unsure, but I was finally getting it. I said, "Because you can't understand everything at once. It's too much, so you pretend there are parts."

The rabbi smiled. "To know things is to know they are one. Well said."

I told Rocco I'd meet him outside the store, and watched as Rabbi Mendy counted out my money.

A Talk with my Advisor

First I bought some stuff for divination club: a new teacup for tasseography, a Rider-Waite Tarot deck which Goldberry had insisted I own. Candles and incense. Rocco bought a krypton bulb flashlight and a FDNY sweatshirt. At the bookstore we ran into Robbie and Balaram in the New Age section, laughing at how silly some of the occult books were. Balaram bought a book on Indian sculpture; Robbie bought a graphic novel; I went to the ancient history section. I was looking for something on ancient Jewish or Christian history, some place to look up Simon Magus, or even Yeishu ben Pandeira. I used up the rest of the hundred on a few books that didn't look that great, while Rocco bought a travel book about Italy.

"Let's practice again," Robbie said as we left the bookstore. "If we're really good, maybe they'll let us go out during the trip to Alexandria."

"The Dean said…" Balaram began.

Robbie rolled his eyes. "Yeah, yeah, the Dean said. It'll be fun, though. Let's practice. Come on, Simon, Rocco?"

"You first, Radish," Rocco said.

"That's Ravitz."

"I got you. Radish."

"Cut it out."

"OK," Rocco said. "You first, Cucumber."

"Sure. You hold my stuff." He thrust it at Rocco, who grinned and took it.

Robbie pointed at an oblong public-information kiosk about ten yards away. A young black woman, maybe twenty, was on a swivel chair inside, wearing a puce suit.

"How will you get in there?" Balaram asked. "It's locked, I bet. You'll have to climb over."

"So I'll climb. No one will notice. That's the point."

"If someone sees you, you'll get in trouble," Rocco said.

"No one will see me. That's the point. Come on, guys."

"Let's do something easier first," I suggested.

"No, I got it," Robbie said. He walked toward the kiosk. It was working, I thought. We watched out of the corners of our eyes so that we wouldn't expose him by looking directly. People were stepping around him without looking at him.

Robbie reached the counter.

"Go man go," Rocco whispered.

Robbie walked around the counter till he was behind the girl. He turned and smirked at us. Then he rolled belly-first onto the counter and started to climb over. She didn't notice. No one nearby looked at him. But he stopped partway. His big gray coat was caught on something, maybe a nail. He stopped, pulling at it.

This must have distracted him. An old couple walking by noticed him and pointed.

"Hey!" the old woman shouted.

The girl swiveled her chair.

Robbie smiled at her weakly.

"Security!" she called. A large mall guard came trotting in their direction.

"Oh, geez," Rocco said. "Let's get him out of there." He started to run, and so did I.

"Wait!" Balaram shouted. "Use magic!"

He was right. "The coat," I said.

"The guard," Rocco said.

"The girl," Balaram said.

We all paused to gather our thoughts. I imagined the coat flapping in the air, free of what it was caught on. As I watched, Robbie tugged and it came loose. Rocco said something in Italian; the guard stumbled, wobbled off course, crashed into an empty baby carriage and fell to his knees. Balaram hummed and breathed, and the girl, dialling the phone for help, shook her head and hung up as if she had misdialled.

As Robbie tumbled back out of the kiosk and started to run into the crowd, Mr. Bannerjee suddenly appeared in front of him, holding out a hand to stop him. We approached. Robbie was panting. Mr. Bannerjee went and helped up the guard.

"Very sorry," he said. "This boy is learning-disabled. Autistic. It is a school field trip from Smoot Special Education Center. Acceptable I will take charge of him now. You won't mind this, I hope?"

"Sure," said the guard, brushing off his knees. "No problem. It happens."

Mr. Bannerjee went to the young woman. "In case of anything missing, you will please telephone me. Here is my business card."

She quickly agreed. Mr. Bannerjee herded us to the food court. "Practice is good, also fast response times," he said. "You did a lot with no preparation. However, you were seen and confronted. Fine of twenty dollars each."

"Each?" Rocco shouted. "Hey!"

"I think we all spent our money," I said.

"No, I have some left," Balaram said, and paid.

"The rest of you will work instead," said Mr. Bannerjee. "Sweeping the school roof. Four dollars an hour."

"That's not minimum wage," Rocco said.

"It is at School of the Ages," said Mr. Bannerjee. "Report to me after vacation, first afternoon after lunch."

"Your business card," said Robbie.

"Yes."

"What does it look like?"

Mr. Bannerjee handed him one. It was blank.

*

There was one more memento analysis class before vacation. After dinner, I went to the meditation hall to clear my head. The air was still and quiet. The flickering candlelight made me calm and sleepy. As I was starting to drift off, Maestro Morgan passed by, walking among the pews. I nodded to him, and he kept going. I visualized the triangle and tried to change its shape. Yet I found in my mind that it was duplicating, fitting together sides to form a pyramid, and then two translucent pyramids end to end – a shining crystal.

Someone was sitting next to me. The crystal was gone from my thoughts.

"You are troubled, Simon," said Dr. Archer. "You have not informed Miss Tinker of the reason yet. She has told me that this does not bother her, but I believe that it does. You must tell her. Then you must tell me. FPTA – first partner, then advisor."

"I can't," I said.

"Some force compels you to silence?" asked Dr. Archer. "Or is it embarrassment, or stubbornness?"

I had thought being in the meditation hall would protect me from the ghost that haunted me, but as I considered telling Dr. Archer what was going on, I felt claws at my throat. "It's OK," I said. "There's no problem."

"I know that there is," he said. "You are seeking out this place to assist you to gather yourself to resist. Moreover, where once you were boldly the first to arrive for my seminar, now you wish to avoid it."

"No, I'm coming to class."

"You are," said Dr. Archer, "because you are determined and responsible. However, you do not wish to come to class. Indubitably there is a reason for this."

"I'm not afraid," I said. I wanted to yell, but not in that place.

"Indeed not," Dr. Archer said. "You wish to avoid class not because you fear to go, but because you feel you are facing a problem too great for your strength, and do not wish others to become entangled and similarly injured. I do not ask what the threat is, nor do I mean I to guess. I will be content to advise you that you may attend class without incident this evening."

"How can you know that without knowing what's going on?"

"Life is a stream," he said. "When I stand within it, I cannot see an end, nor a destination, nor even an origin, but I can feel which way it flows, and how great is the turbulence."

I took a while to think about what he said. "This is because you're a high sorcerer."

"Yes."

"And you can't change anything?"

"On the contrary. Would you like me to identify and combat

the menaces you face?"

"No."

"Why not?"

"Because I have to do that."

"Then you may describe each peril, in turn, and I will instruct you in the manner by which you may confront it. What do you say?"

It was hard to answer. "I guess not."

"I thought as much. But another question now enters your mind. Speak it."

Just like that, there was indeed another question. "This thing you do, knowing what's coming, but not exactly – is that something I can learn to do?"

Dr. Archer apparently didn't have the answer to that question ready. He replied hesitantly. "It is a matter of your goals, and your mood. At present I perceive that your main talents are action and improvisation. You do not yet possess the calm disposition a high sorcerer generally requires. But age will change this, as it changed your father."

I remembered my father saying he had been wilder when he was young. There were plenty of ways Dr. Archer could have learned my family history, so I didn't challenge how he knew. Instead I asked, "So I'll be a sorcerer?"

"I think so, yes."

"But I'll never be as strong as you are?"

Dr. Archer stared at me coldly. "Is a comparison relevant? When you are my age, I will be dead. However, I am here to speak of you, not of myself. Of my own doings I will say only that while in Vienna I consulted the diviner, Johanna Strauss, regarding each of my students. While she does not obtain specific facts in most instances, she is highly effective at describing states of mind. She recommended that you be withdrawn from Memento Analysis. I will not do this, however, unless you request it. Would it relieve your worries?"

I thought about this. It was true that Yeishu ben Pandeira was bound to a memento in that collection, and would keep tempting me to steal the memento. But then, staying away wouldn't help. The ghost had even used its power against Balaram's summoned spirit, a long distance away.

"No," I said. "No, that wouldn't help anything."

Dr. Archer sat watching me. "We should go to the sacristy, then," he concluded.

Our Bargain

I gathered my books and followed Dr. Archer downstairs to the icy-cold classroom.

The attack came the moment I stepped over the threshold into the outer chamber.

YOU MUST FIND RAV YEHOSHUA. The voice was so deafening that I stopped and leaned against the wall, unable to advance into the sacristy itself to join the class. My knees shook, and my arms went limp, and my school bag slipped off my shoulders.

Is his spirit in a memento? I countered.

NO.

Then how do I find him?

THAT IS YOUR CONCERN, SIMON MAGUS. YOU MUST FIND A WAY.

I'll try, I said, but you must meet my conditions.

NAME THEM.

First, you leave me alone until the end of the year, so I can work out a way to do it, and even ask for some help from my friends, without you bothering me.

NO.

Six months.

THREE MONTHS.

All right. Second condition, you swear not to attack anyone else.

I WILL NOT SWEAR, said Yeishu ben Pandeira. HASHEM HAS COMMANDED THAT NO JEW SHALL USE HIS NAME IN THAT WAY.

OK, promise, then.

I PROMISE TO SPEAK OF THESE MATTERS ONLY TO YOU.

Third, let me talk to other spirits for practice, and don't interfere.

NO. YOU GIVE TOO LITTLE.

What do you want, then?

TAKE MY CRYSTAL AND HOLD IT SAFE.

I can't. They'll catch me.

YOU MUST.

Then you promise you won't help me with magic.

I WILL MAKE YOU STRONG.

No, I don't want your help. I want to do it myself.

YOU WILL TAKE THE CRYSTAL, AND I WILL PROMISE NOT TO HELP YOU.

Agreed.

Just like that, Yeishu ben Pandeira left my mind. I felt calm, clean, and pleasantly empty. My strength came back. I picked up my school bag and carried it into the sacristy.

"Where were you?" Goldberry asked.

"Bathroom," I said.

Dr. Archer was moving around the room, placing mementos on the tables. Most looked familiar, but a few that I didn't recognize, I guessed about. "They're from the center pile," I said. "The yellow light pile. Medium difficulty."

He gave the harder ones to tables with older students; not one went to the first-year students, not even Leah or Mermelstein. When I looked at my enemy, he wouldn't meet my eyes. He hung his head and turned away. This was a new attitude for him, embarrassed rather than angry. I wondered why, then remembered: he was missing teeth after our last fight. Perhaps the other boys in the Cabala school were teasing him about it. Even though he had picked that fight, I still felt bad, especially because his power was real, while mine had come from an evil spirit.

Dr. Archer gave us our mementos, and I picked one and started to whisper to it.

*

After class, Leah left at once. William Goodenough moved toward Goldberry and gave me a look. Remembering my agreement with him, I nodded and stepped away and found myself next to Mermelstein. Relieved of the burden of Yeishu ben Pandeira haunting me, I found I had the courage to talk to him.

"Mermelstein," I said. "Yakov."

He grunted. "What do you want?" He started to add, *apikoros*, then stopped himself. "What is it?" he growled.

"I'm sorry," I said. "about your teeth. I didn't mean to do that."

"You don't know what you're doing?" Mermelstein said.

"No, maybe not," I said, watching Goodenough escort Goldberry out of the room. "What would it take for us to stop fighting? Next time it could be worse."

He shrugged. "Surrender to me."

"Let's say I do. Then what?"

"Then stay out of my way."

"I can't," I said. "Even if I try, we'll keep running into each other. The school's that way."

It was just the two of us in the room, and Dr. Archer, who was putting the mementos away.

"Why don't you promise something to me if I surrender to you?"

"That's not how it works."

"Promise me you and your friends will stop attacking…my friend."

He set his books down on the table. "Your stupid roommate wants to fight me," Mermelstein said. "You'll have to call him off."

"I can only promise to try, and I will. I was already doing that anyway."

"You were." It wasn't a question; all the same, I could tell he was surprised.

"But that's not who I meant."

Mermelstein sniffed. "I don't attack the Ritz girl. I never did."

"Who does?"

"I don't know."

"Then you find out, and you try to stop them, and then we'll have a deal."

He scowled. "I won't protect her. That would be a disgrace. Let her fight for herself."

"No deal, then."

"All right." He picked up his books. "Then you and I are still enemies."

"No," I said. "I really don't think we are."

Mermelstein left, shaking his head in disgust. I went to get my own knapsack.

"Well done," said Dr. Archer. "Let's go."

"Can I stay a minute, and pick another memento to practice with?"

Dr. Archer froze. His pale cold eyes seemed to study my soul. "You should not unduly burden yourself," he said at last.

"I just need to take a memento," I said. "Please."

"Take what you must," he said. "Have a good vacation."

When he was gone, I went to the cabinet where the mementos were stored, and reached under the red cloth, and my hand fell at once onto the crystal. I put it into my knapsack and ran.

The Trip to Bayside

Although the weather was really too warm, I decided to pack my beaver coat for the vacation week, in case I needed it for something. I also took a few school books, some books from the mall, and the small prayer book Leah had given me. After some sleepless nights, I decided to keep the crystal close to me also. Borrowing a needle and thread from Goldberry, I sewed an extra pocket inside my school bag, hid the crystal in it, and loosely sewed it shut.

There was no reason to say goodbye on the bus trip, since we would mostly see each other during the vacation. Goldberry didn't talk much: she was getting ready to see her sick mother, and definitely argue with her father, I didn't want to distract her.

Although the ride was short, one thing still troubled me. It happened when Robbie went to sit by Leah, to take a shot at her friendship one last time before vacation really started. I was sitting about two seats back and saw and heard the whole thing.

"Hi, what's up?" Robbie said.

"Hello." She looked away.

"Looking forward to a little break from studying?"

"It doesn't matter."

"You mean, you'll study anyway? Or you never studied in the first place?" He tried to laugh at his irony, but she wouldn't laugh with him. Neither did I: he was trying so hard I felt terrible.

"I guess you always study," Robbie continued. "That's cool. I never used to study much, but I like learning magic."

"I see." She looked out the window.

Robbie was frustrated. He'd done this many times before, but he didn't give up easily. "Hey, c'mon, talk to me. We're friends, aren't we? I mean, we should be. Talk to me!"

She looked down. "I really don't have a lot to say. I'm sorry."

"We're friends. Aren't we friends?"

Leah winced. I didn't know which of the two I felt more embarrassed for.

"But you talk to Simon, don't you?" he pressed. "You talk to him. Why don't you talk to me? Simon's a good guy, I'm a good guy."

I could see in Leah's face that he was pushing her too hard. "You don't know me," she said. "You can't."

"That's right, because you won't let me. That's not cool."

Leah looked at him frankly. "I have nothing against you as a person," she said, "but you are wasting your time."

"Because you like Simon."

Ouch. I didn't want to hear the answer to that one, but I was going to.

"Because some things aren't a good idea."

"Okay, true. But why in this case?"

"Please stop."

"No, come on. Do you think I'm ugly?"

Leah's face was getting pinched with frustration. I considered whether to get involved, but since I was interested in her myself, it would have looked bad to them both.

"Then I'm stupid. Is that it?"

"You aren't stupid."

"Then I'm not Jewish enough? That can't be it. Simon's less Jewish than me."

Now he was getting on my nerves as well as hers. I was tempted to stand up and tell him to leave me out of it already. But of course, I shouldn't have been listening.

"Robbie," Leah said. "You need to leave me alone now." Her tone of voice was dangerous. Robbie couldn't have missed that. There was a note of power in her voice that was far from a little girl's. It wasn't a command, just a warning. Yet there was so much energy in those eight words that it would have been foolish of him to stay. He slid out of the seat.

"Okay, okay,' he said. "Geez. I'm not looking for a fight. Exactly the opposite."

I wished I could help him, explain to him, but my eavesdropping was wrong, and not only that, I didn't even know why Leah was so cold to him. Robbie was big, loud, and clumsy, but he was also the most generous, good-hearted person I had ever met. I felt terrible that I might be the cause of Robbie's disappointment. If she wasn't friendly to him because she liked me, that really wasn't fair to him. I didn't want to see my roommate unhappy because of me, but then, I couldn't stop liking Leah either. Somehow, in the end, I didn't think it was really about me. No matter how interested in Leah Robbie was, they just weren't well-matched. They looked and sounded wrong together.

In a way it was a relief to be worrying about these things. Before making a deal with Yeishu ben Pandeira to leave me alone, I had been dizzy, confused, afraid for weeks. That deal had bought me some time to plan, to look things up, to enjoy my vacation.

And yet, I had stolen the crystal memento. Dr. Archer had told me to do what I had to do, which was kind of a permission, but he would have refused me if he had known what I was planning. When he found it was gone, he had no better suspect than me. What would he do when he figured it out? Or did he know already? What was it he had said? "You should not unduly burden yourself."

He knew. He knew I was going to do something dangerous. What else could that have meant? When he found out Yeishu ben Pandeira was missing, he would trace it back to me. And then what? Would I be expelled? But I had permission to take a memento. How serious a violation was it to take from a different pile than he'd expected? I hoped that I had the vacation to figure out what to do.

Gradually the bus dropped off Leah, Mermelstein, Meir, and the rest of the Brooklyn kids. Then it went over the Brooklyn Bridge to Manhattan and dropped Rocco, then Robbie, who didn't say goodbye to me, and Max and Daniel, and finally, in the Upper West Side, Goldberry. She stopped by me on her way off the bus. We hugged. "Call me tonight, tell me how your mom is doing," I said.

"Will do. Bye."

I was the last one on the bus, since Balaram had gone in his parents' minivan. I went and sat by Mr. Saluto, the driver. He tipped his cap to me and smiled.

"Mr. Saluto," I said. "Can you tell me a secret?"

"I know a few secrets," he said. "Most of 'em are secret, though. You know. Secret? Can't tell."

"No, this is your secret, I think. I think it's up to you."

"Oh, me," he said. "Mr. Saluto's secret. Sounds like a dimestore novel."

"I just want to know how the bus travels so far so fast."

"Oh, that's not a secret," he said. "Good engine, it is. She's old, but I keep her in good condition."

"What kind of engine?"

"Eighteen eighty-five Aethermatic. Empyrean fire-injected. Elemental air pressurized. Used to belong to the Prince of Wales."

"Charles?"

"Nah. Edward."

He looked away from me and began braking. The bus pulled up on my street. I was back in Bayside, where I had grown up.

My Parents' House

As I walked up the hill toward my parent's house, I saw five faces in the living-room window. They were lined up by age: Leo, Cougar, Pink Panther, Cheetah, and Jag. All were looking directly at me, as if to say, What are you doing here?

When I unlocked the door and stepped in, holding my school bag and the wrapped package containing the beaver coat, they came, mewing and squirming around my legs.

"That's more like it," I said.

Then they turned and led me to the kitchen, where the food dishes sat empty.

I scratched Cougar's head when he jumped on the counter to whine at me. After I dropped my things on the living room couch, it took me a moment to remember where the cat food cans and the can opener were stored.

Wait a minute," I said to myself as I opened the first can. "My parents' house. Three months go by, and it's not my house anymore?"

I realized it wasn't. My parents would always be my parents, but from then on, I could only live where magic was, at a place like School of the Ages.

I called to my parents, but no one answered, so they were both probably at work. I had been thinking they'd take the day off for my return to the house, but they hadn't.

I was hungry, so after I fed turkey in gravy to all the cats, I got a can of oyster soup from the pantry, cut it open, and put it on to heat. Would magic really work here, in this very normal and ordinary place? I had spent three months living in an ancient castle with no electricity, no phones, no TV, where you cooked over a fire and read by the light of candles and showers were always cold. There, magic worked. Would it work here?

I had done spells here, of course, but kind of by accident, never expecting them to work. I had done magic at Green Acres Mall, but there were other magicians around then. Here, a house I'd lived in most of my childhood, could I make something happen?

Yes, in a way, of course I could. Magic means you try to make something happen, and it does. The world is made up of forces that push on each other. Most of the time you don't see what the forces are that make things happen the way they do. You forget to do something, or you do something you didn't mean to. Why do you forget, or why do you do it? You can't know. Some magic is that way. You can't be sure.

I had just been cutting the edge of the can with the can opener. That's something most people can do. But did you ever have a day when you just can't get the can opener to cut right? Or when the can keeps slipping out of your hands no matter what you do? Why does it happen? Because you're worried or tired, or didn't eat enough? Because someone didn't clean the can opener? Or is it because there's some pattern in the stars that says you're having a bad day? Or there's an invisible spirit nearby that wants the can to stay shut or just doesn't like your face? Or, somewhere in the distance, an enemy is thinking about you?

I had forgotten the taste of canned soup. I ate it fast, then went and took my bag and folded coat upstairs. My bed was freshly made. The room was neat, but then, I had left it that way. By the phone next to my bed was a brochure for a river cruise around Manhattan Island, starting from Chelsea Pier. I looked at it for a while, then put it down and sat on the bed and picked up the cordless handset phone and put it down again. Who would I call? Robbie was probably too upset. Goldberry was with her sick mother. Leah… No, it was too soon. We'd just gotten home.

I called my mother's office, in a Manhattan hotel.

"Leicester!" she said, sad and cheerful at once. "You're home safe."

"Everything's OK," I said. "I fed the cats. But listen, can I invite one other family to come on the cruise?"

*

Once I got to my parent's house, I gradually felt some of the weight of worry from school fade, but one worry remained: the crystal memento. Finally I went upstairs and took it out of the hiding-place inside my school bag to look at it seriously for the first time.

It was opaque and white, with some smooth surfaces that were shiny, and some jagged – solid white surfaces, as if pieces had been snapped off against the grain. Cool to the touch, it was small enough to be hidden in my fist. I brought it close to my face, to listen, smell, even taste it. Nothing happened. It was dull, dead. Yeishu ben Pandeira was keeping his end of the bargain, leaving me alone, giving me time to sort things out. But was the spirit watching me? And would he resurface if I tried to talk about him and our bargain?

In a few hours my parents would be home. Should I tell them about it? Could my mother handle the news of how much danger I was facing? Could I tell my father without my mother finding out? And then, the rule was clear for magical problems: FPTA – first partner, then advisor. But Goldberry was with her sick mother, and in her father's house, she couldn't have privacy. Without going to Goldberry first, I couldn't go to Dr. Archer. It would be an insult to the partnership.

So there was still no one I could talk to. I went over the list of everything that had happened at school that was worth talking about, in hope of finding something I could tell my parents about. There was very little I felt comfortable telling them. Maybe had they been magicians, I would have been willing to risk more. The problem was that when you tell someone something about magic, you involve that person. It's an aspect of the law of sympathy, which Mr. Bannerjee (not Dr. Chatterjee, judging from the style of talking) had taught us one day in magic theory class.

"Understanding," he had said, "that when there is contact between objects, a connection remains after the contact. So that if you use a pencil and lay it down, a link remains between you and the pencil, which others may uncover and use; Some connections being stronger; parts of the body being very strong; also, very strong the metal objects such as rings and watches. In interpersonal relations the family contacts are strongest, and the bonds involving people in love. In comic books the Superman and the Spider-Man. It seems that those closest to them are harmed. Also in magic the same is true. When you act, others in your life have the chance to feel also the effect."

I had never imagined I would be in this position, aged 13 going on 14 and not telling my parents my problems because I was protecting them from danger. I lay in bed a long time thinking about it. Suddenly I realized I was actually holding the crystal between my hands, cupping it, hiding it even though there was no one there to see it. It would be so much easier if I didn't have the burden. Yeishu ben Pandeira had offered to make me powerful if I would help him. I was going to help him anyway. Why not take the power? What was it that made me refuse? I decided it was thinking that the power wouldn't be real if someone else gave it to me; it wouldn't really be mine. It could go away any time, leaving me a mess.

And then, it was more than that, too. Yeishu ben Pandeira felt wrong to me. This thing he'd done, trying to be Moshiach and failing, had left him wrong somehow: too desperate, too out-of-balance. And what's more, Yeishu ben Pandeira didn't seem to understand my identity. He thought I really was Simon Magus. Simon Magus, another false Moshiach, another heretic, another Yeishu.

Nowhere in my books had I found this Rabbi Yehoshua ben Perachyah he wanted me to go to. Yeishu ben Pandeira wasn't Jesus, and he wasn't in any Christian scripture. I would need Jewish scripture for that, and I couldn't do it alone.

I Ask for Help, Part One

You can't fool your parents. They knew I was tense and nervous. My mother asked me if I wanted to quit magic school.

I told her, "That's impossible."

My father said, "It's obvious Leicester doesn't want to."

I said, "I can't, it's what I am, you understand?"

My mother said, "No you are what you want to be. You can be anything you want, Leicester. You're still young. I don't mean you shouldn't do this magic thing, but you don't have to. You can still be friends with Goldberry and those other people."

"I'm not going to quit. You didn't raise a quitter."

"Martin, where did he get that silly macho thing from?"

"Maybe from Goldberry."

I yelled at him to shut up.

"I was just joking. Don't raise your voice to me."

"OK, I'm sorry."

"Everyone's fair game for my jokes, even your mother."

"Just you try it, Martin, and I'll start sleeping in ski pants."

"Now, Magdalene. Armor is a state of mind."

"Will you both cut out the dirty jokes?"

"What the heck happened at school?" my father asked.

"It's complicated. I'll tell you what I can, when I can."

"Let's contact Dr. Archer," said my mother.

"How, by sending up smoke signals?" my father quipped.

"Forget it," I said. "He's in Vienna, and anyway, butt out."

"Some of the other parents probably know how to call the school," my mother said. "Let's call the Tinkers. Isn't Clive Tinker the head of the alumni board?"

I shouted, "Don't call him. He'd make it one of my favours."

My father said, "Why should he? I'm just asking him a simple question. Anyway, it's me asking, not you. So I'll make the bargain with him."

"What are you, stupid? Do you know how strong he is?"

"I don't really care," my father said. "When I was four years old I spent eight hours in a wild elephant's mouth. No Upper East Side millionaire is going to scare me in the slightest."

'"Eight hours in an elephant's mouth? What happened?"

"Some other time," he said.

My mother said, "Call the Ravitzes or the Dasses."

Then my father said, "I think Simon can get us in touch with Dr. Archer, right?"

"Maybe," I said, "but I don't want to. Just drop it, let it go."

My mother said, "Then forget Dr. Archer. Let's just talk to the other families. They were nice before when we called them."

"Just let me handle it," I said.

"Well," my father said, "maybe, and only maybe, we'll chalk it up to typical teenage worries and give you some space. But you have to explain this one to us."

He had a letter on School of the Ages stationery.

"They want chaperones for the spring time travel trip. Practicing magicians only, so that leaves us out, but explain to me where and when and what the risks are."

I told him the trip was to ancient Egypt to see the Lighthouse of Pharos at Alexandria. I explained there was no risk for me because first-year students aren't allowed out of the school building. I explained the principles of concealment and universal language. They asked me what I could handle. I said some of one and none of the other, but there was still time still before the trip.

"If I could go back in time," my father said, "I would skip eating your mother's cream of wheat this morning."

"Put a sock in it, Martin," my mother said.

"Oh really?" he said. "You forget that I own ski pants, too."

"Can you really do these things?" she asked. "Can you show us?"

"I'm not a circus performer."

"What?"

"I mean that you'd make me too nervous."

The phone rang. My mother went to get it. She called my father to the phone and came back. While he was on the phone, she explained that she wanted to be supportive, but it was really scary for her, and couldn't I just give an inch? I understood she meant, but I also knew it was the usual thing mothers say to teenagers. Finally, my father came back.

"I can't believe it," he said. "Leicester, that was Rabbi Aharon Mermelstein. His family is coming with us on the cruise. But explain to me how you knocked out several of Yakov's front teeth."

*

Late that night I called Goldberry's pager. She called me back.

"How's your mom?" I asked.

"You had to call me away from her to ask me that, I suppose," she snapped.

"No. Forget it. Just go back to her. Will she come on the cruise?"

"Don't know. My father and me, at this point."

"He wants to come?"

"It's his duty to protect me, I suppose. But I think he has something else in mind."

"What?"

"Don't know, sorry."

"No, that's OK," I said. "Go back to your mother."

She paused for a moment. "You know, that wasn't fair, what I said. You are trying to help. That thing we did with Balaram."

"Well," I said, "I need some help too. I know you don't have time, but if I don't tell you first..." I didn't finish.

She waited a long time before saying, "You want to tell me on the phone? You just had a whole week seeing me every day, you know."

"I know. But it's easier away from school."

"Right," Goldberry said. "Well, then, it's your turn. Come up and see me tomorrow."

"All right."

"You want me to send a car for you?"

"No, that's okay. I can handle it."

We hung up. I felt better knowing I was going to tell her about Yeishu ben Pandeira. I had realized that I could never do what he wanted by myself. Going to my school bag, I reached for the crystal in its secret pocket. Instead, my hand fell on the prayer book Leah had given me. I left it on my bedside table, and that night, whenever I woke up, I touched it to make sure it was real.

In the morning, after my parents were gone, I got on the express bus to Manhattan. Then I walked the long way from the bus stop up

Fifth Avenue, past the high-rises and shuttered delis, to her street. The Upper East Side was cool and quiet at that time of day, with little traffic and few pedestrians. From there I used a payphone near the French Consulate to call Goldberry's house. Clive Tinker answered.

"Hello, sir," I said. "This is Simon. I'm calling to thank you for agreeing to come on the cruise."

"You're welcome." His voice was cold; he sounded tired.

"How is Mrs. Tinker?"

"Not well," he said. "I'm a bit busy. Hold for Goldberry."

She came on the phone "Better not to come up today. He's in a mood. I'll be down instead."

We met in the street outside her building. She introduced me to the doorman and told him I was to be admitted at all hours. "Sure," he said, but gave me a warning look. We walked a few blocks to a public playground and sat on a bench. As I began to speak, I no longer felt the claws at my throat. The ghost was no longer preventing me from speaking about him. "You remember on the first day at school, when I heard that ghost," I said.

"Mister I-Want-Forgiveness. Right. What came of him?"

"He's been haunting me. He's in one of the mementos from Israel."

Her eyes widened.

"He thinks I'm the real Simon Magus. He's some kind of false Moshiach named Yeishu ben Pandeira."

"Crikey," Goldberry said.

"He made me promise to help him get forgiveness from a man named Rabbi Yehoshua ben Perachyah."

"What do you get out of it?"

"He offered me power, but I turned him down. But I did use

his power a few times first."

"When?"

"The first time was on the basketball court, during intramurals. And I used it in the magical duel with Mermelstein in the kosher dining hall. Oh, and it was Yeishu ben Pandeira who drove away the spirit that Balaram summoned."

Goldberry nodded. "That all fits. But what do you get out of helping him?"

"Nothing except that he stops haunting me."

She rolled her eyes. "Well, that's a rotten deal. Anything else, then?"

"Well, I made an arrangement that he would leave me alone for a while. Before that, I couldn't even talk about it without him starting to choke me out."

"Right."

"And as soon as I made that deal, I kind of made up with Mermelstein. Kind of."

"Kind of how?"

"Mermelstein wanted me to surrender to him. So I said I would only if he would... do something for me. But he won't."

"Do what for you?"

"It doesn't matter."

"It matters. Tell me all of it, Simon."

"I wanted him to make the Cabala school kids lay off Leah."

"You ass," she said quietly. "No, really."

"That was it."

She flared. "And what made that your business, you stupid boy?"

"I don't know. I just..."

"You're just a fool is what you are."

I wasn't sure if she was angry or sad. I knew she wasn't jealous; she knew something about Leah that she wasn't telling me. She got up, paced around the bench, sat again.

"Tell me everything else, then."

"Ogopogo also mentioned Yehoshua ben Perachyah. Oh, and Mermelstein's coming on the cruise."

"Mm-hmm. Is that all?"

"And I took the memento with Yeishu ben Pandeira in it," I finished. "I have it here in my coat pocket."

Goldberry swallowed, thought for a little while. "Honestly, Simon, I don't know how you could get in so bloody much trouble and hide it all from me. You didn't tell anyone else, did you?"

"No. But I do need to tell some more people. I need help."

"So, whom to tell then? That great git of a roommate of yours, I suppose, for starters. And then…"

"And then Mermelstein."

"Come again?"

"I need someone inside the Cabala school to help."

"Yes. But you choose him because…"

"I don't know exactly," I said. "But I have a feeling he's the person I need."

Goldberry thought about that for a while. "It could be," she finally said. "Let me look into it a bit. Hang on." She began rifling through her small black handbag. "Right, I've been wanting to try out this deck." She took out a tarot pack I hadn't seen before. The box read *Tarot in de Herstelde Orde*.

"Where'd you get it?"

"My uncle sent it from London."

"Your uncle?"

"Uncle Hugh. A stuffy git, but he has sources." She peeled open the plastic, freeing a deck of plain-backed cards with lettering in … I wasn't sure what language. I asked.

"It's Dutch," Goldberry said. "Never mind, I know the pictures. I can't lay out a cross in this wind, though. Let's go inside."

We went onto York Avenue and found a coffee shop. Goldberry took black coffee, no sugar, and I got a hot chocolate. She did a tarot reading. It was mostly swords cards. The Page of Swords showed up as "a problem in the past that is coming to an end." Goldberry said Mermelstein was a good example of a page of swords: a young, inexperienced man who gets into a lot of conflicts. In the slot for future problems was a card called The Lovers, showing a woman standing between an old man and a young one.

"She's choosing between the excitement of youth and the wisdom of experience," Goldberry explained. "It means you have a difficult choice coming up. But that's the problem. We all always do, don't we?"

"So it looks like I should involve Mermelstein, or not?"

"It looks like he's involved," Goldberry explained. "So it might as well be on our terms. Let's talk to him."

After the reading, Goldberry said she wanted to go back to her mother, and she'd call me later. I didn't want to go home yet, so I got on a train to Forest Hills to go to the movies. Using the power of concealment, I walked past the ticket-checker and directly into the theater. When the movie was over, I went back and bought a ticket for it. Then I took a bus home.

Before the Cruise

That night, late, the phone by my bedside rang. After three rings, my parents didn't pick up, so I did.

"Simon," Goldberry said. "Hang on a tick."

There was a muffled sound as the phone was passed. The next speaker was a dignified British woman. "How are you, Simon? This is Rosemary Tinker."

"Hello, Ma'am." I was surprised and decided not to hide it. "Are you feeling all right? Can I help with something?"

"I know you're helping me already, by helping my Goldberry," she said. "I was wondering how you liked my gift."

"The coat?" I asked.

"Yes indeed. It's quite warm, isn't it? Do you wear it often?"

"Actually no ma'am, I don't. I think it wouldn't be as good if I used it all the time."

"Oh, no," she said. "Use it when you need it, dear. Just mind the curse."

"The curse?" My stomach might have fallen down to my ankles if I were standing. "What curse?"

"Oh, the curse of the blue-blooded leeches, dear Simon. They suck out your red blood, and they pump blue blood back into your veins."

"What?" It didn't make sense. Then I heard Goldberry laughing.

"I was joking, dear," Mrs. Tinker said.

"Do you need something in trade for the coat?" I asked her.

"No," she replied. "It is a gift. I'm not Clive, you know. I know you'll be at hand if I need something, before I even tell you I need it."

"You know the future that well?"

"Oh, I won't say I don't have a curve thrown at me now and again, but I know what the future holds, by and large."

"For everyone?"

"No, no. Only for everyone I need to know about. Now, then, here's my daughter."

"Simon," Goldberry said. "Wear the coat during the cruise, will you?"

*

The next Sunday we drove into the city and parked at Chelsea Piers. I kept the package with the beaver coat under my arm as we waited at the arranged meeting place, a coffee bar between the parking lot and one of the piers. The weather was cold and clear.

"Can I see you in your new coat?" my mother asked.

"It's sort of an old coat. Goldberry's grandfather on her mother's side used to own it."

"Put it on, Leicester."

"On the boat."

My father said, "I can't get over the Mermelsteins agreeing to come. Yakov's father is a solid citizen, but Yakov himself…"

"Don't say it," I interrupted. "He reads minds."

"Poppycock," my father said. "He's thirteen. You want to be scared of him, fine, but I'm not afraid of boys."

"Scared?" I said. "I'm not scared."

A commotion outside the entrance announced the arrival of the Ravitz family. Robbie's mother, Rhea Ravitz, was a tall redhead with freckles, wearing black slacks and a flower print blouse under a tan overcoat. His father, Rolando Ravitz, was a big dark-haired man with a ponytail and a black pinstripe suit. He went from person to person, squeezing hands. To my surprise, he had a light Spanish accent. Mrs. Ravitz ordered two triple espressos. Mr. Ravitz began to jabber at my father about the stock market. Robbie and I stood staring at each other.

"You have to help me with Leah," he said.

"Who?" asked my mother.

"Shut up," I told Robbie. "Let's walk a little."

We got outside into the cool air. There were some people in the parking lot, but no one close enough to listen.

"How about it?" he asked.

"I heard you on the bus," I said.

He looked away for a moment. "Hey," he said at last. "I mean… It's just so frustrating."

"That's because it isn't right."

"And you and her is right?"

"I don't know. We may just be friends. It's hard to get to know her."

"Well, you're doing better than me."

"Sure," I said. "But I think she isn't really ready. You're pushing really hard, Robbie."

"So I'll ease up for a while."

"Robbie," I said. "You're a good guy. Everyone knows that. Leah knows that. But everyone knows you like her because she's pretty."

"That's bull, man," Robbie shouted. "I know she's really smart, and..."

I waited.

"Come on, man. Everyone likes a pretty girl. You don't notice that a girl is good-looking?"

"Sure I do. And Leah is the prettiest. But there are lots of pretty girls."

"Not at School of the Ages," Robbie said. He looked over my shoulder. "Whoa. Those are Goldberry's folks?"

Turning, I saw Goldberry, elegant in a long, deep-blue skirt and matching jacket. I'd just said Leah was the prettiest, but my partner wasn't someone you could ignore, either. With her was her father, Clive Tinker, striking in his suede jacket and sunglasses, holding his wife's hand. Rosemary Tinker was tall, the same height as her husband, pale and dressed in a floor-length mink and matching hat. Though she was still far from us, somehow I could see her dark eyes sparkling like wells full of stars.

I watched Clive Tinker whisper in his wife's ear as they approached.

"I'll get my folks," Robbie said. "Whoa. These two are big-time."

I had to agree. If you like old-time movie stars, it was like Cary Grant and Audrey Hepburn, only taller.

"I see you've that old coat now," Clive Tinker said as we shook hands.

He was right. I was wearing the multihued beaver coat. I had no memory of putting it on.

"Better you than me, I expect," Mr. Tinker added.

"It wouldn't fit you," I blurted. Don't ask me why.

"Cle-ver," Goldberry said.

He took a deep breath, shook his head, then introduced his wife.

"I feel as if I've known you a long time," Mrs. Tinker told me. "I believe you are a good partner for my Goldberry."

"I want to be," I said. "She's a good partner."

"Let's not be sentimental," said Goldberry, rolling her eyes. "Let's get on the boat, please."

"The fact is," Clive Tinker interrupted, "you and my daughter are due to endanger each other quite a bit."

"But danger is part of magic," I said.

"It is if you think it is," he replied. "But who am I to teach you? Let Archer see to it."

"He does a good job," I said, stung by his tone.

Clive Tinker turned to his daughter. "Call off the dogs, will you?"

"Oh forget it Simon," she said. "He's incorrigible. Who are we waiting for?"

"The Mermelsteins. The Dasses cancelled, and we couldn't reach the Vitellos."

"The Mermelsteins?" blurted Mr. Tinker. "Good God! What did you invite them for? Don't seat me downwind."

"Clive," Mrs. Tinker scolded.

"If you want to know why," I said, "we can trade information."

"Hmm," he said. "You're brave, Simon. Not on your home turf today, and still ready to bargain? No, thank you. I have other ways of getting my information."

My parents and the Ravitzes came out with Robbie. Everyone said hello and shook hands.

"We set sail in ten minutes," my father said. "I hope the Mermelsteins are still coming."

We stood a while waiting. Rolando Ravitz began to talk stocks with Clive Tinker, who replied with polite impatience. After a few minutes, I spotted a black limousine turning a corner in the parking lot. It was a little bit dented and battered; I recognized it as the limo used by the Mermelsteins many months back. "There they are," I said.

"Who's Leah?" my mother whispered in my ear.

"Goldberry's roommate," I whispered back.

"So? Do you know her?"

"Yes. Please drop it."

The Cruise

The limo contained Rabbi Aharon Mermelstein, his wife, and Yakov. Rebbetzin Sharon Mermelstein was a stout woman in a dark burgundy skirt and jacket, with a black wig and a burgundy hat. She nodded and said hello to everyone, but did not shake hands. Mermelstein himself did not smile, but he did shake hands with all the males in the group. He looked a little cranky, but not as hostile as I had seen before. One reason for his change of mood occurred to me; it was only about two days since vacation, but his missing teeth had been replaced.

"What's that coat?" he asked me bluntly. "Are you an Eskimo?"

"Long story," I said.

We boarded together, my parents presenting all the tickets. The crew guided us to dining room space inside, enclosed mainly by big glass windows, and said we could go topside once the ship had put out. The women sat, the men went to the bar, and we students were left to our own devices. We sat at a separate table from the adults.

"Let's get some sodas," I said.

"Sure," said Robbie. He went for four Cokes, one diet Coke for Goldberry, who never took sugar. They had leftover Coca-Cola that was kosher for Passover, so Mermelstein could drink it.

"What's all this about?" he asked me. "Why invite us here? We're not your kind."

"We're all magic students. We all go to School of the Ages. That makes us the same kind. And your father is a nice man, Mermelstein, even if you aren't most of the time."

"All right," he said. "So we go to the same school. What's your point?"

"I need your help, and Robbie's," I said. "Robbie, I'll tell you where you fit in in a minute."

"Help with what?" Mermelstein grunted. "I told you I have nothing to do with the Ritz girl."

"Because she's an *apikoros*."

"Close enough."

"Well," I said, "I think I've figured out why you used to call me that, and now you don't. Or do you know why?"

He rubbed his chin, letting his lips part slightly so that I saw the new teeth, more white and smooth than his own natural yellow ones. "You looked like one," he said thoughtfully. "It was all over you. Now, you just look like a boy."

"I was being haunted by a real *apikoros*," I said. "That's what you saw. It's a ghost connected to one of the mementos from Israel."

"Whoa," said Robbie. "For how long?"

"Since we started school. I asked you about it one time. On the first day, actually."

"Oh, yeah. I forgot about that." Robbie looked at Goldberry. "You knew about it?"

"He just told me a day ago," she replied. "Simon mentioned the ghost to me once, then dropped it. I thought it went away."

"How do you know about this ghost?" Mermelstein asked.

"I'll tell you his name: it's Yeishu ben Pandeira."

Mermelstein sneered, again showing his mismatched teeth. "That's rich. The boy is haunted by Jesus."

"Pardon?" This from Goldberry.

"Yeishu is Hebrew for Jesus. No, it's not the same person as in the Christian Bible, but the same kind of person. Yeishu is a heretic."

"A false Moshiach," I said.

"That's it. You looked this up?"

"Not very well," I admitted. "That's why I need you. I made a deal to get rid of this ghost. But I have to get some rabbi to forgive him. The rabbi's name is …um… Yehoshua ben Perachyah. I need you to look it all up."

"That's all you need from me?"

"Maybe. I don't know."

"And what do I get?"

"What you want," I said. "I'll surrender to you in public."

"Whoa," said Robbie.

"Let's clear off," Goldberry told him. "I'll explain the rest of it to you."

"Let me think," said Mermelstein. He thought. I paced. A short distance away, Goldberry was explaining to Robbie about the crystal and the haunting. From where it was, it looked like his eyes were bulging.

"No," Mermelstein said finally. "I don't want you to surrender to me."

"Why not?"

"Because I haven't beaten you."

"You would have," I admitted. "Yeishu ben Pandeira was helping me to fight you."

"When?"

"That time in the dining hall."

Mermelstein's eyes widened. "That's what the spirit told you? What a stinking liar! It was you, believe me. That teacher of yours, Archer, he's in charge of fighting for the school. You may not know much, but no one wants to mess with you."

"Because of Dr. Archer?"

"Because anyone he advises is going to be hard to beat."

"But he didn't teach me anything about fighting."

Mermelstein shrugged. "You don't see it, I guess," he said. "You're just like him when you fight. Same voice, same look in your eye. You give an order and don't back up an inch. In yeshiva they call you the first-born son of Archer."

"But I'm not," I said. "I'm the seventh son of a seventh son, actually."

Mermelstein's voice dropped. "So am I."

Goldberry and Robbie came back, my roommate with a new can of soda.

"I am totally blown away," Robbie said. "I can't believe you hid this from us so long."

"I had no choice."

"Let's go up on deck," Goldberry suggested. "It's okay now."

The four of us went topside. Indeed, while we were talking, the ship had pulled away from the dock and was headed south, with the piers sliding away on our left. The top deck was a good distance above the water, and a cold wind whipped around all of us. Up ahead, we could see the shining lines of the Twin Towers. Many of the other people on the ship, mainly tourists, were also topside, standing along the rails, sipping their drinks at the small metal-frame tables, or snapping photos. None of us talked for a while. Then Robbie went over to Mermelstein.

"Hey, no hard feelings," he said. He offered a handshake. "If you're in this with us, let's try to get along."

Mermelstein looked at his extended hand for a moment, then shrugged and took it. "You have guts," he said. "Brains you need, but guts you have."

"That sounds about right," said Robbie. "I'm going for another Coke. Come?"

They left me and Goldberry together. The Twin Towers were now north of us, behind us as we continued on our course, and we could see to the south the distant speck that was Liberty Island.

"It's an amazing magic you did, getting him in with us," Goldberry told me.

"Your mother looks all right," I said.

"She is when she needs to be. She wants you to go and sit with her later." Goldberry looked at a stout European couple who were at the prow of the ship, out of earshot. "Shove off," she whispered, gesturing at them. Though they couldn't have heard her, they casually strode away and headed below decks.

We walked together to the prow of the ship, watching then as the green dot that was the Statue of Liberty began to take shape in the distance. The wind beat at our faces, and we held hands.

After the Cruise

After the cruise, my head was whirling with changes, my new uneasy alliance with Mermelstein being the principal one. Now we had a genuine plan of action, I felt some pressure was off. I had something else to do.

Before calling, I looked at the small prayer book she had given me. In an embarrassing second, I forgot that Hebrew books open from what would be the back cover of an English-language book. Scanning the Hebrew, I found too little I could grasp, only a few familiar words. Admittedly beaten, I hesitated before dialling. But I knew I was going to call, and I knew what I had to say. There was nothing to fear, was there?

I dialled. It rang many times. A woman picked up.

"Mrs. Ritz," I said. "Is Leah at home please?"

The phone receiver was set down at once. After less than a minute, Leah answered. "Hello, Simon."

"Hi! How is your vacation going?"

"It's quiet. Just me and my mother, actually."

Her father, I remembered, had died a few years earlier. "You're reading and studying?"

"Yes, mostly. What about you?"

I told her what I had been doing. Then slowly, I explained my secret problem, then what I was planning. Her answer surprised me.

"I knew you were being haunted," she admitted. "But I wasn't sure you knew it. I thought it might be a guardian spirit, like a relative who died."

"But why didn't you say anything?"

She took a while to consider her answer, then said, "Things happen for a reason, Simon. When you don't know the reason, it's best not to interfere. But if you're asking me to help, that's different."

"Then you'll help."

"Yes. But we have to make a bargain."

This was my second surprise of the conversation. Leah was more like a friend. I had never considered she would bargain.

I tried to think what I could offer. "What would you like? I mean, what's my end?"

"I think..." she said. "I think you must promise me to look at the siddur I gave you every day."

"I will," I said. *Siddur* means prayer book. "But I really don't understand anything in it."

"You will," she said.

"I don't see how that helps you, exactly," I said.

"It's *chesed*," Leah explained. "For me, it is."

"*Chesed*. Hebrew for a good deed."

"For being good and kind to people, yes."

"Should we..." I surprised myself by asking. "Should we get together before school starts again?"

Her voice was quieter. "If Goldberry is there, maybe I can go. You could have her call me."

I ended the call soon after, and called Goldberry.

"Use me as a chaperone?" she said disgustedly. "Oh, good idea.

No thank you. And for the record, I don't know why you pulled poor Leah into this adventure of ours. Is it her lips? Or her eyes?"

"No," I said, though I wasn't sure. "It was… She knows about these things, and I just don't want to keep secrets from her."

"Simon," Goldberry said, "It's not smart to get Leah involved with spirits. Didn't you ever wonder why she takes so long with the mementos?"

"Sure, but…"

"But you didn't wonder very hard, then, did you?"

"Why, then?"

"Honestly, boys are such idiots. She wants to find her father."

"Who died?"

"She wants to talk to his spirit, yes. And that could get her into trouble."

"Her father?"

"No, her father wouldn't hurt her. But the other spirits she deals with might."

"Well, there are some bad ones," I said. "I should know. But…"

"But nothing. You're an ass, Simon, seriously. I'm going to hang up now. I'll talk to you in a few days."

*

Getting back to school was good. Everyone seemed refreshed, and stories were being exchanged about using magic over the break. Robbie had learned a new trick from a water spirit, so he said. He could judge the health of fish in a tank at a glance and know which one to buy, either as a pet or as food. Rocco, meanwhile, had explored several fire stations without being noticed, while Balaram said he was getting better at universal language and had been watching and understanding Punjabi TV shows.

The week went fast, and then we were scheduled for the first session of sweeping the school roof. Robbie, Rocco, and I met Mr. Bannerjee in the fourth-floor classroom where we studied Asian history. He arrived with a pushcart containing a large plastic bin, many plastic bags, and several brooms and dustpans.

"First, to remember," he said. "Not to sweep anything off the roof. We do not want dust and garbage in the grass below. Next, not to use magic for this activity."

"That's not possible," Robbie said.

"Please to explain," said Mr. Bannerjee.

"Everything we do is magic. Magic is just change, like the influence of your attitude."

"Magic is change only," said Mr. Bannerjee. "This is a very interesting attitude. And so I suppose no skill is required."

"Skill is required to do well," I said.

"All right," said Mr. Bannerjee. "Please to do well with the brooms. Two hours solid work. Sweep garbage into dustpans, then into bags. The filling of three bags is expected. Stay away from the sloping parts of the roof, of course. Also, not to go near the hutch on the south side, that is blocked with police tape. Various reasons for this involve both physical and emotional injury. This is not a test or a challenge. I am quite serious about it."

We knew that when Mr. Bannerjee dropped his odd way of talking and spoke in normal English sentences, he was indeed serious. None of us considered disobeying him. He left us to get started.

From the rooftop you could see very far. Over the sea of trees that framed the island there hung a chilly early-spring sky. The skyline of Manhattan was close by. On the horizon was a green line of ocean.

The roof itself was flat gray and brown stone with gravelly patches. It was very broad and unevenly shaped, with many projecting sections. Waist-high battlements ran along the edges. Exploring, we located various structures, including a belfry, many chimney pipes, the police-taped hutch, and three striking stone gargoyles, each about six feet high. Each resembled a twisted man with the snarling face of a male orangutan, but their clawed hands were in different positions. One covered its eyes, one its ears, and one its mouth.

"See no evil, hear no evil, speak no evil," Robbie said. "Nice."

"They have names," Rocco said. "Look at their bellies."

Names were chiseled on the navels of the three gargoyles. The chisel marks were far newer than the statues themselves. The one with covered eyes was "Kalkas." The one with covered ears was "Humperdink." The one with covered mouth was "Ellen James."

"I don't get those names," Rocco said. "Oh well, let's get to work."

We decided to pick a section near the Manhattan side and work together there. We swept dust, sand, broken glass, and crumpled dry leaves into the black plastic bags. It was chilly, and a light wind made it hard to keep the dust where we wanted it. Robbie talked about summoning an elemental prince of earth to give information about the gargoyles.

"We could just ask a teacher," I suggested.

"Got to practice, man," he answered.

After an hour, we were all tired and thirsty.

"Wait a minute," Rocco said. He closed his eyes, concentrating, then walked over to the gargoyles, circling around behind them. He knelt behind Humperdink, then stood and came back to us holding a large bottle of spring water. "Had a feeling that would be there," he said.

"Dude, you just conjured that out of thin air," Robbie said.

"Nah," said Rocco. "Must have been there already."

We shared the water and went back to sweeping.

After Mr. Bannerjee came to collect us, we hauled the bags down one floor to a large garbage chute.

"How does the school's garbage get taken away?" Robbie asked.

"Please to ask me after two years," said Mr. Bannerjee.

We had a snack, and then Rocco went off to study, and Robbie and I went to a meeting. We used the alcove outside the sacristy, the room with the mementos. Goldberry and Leah were already there. About ten minutes late, Mermelstein finally arrived. He shut the outer door and said something under his breath.

"It wasn't easy," he growled.

The Meeting

"Finally," Mermelstein said, "I found a reference in a book called *Tosefta*, from the *Baraitas*, to this Yeishu ben Pandeira. It says he was a heretic, which we knew already, and he was also called Yeishu ha-Notzri. It says that Rabbi Yehoshua ben Perachyah repelled him with his hands."

I had heard that before. "Where?" I asked. "When?"

"It says in Egypt," said Mermelstein. "The exact year is not given, or I can't find it."

"The school trip," Robbie said. "Would Rabbi Yehoshua ben Perachyah still be around then?"

"I don't know," said Mermelstein. "I don't understand the text so well."

"I'll look," Leah said.

"Nonsense," said Mermelstein. "I won't put that kind of *sefar* in your hands."

"You won't let her embarrass you, you mean," Goldberry snapped.

"She shouldn't be here," Mermelstein replied. "Not you, either."

"Enough," I said. "Mermelstein, if you bring the book here, we can all work on it together."

"How?" he replied. "Universal language doesn't work with books, and none of you knows enough Hebrew. Even I don't."

"Let me try," Leah said.

"I won't bring the book to you."

"I have *Tosefta* at home," said Leah. "Mother will bring it to me."

Mermelstein scowled, but gave up.

"Let's talk about a plan of action," Goldberry said. "I for one am convinced that the trip is going to be the right time for what we need to do."

"How do you know?" asked Robbie.

"They always work out like that," she explained. "Each year's trip is selected by a complicated calculation with everyone's astrology. My father told me that people in his day were always nipping off to settle their personal business during the school field trips."

"They expect it?" I said.

"Well, we're not supposed to do it, being first-years. But I know they look at everyone's charts as well as conditions at the time and place of the trip."

"What about changes in the constellations?" Robbie said.

"They could," Mermelstein said. "In our *Beit Midrash* we have books of Chaldean astrology. They show the night skies thousands of years ago."

"So we won't be the only ones with something personal to do in Alexandria?" I said.

"Oh God, no!" Goldberry said. "Some of the fifth-years will probably steal Alexander's bones, or something like that."

"Way cool," Robbie said.

"It's not good to rob graves," Leah said.

"So first we have to figure out how to sneak out of school," Goldberry said. "My father wouldn't tell me that, of course. And then, once we're out, what do we do?"

"Sneaking out will be my department," Robbie said. "We'll need a secret exit or something, because our concealment magic won't fool the teachers."

"And as for what we do once we get to Alexandria – leave that to Simon and me to plan."

There was a long silence.

"I want to go," Mermelstein said.

"Why?" Goldberry asked.

"I want to meet Rabbi Yehoshua ben Perachyah."

"It wasn't part of our original agreement."

"You don't want me to go?" he said, offended.

"No, it's not that," I corrected. "But I think our original deal isn't good enough if you're going to take such a big risk."

"What deal?" Leah asked.

"I'll surrender to him publicly," I said.

"Oh, who cares?" Goldberry said. "Get over it, you two."

"Don't order me," said Mermelstein. "Anyway, I don't want a new deal. The old one is off, too. I told you that on the boat. It was stupid. You'll surrender when I beat you. Right now, I'm going with you. Show me the memento."

I had the crystal in my jeans pocket, in a cloth pouch I had gotten from my mother. I took it out and handed it to Mermelstein.

"I can tell" he said. "This thing feels bad to me. The spirit of an *apikoros* is bound to it, just as you say."

"But somehow Yeishu ben Pandeira chose me to haunt as soon as I got here. I don't get why, even now."

"Because Yeishu ben Pandeira thinks you're Simon Magus," Goldberry speculated. "He thinks you're the heretic you named yourself after, the one who fought the disciples of Jesus. He thinks you're strong enough to help him."

"But I'm nothing like Simon Magus," I protested.

"Simon," Leah said, "what if you are Simon Magus? What if he does recognize you?"

"How?"

"We're going to the past," she said.

"Hey, that's right," Robbie put in. "Maybe you'll grow up to be Simon Magus on some future trip to the past. Uh… I mean…"

"Some trip I make when I'm older and stronger," I clarified.

"Yeah, that."

"So," said Mermelstein, "you go to the past now, meet Yeishu ben Pandeira, pretend to be Simon Magus, he thinks you're the real Simon Magus, and recognizes you a thousand years later."

"Wait a tick," Goldberry said. "Simon gets recognized for doing something that he wouldn't have done in the first place if he wasn't recognized for doing it."

"That's stupid."

"Or," said Leah, "he really is the only Simon Magus. The whole story is very old. People change stories over time. Who really knows how the stories get started?"

That blew my mind. "Look," I said, "here's what we need to do. Robbie, you find a way for us to sneak out of school. Better yet, find two, in case one doesn't work. Leah, you can get that book and take over research. Mermelstein, you brush up however you can on what we need to do to survive. And Goldberry and I will plan the rest."

*

We separated near the dining hall. As I headed in, I realized that Dr. Archer wanted to see me. Was it about the crystal? Or was it just an ordinary meeting to discuss my progress? I went upstairs to his office.

"I am informed," he said, "that your parents arranged a get-together of several families during the vacation."

"Yes, I… I'm sorry that we didn't invite you."

"Invite me?" He looked puzzled. "I don't understand why…. Ah, yes. I was in Vienna and could not have come. Besides, Clive Tinker…" He trailed off. "My question is more about the inclusion of the Mermelsteins. What purpose was served? Don't lie to me, Simon."

"I needed his help to look something up."

"Why him specifically?"

"Dr. Archer," I said, "I don't think it's a coincidence that Mermelstein and I had the same second interview. I don't know just what to expect, but something has to be going on with us."

"Perhaps," said Dr. Archer.

"Perhaps?" I said. "Don't you know? Didn't you even kind of plan it that way?"

"I have other concerns," he said. "You have noticed that I am distracted. A matter is afoot in Europe. I know that if I were to probe your doings thoroughly, some mischief would be uncovered. Tell me of your progress with concealment and universal language."

I told him what I had learned and about the practicing I had done. He said it was satisfactory and asked me about continuous defense, the third principle.

"We haven't had a lesson about it yet," I explained.

"Of course, of course – meditation being required at a certain level. Maestro Morgan," he said, tilting his head. "Yes, all right."

"You were talking to Maestro Morgan?" I asked. "Telepathy?"

"Talking?" he said. "Telepathy? This is a practice that leads to unguarded thoughts, and to the extirpation of minds. A thought occurred to Maestro Morgan, and it then occurred to me what his reply might be."

"Can you teach me that?"

"Thought trading is a sorcerous skill, which you already possess. You have contacted me in this manner. You were at home, and I telephoned you later that day. I also called you to me today without a written message, if you recall."

"But that day," I said, "I burned an inscribed candle, and…"

"A prop," he said. "Simon, I must end the interview for the time being. Someone is coming to see me."

A moment later, I was outside. I walked down the hall, then stopped and tilted my head.

Dr. Archer, I thought, who came to see you?

I realized that it was annoying for me to interrupt him, and kept walking, then stopped again. Goldberry, I thought. Done with your essay yet?

I realized she wasn't, and I should go and help her out.

Continuous Defense

Robbie asked around and came up with two ways to sneak out of school. Neither one seemed that great. On the roof there were two metal posts by the back which were spaced perfectly for attaching a rope ladder. He said he'd heard some older students had one, and he was trying to find out who. The other way out of school was to go through an always locked first floor room marked H.O.L., which had a gigantic padlock.

"Opening locks is easy magic," he said. "We'll figure it out."

"Why is the room locked?" I asked. "What's in it?"

"It's locked to keep people from getting out," he said.

"Or it could be locked for some other reason. Someone could be trying to get you in trouble. We need to check it out later."

"No prob. I'm on it. One helpful spirit coming up."

"Wait," I said. "I have a better idea."

At that night's meeting of the divination club, I asked if anyone could check something for me.

"Ask your partner," said Irene in a bored voice.

"I'm too close to it," Goldberry said, as I'd arranged with her. "We'd appreciate it, really."

"All right," Irene said, rolling her eyes. She poured me a cup of tea. I gulped it down – it was hot. Then she studied the leaves at the bottom. Mina leaned over to look also.

"The spirits have explained that you are all going to die," Mina said grimly.

"Come on," Goldberry snapped.

"Don't bother," said Irene. "Freshmen have no sense of humour: too self-involved. There's a rabbit. You'll be on the run and have to stay alert. And the moon. Travel by night. And a handsome man. That's not you, Simon."

"Anything about a locked room?"

"I would have said, wouldn't I? Locked rooms, what foolishness. I would ask you what this is all about, but luckily for you, I don't care."

"Let me," said Lakshmi. "Simon, what's your *lagna*?"

"No astrology," Goldberry said.

"You must not want the truth." Lakshmi shrugged.

We got back to Goldberry's room to find Leah out, and inside – Goodenough.

"You could just leave a note, you know," Goldberry scolded.

"Never mind that," he said. "You first-years are up to something."

"So are you," I said. "So what?"

"We're supposed to have a truce, little man," Goodenough smirked.

"That goes both ways," I shot back. "Keep out of our business."

"No sorry," Goodenough said. "I want in. Whatever you're doing, I'm part of it now. You know you need my help."

"So you can report it all to Mr. Tinker," I said.

"Not at all," he said. "I want in because I care for Goldberry."

"Very touching, I'm sure," she said. "But for my curiosity, which of a hundred possible ways did you find out?"

"Why," he said, "Simon here just admitted it. You're like a brick wall against brute force magic, little man, but a bit too easy to fool. Now, what's the game?"

Goldberry and I looked at each other.

"We have a plan to heal Goldberry's mother," I said. "At a time and place we don't know yet, we have to leave the school and go some other place. A spirit promised to come and tell us when."

Goodenough rolled his eyes. "That's your big plan? Hmph. You first-years really do get up to nonsense. All right, if that's on the level, I'm in."

"One condition."

"Really?"

"You tell no one till it's over."

"Oh, all right. Killjoy."

When he was gone, I said to Goldberry, "At least he didn't find out about the other plan. Do you believe his reason for getting involved?"

"I think I do," said Goldberry. "He's been rather nice to me."

The next day in meditation, Maestro Morgan kept the first-years after the regular session and told us to try something new, a rotating cylinder.

"Once you see it," he proclaimed, "enlarge it, till it is taller and bigger than you are. See how it hangs in the air nearby you. Not a pyramid, Cohen. We aren't in Egypt yet! a cylinder. Now the whirling spinning cylinder, it moves closer, and now you are inside it. It is transparent, and you can sense everything around you, but you are also enclosed. Visualize this!"

"Cool," Robbie said near me. I hadn't realized he was awake.

"In the days to come," said Maestro Morgan, "you must retain the cylinder in its position. You may make it larger, if you wish. A part of your mind is to be devoted to the cylinder."

"How can we think about the cylinder and study?" Daniel Cohen complained.

"Your mind has the power to do many things at once, if it is properly trained," answered the Maestro. "When a task can be performed without concentration, it becomes routine. For example, you can walk, talk, think, and chew gum all at once, because some of these actions do not task your conscious mind. Do you think about how to move your lips and jaws and tongue as you chew?"

"You can think about it if you want to," I said, "but you don't have to."

"Indeed, Simon. But I shall mention another task: playing the piano. One hand carries the melody, the other the harmony. To play well, you cannot put your thought on either hand, or the other will halt its motion. Instead, the actions of the two hands become blended into a single activity. It is not half your mind on harmony, half on melody. It is your whole mind applied to the joint task of harmony and melody together."

"So instead of dividing your attention between the cylinder and studying," Rocco said, "or talking, or whatever, you just do the cylinder and that thing like it's a single thing."

"The cylinder must become to you as routine and unexamined as chewing gum."

We worked on the cylinder. It wasn't as hard as I expected. Maestro Morgan, who seemed always to know how we were doing, made some comments. One kid had failed to enclose his feet. Another kid made it so big across that he was having trouble keeping it in his mind. That was the sort of thing we were dealing with.

"Your cylinder must defend you," Maestro Morgan said finally. "Its purpose is to delay magical attacks upon you so that you have time to respond. I shall now attack one of you. Respond by dropping to the floor, and the attack will stop." He turned his back. We all thought about our cylinders.

A row back from me, Goldberry dropped to the floor.

"Crikey," she said, "that bloody hurt."

"You were not well-defended," said Maestro Morgan without turning.

Across the aisle from me, Balaram dropped to his knees.

"Was there pain?" asked Maestro Morgan.

"Not really," he said. "I was…"

A bright flash against my cylinder pulled my attention away. I closed my eyes to examine the cylinder again and got a vision of the Maestro's attack: a machinegun floating next to me blazing away at my chest. I imagined my hand swatting the machinegun in the back, turning it around. In my mind's eye the gun spun partway, then swiveled back at me again. Suddenly beside it appeared a dozen more. As they began to fire I threw myself down.

"You didn't understand my attack well enough to reverse it," said Maestro Morgan. "A noble effort, but defense is today's lesson."

He went on with the attacks as we lay there. Suddenly, I felt hot stings upon my chest and face. It hurt horribly. I had let my cylinder fall, feeling safe. I wasn't the only one: more kids around me were groaning.

I tried but couldn't re-form my cylinder. The attack hurt too much, and it didn't let up. I managed to make the triangle and tried to use it like a shield to block the painful burning stings. It didn't work, but Maestro Morgan let up anyway.

…………………………………………………………………………

"Mermelstein," he said. "Ritz. Dass. Rocco. Well done. Simon, a good effort, but you were unwise to drop your defenses. Ravitz, the attack was not actually fire, so visualizing water did not serve. Tinker, why did you switch to a cone?"

"My mother taught me that."

"A cylinder is, in my view, more easily expanded. Very well. Continue your practice."

*

As I walked into magic theory class, I felt the stone floor beneath me turn muddy and slippery. I fell. My cylinder wasn't up, of course.

"Please to maintain defense," said Mr. Bannerjee.

"Sorry." Of course, the stone was unchanged; the attack had been mental.

As I walked into construction class, Rabbi Horn flung a gigantic black beetle at me. My cylinder was down. It landed on my cheek and sank slashing pincers into my eyelid. I clawed at my face and fell onto a table. The beetle fell off. My eyelid wasn't really injured, but there was a throbbing pain.

"Got to protect yourself, kiddo," said Rabbi Horn. He held in his hand a black model of a huge insect.

"That's cool," I said as I got up. "Can you teach me that?"

"Let's talk after class."

After class, Rabbi Horn gave me and a few other kids instructions on how to construct what he called "the bug toy."

"Don't work on it anywhere near me," Goldberry said. "Ugh."

Working with a toy rubber insect, spray fixative, and a variety of magic words and techniques, I sat with Robbie making a bug toy of my own. I tried it out during intramurals, where Rocco's team was getting smashed at field hockey by Finkel's team. Standing on the sidelines, I hurled the bug at Shifrin, one of Finkel's defenders, a tall, skinny third-year boy with a sweaty beard. He swatted at his face, and Rocco got the ball past him and shot for a goal.

"Nice trick," Shifrin told me after the game. "I forgot about that one. You can try multiplying it, you know. Just think about a swarm of bees or something."

Rocco, Robbie and I went to the roof for our second session of sweeping. The weather was still turning, and it was warm enough for us to work in shirt sleeves. Sweeping by one edge, I looked off into the distance, imagining the trees gone, the Manhattan skyline gone, and a single tower, hidden in shadow, and from it a red beam burning into the distant gray clouds.

As the days went by, and we all grew better with the cylinder, some nervousness went away. With your cylinder in place, you knew you had time to think and react. With your cylinder in place, it was as if time slowed down a little, so you could go through your options and decide how to respond. But it wasn't just responding to attacks we got better at. With the cylinder up, you had a little space in yourself that would soak up all sorts of worries, leaving your head clear, and the rest of you able to think things out. So the cylinder defended us mainly against being distracted. It created a safe zone and left our minds free.

With only a few days before the Alexandria trip, I began to feel confident enough about this and I got an idea. When Dr. Archer was giving magic theory class, I raised my hand. "Can the cylinder protect you from spirits?" I asked. "Or just from live magicians?"

"By the cylinder," said Dr. Archer, "I presume that you are referring to the principle of continuous defense. Maestro Morgan has encouraged you to conceptualize it in cylindrical form. Well enough. I am not certain what you regard to be a live magician, but continuous defense does allow for protection from non-physical attacks, such as you may use in duels with each other. Also, it may give you some warning of an impending physical attack against you."

"But it won't stop a bullet," said Goldberry.

"Continuous defense is not congruent with a force field," said Dr. Archer. "A magician with sufficient experience might respond to being the target of a bullet by an act of misdirection against the sniper."

"Misdirection?" she asked.

"Causing the sniper to fire inaccurately by any number of means. And there are other options for overcoming a foe who is conventionally armed. One cannot halt the trajectory of a bullet, however, by use of continuous defense."

"But does it protect against spirits?" I repeated.

"In certain contexts, protection is afforded. Not in every case." He then resumed his lecture.

That was good enough for me. During our next Memento Analysis class, when the mementos from Israel were laid out, I went to the yellow pile and, trusting my instinct, selected one. Dr. Archer observed me coldly and said nothing.

The memento, a lump of sandstone with a faded symbol on it, was cool in my hand. Studying it, I made sure that it had what I had expected to find: small flecks of the same kind of crystal that composed the large piece I now carried with me all the time. I adjusted my cylinder in my mind, perfecting its shape and its rotation, smoothing its surface. Then I sent a mental greeting to the spirit bound to the memento in my hand.

"Simon Magus," the spirit replied.

I kept calm at the knowledge that the spirit recognized me. I had expected it.

"Suppose that to be my name," I answered. "You must tell me yours."

"I am known as Naqai," said the spirit. "You well know that I am a follower of Yeishu, the Moshiach."

"You're talking about Yeishu ben Pandeira," I said. "Yes, I know him. Did he tell you about me?"

"I know you," answered Naqai, "because I met you myself, many ages ago."

"Where?" I asked.

"Give me your eyes," the spirit said, "and I will show you."

My mind was divided between my struggle with Naqai and the cylinder. I could feel the spirit clawing at the edges of my continuous defense, trying to strip away the smoothness of the cylinder, to crack it, to enter my body and possess it.

"You did not control me those ages ago," I argued. "You will not control me now."

"Sad is your life, Simon Magus. There is much shame for you in days to come."

"I didn't ask you that. I asked you, where did we meet?"

"In Alexandria," responded Naqai.

"Goodbye," I said. I hung up on him and returned to the world.

I opened my eyes and saw Dr. Archer leaning over me. "You were successful," he said, "in contacting this spirit?"

I considered denying it, but he was hard to lie to. "Yes. It's an Alexandrian Jew named Naqai."

"I was not able to contact this spirit," said Dr. Archer. "Perhaps the name will be of some assistance on my next attempt." He extended his hand. I gave him the memento. "Curious," said Dr. Archer, "that you selected this stone to study."

"There was nothing left in the green pile that I hadn't already tried," I said.

"Indeed," said Dr. Archer.

Later that evening, I told Goldberry and Robbie what I had done. "This seems to confirm that we're doing the right thing, going to Alexandria."

"Dude," said Robbie, "I wish I was in your class. I'd love to try that."

"It's really hard," Goldberry said. "I haven't tried the yellow pile yet. Almost no one has, except Simon."

I didn't add anything else, but I knew that I was more than willing to give the whole thing up. I'd never had a choice, though: Yeishu ben Pandeira had begun haunting me from the moment I entered the school.

*

The blow fell at lunchtime the following day. The cafeteria was full of students eating and talking. I was sitting with Goldberry and Leah when I felt a push against my cylinder. I turned and saw Donovan Archer standing beside me. It didn't look like Donovan, though. Donovan was calm and quiet; this time, his eyes were wild and fearful.

"Simon Magus," he said. "My master would speak with you. But first, tell me which of these females is Helen? For after two thousand years I cannot recall her features."

Helen was the legendary female disciple of Simon Magus, who claimed to be the reborn Helen of Troy. But I had no time to think about this. I had never seen a person so thoroughly controlled by a spirit. How had this happened to Donovan, a fourth-year student?

"Who are you?" I asked.

"It is Neitzer who speaks," Donovan's voice said. "All of us are here, occupying this form. Mattai, Naqai, Buni, and Todah bid you greeting."

"Well, bloody well get out of there," Goldberry snapped. "That body doesn't belong to you." Her hazel eyes blazed, and I mean it literally. I saw the image of flames where her irises normally were. Whatever she did made Donovan's eyes dart left and right with anxiety, but then he calmed down.

"This is as it should be," answered Donovan in a slightly different tone. Perhaps a different disciple was now speaking through him. "Because we have been so long without physical form, all of us were required to make the effort to dwell within this poor student. You must contact my master."

"You will expose my bargain with your master," I said. "You possess a person with powerful friends, and you have come to a public place. We will be noticed soon. Get out."

"This form suits me, at present," said a voice more like Naqai's. "I shall not leave it." Then his eyes snapped directly to Leah, who was praying in a language I had not heard before.

"No female may pray in this manner," Naqai whined.

Donovan's expression changed. "You must stop," said a deeper voice. "Contact the master."

"First, get out of the body you are possessing," I commanded.

Donovan's body got up and ran out of the dining room. I ran out after him, but once he had turned a corner ahead of me, I lost him. The girls came up behind me after a few moments.

"Donovan is holding all the mementos," Goldberry said. "That's why it was so hard to drive those spirits out. Disciples of Yeishu, are they?"

I nodded. "What language was that?" I asked.

"Aramaic," said Leah. "I prayed to Hashem using the name *Havaya Tseva-Ot*, a name that has great power for a true believer. It should have worked, except that there were so many of them all fighting back at once. I'd need more time, or someone to help me. My father could have done it."

We searched the school for Donovan, but couldn't even find anyone who had seen him. As a fourth-year student, he could enter places we weren't permitted or were physically unable to enter or couldn't even see. It was a terrible situation. We hated to see our friend possessed, but even worse, when he was finally located, and his condition discovered, we would be exposed too. It was only a few days from the Alexandria trip, but would it be soon enough?

"Let's go somewhere private," I said.

Leah and I went to my room. Robbie was there, asleep and snoring. Goldberry hung back to look for Donovan a little more.

"Tell me that name again," I asked Leah as I sat on the bed and she sat on a chair.

"*Havaya Tseva-Ot*. But you must be a believer, and you must have a level of understanding."

"I believe in you," I said. "I know it's true because you know it's true."

"It's not the same," she said. "But all faith has value before God."

I took out the crystal and rubbed it gently. "Talk to me," I said into the spirit world.

AT LAST, answered Yeishu ben Pandeira. YOU HAVE MADE ME WAIT MANY MONTHS. I CAN WAIT NO LONGER. I MUST KNOW HOW YOU WILL WIN ME FORGIVENESS.

I'm going back to your time, I thought back. Rabbi Yehoshua is still alive then. I'll ask him to forgive you. I'm keeping my end of the bargain. Then you'll go away, and never haunt me again.

I CAN GIVE YOU POWER, answered the ghost in the crystal. IT IS NOT WISE TO DISMISS ME.

You can't give me power, I answered. The power is mine, and I know its name, *Havaya Tseva-Ot*, and by this name I command you to leave me in peace once I've done what you asked.

THAT NAME SHOULD NOT BE IN YOUR THOUGHTS, answered Yeishu ben Pandeira in what felt like a hiss. YOU DO NOT KNOW ITS MEANING.

I made a bargain with you, and I will keep it, I answered. But by that name, *Havaya Tseva-Ot*, you will never haunt me again.

FOOL, answered Yeishu ben Pandeira. YOU SPEAK THE NAME OF HASHEM UNTO HIS PROPHET? AND YOU BELIEVE YOU WILL FRIGHTEN ME?

Good-bye, I thought.

I came back to our world, and found one of my hands on the crystal, and the other in Leah's. She was touching my cheek with her own free hand.

"You're bleeding," she said.

I felt tears on my cheeks. No, not tears. I was bleeding from my eyes.

"We'll win," she said. "All of us together. We'll win."

I lifted her hand to my lips and kissed it. "I love you," I said.

"I would love you back," she said, "if we had time."

Final Preparations

Two days before the time travel trip, there was still no sign of Donovan, and no word from Dr. Archer either. Perhaps no one noticed because of the excitement all over the school from the second year up, and grumbling from first-years about being stuck in the building. All school lessons were connected to the place and time, to make sure we knew either what to do or, for first-years, what we were missing.

Here are some things I heard, overheard, or heard rumours about as the trip got closer.

1) Kids were going to steal the bones of Alexander the Great from his tomb.
2) Some kid was going to go around and ask everyone he met, "Are you a Hyksos?"
3) There were plans to take digital camera photos of various things, even though the Dean warned us that time travel destroyed just about every kind of recording device.
4) A group of kids were going to copy the lost plays of Sophocles, in Greek, from the Library of Alexandria
5) Getting drunk on unmixed Greek wine came up a lot.
6) One boy wanted to be his own ancestor by … well, as often as he could

7) Plenty of kids wanted to mark things so they could go back to 2001 and see if their marks had lasted
8) Bringing home Roman coins was permitted, so lots of kids planned that.
9) Taking soil samples for scientific analysis was on a few people's list.
10) Taking water samples was on the list, too.
11) One of the girls was going to try to find out if dinosaurs were still alive in that time.
12) A few kids said they were going to see the Great Pyramid and the Sphinx, and couldn't seem to grasp that the Valley of the Kings was too far from Alexandria for one day's travel.
13) A group was scheduled to climb to the top of the Pharos, the Lighthouse.
14) It wasn't allowed to bring home a mummified cat or crane, but some kids thought they could still pull it off.
15) It was allowed to buy kohl (Egyptian makeup) for girlfriends or mothers.

Mermelstein was our source of information about planning in AAC. From him we mainly needed to learn if there were plans for groups to go to the Jewish quarter. Such groups might see us and perhaps interfere.

Ancient Alexandria, we had learned in class, had one of the largest Jewish communities in the ancient world. And the time when Egyptians had enslaved Jews was already centuries past. Under Roman rule, Jews often enjoyed advantages under law – such as exemption from the Roman state religion – because their skill at business made them good for the economy of the Empire. Here, in fact, was one of the historical roots of European anti-Semitism, said Professor Bright.

He described the resentment of Pagan Romans against Jews for their political advantages and connection to the wealthy classes.

Professor Bright also reminded us that the Egyptians of that time were not Arabs or Muslims. Arabs as a people came from the Arabian peninsula and hadn't yet spread so far west. There were no Muslims, just as there were no Christians, because those religions hadn't been founded yet. In the time we were visiting, Jesus might be alive, hundreds of miles away, but Mohammed's birth was more than 600 years away. Dr. Chatterjee added in Magic Theory class that Hindu faith was already millennia old and had helped to shape Jewish mysticism. The Cabala school kids went and complained to their other teachers about this claim.

Anyway, with Alexandria's Jewish community being so large, the Cabala students were definitely interested to go there. However, Mermelstein, who was well-connected, said no one had made the connection we had, and no one was looking for Rabbi Yehoshua ben Perachyah. We would have to keep our eyes peeled while we were there, but we had at least a shot at going undetected.

We had decided to dress in simple robes with hoods, except for me in the beaver pelt coat. Under our robes would be light summer clothing. None of us would feel or look comfortable in the actual clothing of the place and time. Each of us would carry a staff, and the girls would keep covered, disguised as males for as long as possible. The job of putting the outfits together was given to Robbie and the girls.

The day before the trip, we did our last stint sweeping the roof. With all the dust and garbage from the city, it was just as dirty every time we went up there, and we worked steadily without making much of an impact, even though we had help this time – some older kids also being punished by Mr. Bannerjee. During our breaks, we looked at the Manhattan skyline on one side, and downtown Brooklyn on the other side, and imagined instead the calm, dark seas of the Mediterranean, and stars overhead, two thousand years older than the ones we knew.

It was hard to sleep that night, unless you were Robbie. Annoyed by his snoring, I went out to wander the hallways, trying to decide what I would do and say in Alexandria. We had a map I'd downloaded and printed from the Internet over the holiday, although it was a modern map of the ancient city and might not be accurate. We knew where in the city the Jewish neighbourhood was, but our route would depend upon where the school was when we reached the past, and no one who knew that information was willing to share it.

I turned a corner and nearly crashed into Dr. Archer.

"Simon," he said. "I meant to speak to you. Let's go to the dining hall."

Saying nothing, I followed him. I didn't want to lie to Dr. Archer. In fact, I wasn't sure I could. I had only been hoping to avoid him. Now, at the last minute, I had failed.

We sat in the dining hall. There were a lot of kids up and having late-night snacks or talking. Dr. Archer got an orange from the fresh fruit basket and split it for us to eat as we talked.

"I finally found Donovan," he said. "You saw him recently?"

"Yes."

"And were you aware that he was possessed?"

"Yes."

"But you didn't tell me about it?"

"We tried to cast out the spirits ourselves."

"I see." Dr. Archer didn't seem angry, or even hurt. He was just analyzing my responses. "Then you knew that there were three spirits possessing him."

"I knew there were several. Spirits lie, so..."

Dr. Archer nodded. "Spirits lie. These are very deceptive. They claim to be the disciples of Jesus."

I paused. Was Dr. Archer testing me, to see if I would correct his misstatements? Or was he actually not clear on what was happening?

"In fact," said Dr. Archer, "I am partially responsible for what happened to Donovan. I asked him to investigate several of the mementos. I was concerned because one memento is missing. I thought perhaps these spirits knew what happened to it. Then they began naming students in our class, blaming almost all of them for the theft. They must have taken information about the class from Donovan's memory."

I nodded. "Then...they included me?"

"No," said Dr. Archer. "None of the first-year students were mentioned. But all the same, I wished to warn everyone in the class that there are mementos in the collection too dangerous for a student to handle. I warned you of this before, but teenagers are notoriously difficult to convince. Now at least, I have evidence to support my assertion."

"How's Donovan?"

"He has lost some memory," Dr. Archer said, "and he's hungry. The spirits didn't let him eat. After a night's sleep, however, he should be well enough to go on the trip tomorrow. But tell me something else, Simon."

I waited for the question.

"Is it true that you have repaired your relationship with Yakov

Mermelstein?"

"I think so."

He nodded gravely. "To achieve Rabbi Mermelstein's intention to civilize his son, it was necessary to bring him together with a stronger magician of his own age. I wasn't certain whether to use you in this context, but the Dean decided that the second interview appointments would coincide. I believe I should thank you, on behalf of Rabbi Aharon."

"I don't understand. I'm not stronger than Mermelstein. He can do a lot of things I can't do, with his knowledge of Cabala."

"I am not referring to you, Simon. Nevertheless, whenever the students I sponsor are of use to friends of the school such as Rabbi Mermelstein…" He trailed off. "Well, I must go. I still need to find Dempsey."

When he was gone, strangely enough, I felt better. I was relieved that Donovan was okay, assuming that all four of the spirits had been driven out of him, even if Dr. Archer only mentioned three. Either my advisor didn't know what I had been up to, or he was letting it happen for some reason. I felt that I was going to be able to go ahead the next day without worrying about being stopped.

I woke up a few minutes after falling asleep. Who was the stronger magician Mermelstein had been brought into contact with?

"My God," I whispered. "Leah. He meant Leah. But..."

I heard a grinding noise. It was far off, echoing, loud. It was kind of like a car starting, magnified a thousand times. It went on for several minutes, then died down, becoming a steady chug, and then a hum. A cold wind blew across my face. That was impossible, since I was inside a stone building, but it happened. Then came a hot wind, and then a cold, alternating, hot and cold, hot and cold.

Finally it was just a slow, steady hot wind.

I rolled out of bed and hit Robbie in the stomach. "Wake up. We're doing it."

"We're what?"

"We're traveling in time. Right now."

H.O.L.

When we were dressed and out in the hall, there was a real crush of kids headed for the staircase toward the roof. We couldn't get to the top, though – something was holding up the kids in front of us.

"Come on, man," Robbie whined. "I want to see what's going on."

"Maybe you can't be outside the building when it time-travels," I suggested.

"You can't," said an older student. I finally recognized Shifrin, who was pressed up against the stone wall above us in the staircase.

"Why? What happens to you?" Robbie asked.

"What, you think anyone wants to find out?"

Shifrin had a point. We waited, pressed up against the walls, sweating. After a long while, there was a disturbance in the hallway below the stairs. The kids started to clear out of the way, making room for a teacher, I thought. Finally a small figure in a hooded robe came partway up the steps, by chance stopping right by me. The hood came down – it was Ms. Roosevelt-Wilson, the registrar. She was probably there because no one else was available, I thought, not liking the annoyed look on her face.

"Don't gather here. You were told not to do this," she snapped.

"By who?" one of the yeshiva boys shouted.

"By whom," she corrected. "Now make a path. Let me get to the door." She brandished a large bronze key as she made her way up the dim staircase. Now I was beginning to smell something besides the body odour of sweaty kids. I was smelling sea air. It was cleaner and fresher than the sea air dockside in New York. I could smell the warmth and the sunlight in it.

Light and more salt air streamed down the stairway. The kids almost trampled each other climbing to the. roof. As I passed, I noticed Ms. Roosevelt-Wilson pressed against the wall by the door, looking miserable. I gave her a sympathetic glance. She looked at me with a twisted smile and rolled her eyes.

Finally I came up into the sunlight. It was early morning, and the sky was crimson, pumpkin-orange, colours I'd never seen in the sky before. With the sea air came the smell of fish, and the calls of seabirds. From the top of the stairs, I followed the rush of kids to the eastern edge of the roof.

We were on one tip of an island surrounded by ocean. From the east battlement of the school, I saw the Pharos, the Lighthouse, at once. It looked to be a mile or so away. There was nothing near it anywhere close in size, so I saw the whole structure, from the pillared turret, smoldering and smoking, with the statue on top, to the cylindrical central shaft, topped by battlements, to the nearly rectangular, broadening fortress base, all shining sandy-pale and orange in the morning sun. It was set on an irregularly-shaped beach and surrounded by a square, columned structure that could have been a fortress or a temple with its mix of columns and windows. As I watched, dots that were people and carts moved in and out of the lighthouse's outer structure and onto a brown road that wound along a narrow peninsula to join the larger island of Pharos.

"In the evening, just before we leave," said Ms. Roosevelt-Wilson, sounding bored, "many of us may wish to congregate here on the roof to observe the light of the Pharos at its height. To our north is the Mediterranean, to our southeast the Great Harbor, to our southwest the greater part of the island of Pharos. If you go to the south side of the building and overlook the Egyptian village, the largest structures you will see will be the Temple of Isis, and the Roman-built fortification which guards the Heptastadion, the mole leading to the mainland."

A mole, I remembered from history class, was a road constructed by piling rocks and dirt into water until they topped the surface. It was a laboriously constructed artificial island, used as a bridge. Since the school had put down on the island of Pharos, everyone going into the city would have to cross over the mole to get into the city.

There was no time, though, to explore. Tearing myself away from the Pharos, I roamed over the roof, gathering up my team, except for Mermelstein, who gestured that he would meet us downstairs. Goldberry had come sleepily up the stairs, yawning and holding Goodenough's elbow. As Robbie, Leah, and I approached, he said, "Poor children. Leaving already? If you can't go explore, you can't even stand to look, can you?"

"You missed the trips last year, Goodenough," I said.

He winked at me. "Are you sure?"

"See you downstairs in a tick," said Goldberry. "Just going to look at the Lighthouse a bit."

*

"This is as close to Egyptian clothes as we can get," Mermelstein said. "They're extra clothes from the supply at my school. I brought the hooded robes with Egyptian cotton. The girls should not show their faces or arms in the Jewish Quarter."

"It looks fine," said Leah.

"I'm going to wear this," I said, taking out my beaver coat.

"It's too hot," Mermelstein said. "That's for below freezing weather."

"No, this coat feels good in every weather."

"That's the magic coat," Robbie said. "Roomie, I'm disappointed you didn't show it to me before the cruise. Where'd you get it?"

"My mother," Goldberry said. "It's not his fault. The coat is designed to be forgotten except when you need it. You forget you have it for months at a time. Until I saw it in Simon's hand, I forgot it existed. Maybe my mother did, too, till she needed a gift for him."

I hadn't heard any of this before. Apparently there were things about the coat Goldberry hadn't remembered until she needed to say them.

"Anyway I got us something else," Robbie said, changing the subject quickly. "In the broom closet off the gym."

The gym was empty except for an older girl we didn't know, shooting baskets. Everyone was dressing up and going out, so she had no reason to be suspicious of our outfits, and she ignored us. In the broom closet, mixed with the brooms, were a half-dozen staffs, long wooden rods, polished smooth, painted red, green, orange, purple, bigger at one end than the other.

"Stylish," said Goldberry, rolling her eyes.

"They look like pool cues," I said.

"Yeah, well," said Robbie. "But I did all the rituals and stuff like Rabbi Horn taught."

"I didn't know there was a pool table at School of the Ages," I added.

"Well, actually…"

"Never mind," said Goldberry. Everyone took a staff, and we left one behind.

"I have something for us," Leah said. She went into the closet. In the blackest shadows of the corner she groped, as if she could not remember where she had left the object. Finally she came out holding a large leather satchel. Inside were five denim canteens, each sloshing with water.

"I never saw that in there," Robbie protested. "I was in there this morning."

Leah didn't reply, but handed each of us a canteen.

"We shouldn't need food," I said. "We want to get where we're going and back fast. As for the other things we have to remember – the three principles. Continuous defense, no one gets caught without a chance to react. Universal language for conversation, but avoid talking too much because we'll look and sound strange. Stay by Leah and Mermelstein for translating Hebrew writing. Latin, Greek, and Hieroglyphics, Egyptian writing, we just have to get around. Last principle, concealment. No one should see us except who we talk to. If we need to talk secretly, use English. English did not even exist at that time, so no one can possibly understand it."

"Okay," said Robbie. "Let's go."

We had decided to try the roof first. Again, with the hoods up, no one knew who we were anyway. I went up first to scout. I knew where the rungs for the rope ladder were, but there was no chance of going down that way. At least a dozen kids, mostly kids we knew, were hanging out on the roof, and there were also some teachers who knew us, including Rabbi Mendy and Dr. Lehman.

I climbed back down. "We'll have to go the other way." We lit candles and headed downstairs.

Fortunately, the halls weren't crowded. Kids were either headed out of the building exploring, or on the roof. Still, we got lost in the dark corridors searching for the secret exit. At last we found the small wooden door with the round sign on it. The sign read "H.O.L." The door was padlocked. The lock was hard, heavy, dusty, and slightly rusted. A planter full of dirt stood nearby. There was no plant. I jiggled the lock. It didn't budge.

"Ideas?" I asked.

"A hammer," Robbie said.

"A hammer won't open that lock," said Mermelstein. "You'd need a bomb."

I studied the padlock. A broad metal latch was affixed to the door and the doorframe. The padlock closed the latch.

"Can we get the latch off instead of opening the lock?" I asked. I studied it and could answer my own question. The latch was bolted to the door. The bolts were in solidly. I felt stupid. We should have checked out the door in advance and planned how we were going to open the lock.

"Get a fire spirit to melt the metal," said Robbie.

"Do you have one in your pocket?" said Mermelstein.

"Wait a tick," said Goldberry. "I've a feeling there's a key nearby."

"Why?"

"I saw a key in my morning tea leaves," she said

"There," said Leah. She looked at the planter.

Mermelstein and I began to dig in the soil.

"Start at the bottom," said Leah.

Mermelstein ignored her, but I sank my hands to the bottom and began breaking up cold clumps of soil. No luck.

"Dump it out," said Robbie.

"Only if you clean it up," Mermelstein snapped.

"No," Leah said. "You don't have to dump it out."

"It's not in here," I said. The soil was getting under my nails.

"I know," said Goldberry. "Stand back, you two."

We did. Goldberry tilted the planter slightly and felt along the underside. She peeled off a piece of duct tape and found a padlock key underneath.

"Oy gevalt," said Mermelstein.

"A bomb indeed," said Goldberry. "I suppose whoever is in charge of the door keeps an extra key handy for emergencies." She took the key to the padlock and fit it in smoothly, turned, and the lock snapped open. "Easy enough, when you aren't a bloody idiot."

Robbie and I nudged the door open with a slow, steady creak. There was no light on the other side. Our candles showed a stone floor, bare walls, and a small wooden table. There might have been a door on the far side, but it wasn't clear. The candles weren't shedding light as far into the room as they should have been.

Something on the table was twitching. The shadowy thing wasn't visibly shifting its position, but we could hear its dry scratching sounds on the surface of the wood.

I felt again as I had felt at Lake Okanagan months ago: it was like I was falling into a new, distant world. The magic in this room was strong, beyond daily experience, even for a magician.

"What is that?" asked Robbie. He held up his handle, shedding light on the table.

"It's H.O.L.," said Goldberry. She stepped in, and I followed.

It was a hat, one of those triangular hats like you see in pictures of Robin Hood, but made of a red and green tartan fabric like a

Scotsman's kilt. It was definitely twitching.

"Everyone get inside," Mermelstein said, obeying himself. "Shut the door. We can't leave it open for long."

He was right. So far as we knew, no one came much to this part of the school, but leaving the door open would attract the attention of anyone who passed by.

"We'll leave the lock inside by the door," I said.

The moment the door shut, the hat leapt off the table and bounced off Mermelstein's head, loosening his yarmulke. He tried to swat it and missed. Next it smacked into Goldberry's head, then Robbie's. He caught it. It jerked and shook in his hand, but he held on and went to put it on the table.

Leah was moving around to the far side of the room, looking for another door. As Robbie set the hat down on the table, he noticed there were two hats in his hand.

"What the heck?" he said.

The first hat jumped off the table at my head and nearly poked me in the eye. I smacked it away.

Now there were two hats, plus the one on the table. One hat jumped at me, the other at Goldberry. I dodged, and she jumped, and the hats hit the floor, and now there were five. No, six, when Mermelstein punched away the one Robbie had put on the table.

"If we hit them, or they fall, they duplicate," Goldberry said.

"A magic like this, I never heard of," said Mermelstein.

Hats were now leaping at all of us except Leah. Whether we struck back or not, they hit the floor and doubled.

"No wonder this room was locked," Robbie said. "What a messed-up curse."

Before long, the room would be filled with bouncing hats. If you touched one, it doubled. If you didn't, it jumped at you, and wherever it landed, it doubled. We could expect the room to be so full of hats that we couldn't move, squeezing us and crushing us like in a garbage compactor.

"Can we burn them?" Robbie asked.

"With what?" snapped Mermelstein. "Candles?"

"I'll try to summon a…"

"Summon something with this going on?" Goldberry growled. "Are you mad?"

"No, I…" A tartan Robin Hood hat struck him on the cheek and fell as two hats and landed as four hats.

Someone needed to think it out. I stepped back to the wall and put up the hood of my beaver coat and put my hands in my pockets. Being in the coat was like crawling into a dark safe space where no one could see me and no one could touch me. The noise and bouncing hats didn't bother me.

There must be a way to get rid of the hats, I thought, because if you touch them they multiply. Is there a way to touch them that will make them keep still? How do you get a hat to keep still?

I imagined discussing it with Dr. Archer.

Simon: How do you get a hat to keep still?

Dr. Archer: In what capacity? Still as in unmoving? Or unchanging?

Simon: Unmoving.

Dr. Archer: Then do not move it. Is this a riddle? Or perhaps a metaphor. What does "hat" signify in this context?

Simon: What?

But how could Dr. Archer say in my imagination something I couldn't understand? I realized, to my regret, that I wasn't imagining his voice.

Dr. Archer: Where are you, Simon?

Simon: It's a metaphor. It's…

Dr. Archer: I cannot assist you. I am miles away and have others in my care.

Simon: Are we speaking telepathically?

Dr. Archer: Yes. We are not merely thought-trading. I sense that you are using some magical object to empower this action. Again, you must at once tell me your location.

Simon: No, no, that's all right. I think I have it.

I put down the hood of the coat. Dr. Archer was gone from my head, but I had a new idea. Not a moment too soon: my friends were knee-deep in hats, their faces covered, except for Leah, whom I couldn't see.

"Put one on," I called.

"It might turn one of us into a hat," protested Mermelstein.

"You'd look better that way," said Goldberry. "Easier to wash." Trusting me, she grabbed a hat and pulled it on tightly. It seemed to be tugging itself off her head, almost knocking her over, but then it crumbled into dust.

"Good one," Robbie said. He grabbed a hat in each hand and put both on, one over the other.

We kept on that way, and gradually the number of hats in the room diminished. A solid forty-five minutes later, we were covered with tartan-coloured dust, but down to one hat, which was in Robbie's hand.

"Destroy it," Mermelstein said.

"They saved the thing for a reason," I said. "Just put it on the table where it was."

Alexandria

The outer door we left unlocked. As with the inner door, we had to hope that no one noticed, or that if they did, they blamed it on other kids. From there we had to make our way around the school building without being noticed. School of the Ages had sensibly been placed away from other buildings, on a solid beach, and there was a field of tall yellow crabgrass nearby. Using that as cover, we got away from the school without anyone on the roof reacting to our movements. Again, wearing hooded cloaks, it wasn't obvious who we were, unless you had seen my beaver-pelt coat, which, except for Balaram, no one on the roof had.

Walking east through the crabgrass and reeds, we found a dirt path headed into the village. After about twenty minutes this path met a paved Roman road, and the smell of sea air became mixed with other, less pleasant odours: manure, maybe, or worse.

Soon we saw some people for the first time – two Egyptian men driving an ox-cart. They were very dark, with shaved heads, wearing lightweight white skirts, with straps going over their shoulders. The ox was white and had twisted horns. Our power of concealment worked, and they didn't notice us. Then we saw more and more Egyptians. Most of the men looked about the same as the first two we saw. The women were a little more covered, in the same white linen, but cut in dresses that covered their breasts and the tops of their arms and left their shoulders exposed. Children dressed pretty much like their parents. The dirt road ran into a village made of sun-dried brick houses. Instead of doors and curtains, they had large reed mats hanging over all the openings. I was surprised to see that the buildings were two or three stories high, like the house I lived in.

The school maps had told us about this Egyptian village. We needed to go through it and keep heading south. If we passed the Temple of Isis, we were going right and would soon reach the Heptastadion, the bridge to the mainland.

None of us knew what the temple of Isis would look like, but as we walked unnoticed through the village, trying not to be distracted by the smell and the flies, we looked for a more impressive building, and soon saw one – taller than the surrounding houses and shops. It had a high front porch area with a rectangle of brightly painted pillars, amidst which some better-dressed Egyptians were mingling. The men had jewels on their belts, and the women wore flowing white cloaks over their shoulders.

We knew better than to stay near the temple, since other School of the Ages kids might be exploring there, so we kept moving, headed for the Heptastadion. The plan was to try to walk right near a group of people or a large wagon, and blend in with them if possible. As we mixed in with larger groups of Egyptians, I noticed how sweet they smelt, rubbed down with perfumes and scented oils. It was hard to accept how much obvious makeup they wore, including the eye makeup of the men. Some children were running around naked.

We reached the Heptastadion. It was like a big dirt road, very crowded with Egyptians and also with a few Romans in white and purple, as well as their slaves in simpler white knee-length shirts.

Most people were headed into the city, not onto the island. We easily blended into the dense crowds, keeping to the center of the southbound traffic so we wouldn't be pushed too close to the water. We didn't see anyone from school, but they were using the power of concealment, too, so we wouldn't notice them unless we were specifically trying to or knew them well.

There was a glut of wagons and pedestrians where the mole touched the mainland, making it harder to concentrate on concealment. Finally we got through and onto a road made of paved stones. There were more stone buildings here, with smooth walls and columns covered with bright paint. We also saw more Romans and other foreigners mixed in with the Egyptians. Consulting Robbie's compass, we located east and started in that direction. We tried to pass midway between the crowded, smelly dock area along the coast and the crowded, extra-smelly market square that began right where the Heptastadion ended. The sea-air smell had been replaced by the mixed odours of animals, cooking food, perfume, and dung. Eventually we wound up on a large paved road which our maps told us was Canopic Street. It was one of the most important routes through Alexandria and ran east-west the full length of the city between the Moon Gate on the west side, and the Canopic Gate to the east. Most of the tourist attractions, for the people of the time as well as for School of the Ages students, were north of Canopic Street, so if we stayed there, we had a good chance of not being seen by our schoolmates as they crowded to the Library, the Museum, Cleopatra's Needle, and so on. After a couple of miles, with all of us getting very tired and footsore and tapping our canteens often, we reached a large intersection with a north-south street I had forgotten the name of.

....

Professor Bright had told us that the old Roman maps of Alexandria were considered to be very accurate, if full of lacunae (that is gaps), so we were trying to stick to them as long as possible and not risk asking for directions. We could all use universal language, but all of us could lose concentration or forget, and we didn't want to attract attention. At one point Robbie slipped between two buildings and refilled his canteen from a large bottle of spring water he had been carrying inside his robe. I was worried he was going to leave it in the street and create a major crisis in archaeology, but he saved the bottle to throw away back in 2001.

At last we saw signs that we were entering the Jewish settlement. We saw bearded men wearing what was basically a double set of robes, the first like a long nightshirt, the second a cloth jacket with floppy sleeves. They had blue belts and were wearing trapezoidal hats. The women were also covered in white cloth and had their heads wrapped in scarves.

"It's time to take the risk and ask someone," I told my team. We had agreed that Mermelstein would do this. He was a lot paler, didn't have much beard, but he looked enough like the people on the street not to attract too much attention. He nodded and approached a wealthy-looking Jewish man and asked, in Hebrew he had prepared in advance to resemble the Hebrew of the Torah, where to find Rabbi Yehoshua ben Perachyah. We hoped his pronunciation was okay, since Hebrew had changed little from Biblical times to modern.

Mermelstein came back to us sweaty and annoyed. "He told me where to go," he said, "but I didn't understand him. He doesn't pronounce right, and what are those places he said?"

"Use universal language," I told him.

"Oh, all right." It had been a point of pride for Mermelstein to get directions with the Hebrew he actually knew, but he let it go and went to try again with another man in the street. Meanwhile, Leah went and asked a girl carrying a jug of wine on her shoulder. I figured it was wine because I saw some slosh out.

Between them, my teammates got us directions to a synagogue. We had to take a lot of smaller paths, some narrow and twisting, amidst buildings made, like those of the Egyptians, of mud bricks. Children and donkeys moved across our path. These children were fully dressed. The smells of cooking food reminded me of how hungry I was.

Finally we came out of an alley between two houses and reached a public square. The synagogue could clearly be identified by its higher, smoother walls, broad wooden doors (the first wood we'd seen in a while) and carvings of the Star of David. We stepped up to the doors and were about to push them open when they opened from inside, and two men in colorful robes stood in the doorway, blocking us.

"This is a house of faith," said the older of the two, a gray-bearded man. "What is your business here?"

"I am Simon," I answered. I was still clumsy with universal language, and must have sounded foreign or stupid to him. "I have come to see the great rabbi, Yehoshua ben Perachyah."

"Come from foreign parts," said the younger bearded man. "Why should he speak to you?"

I could barely think about my answer. I was too excited. The plan was working! The man was actually here!

"I come humbly to ask help from a man of God. I am not from foreign parts. My journey began on the Isle of Pharos."

"Humbly? Dressed in skins like a wild man, with a staff of many colours? And you hide your face also."

"I hide my face because there are people in the city who would stop me. I will show it to the rabbi."

"Simon," said the older man. "Not the heretic Simon Magus? For he and other heretics have been known to lay challenges at the feet of great *rebbeim* in the past."

"Some have called me by that name, and I have used it, but it is not my real name. I have come not to challenge anyone, but to ask the rabbi for forgiveness."

The men stepped back into the shadows and held a whispered conference. Then they returned to the threshold again. "You may not enter."

I turned to my companions and said in English, "How do you want to work this?"

"We could beg them," Robbie said.

"Or knock them down," Mermelstein added.

"Or we can distract them, and you sneak in," said Goldberry.

"Guys," said Leah, "Coming up behind us…"

We turned. I saw a group of six men in simple robes and sandals, their arms and legs free, their heads covered with black yarmulkes. Their beards were scraggly, and they looked dusty. Their eyes were a little crazy, especially those of the leader. All the men were young, but he was the oldest at about thirty, and his eyes were commanding, Olive brown, they carried a mix of wildness and wisdom. "Neitzer, Todah, Buni, stand ready," he said. "Mattai, Naqai, stand close to me."

The temple doors slammed. These men were even less welcome than we were, and my group was alone, confronted by theirs.

"It couldn't be," Robbie said.

"Stand aside, heretic," the leader challenged.

"Look who's talking," I answered. "I know you, Yeishu ben Pandeira."

"Foreign sorcerer, you do not belong here. In the name of the Lord, be gone from this place."

"I'll go when I've accomplished what I came for," I answered. "I'm not your friend, Yeishu, but I know you well, and I've come here to help you."

"You lie like a serpent," Yeishu barked. "For are you not Simon Magus, the lying magician who is cast out of each town for his false teachings?"

"I'm Simon," I answered. "And through my knowledge of the future, I know that after your death, your spirit will be restless, because Rabbi Yehoshua ben Perachyah has not forgiven you. I am here to win you his forgiveness."

"And they will march you around for forty days," said Mermelstein, "and a herald will go in front of you, proclaiming you a treasonous deceiver."

"And on Pesach eve, you will be stoned to death," Leah added. Her voice was quiet, but it seemed to echo. I loved that about her.

"The end of your life will suck," Robbie said in English. Goldberry kicked him in the foot.

"Liars!" he spat. "False people! I am come to forgive Rabbi Yehoshua for rejecting my guidance."

"Good luck with that," Goldberry snorted.

"Of course," said a follower, a short man with heavy brows whose voice I recognized from his possession of Donovan Archer. "The heretic keeps women with him as acolytes and whores."

"Shut your mouth, Mattai!" I shouted at him.

"Is this not the whore Helen, reborn spirit of the whore of Troy?"

Mattai snapped. 'Look, he has two females with him."

"They are my friends and companions," I said, hoping Goldberry wouldn't blow up at him. "This is Helen." I reached back and squeezed a hand – Leah's. Tiny and soft and gentle, it still gave me strength.

"Whore," said Yeishu.

"She is not," said Mermelstein, "and the other is not either."

I thanked Mermelstein in English.

Yeishu drew himself up and held forth a trembling hand. "Stand aside, foreign wizard, and begone!" he hissed. "Get behind me, serpent!"

He was strong-willed, and his command might have beaten me, if I had never met him before. However, I had known him for a long time, and had him living basically inside my mind, and I was practiced in resisting him.

"No," I said. "I'll go when I'm finished here. You can wait outside, or just leave. You should go, Yeishu. I'm only here to help you."

Yeishu paused, maybe reconsidering. "It is said," he rumbled, "that Simon Magus seeks to win followers and their money by trickery and magic."

"That has been said," I answered. "But the Simon Magus who stands before you acts only to help others."

"It has been said that Simon Magus falsely claims that his power comes from the Lord."

"All power comes from God," I said. "And haven't you claimed the same thing yourself?"

"For me it is true."

"It's also true for me, and everyone else."

"But," he said, "the Lord speaks to me. Not to you?"

"Not the way you mean," I said. "But I don't know a better way to explain things than to talk about God."

"Then we must be tested against one another," he said calmly, "to learn who is favored in the eyes of the Lord."

"Oh, please," Goldberry snapped. She had been listening to us babble for too long. "We don't care about that. We just need to see Rabbi Yehoshua."

"I will not permit it," Ycishu declared.

A magical battle between my team and his could turn out badly. They were older, and outnumbered us by one, so if they really knew magic, they might easily beat us. The Biblical confrontation between Simon Magus and the disciples of Jesus had not gone well for Simon, and this one might be just as bad for the false Simon, me.

"What do you think, guys?" I asked in English.

"Fight," said Mermelstein.

"Fight," said Robbie.

I waited for the girls.

"We have to fight," Leah said, very softly. I didn't like the sadness in her voice.

I looked to Goldberry.

"Oh, all right," she said.

In one coat pocket I had my toy bug. I slipped it into my hand, scanned the disciples, found Mattai, and threw a handful of beetles at his face. He fell to one knee, scraping at his cheeks and eyebrows.

"Peace, brother," said Yeishu. He raised his staff over Mattai's head. Mattai stopped groping, but kept his head bowed. He was out of the fight, but not for long, I thought.

"Let's fight," I said.

....

Team vs. Team

"Yakov," I said, "Attack them like when you fought me."

"Good idea," he said.

He said something under his breath and gestured at Buni, the tallest of the disciples. Watching it happen, instead of feeling it myself, I kind of imagined Mermelstein being *Darth Vader.* Like, "Where are the Death Star plans, *apikoros*?" Funny how you get thoughts like that at really dangerous moments.

One by one my team went with simple attacks they'd picked up at school. Todah's robe started burning along the trailing edge. That was something Robbie had learned from a fire elemental he'd summoned. Goldberry was doing against Naqai the trick to suck energy out of your enemy that we'd learned from Dr. Chatterjee. I remembered that it wasn't very useful, and wished she knew something better.

I don't know what Leah did, but one disciple, Neitzer, who had a dirty beard, dropped to his knees, sobbing. As for me, I threw my bug attack right at Yeishu himself.

None of our attacks worked well. Buni just closed his eyes and shook off Mermelstein's choke. Todah kicked his robes until the fire went out. Goldberry lost her concentration, and Naqai laughed. Neitzer got to his feet, rubbing tears from his eyes. And Yeishu didn't feel my bug trick at all. I should have known – he'd already protected

Mattai from it.

Our first tries had failed. I remembered, again, as Mattai stepped beside his leader, that they outnumbered us, so if they counter-attacked, one of us was going to be hit extra-hard. That would of course be the leader, me. I preferred it that way, but I needed to keep my head clear so I could help the rest of the team.

I put my hood up, using the magic of the beaver-pelt coat to clear my mind of distractions. Then I mentally strengthened my cylinder. I did that just in time, because an image of leaping flames came into my thoughts. There was no fire in front of me: it was a psychic attack by Yeishu. Still, if I hadn't been ready to defend, I would have felt the pain of being burned. The flames ate away at my cylinder of continuous defense. It got worse. Mattai also threw the image of fire at me, and he and his master wreathed me in flames, burning away my cylinder from both sides.

I had to focus on defending against this attack, and I couldn't help my team, but with the added mental stability the coat gave me, I could at least look and see how they were doing. I saw that Robbie and Leah were unaffected by the fire attacks of their adversaries, but Mermelstein was sweating, and Goldberry was hugging herself with pain. Someone, perhaps Naqai, was torturing my beautiful partner! I wanted to rush him, to beat him with my fists, but the calmer part of my mind told me I couldn't afford to lose control of myself. To my relief, Leah went and took her arm and held her close, protecting her.

I was holding off the attack, but I needed to do better. I had to stop Yeishu and Mattai. I closed my eyes and envisioned my cylinder. A lot of it had burned away, and the flames were close to me now. I envisioned the outer surface of the cylinder turning to stone, stone so hard and cold that nothing could burn or melt it. In my mind's eye,

I pushed this rock surface outward, forcing the fire further from me. Then I imagined cold water, the chilly front of a Long Beach wave at high tide, coming up from behind me and rushing forward over the paving stones and splashing all around the fire, extinguishing it.

Yeishu and Mattai were strong, especially together, and my wave kept burning away as it crashed against them. But finally they gave up, and the fire went away, and I opened my eyes.

There was steam in the air. The fire and the water weren't real, but there was steam. I hadn't expected any part of the battle to show in the real world. Neither had Yeishu, apparently, because his eyes were wider than before. I decide to try to shake his confidence.

"The fires of Hell won't burn me," I said. "I am Simon Magus."

"You can't burn me either," Robbie said. "I'm a personal friend of Axolotl, the Salamander Knight. So there."

"All men must fear Hell," answered Yeishu, "and especially those who speak with demons."

"Axolotl, the Salamander Knight," Goldberry sneered in English. "Give me a break." She was shaky, though, still hugging herself, remembering the pain. I put my arm around her for a moment.

Both teams drew back at this point to plan some strategy.

"These guys are really too tough for us," I said. "We need to look stronger than we actually are so they back off. We don't really have to win. A tie is fine."

"I'll summon somebody," Robbie said.

"Who?" Mermelstein snapped. "You couldn't summon a rat in a garbage dump."

"Just watch me, big mouth. I know a spirit, I can personally guarantee I have summoned before who exists in this time."

....

"Who?"

"Mr. N. Otis, of course. The South Wind. The Greeks wrote about him centuries before this."

I thought a second. He was easy to summon in our time, because he was a recruiter for School of the Ages. But what was he doing two thousand years earlier? "Go ahead," I said.

Robbie took out some sidewalk chalk and started drawing symbols on the ground and humming. I had never seen him summon before, because I had always halfway thought he was faking and didn't want him to be embarrassed in front of me. But it seemed like he actually knew his business. Soon he was done, except for some quiet humming.

I started to hum in the same way, and my team joined in, even Mermelstein. Soon we felt a slow, hot breeze on our faces. A man was trudging his way up the street toward us. He was wearing flowing silk garments, a turban, and shoes with curled-up toes. He looked a little pudgy. It wasn't Mr. N. Otis. He walked up to our group, gazed nonchalantly down at the chalk symbols, and raised one hand. A breeze brushed over the chalk, smearing the pattern.

"Better not to leave that lying around," he said. I didn't recognize the language, although since he was a spirit, I could understand him.

"You're not N. Otis," said Robbie.

"Notus? No, he is deeper in Africa, spreading a fire in the tall-grassed plain. I am Eurus, East Wind Wanax."

This made sense. He was dressed like a wealthy Persian merchant, as if he had come from the East. The arrival of Eurus had caught the attention of almost everyone in the area, and many men and women were gathered, watching, with superstitious fear in their eyes, to see what would happen.

"These are my enemies," said Robbie, gesturing at Yeishu and his disciples. "The fools doubt the power of my master, Simon Magus. Call up a fierce dust storm so that they will fear his might."

"Who, me?" answered Eurus. "That sounds like my brother Boreas, the North Wind. I'm a slow, hot wind. Anyway, this isn't Scythia, you know."

I studied Eurus. He was stout, red-faced, with a curly black beard. Then I glanced at Yeishu and his followers to see what they were up to. They were now praying and chanting, maybe also summoning something. Whatever they could call would be worse than Eurus.

"Robbie, you better come up with something," I warned.

The East Wind yawned. His hot breath felt like the heat from slowly opening an oven.

"Burn them with stinging sands," Robbie tried.

"What, before midday?" said Eurus.

"Stir the nearby river to overflow its banks."

"Absolutely not! It's not flood season."

"He's bloody lazy," Goldberry said in English. "The East Wind always did have that reputation."

"Don't get me started on the reputation of a half-blood Pict," Eurus drawled at her. He turned back to Robbie. "Now, if you don't have anything sensible for me to do, I'll be on my way. The Seleucids are having chariot races I'd quite like to watch."

"Tell him," said Leah, "to bring back long-forgotten memories, as if at the edge of sleep."

"Can you do that?" Robbie asked Eurus.

"Oh, that's easy," said the East Wind. He raised his hands, palms spread, sucked in a breath, cupped his mouth into a long oval O shaped like a mango, and exhaled slowly. A warm breeze washed over all of us. Eyes drooped, hands fell to sides. "Father," I heard Leah say. Then I fell away, out of Egypt, out of the sun.

I was on my back and couldn't move. My arms and legs were weak and floppy. A heavy blanket lay across me. It was dawn, maybe. The room was full of gray light that crept through the wooden slats surrounding my bed. It wasn't a bed. It was a crib. A shadow passed alongside the crib. A four-legged shadow sat on the rail of the crib. Its eyes glinted. Of course, it was a cat, a huge tabby with long gleaming whiskers. I didn't recognize it. It looked at me and licked its paw and rubbed the paw across its scalp and looked at me.

I was an infant. This cat was big, and it gazed at me with a sort of ironic sadness.

"Unlucky in love," it said in plain English.

I woke up. I was in Egypt. The sun beat down on me. Was that a real memory? Had a cat spoken to me when I was an infant, too young to understand what was happening?

When I had shaken off the dream, I looked around. Mermelstein was completely knocked out. Goldberry was wiping tears. Two of the disciples, Naqai and Buni, were out cold. Yeishu ben Pandeira was shaking. Eurus was gone, like the wind... Well, how else would he leave?

Also, I realized that a crowd had now formed. Men and women in Jewish garments, a few Egyptian labourers and a couple of Roman soldiers, were on the periphery of our fight. Maybe the dream had smitten them too, or maybe not.

Yeishu now straightened. "You are a mighty wizard, Simon Magus," he shouted. "But my power is from the Lord." He raised a big staff, about four feet long, and Mattai and Todah and Neitzer raised theirs, and all of them threw down the staffs, which shook, wriggled, and became huge brown snakes.

"Guys," I said in English. "Got any ideas for snakes?"

"Bigger snakes," said Goldberry.

I nudged Mermelstein, who was still out of it. The snakes were easing across the ground toward us, their heads raised and bobbing, tongues flicking.

"*Oy vey*," Mermelstein said. "Help me." He said a string of words I didn't understand and threw down his staff, and so did Goldberry and Leah, and then I did. All four staffs changed into big green snakes. They rushed at the brown snakes and tangled them. The snakes thrashed together in the dirt and across the cobblestones.

"I would have made a mongoose," Robbie said.

"I didn't know you could do that," I told Mermelstein.

"We all did it," he said. "But it's easier for me here, so close to where Moshe did it centuries ago. Back in Brooklyn, forget it."

There wasn't time for more talk. A rumbling sound was coming from the east, accompanied by shouts and screams from the same direction.

"We have divined your secret enemies, Simon Magus. We have called a terrible foe against you," cried Yeishu. "You must flee."

The rumble got noisier and divided into echoing heavy strides of feet that weren't human. Coming at us from the north were bobbing heads, huge spherical brown and white bodies, scaly back-bent legs, rustling feathers – ostriches, more than a dozen, charging us as if to attack.

Birds, you will remember, have never liked me.

Even a single angry ostrich could probably kick us all to death. Many ostriches were coming.

That sounds funny, doesn't it? Seriously, who would ever expect to be attacked by a gang of ostriches? But their magic had picked up on my vulnerability and had used it against us.

Time does slow down for you when you see danger coming. It seemed like I had a lot of time to think about magical responses to this attack. I went down the list to see if I could accomplish any of them.

1) Kill the ostriches. No, no killers were on my team; we didn't have the right personality to try that kind of magic.

2) Scare the ostriches. Well, how? What do ostriches see, hear, or smell? What scares them?

3) Teleport the ostriches away. No way could my team do that in the first year of magic school.

4) Turn invisible. We knew how to be unnoticed, but only to people who weren't looking for us. The ostriches, and Yeishu's group, knew where we were.

5) Put up a magic wall the ostriches would bounce off. My team might be up to that some day, but not now.

6) Run away. No, outrunning ostriches was impossible without a car. Getting into a nearby building where they couldn't follow was possible, but would end a duel we couldn't afford to lose.

7) Misdirect the ostriches. Make them run the wrong way. Good idea, but how do ostriches think? How do you mess with their heads?

8) Make something come and fight them for us. But what? Other ostriches? Elephants? Lions?

9) Put up my hood, use telepathy, and ask Dr. Archer for help. Fail the mission, get us all expelled, but live… No, that wasn't right for me.

The answer was to get something to fight the ostriches for us. We couldn't summon animals, or spirits, though – not under this pressure. Then, what?

....

I had it! I'd figured it out in only a few seconds, too. I realized it was all the meditation I'd done that helped me to focus and think so quickly, and thanked Maestro Morgan in my thoughts.

"Guys," I said. "Who's the leader of those Roman soldiers over there?"

"The guy with the shiny armour and the gray hair," Goldberry said. "The one who looks cleaner."

"Help me," I said. "He needs to make his men stop the ostriches."

A group of seven or eight soldiers were in the crowd about ten yards away, probably drawn by the fight. They were wearing breastplates and helmets with stiff tassels on top and had leather skirts going down to their knees and leather sandals covering them to mid-calf. They were leaning on long spears and also carrying short swords. All the men were deeply tanned and had dark, hardened faces. They looked like longshoremen or dock workers; they were nobody to mess with. The officer, who had gray hair, looked pretty tough, too I tried to focus on him and try to project into his head the image of his men using their spears against the ostriches. I remembered that I had spoken to the spirit of a Roman soldier before, in one of the mementos from the Holy Land, months before. Maybe their minds were alike enough that I could speak to them the same way. I hoped my teammates were helping me.

It worked! The officer called out sharply in Latin, and the soldiers I could see, as well as more I hadn't seen, sorted themselves out of the crowd and formed a line crossing the ostriches' path of approach. They braced their long spears against the ground, forming a wall of spear points. This might have been designed to stop cavalry, but it worked even better against wild ostriches. The lead ostrich spotted the obstacle and immediately veered away from it. Those coming up behind imitated it, and the whole gang of ostriches was detoured away from us. The soldiers, at a command from their leader, broke ranks to pursue.

Robbie grinned at me. "Nice going, dude. Hey, you think ostrich meat tastes good?"

"It tastes like a good steak," Goldberry said.

"I wouldn't eat that," said Mermelstein.

"Guys," I told my team, "we need to end this fight. Someone will get hurt if we don't."

"Tell that to him," Mermelstein growled, looking at Yeishu. He didn't point. I'd learned that in Orthodox Judaism, it is forbidden to point at people, even when counting.

Mermelstein was being sarcastic, but I thought he was right.

"Enough fighting." I took a few steps toward Yeishu. "We need to end the fight. What will it take?"

Yeishu stared at me, as if trying to peer through my flesh to see the soul inside. Finally he said, "Has not Simon Magus boasted that his consort Helen can fly?"

Rabbi Yehoshua

I looked at my team. I'd made a split-second choice about ten minutes earlier, and so Leah was playing the part of Helen.

"Does anyone have a clue about that?" I asked.

"Remember I tried to summon the air spirit Nicholotus who teaches you," Robbie said. "But I never could get him to show up."

"Can we fake it somehow? Like throw something in the air and make it look like her?" I looked at Leah. She was biting her lip and had a determined, thoughtful look on her face.

"Maybe," she said. "If you all help me."

"You can fly?" Mermelstein sputtered.

"No. But levitation is different. Going straight up, during serious prayer, well… maybe. With God's help, it is possible."

Mermelstein seemed to struggle within himself. Finally, he said, "Yes. With God's help it is possible. But this is something that can't be done with thinking. It is only with faith."

"We pray," Leah said. "If it is God's will."

Pray? I thought. I can meditate, but how do I pray? I had never done that. I believed in God, because of studying magic, but I never thought of God as someone in space who listened to prayers and granted them. Whatever needed to be done, I tried to do it, or asked a person I thought could do it. Asking God for help – that never worked, right?

So while my team was praying, I was lost. The best I could think of was to meditate, and imagine a cylinder around Leah, and lift the cylinder in the air, and visualize her rising along with it.

Something was happening. She was rising in the air. Her head was bowed; her eyelids were lowered, fluttering. I saw white under the lovely dark eyelashes.

How could she? I mean, the girl I loved; How? Two feet, five feet, ten feet in the air, her slim shape in the rolling robe, her lovely skin and flowing hair, the hands delicate like tulips, my love my Leah rising into the sky in the enfolding grasp of God.

Behind me a voice cried out in Hebrew, or Aramaic, or who knew what language?

She fell with a crashing thump.

A tall, rigidly upright man with a long white beard appeared in dark robes, with a box-like headdress.

"All of you here, now!" This I understood, as universal language began to work, even as I rushed to Leah, a split-second ahead of the others.

I said her name. She wasn't moving, but her chest worked a little. I saw blood on her lips. "Leah," I said again.

She smiled. Her eyes were closed. "Simon," she said. "I will always be with you."

Then men came and lifted her up, pulling her hand from Goldberry's, Robbie punched them, they didn't notice.

"Now," said the white-bearded man. "That is enough of the fighting outside the temple. The leaders come inside with me now."

"Leah." I watched the men carry her to a nearby house, where women waited in the doorway. I tasted wet salt.

....

"That one will be tended to. Come, boy. Yeishu! Come inside now!"

"Leah," I said.

He took me by the elbow, and Yeishu by the back of the head, and guided us over the threshold into his sanctum. It was baking hot inside, and dark but for small lamps of burning oil.

"Summoning evil spirits in the shapes of great birds and Persians," said the old man. "Shouting in the public spaces about fire and magic. Public disputes between two heretics, stirring up the Romans? This I cannot permit. Yeishu I know well, who has followed me for many months, but you, foreign boy, tell me your business."

I was still crying, and my words didn't come out right. "Rav Yehoshua, maybe I was fighting Yeishu, but I came here to persuade you to forgive him."

"He spoke to me in vulgar words about women. Why should I forgive this?"

"No, Rebbe," he said. "Rav Yehoshua, my words had an unintended double meaning. I meant no disrespect."

"Let us," said Rabbi Yehoshua ben Perachyah said, "suppose I misheard you. But how can you go about the city claiming you are the Moshiach? If this were true, everyone would know it, without a word from your tongue."

"Please, Rebbe. Never have we needed the Moshiach more than in these ruinous times. I hear Hashem in my heart, calling upon me to help my fellow Jews. If you were truly the Moshiach, what would you feel?"

"I don't know," said the old rabbi.

"Rav Yehoshua," I said, "please forgive him. His ghost is

tormenting me."

"How so? He lives."

I couldn't possibly explain time travel to him. I had decided long ago just to act confused myself. "I can only say that it's true," I answered. "For many weeks the ghost of Yeishu ben Pandeira has been speaking to me."

"Then," said the rabbi, "Yeishu, you are not the Moshiach. If you do not withdraw these claims, I think that the people will stone you in time. You must go forth among the Jews, and be forgiven by them for your calumnies. Return in one year, and I will then forgive you."

"Thank you, Rebbe."

"Go."

Yeishu smiled and clapped his hands and ran out of the *shul.*

"Now, as to you," he said, "you are only a boy, and you have no learning."

"Rav Yehoshua," I began. "Rebbe, you're right. But please heal Leah."

He stroked his beard. "I cannot," he said. "I feel that the girl's spirit is not in her body. I feel it is being called somewhere else. Another place, another time?"

"She's dead?" I shrieked.

"You, necromancer, should know not all spirits leave our lives at death. Hers is a wise and busy soul, I sense, and you are not the only one who watches over her. Mourn, but speak to her, and she will hear."

"It's not fair," I said. "She was only trying to help me."

"Fair," said Rabbi Yehoshua with a gentle laugh. "Why speak to me about what is fair? I am a Jew. Talk to Hashem about what is fair. Only Hashem is wise enough to explain our suffering."

....

"I killed her," I said. "She fell, because I didn't pray."

"Ah," he said. "I forgot that you are Simon Magus. Perhaps, like Yeishu, you believe you know what Hashem wants?"

"No," I sobbed.

"When you know what Hashem wants, then you know why the girl fell. Consider – did Hashem want her to fly?"

"No. No, I did."

"What you want, or what you pray for, doesn't make Hashem take action. You do not rule; Hashem rules. That is why you are here, and why I am here. Unless you broke her neck with your hands, why are you a killer?"

"Because I didn't believe."

"Do you believe you are here? Do you believe you are in the room with me? What, is this a dream?" There was a scuffling noise from outside, and the doors creaked open. Rabbi Yehoshua looked up. "Someone is here for you. Someone who is better suited to tend you than I am."

I turned, following his gaze, and saw Dr. Archer. Then, behind him, I saw the Dean. The rest of my team was behind them.

"Oh, no," I said.

"These are my students," said the Dean. "They should not be here."

"Since when are students ever where they are supposed to be?" answered the old rabbi. "Still, if they are in the wrong place, it was for a good reason. They have helped me to reclaim one of my own pupils who was far astray. I should give a reward, but I'm no Roman. I don't keep riches. Only Hashem's word is real wealth in days of exile."

"I will take my students back and punish them for the intrusion," said the Dean. "Please excuse us."

"Do as you like with your students," said Rabbi Yehoshua, "if they have broken your rules. But first let me speak to these others. Come, children."

My team crossed the room, passing through the oil smoke, to stand before the white-bearded rabbi. "What's your name?" he asked Mermelstein. "You are a Jew, yes?"

"Yakov," he said. "I am a Jew."

The rabbi reached to the floor and wrenched out a cobblestone with his wizened hand. "Build your home with this stone in the foundation," he said. "Then your sons will be holy men."

"Thank you, Rebbe," said Mermelstein.

The old man looked at Robbie. "You are also a Jew, I think, but not the same way. What is your name?"

"Aaron is the Hebrew name that my rabbi at home gave me."

"You are the one that called the spirit. Come close to me, and I will whisper a word in your ear." Robbie complied. "Now," said the rabbi, "if you say that word, no fire will burn you, or not easily. But don't repeat it to anyone."

Yehoshua ben Perachyah turned to Goldberry. "You are not a Jew," he said. "You look like a Roman. What do I have for you? Ah, I know." From the folds of his robe he produced a tiny comb made of seashell. "I got this for my little daughter this morning, but you may keep it."

"Thank you, Rabbi," said Goldberry, although she looked annoyed at receiving a little girl's gift.

"You," he said to me. "I have delayed long enough, and what you needed to do you have done. Now, give me that crystal from your coat."

It was hidden, but I didn't question how he knew about it. I handed it to him. He handled it, mumbled a little, and handed it back. "Don't lose this," he said.

"Will Yeishu's ghost…?" I began.

Yehoshua ben Perachyah ignored me and looked at the Dean. "Your students have in them no wickedness," he said. "I could use more like these myself."

Aftermath

Several hours later, we were all in the conference room, where I had first been interviewed. All of us were there except Leah. Two of the rabbi's helpers had brought her body over the mole in an oxcart. We didn't know what happened to it after that. The teachers left us in the room. We had very little conversation. Here's what there was.

"I didn't want her to die," Mermelstein said. "No one would wish that for a fellow Jew, even a wrong-headed one."

"Just shut up," Robbie said. "This isn't about being a good Jew or not. This is about loving someone."

"All right, all right," Mermelstein said. "I know that. I was only just saying it. I know I acted like it, but I wasn't one of the people who were against her. That's all."

"Thank you, Yakov," I said, trying to cut off the conversation before it turned into a fight.

I didn't feel the return to the present the same way I had felt the trip back in time. Maybe returning was different. I was able to tell that we were back only by looking at my watch, because I knew when, in New York time, we were supposed to be back.

Finally the door opened, admitting the Dean, Dr. Archer, Rabbi Shulman, and Maestro Morgan, all of our advisors. They sat.

"I don't want to expel you," said the Dean. "I believe that I have to. Violation of our rules has caused a student's death."

"Her death is a great punishment for all four of them," Dr. Archer said, supporting us. "I agree we must take some action, however."

"Let me die instead," Robbie said. "God, I loved her."

"We all loved her," I said. It was more polite to include Mermelstein, because at least he was trying to be decent about it.

"You can expel me," Goldberry said. "Let me take the blame, and keep these three. I can get into Citadel d'If next year."

"Expel me," Mermelstein said. "I never wanted to come here. I can learn at home."

I looked at my remaining team. All three were crying. Rabbi Shulman began to harangue at Mermelstein in Yiddish, but I didn't want to pay attention, so I shut off universal language.

"I think we all know this is my fault," I said. "You have to expel me, because I got the rest of them into the mess. Also, I stole the crystal."

"Not precisely," said Dr. Archer. "You were given permission to take a piece to practice with. Your deceptive use of my permission is willful and foolish, but not egregious."

"Dr. Archer," I said. "Why are you helping me? You should be the most angry of all! I lied to you, I hid things from you, and it's my fault Donovan was possessed, too!"

He looked thoughtful. "Fault?" he said. "Donovan was caught up in a complex matter that resulted from student access to dangerous mementos. I was not aware that you instigated the matter."

"It's my fault. I tried to handle Yeishu on my own."

"Simon is right," the Dean interrupted, "that he is logically the student we ought to expel. However, I think some question exists as to the appropriateness of these mementos being supplied to us for student use. My understanding, based on what you told me, Simon, during the return trip, is that Yeishu began to haunt you long before you handled his memento. This was therefore an extremely powerful and malevolent spirit. The strongest mementos housed in our regular collection, such as the memento in the entrance hall which secures the Founder, do not bind spirits of this magnitude. This being the case, I do not think the crystal containing Yeishu should have left Israel at all. Yeishu is gone from it now, I assume?"

"Yes," I said. "Rabbi Yehoshua took care of that for me."

"Keep it," said Dr. Archer quickly. "Dean, I don't wish to expel Simon. I need him."

"Expel me," said Goldberry.

"Expel me," said Mermelstein.

"Expel me," said Robbie. "I'll check out that other school, the one in Miami, where Dr. Phillips' nephew works."

Rabbi Shulman pursed his lips. "A moment," he said.

The door opened, and then the sky opened under our feet for a moment. Or, that's how I felt the first time I saw the man. He was small, a stooped elderly gentleman in a black suit, wide-brimmed black hat, a long white beard. His eyes looked directly at everything and everyone at all times. His face was deeply wrinkled, thoughtful, calm, distracted but not worried, youthful in energy although his body was slow-moving and bent.

The Rambal.

"Rabbi Lichtman," said the Dean. "Thank you for coming."

Was he more like Rabbi Yehoshua ben Perachyah, or more unlike? I was so tired, my mind awhirl with thoughts.

....

"Rambal," I said. "Bring her back to me."

"I wish," he said. Then he stopped talking and settled into a chair. "I wish you were the first one to say those words to me. Or even the first one today."

"I don't care if I get expelled. Nothing matters but Leah."

"Wise of you to say that," he said. "To say that to me. You know who I am?"

"You're a great Cabala teacher," said Robbie suddenly.

"Great? *Nu*, famous maybe. Hashem alone is great. But I mean to say." He stopped talking and looked around, unmoving. "I mean to say, who I am to Leah Ritz. You know?" He looked at Goldberry. "Maybe you know?"

Goldberry shook her head.

"Take a good guess."

"Her grandfather?" Goldberry tried.

"Great-great," said the Rambal. "Hmm. Great-great grandfather. This surprises you, I suppose."

"Whoa," said Robbie.

"I take that as yes. So anything concerning her, it is a serious matter for me. And this is why I made known to you, Dean, what was suspected of her future, that she would not marry."

"Rebbe," said Mermelstein, "she's your blood, and you allowed…"

"Allowed?" he said. "Allowed her to die?"

"Allowed her to study Talmud," Mermelstein finished.

"And allowed everyone to attack her," I added.

"I don't rule the world, or control the people," said the Rambal. "People become who they become. My great grand-daughter, Chana, married Avrohom Ritz. He was a difficult man, but no man ever loved his family more. Some things, you accept. I brought her here to watch over her in her last year."

"It was believed," Dr. Archer added, "that she would die."

"What?" cried the Dean. "I should have been told!"

"It was known to four individuals," said Dr. Archer. "To the Rambal; to me; to Chana Ritz; and, on my judgment, to Goldberry Tinker."

"Why?" I shouted.

"For her protection, Simon. And for protection of the secret. Given her talents at divination, Goldberry would have suspected and, lacking guidance, informed others."

"I never knew who Leah's advisor was," said Goldberry. "Nobody did. But it was you."

"I was her advisor," the Rambal confirmed. "And that, Dean, has brought me to the matter of whom you must expel. There is a complication."

"Post facto, I presume," said the Dean.

"Not at all," said the Rambal. "The night before the trip, Leah asked my permission to go, with her friends, to meet the great rabbi, and it was granted. She was a moral child and did not wish to disobey her elders."

"You gave permission," the Dean said. "All the children had permission?"

"It could be so construed," said Dr. Archer.

"Very well," said the Dean. "There shall be no expulsion from School of the Ages today. The four of you are assigned to clean the general dining hall after dinner from now until the end of June. Go and get some sleep."

"Sleep," Robbie said "How can we sleep, when she's dead?"

"And it's my fault," I added. "I should never sleep again."

"Your fault, your fault." The rabbi clicked his tongue. "That *dybbuk*, so to speak, was in your head. Was that because of your error?"

"Because of my weakness."

"And then, I gave her permission to go. Is it then my fault?"

"It was my idea."

"Then why did I give permission?"

"Yes, why did you?" Goldberry interjected. "No disrespect, Rabbi Lichtman, but why did you, if you knew she would die?"

He shrugged. "It was what she wanted. A child like that, who so loves the Talmud, who will deny?"

"You could have prevented her death!"

"Perhaps in one place," said the Rabbi, "but not in every place. It is not for me to decide how long anyone lives. It is for me to see that life is lived according to *halacha*, good principles."

She shook her head, not understanding. "What good is all your magic then, if you don't do anything with it?"

The rabbi turned away, looking at the universe.

"The good of magic," Dr. Archer said, "is not principally in doing, but in knowing what ought to be done."

Interlude

We agreed among the four of us not to talk about the incident more than we had to. The other students knew something was up: Leah, a school celebrity for her beauty and her enemies, was gone, and Goldberry had no roommate. Robbie, a notorious bigmouth, was scarcely talking to anyone. Donovan Archer, one of the best-liked kids in his own year, had also become quite withdrawn. The Divination Club worked double-time to figure out the details.

Robbie and I told Rocco and Balaram, our remaining friends who weren't there, the barest outline of the story. Goldberry told Goodenough to mind his own business; she didn't want the story to get back to her father. I quit intramurals. We cleaned the cafeteria for an hour and a half each night. We all kept our grades where they had been, between 70 and 90.

End of Summer

(Written in Prague, 2/20-23/06)

The summer passed. We learned. Sometimes – often – I cried because Leah was gone. I held the crystal in my hand at night, and carried her prayer book in my shirt pocket by day. Then on a morning in September, someone shook me awake. I blinked at Balaram leaning over my bed.

"*Deviji* says it is today."

"Today."

"You must wake Goldberry," he said.

"And Goodenough," I added. "William Goodenough. I promised him."

"I don't know his room," Balaram said.

"Goldberry knows. Give me a minute."

I threw on my shirt and jeans. Then I took my beaver coat. We went and woke Goldberry up. She was wearing black satin pajamas. "Get out," she said.

"Where's Goodenough?" I asked.

She told me where his room was, and I took Balaram and went to wake him up. He appeared at once when I pounded on his door. He was fully dressed in a blue shirt, slacks and tie.

"Oh. It's you," he said, giving a half-grin. "Come to worship at my feet?"

"If you want to protect Goldberry," I said, "this is the day. According to our bargain, I had to include you."

"Right," he said. "I'll get my magic wand."

He shut the door in my face. I heard a bumping noise, then he came out again, holding a cell phone with a magic wand sticker on the front. "Let's go."

As we walked, he added, "What's with the fur coat? Bit too hot for September?"

"I have my reasons."

"*Deviji* says we should get to Manhattan soon," Balaram said.

"How?" I wondered.

"I'll call for a ride," said Goodenough. "Meet me out front."

We collected Goldberry, dressed in black jeans and grey sweatshirt. "I threw some tarot," she said. "Death came up each time, and a tower struck by lightning."

"A tower?"

"Yes. Great disaster, lives and fortunes ruined."

"Not good," Balaram said. "Deviji is advising me not to go with you, I may be killed."

"You can stay," I said.

"No, I'll go. I'm curious. I believe in God, and God will protect me."

We made our way to the entrance, passing through the main hall. There, although light was limited, I paused for a moment to look at the seven pillars: faith, perception, balance, wisdom, receptiveness, judgment, and discipline. Despite doing my best to follow them, I had still gone through the most painful year of my life, lost the only girl I would ever love, and nearly gotten kicked out of school.

We were headed for another mistake, I knew, interfering with the problems of adult magicians stronger than we were, risking the lives of kids who weren't really involved, but I was loyal to Goldberry and had to help her.

Goodenough was outside, holding the magic wand. As we watched, a white Mercedes emerged from the trees and pulled up in front of the school. "Our ride," he said.

"That was fast," said Goldberry.

Behind the wheel of the car sat a short man wearing what looked like a wrestler's mask. He popped out of the car and opened the back door, gesturing for us to climb in.

"My chauffeur," said Goodenough.

"Why the mask?" asked Goldberry.

"He doesn't have a face," Goodenough said. He smirked. I wasn't sure he was kidding. "Works for my dad, actually," Goodenough said as he climbed into the front seat.

The car swung round, plunged into the trees, and passed through darkness into the brown light of the Battery Tunnel. We came out into a street crowded with traffic and were stuck at a light. There was an overpass nearby, and on our right was the Battery Tunnel garage, ugly brick and metal fencing. Horns blew.

"*Deviji* is…" said Balaram. "*Deviji* has run away. What?"

I felt it, then: a vibration in the air. The doors of the Mercedes sprang open on their own. The chauffeur leapt out from the driver's side and blinked out of sight. Now we were all standing in the road where the car had been. I felt the heat pressing against my face and hands. There was a roaring sound in the air. I knew what it was. It was a jetliner.

"A plane?" I said. "There shouldn't be any planes so close to the city." I spun around in place, trying to spot it in the air.

"Oh, mum," Goldberry said. "Is this what you saw? You knew this was coming?"

"Goldberry," I said. "Where will your father be right now?"

She checked her watch. "It's 8:45, he should be… He has a securities office in the South Tower of World Trade Center."

We were standing in the street, with cars all around us, none of them moving. I grabbed Goldberry and tugged her toward the sidewalk as the car horns blared still. A cab ahead, suddenly shut down its engine. The driver climbed out of the cab and was staring south and east of us. I followed his gaze. I saw a jet approaching the Twin Towers. Vaguely I heard Balaram praying as he staggered to the sidewalk behind us.

Om bhur bhuwah swaha, he prayed.

"Get out," Goldberry said huskily, as if her father could hear.

The plane was too low and not turning. Its engines whined. It shouldn't have been so loud, as far away as we were, but I heard it.

"Goddamn spirit ran away," Goodenough yelled into his cell phone as he stared.

"Get out!"

Tat savitur varenyam

Mr. Tinker, I thought. Get out of there.

Bhargo devasaya, dheemahee

The plane dove into one of the towers. Windows shattered. Fire and smoke erupted. A wave of fuel smell choked me. The sky screamed. It was like watching a volcano erupt. The horns blowing stopped.

Dhiyo yo na prachodayat.

Balaram fell to his knees.

Goldberry began to cry. Then I did. So did the cab driver.

"The tower struck by lightning," Goldberry whispered. "Great disaster, lives and fortunes ruined." She snatched Goodenough's phone. People were climbing out of their cars, running in all directions. Goldberry was dialling over and over. "No service!"

"The spirits are running," Goodenough said. "My chauffeur, Balaram's guide. They're afraid."

"Which tower was it that was hit?" I asked.

"Let's go get him out."

Flame and smoke rose from the tower, but the city was quiet.

"Let's go," Goldberry repeated.

"All right," Goodenough said.

"I'm with you," Balaram said.

I knew my own parents were safe, my father in Brooklyn, my mother in Midtown, on Park Avenue. Goldberry's father was the only person I knew who worked in the World Trade Center.

We started walking. Debris was falling, mostly dust. People were walking heedlessly, staring up at the trail of smoke emerging from the tower. I heard people shouting and cursing. No one was obeying traffic laws. At last it came to me what to do. I pulled up the hood of the beaver coat.

Mr. Tinker.

What? Who's that? Get out of my head. There's a...

I know. A plane hit the other tower. Get out. We're here, Goldberry and me, to help you. Get out. Meet us somewhere.

You brought Goldberry here? You ass!

I came to help her. William Goodenough is here, too. All the spirits are running away. It's serious. Where can you meet us?

Just a… Wait a minute.

He broke contact with me. I told Goldberry what had happened.

"He's stubborn, all right," she said. "He'll try to figure it out on his own first. Let's go."

Still walking, we passed by a Manhattan bus that had pulled over. People were pushing their way out by both exits. I heard them cursing the driver. A homeless man in a torn denim jacket leaned against a wall. "It's the end of the world," he blurted. I put my hood down.

Then I heard sirens from everywhere. They must have been there before, but with the hood up, I had blocked them out. Goldberry and I pulled each other to the curb as a fire engine, an ambulance, and two police cruisers zagged down Broadway. I looked around. "Where's Balaram?"

"He went to a payphone," Goodenough said. He was struggling with his cell phone, cursing at it.

"Another one," Goldberry said.

"Another phone?" I asked. But I could hear it.

"Another plane!" someone on the curb shouted. "Holy shit!"

"I heard that one hit the White House," a woman shouted. "It's on the radio!"

Another jet was approaching, the whine of its engines clawing at our bones. We were crazy to be walking closer, and we began to run, as if we could get there first and somehow hold the plane back.

"It's an attack," someone shouted.

A young blond couple came running up to us. "There is no subway," they said with German accents. "How can we get out of here?"

"Keep going up Broadway," I said. 'It goes all the way uptown." I stopped, looked at my watch. How long since I told Clive Tinker to get out? It was 9:02 when the second plane hit. There was a flash of flame, and then the boom washed over us. I staggered and fell to the sidewalk. A young black girl in a school uniform ran up to us crying.

"It's the Devil," she said.

I got the idea to raise my hood again. I was running now, and Goldberry was pulling my hand. We lost Goodenough in the crowd. I could still hear sirens in the air everywhere.

Dr. Archer.

It is as I expected that you are in the midst of the great trouble.

Couldn't this be stopped, with all the magic you have, you and the Rambal and the Dean?

Help those you can. The matter is vaster in scope than any of us can grasp. We will speak later. It is time now to act.

Crowds of people were streaming up Broadway. Dust and smoke were everywhere. We couldn't push forward. I saw that the young girl was nearby, and pulled Goldberry to her and took her hand.

"Any more kids with you?" I asked.

"I was going to school," she said.

"Just stay with us till we find a policeman."

She nodded. I looked around for anyone else to help. It was hard to see through the smoke. More sirens were howling in all directions. I kicked something as I walked – an abandoned cell phone. I picked it up and tried to dial. No service. Goodenough and Balaram appeared beside us.

"Crazy, you two, running off," Goodenough said. He grabbed Goldberry's hand, stopping her progress.

"How'd you find us?" I asked.

"I'm lucky. And I'm a magician, after all. Who's this?" He looked at the girl.

....

"Michelle," she said. She had a missing front tooth.

"Get out of here," he rasped, making a fierce gesture with his right hand.

Michelle cursed him and leapt into the air and swirled away like a leaf on the wind.

"Plenty of nasty spirits around today," he said flatly. "Come on, Goldberry, where's your father?"

"How should I know? You bloody ask him!"

"Let's stay put, or he'll never find us."

"I called my parents," Balaram said. "They are calling everyone else they can. Let's get over here, in front of this deli."

We all went where he pointed, out of the way of the crowds. I decided to try something and went into the deli, where a clerk was bundling money from the register into a black backpack.

"Let me have some facemasks," I said. "In the drawer there."

"No masks," he said. But he opened the drawer, and there they were, six facemasks like construction workers wear.

"Thanks," I said. I took five of them and handed him a $10 bill. He put on the sixth one.

"That's freaky," he said. "They weren't there before."

Back outside, I gave one mask to each of my friends. Breathing was still tough, with all the dust. "Your father will find us," I said. "Let's see whom we can help."

A little boy, about 3, in overalls, was running away from his mother who was holding an infant in a sling at her breast. Balaram blocked the boy's path and herded him back to his mother.

An old woman crying, staggered across the road. Goodenough took her arm and held her till he saw a policeman leading some people away and joined her to that group.

A man sank onto the curb vomiting. I gave him water and the last spare face mask. He leaned on me for about a block, then got moving on his own.

Goldberry helped a confused French couple with walking directions for the Brooklyn Bridge. She wasn't using universal language; her French was excellent.

The people kept staggering past. Are the subways running? Are the buses running? What happened? Are they evacuating the city? Where is the cab? Can I get to Jersey, to Staten Island, to Connecticut, to the airport? Did they hit the White House? Who did this? Will the towers go down? The fire, the smoke, asbestos, is there asbestos? Listen to the sirens, the fire trucks. You kids should clear out, come with me. No, my dad is coming, Goldberry said, we have to wait for him. A group of cops on foot ran past us headed for the Twin Towers. Leaning back against the wall, I saw small objects falling from the upper floors of the towers. That had to be debris, couldn't be people?

Dad, Goldberry said, crying.

My God! someone shouted. Adults wailing like babies. One tower was collapsing, collapsing under its own weight.

"Can't be," Goodenough shouted, coughing under the mask. "Plane hit the Empire State Building, but it didn't go down. This one can't…"

"Cover your eyes!" Balaram shouted. "Cover your faces!"

A wave of dust and smoke was rolling up the street toward us. I pulled Goldberry down, squatted on the street facing away, held her head into my chest. She was sobbing, "Mum! Is this what you saw?"

The dust cloud rolled past. Dust coated everything. An old Chinese lady without a mask, with a face like a painted ghost, slumped against a wall and passed out. Balaram and Goodenough dragged her by the armpits into a nearby shop. They came out with a handful of surgical masks and started giving them out to people. A shop clerk, a chubby Mexican woman, came out also with a large box of masks and started handing them out too.

It was a few moments later that Clive Tinker came striding out of the hanging dust, his blue suit covered with grime, his face grim, one hand clutching an attaché case.

"Who have we?" he said, counting us, as Goldberry ran to him and buried her face in his chest. "Right, four, plus me. Let's get going. West Broadway and Houston, Spanish Restaurant. Move."

We followed as best we could, losing him once or twice. Then we spotted a restaurant called El Sombrero Negro, and rushed toward it, opened the door, stepped in and entered the lobby of the Empire State Building.

"That was good," Goodenough said to Mr. Tinker.

"And it will cost me," he said darkly. "Come on. I have an office upstairs."

With Mr. Tinker

The office of Tinker Investments had a reception area, a large office, and two small offices. The workers, a British man and woman in their twenties, left as soon as Mr. Tinker arrived.

"We'll be safe here," he said. "No more airliners will strike this building. Now, as to why you are in the city at all, that is a matter that brooks no further delay." He whirled on his daughter, but had to wait. She was kneeling over a wastebasket, throwing up. I felt like puking also.

"The three of you," he said to Goodenough and Balaram and me. "Call your parents."

"They don't know we're in the city," I said, coughing. "Why worry them?"

"You?" he answered. "You can't talk at all."

He was right. Words wouldn't come to me at all. My mouth was working, but I couldn't seem to hold onto an idea once I'd begun to say it. This simple but overwhelming act of magic reminded me, even more strongly than the translocation some twenty blocks north, that he was a master magician on his own turf.

Goldberry managed, through tears, to explain that a spirit summoned by Balaram had told us we could heal her mother by coming to Manhattan at a specific time.

"You trusted some low-grade spirit called up by a first-year summoning student?" he thundered. He whirled on Balaram, who was dialling the phone. "This was your idea?"

"Not mine," Balaram said. "The spirit explained that…"

"Idiot," he snapped.

I wanted to talk, but couldn't. I grabbed Mr. Tinker's wrist.

"Sit down," he growled. I felt my legs giving way, but this time I resisted. We had helped people! We didn't deserve this. I wobbled, but I kept my feet under me. Hoping it would help, I put up the hood of the beaver coat.

It didn't help. I was sweating and shaking. I took off the coat and let it fall. It was covered with ash and soot, fouled beyond recognition. Whatever magic it had was no longer working, at least for now.

"Let Simon go," Goldberry said. "He was only helping me. As a matter of fact, seeing that he could have died…"

"Yes, yes. He gave his life to you. That's one, boy."

"It's two," I said. I let go his wrist. Either I'd shaken off his spell, or he let it go.

"Two?" Clive Tinker visibly shut down. He settled into a chair himself. Balaram, out of the spotlight, began dialling again.

"Two?" Goldberry echoed.

"There was a girl at school," I said quietly. "I loved her. She was like life to me. I had to choose, her or Goldberry, to do something dangerous. I chose her. She was killed."

Clive Tinker seemed at a loss for words. "A student was killed?"

"They knew," Goldberry said. "Dr. Archer told me at the beginning of the year, to look out for her while I could."

"The Rambal foresaw it," I added. "She was his great-great-granddaughter. He protected us from being expelled."

"Interesting," said Goodenough, emerging from the adjoining office where he had been making calls. "The word was out she wasn't safe to know, but no one said why or where."

"That's why I was admitted," Goldberry added. "To take care of her."

Clive Tinker shook his head. "Not true. You were admitted on merit." He seemed to be thinking about this and what it meant. I saw something change in his face. "You're *my daughter*. It's your heritage." He paused. "Good God. I've been far too preoccupied with your mother's illness. I had no idea what was going on at the school."

"I hope we helped her," I said. "We helped whoever we could, but it was for her. I think if not for Goldberry being in the city, you'd have stayed in the tower, and you would have died."

He thought about that. "You're right," he said. "Then your debt to me is two-thirds settled. One for the girl, one for helping Goldberry today. God. You are only children, and what you did…" He stood a moment. "Your parents are all well. They'll get home safely. I'll take you home in a few hours. All of you. Right now, we're safest here."

"Why did they do it?" Goldberry said. "Whoever it was. Why did they do it?"

"Let's see the news," he said. There was a TV in his office, and we watched as the reports came in.

The Last Day of School

The last day of school, we got our report cards for the year. Instead of taking the bus back, Goldberry and I were going to be picked up in a Mercedes SUV driven by the Tinkers. They came in to help us pack and load the car. Afterwards, Mrs. Tinker said, we would meet my parents at Nobu for dinner arranged by the Tinkers. As we were stowing Goldberry's clothes, to our surprise, Dr. Archer arrived to see us, and met Mr. Tinker, who was standing impatient in the hall. There was a strong contrast between the tall Clive Tinker, in his expensive blue suit, with perfectly styled dark hair, and Dr. Archer, already gray, shorter, in his turtleneck and metal-rimmed glasses, with his icy eyes. "Clive."

"Solomon. Has my daughter yet had her fill of danger, or will you expose her to more?"

"There will be more," said Dr. Archer. "There is no end to peril in the world. Some perils she will seek, and other perils will arise unbidden."

"It's true," said Mr. Tinker. "But your platitudes mean no more to me now than they did when we were friends. If Goldberry is under your tutelage, I expect you to supervise her, and stop day-tripping to the Rhineland."

"Day-tripping," said Dr. Archer. "A curious term you use for business concerning the defense of the school."

"I doubt that," said Mr. Tinker.

"Clive," Mrs. Tinker chided.

"*Gott im Himmel,*" said Dr. Archer coldly.

There was a long silence between the two men.

"I'll call London," Mr. Tinker said. "I'll learn for myself if there's something to your claim."

"I need to see the children," said Dr. Archer. "Goldberry, Simon, if you please."

We followed him to his office.

"Regarding next year's schedule," he said, "Simon, it is necessary for Goldberry to advance in Divination. At present you are still deficient in this subject, although you have attempted it in order to support your partner. You may be enrolled along with her, and risk harming your average with a likely failure; or, if you wish, I may place you in the first level of summoning, with the younger students."

I thought about it. I hated divination, since I was so bad at it, and summoning, Robbie's main interest, intrigued me. On the other hand, I liked having all my classes with Goldberry, and studying and practicing with her.

"I think I should take Divination II," I said. "Maybe I can pass by learning the vocabulary, or something like that."

Dr. Archer scribbled on a card, then showed us our schedules.

"Mediumship," I said.

"It is training to become a trance medium. I believe, Simon, you already have a spirit guide."

I touched the crystal, where it lay under my shirt, and felt Leah's ghost there, close to my heart.

....

Next book in the
School Of The Ages
series is

Level Three's Dream